# Tyranny
## A Demon of Athens Novel

### MARTIN SULEV

# THE DEMON OF ATHENS SERIES

*TYRANNY*
*GOD OF SPARTA*
*SHADOW OF THEBES (2021)*

For my wife.

# MAPS

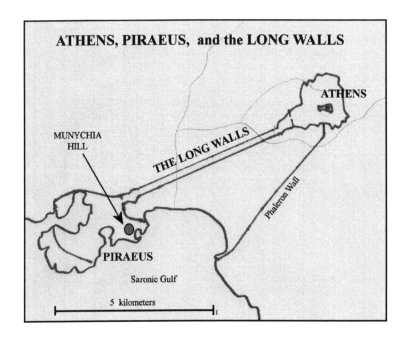

**ATHENS, PIRAEUS, and the LONG WALLS**

ATHENS

MUNYCHIA HILL

THE LONG WALLS

Phaleron Wall

PIRAEUS

Saronic Gulf

5 kilometers

# A NOTE ON SPELLING

For various reasons, transcribing Classical Greek words into English can be quite a challenge. In this book, I have used different conventions in different situations for different reasons. For familiar places such as Thrace and Sicily, I have tended to use conventional English spelling to avoid confusion. In many Greek names, however, I have used "k" instead of "c", as in Alkibiades and Perikles, to better approximate the original pronunciation or Greek spelling. In yet other cases, I made rather arbitrary decisions regarding a particular name (Thrasybulus rather than Thrasyboulos, for example) because I thought it looked nicer on the page. All that is to say, I apologize in advance if my spelling choice in a particular situation differs from what you yourself might have chosen.

M.S.

# Part One

# Fire

*Τω Πλατονι μη πιστε. Ψευστης γαρ εστιν.*

Do not believe Plato, for he is a liar.

All the disciples of Sokrates are enemies of the truth, but Plato is the worst of them.

I hate him.

Word of his death has been slow in reaching me, but I will savour these tidings, late or not, for Plato has ever been my adversary. In this final contest, I have emerged as the victor.

Do you know me, Athenian?

I am an old man now, feeble and nearly toothless, yet there are those who still fear my bite. Many hasten to make the sign against the evil eye at any mention of me. Mothers utter my name to frighten their children, saying that the fire-haired monster will come to run them through with his barbarian blade and eat them raw if they do not do their chores. There are those who know me by other epithets. Blasphemer. The Godless One. Death-bringer. Gorger. But most merely call me *Ô Daimon* - the Demon.

They are right in that last thing, at least, for that is my name.

I am Daimon, son of Nikodromos.

It is an odd name, and was so even in my own time. These days all demons are *kakoi daimones* – evil spirits. What father now would burden his son with such an inauspicious title, like a brand seared on his cheek? It was not always so, but Plato feared me and it was his desire to see my name cursed. The whispers spread from that coward's academy to every household in Athens.

Go to the agora. Talk with any villager in Hellas. Everywhere, superstitious fools are plagued by demons. Any unexpected death or ill-fortune that befalls a home or farmstead is blamed on a demon. Any madness that infects a person is the work of a corrupting spirit, like maggots in rotting flesh. It is always simpler to accuse a demon for the evils of this world than to accept that life is bitter and the Fates are cruel.

And so, people have forgotten. In times past, a demon was not a curse but a protector, the spirit of some ancient hero that guarded a home or village in its time of need. That is all I have ever been. I am the Demon of Athens. And the enemies of Athens feared me.

Know, Athenian, that on land and sea, I was the scourge of your enemies. I protected your fragile democracy, which my father loved so much, though it has only scorned me in return. I worshipped the capricious gods of my ancestors faithfully. I was the spear and shield of the greatest general of our age. Again and again I saved you. I did all that was asked of me. I sacrificed everything.

But before I was your demon, before I was forsaken by you, I was something else. Something less. Something more worthy of your contempt.

I was a thief.

# CHAPTER 1

When I was eleven years old, I stole a knife. I should have been at my lessons, but it was a market day and the bustling agora of Athens struck me as a more attractive proposition than scratching out my letters or fumbling to recite a verse of Homer under the withering stare of my tutor, Iasos. And the agora taught me more than any classroom.

"We have to get back soon, Dammo!" Tibetos said. I laughed and darted off into the crowd, leaving my friend to scamper after me. I would not give up my hard-won freedom so easily. The two of us wove through the throngs, examining with wonder all the sundry wares displayed on the vendors' tables.

One table in particular caught my eye. On it were laid out assorted blades and spear-heads, all nicked and dull from use. The seller was bellowing at a nearby cockfight with an intensity that suggested that he had wagered a considerable sum on the outcome of the contest. As he wiped his sweaty brow, he caught sight of me and Tibetos whispering and stroking the battered weapons. He sized us up with a sniff of disgust. "Be off, slaves!" he growled. He gave a half-hearted swipe at my head and I danced out of range.

The merchant, satisfied with this effort, turned back to the cockfight and resumed his shouting. I glowered at his back, bristling at the insult. I was no slave, though admittedly with my copper hair and dirty clothes I looked like one.

"Come on, Dammo! Let's go," Tibetos said, pulling at my tunic. I was about to turn away. Then my eyes fell on it. Among the vendor's mediocre offerings was a knife that stood out for its quality. I stared at it, a decision coalescing in my mind.

Help your friends. Hurt your enemies. Is that not the code that every Greek learns from childhood? The merchant had chosen to be my enemy.

I glanced at Tibetos and he shook his head, knowing what I intended. But I ignored him. In a swift, practiced movement, I palmed the fine blade and tucked it into my clothes. Without even a glance back at the cursed vendor, I slipped into the crowd with Tibetos right on my heels.

My prize stayed hidden in my tunic until we arrived at our home in the dusty backstreets of the city. Only when we were alone in the storeroom that doubled as our sleeping chamber did I dare remove the knife from its place of concealment. Tibetos let out a low whistle. "It's beautiful," he said in a hushed voice.

Tibetos was our house-slave. His light olive skin and almond-shaped eyes betrayed his Persian ancestry, but he spoke only Greek, for my father had bought him when we were both infants. We had been constant companions ever since.

We turned the knife over, admiring how the light played on the gracefully curving iron blade. The sailor's knife was not large, but solid and well-crafted. I handed it to Tibetos and he touched his thumb to the edge, feeling its sharpness.

"What are you two turd-sniffers looking at?" Tibetos and I both jumped, startled by the intruder's voice. It was my half-brother, Adrastos. We had been so engrossed in examining the knife that we had not noticed him come in.

Adrastos' eyes fell greedily on the knife. "Thieving again? It's mine now, you sacks of dung. Give it to me," Adrastos demanded. He snatched at the blade in Tibetos' hand, but my friend leapt back out of reach.

I forced my way between Adrastos and Tibetos, shoving my brother back. I was larger than most boys my age, but Adrastos was six years older than me and his muscles were like stone under his tunic. "It's mine! If you want it, come and get it!" I said, raising my fists. Adrastos could pummel me with ease, and I expected to meet that fate now.

But my brother retreated one step. "You win, *barbarian*," he taunted me.

I took the bait. "I'm not a barbarian!"

Adrastos smirked. "I don't know why father married her instead of a proper Greek, but your mother is a Thracian whore, so that makes you a barbarian too, you green-eyed Thracian shit. It's the law of Athens."

"I am a Greek!" I protested, my voice rising. I swung a fist at him but it merely glanced off his shoulder. Adrastos punched me hard in the chest and sent me sprawling on my backside.

As I lay gasping for breath, Adrastos ground his foot into my breastbone, pinning me. "Now you have found your proper place, barbarian. Remember it." He spat on me for good measure before walking out of the storeroom.

Tibetos helped me to my feet. "Don't worry about that turd-sniffer, Dammo. He'll get his someday," he said, handing me back the knife.

"I wish it had been today, Tibo," I said, trying to rub some air back into my aching chest.

I soon learned why Adrastos had let me off so easily. As I stepped out of the storeroom with Tibetos in tow, I ran headlong into my father. He stared down at me, a stern expression on his face. Adrastos stood behind him, smiling smugly.

I suppressed a moan. My father had warned me of the consequences if I kept stealing.

"Where is the knife?" my father demanded. I knew better than to try to hide it. My father had once been a *strategos,* a general of Athens, and the authority in his voice was unmistakable. I handed over the spoils that I had only so recently acquired.

"Did you steal this?" he asked. I decided that silence would be my best defence. I clenched my lips and stared back mutely at my father. I could see his anger rising in response to my defiant reticence.

The quiet yet unwavering voice of Tibetos came over my shoulder. "I stole it, Master. I was just showing it to Daimon."

My father narrowed his eyes at me before his gaze shifted over to Tibetos. He pursed his lips as he considered his house boy's confession. But instead of interrogating Tibetos, he addressed his next question to me. "Is this true, Daimon?"

I hazarded a glance at Tibetos. His head was bowed. I swallowed hard, fearing the punishment that would come should I admit to the deed.

"Speak up, boy!" My father's voice echoed like thunder in the courtyard. I bit at my lip and glanced about for any escape.

The unfolding drama had attracted an audience. There was a flash of movement in the corner of my eye. My little sister Melitta's wide-eyed face, framed by a tangled mass of red hair, stuck out from around the corner before disappearing once again, no doubt called back by my mother.

My eldest half-brother, Heliodoros, had also come out into the courtyard. Unlike Adrastos, Heliodoros was kind and generous. He was also a veteran of the phalanx, brave and good. I idolized him. He was staring at me and our eyes locked for a heartbeat. Under his gaze, I suddenly felt ashamed of my cowardice. I let out a breath.

"I stole the knife, Father," I confessed, lifting my chin to meet my father's stare.

A long, growing rumble came from the back of my father's throat. Keeping his eyes locked on me, he spoke. "Both of you! With me!"

My father marched the two of us into the courtyard. He picked up the spear-straight stick that leaned ever-ready at the altar's side. "Tibetos! It is ten strokes of the rod. It is light penance for a slave who lies to his master!" I sucked in a rush of air between my teeth. For all of our past misbehaviour, my father had never meted out such a punishment. Five strokes was the norm.

Tibetos walked past me to the altar, not daring to even look at me. He lifted his tunic, exposing his thighs and buttocks, and then leaned over and put his hands on the edge of the worn rock, bracing himself for his punishment.

The ten lashes of the switch seemed to take an eternity. Tibetos bravely bit his lip for the first five strokes but cried out with each of the remaining ones. I flinched as each snap of the rod left an angry red welt on Tibetos' flesh.

"Tibetos," my father said.

Tibetos straightened up gingerly, his tunic falling back down to cover the bruises of his ordeal. His voice quavered. "Yes, Master?"

"Go and attend to your duties."

"Yes, Master." Tibetos shuffled away to the kitchen, grimacing with each step.

"Daimon!" my father's voice snapped.

I turned my head away from the retreating Tibetos to look at my father. "Yes, Father?"

"It is twenty strokes for you."

"What?" I blurted.

"Ten strokes for stealing the knife, and ten strokes for letting your friend take the blame your own misdeed."

"But I said I did it!"

My father's eyes bore into me. "But why at first did you stay silent?"

I swallowed hard, but I knew better than to argue further. I went to the altar and lifted my tunic.

Heliodoros, his arms crossed across his chest, had watched without expression as Tibetos took his strokes. When my father announced my more severe punishment, my eldest brother pursed his lips in a silent whistle. I ventured a look over towards Heliodoros and he gave me a slow nod while clenching his fist in solidarity.

I was about to nod back when the first stroke whipped across the back of my thighs. I stifled a cry of pain in my throat. Adrastos was standing in the doorway of the kitchen. A pillar obstructed my father's view of him, but I could see him plainly. A sadistic grin split his face from ear to ear. I knew he was waiting for me to cry out. I gritted my teeth, determined not to give him the satisfaction.

It was a near thing. Tears streamed down my face, and I bit down so hard I thought my teeth would break. I lost count of how many times my father had already struck me. All I could do was dig my fingers into the altar and wait for it to end.

Then it was over.

I rose up, my skin screaming at me. My hands were trembling. I turned to face my father.

He looked down at me, his brow creased. "Will you steal again?"

I jutted out my chin just a little. "No, Father," I replied flatly.

My father let out a defeated sigh. "When you're able, go help Neleus in the smithy, boy," he said shaking his head. "I think you will need to spend more time there, if only to keep you from stealing and fighting."

"I can go now, Father," I said, though I winced with each step as I hobbled away. Adrastos was still gloating from the kitchen door. I flashed a sign telling him to go hump a goat, and his smirk vanished. I would pay for it later, but it would be worth it.

In the evening, Heliodoros came to find me as I was cleaning up the smithy that was adjacent to our family compound. It was run by Neleus, my father's former captain, and more and more of my chores involved helping him with his tasks.

"Daimon!" Heliodoros called.

I looked up from my sweeping with a grin, happy to see my oldest brother.

"That was quite a beating you took today, Dammo!" he said.

"I still can't walk straight," I said, grimacing. "And I haven't sat down once all day!"

"I got plenty of thrashings when I was your age, believe me, but I can't remember ever getting twenty!" he said shaking his head in wonder. I shrugged sheepishly.

He leaned in close to me and looked back over his shoulders conspiratorially to make sure that we were the only ones in the smithy. "You were brave not to cry today. You'll make a fine soldier. I'm proud of you." I beamed at his praise, for nothing meant more to me, not even the respect of my father.

Yet a blow lay hidden behind my brother's warm words. "But are you no better than a common thief, Daimon?"

I was an adept thief and bold to the point of recklessness. My exploits increased my standing among the street boys and orphans whose company I preferred, especially because I was generous with my spoils. But my brother's soft words moved me where my father's harsh punishment had failed to do so. I hung my head in shame. "I meant no harm," I said weakly.

"You are the son of a *strategos*. You must be above reproach. You should not steal from your fellow Athenians," my brother admonished gently.

"*They* would not regard *me* as one of their fellows," I said bitterly. It was true. In the eyes of Athenians, non-citizens like me were only marginally more respectable than slaves.

My brother knelt and gripped my shoulders. "You will be someday, Brother. Until then, you must show them your *arête.*"

"My *arête?*"

"Your courage. Your virtue. Your *excellence.* You must show yourself to be better than them," he said.

"And when they still attack me?" I asked.

"Then you can show them your *arête* in other ways," he grinned, tousling my copper hair.

"I will not disappoint you, Heliodoros," I said solemnly. I meant it.

He took my hand and pressed two drachmas into my palm. My fingers wrapped tightly around the cool metal of the coins. "I see you have a good heart from the way you stand up for Tibetos against Adrastos. But pay the vendors next time. And give one of the coins to Tibetos. Few are fortunate enough to have such loyal friends."

"I will," I promised.

"What is it?" my brother asked, detecting the trace of wistfulness in my voice.

"The knife is gone."

"Is it?" my brother said enigmatically. He pulled something out from behind his back. My breath caught in my throat, for in his hand was the knife that had been the cause of my ordeal. "But," he said snatching it away as I reached for it, "Don't let Father see it! I will deny all knowledge of it." He winked at me and handed over the hard-won blade.

Once he had left me to finish my chores, I pondered the knife in my hand. If I kept it, my father would surely find out. But there was someone I could give it to. Someone against whom even my father was powerless.

# CHAPTER 2

Heliodoros was dead.

The demagogue Alkibiades was to blame. Four years earlier, the nest of fools that is the assembly of Athens had voted to undertake that silver-tongued villain's mad plan to conquer Sicily. My father had spoken out against the expedition, but the mob had shouted him down, their lust for Sicily's wealth overwhelming any sense of prudence that may have existed in their hearts.

They should have listened to my father. Sicily became Athens' graveyard.

The traitor Alkibiades was not even there, having already fled to Sparta to escape his political enemies. He did not witness one hundred Athenian triremes set afire in the harbour of Syracuse. His eyes did not have to bear the ignominy of Heliodoros and seven thousand other Athenian brothers, fathers, and sons perishing under the pounding heat of the Sicilian sun.

I did not even know how Heliodoros had died. If he was fortunate, it was by the thrust of a spear or sword, a quick end. If fate had been cruel, and for most it had been, he would have slowly expired while labouring in the open quarries with the other prisoners of war, worked to death under the vengeful eyes of the men of Syracuse, whose country we Athenians had invaded with no provocation at all. My father, in his disgust and sorrow, had retired from politics.

Until today. Today my father was returning to the assembly.

I was sixteen years old and thinking about my dead brother. A jarring bump jolted me out of my ruminations. The donkey-cart I was steering had struck a rut, and I was brought rudely back to the present, my thoughts of Heliodoros already evaporating like morning mist in the growing heat of the day.

Tibetos, walking ahead of the cart, led the donkey by its halter, so there was no real need for me to guide the beast. The slave glanced back at me. As usual, my friend's secretive eyes showed little, but a slight smile told me that he was enjoying the rare opportunity to get out beyond the protective walls of Athens, as was I, despite the poor condition of the road.

In peacetime, the road would have been better maintained, but twenty years of war with Sparta had led to its deterioration. The summer sun had turned the surface as hard as stone, and every depression and rock that the cart rolled over sent a shock up my spine. My teeth still tingling from the last bump, I hopped down and rubbed my aching backside as the cart trundled past. In the back sat my father and Neleus, the blacksmith. They had some hay to soften the jarring bumps, but it still could not have been comfortable.

There was something that bothered me about this journey. "Father, why is this assembly not being held at the Pnyx?" I asked. The location of the assembly was odd. Rather than being held at the hill in the city where such votes usually took place, the Pnyx, the people were convening at the temple of Kolonos, about a mile outside the city walls.

My father turned his head towards my voice, his clouded eyes staring through me. "Because the assembly is a pack of cowards!" he said irritably. His voice had a spark that had been absent for a long time. A plea from his friend Iobates had drawn him out once again to be present at today's assembly, the first my father had attended since the disaster at Sicily. "They're letting themselves be led to slaughter like lambs!" He reconsidered this and then amended his statement, his tone more resigned. "No, I think that lambs would probably put up more of a fight." Beside him, the brawny figure of Neleus snorted in agreement.

My father's response was met by my confused silence. He sighed. "Pisander and the other demagogues are up to something. They know that if they hold the vote outside the city, fewer people will attend. They'll be able to stack the assembly with their supporters and pass whatever law or decree they've been planning. Perhaps they wish to elect new generals? I'm not certain. Whatever it is, they want to increase their influence over the assembly."

My father was the staunchest of democrats, a great ally of the great Perikles himself in his time. He had only contempt for those who thought that democracy was madness, and that rule by the wise few was preferable to the whims of an unpredictable mob. In this, Athens was a microcosm of the war that had already raged for twenty years.

As my father had told me many times, the war between Athens and Sparta was as much a struggle between ideas as it was a battle of arms. All over Hellas, cities were torn apart by politics. Neighbour fought neighbour and father clashed with son. Both Athens and Sparta exploited these divisions. In every city Athens occupied, it drove out the ruling class and established a democracy. If Sparta took control, it overthrew the democracy and installed an oligarchy of men from the old aristocratic families.

But this was Athens. Democracy had reigned for five generations. The majority of citizens would agree with my father. A thought slowly occurred to me. "Why aren't there more people opposing Pisander?"

"They're not here," my father said bitterly. "Our hoplites are scattered all over the Aegean. Our generals are campaigning. There's nobody left but old men like me."

Neleus grunted. "And most of those old men are scared," he said scornfully. The veteran hoplite grunted as he shifted his crippled left leg, the legacy of a Megarian spear-thrust.

"Scared of what?" I asked.

"A dagger in the back, mainly," Neleus replied.

I spent most of my days helping Neleus in his smithy, but in my recent forays into the streets, I could feel the simmering tension. "How can they just murder their opponents?" I asked.

My father grimaced. "Assassins. Street thugs. Gangs of youths from the political clubs. The leaders of the conspiracy are never involved directly, but someone is behind the intimidation. The old families see their opportunity to grab some power, and they are not going to let it slip by."

My father slapped the floor of the cart in exasperation. "By Zeus! The democrats can't unite! Anyone who might have led them has been killed or has gone into hiding. Look what happened to Androkles! Murdered in his own home! An ass, to be sure, but a leader of the people nonetheless. And Bisaltes, killed in the street like a dog! Anyone who speaks out against the anti-democrats is likely to end up the same, so they hide behind their doors like the cowards they are."

"But why don't they fight back?" I asked.

"Pisander is never without his troop of mercenaries protecting him," Neleus answered. "Still, I reckon I could round up enough lads to convince him of the error of his ways. Daimon would be good in a fight, I'm sure!" Neleus winked at me and I grinned back at him.

My father dismissed the idea with a wave. "Bah! The problem is not the leaders. The problem is that no one knows just how many people support their conspiracy. Is it one hundred people? Five hundred? A thousand? How many are there? Everyone is suspicious of everyone else. They're afraid if they reveal their opposition to the wrong person, they'll just end up dead like Androkles, so they just keep voting for whatever motion is put before them. Like sheep."

"Better a live sheep than a dead martyr," Neleus said dryly. "Still, Pisander's head on a pole at the city gate would be a good start, I reckon." My father sniffed but said no more.

The creaking wheels of the cart and the steady rhythm of the donkey's hooves on the packed earth filled the silence. The wide open space was unsettling, for I was more accustomed to roaming the narrow, twisting streets of Athens. The ravages of more than twenty years of war were plain to see. Ruined farm buildings dotted untended fields long choked with weeds and shrubs. The hacked and scorched carcasses of once mighty olive trees watched accusingly as we and other inhabitants of Athens streamed to Kolonos, still half a mile away.

We were not the only ones travelling that day. Sentries were posted at intervals along the route to watch for Spartan patrols and protect citizens should the need arise to retreat back to Athens.

We passed a squadron of a dozen hoplites standing somewhat idly by the side of the road. They were leaning on their spears with their helmets tilted back, watching the procession pass with evident boredom. Most had foregone heavy breastplates for lighter leather cuirasses, but all bore the large, concave *aspis* shields on their backs.

Neleus, the old soldier in him coming out, hailed the group as the cart rattled past. "Fellows! Not the most exciting posting, is it?" he called sociably.

"Can't say so, no," one of them responded in a gravelly voice. The man had an angry scar that ran diagonally across his tanned face from his forehead across the bridge of his nose to his left cheek. His hand rested casually on the sword hanging at his side.

"Are you expecting any action?" Neleus asked, gesturing towards their kit.

"Don't like to be far from my weapons. Never know what's going to happen. A corpse don't bite, as they say." The other members of the man's squad laughed at this.

"That's for sure, friend," Neleus replied. "You're going to Kolonos?"

"Aye."

"The gods be with you, then."

The hoplite said nothing, acknowledging Neleus with the barest dip of his head.

"Odd accent. Where do you think they were from, Nelo?" my father asked as the soldiers receded to our rear.

"Andros?" Neleus ventured.

"I would have said Tenos myself, but you might be right."

"It's hard to find an Athenian soldier in Athens these days," Neleus reflected with resentment. "Just mercenaries and allies of questionable loyalty."

I turned on my heel, wishing to look at the soldiers once more. I cupped my hand over my eyes against the sun. The band of hoplites had not moved, their gazes still fixed on our party of four.

My eyes met those of the scarred man, and I raised my hand in farewell. He did not return the greeting. Instead, he spat casually on the ground to his side and then turned to say something to one of his companions. The other man laughed and regarded our cart with more interest.

A faint ripple of unease tickled my gut, but I dismissed it with a shrug. Let them boil in their armour, I thought. I turned around and ran to catch up with the cart.

"SLAVES ARE NOT ALLOWED in the assembly," the soldier said, barring my path with his spear. I felt my face reddening.

"My *son*," my father stressed the word, "is my guide. Or have you not noticed that I am blind, you fool?"

The guard regarded me doubtfully, but either the authority in my father's voice or the disapproving glower of the brawny Neleus convinced the soldier to raise his spear. Still brooding over the slight, I led my father past the sentry. With his limping gait, Neleus brought up the rear.

We found some space on the right side of the steps and sat down. The temple was situated on a slight rise, with the slope leading up to it forming a natural amphitheatre. The hillside slowly filled up with men taking their places. The hum of hundreds of hushed conversations hung in the air.

My father leaned close to me. "Tell me what you see, Daimon. You will be my eyes today. My ears will keep their own counsel."

I described the scene to him, and he creased his brow in thought. "Do you see Iobates?" he asked.

"Yes, he is near the rostrum." It was easy to pick out the stout figure of my father's old friend, who was in animated discussion with those gathered near him.

Another face on the far side of the crowd made my hackles rise. "Father, Adrastos is here as well." My half-brother sat with a group of other young men, no doubt the clique of young aristocrats who were Adrastos' constant companions. They stood out for their lack of movement, their stone-faced gazes fixed on the rostrum. My father's frown deepened, but he said nothing about my brother's presence.

Something beyond the edge of the crowd caught my attention, pushing aside the ill-will I felt about Adrastos. A quick scan confirmed my suspicions. A knot formed in my stomach.

"Father, something is wrong."

"What?"

"The soldiers have surrounded the assembly."

As Neleus cursed under his breath, I described what I saw to my father, whose face grew more grim with each word.

The loose cordon of soldiers that had controlled entry to the assembly had been considerably reinforced. The perimeter had tightened, and now there was barely a shield's width of space between each man. Disconcertingly, not one of them was looking away from the temple, watching out for the enemy. Instead, they focused on the crowd with a silent, motionless intensity.

My father cursed. "I underestimated the audacity of the enemy. Pisander wants more than just influence. We have been outmanoeuvred, old friend," he said in a low voice to Neleus. The blacksmith let out a frustrated growl.

A trumpet sounded to indicate that the session was beginning.

The trap closed. As soon as the signal had been given, the soldiers reacted. The clatter of movement caused an uneasy stirring to sweep through the crowd. The ripple of confusion became a wave of panic as the soldiers began converging on the assembly, spears lowered and swords drawn. I looked back and saw that more armed men had appeared from within the temple to cut off any chance of escape in that direction.

At a distance of ten or so paces from the edge of the crowd, the soldiers stopped and grounded arms. The majority of the assembly had risen to their feet and were looking around in bewilderment, not knowing what to expect next. A few angry shouts were drowned out by the clamour of fearful voices.

The trumpet sounded again and again. Gradually, the insistent peals had the desired effect. The noise subsided as all eyes turned to the herald standing at the front of the crowd. Another man stood patiently at his side.

In a practiced voice, the herald spoke. "This session of the assembly will now come to order!" There was a stunned silence as those present realized that the assembly was going to take place under the threat of arms. The silence evaporated as the attendees began to protest. The herald repeated his proclamation, his voice cutting through the noise. "This session of the assembly will now come to order! Be seated!"

The soldiers surrounding the temple took two more steps towards the assembly and then halted, tightening the perimeter even further. The meaning was clear. Slowly, the citizens took their seats on the ground and the steps of the temple.

Absurdly, the protocols of an assembly were faithfully adhered to. The purification offerings were made, prayers offered, and the herald pronounced a curse on all traitors of Athens.

His eyes closed, my father bowed his head. "Follow procedure to give it an air of legitimacy," he muttered.

Finally, the herald moved on to the true business of the day. "The Commission for Revision of the Constitution of Athens will present its recommendations for debate. The first motion will be introduced by Pisander, son of Echemus, of the deme Sybridai."

The man beside the herald stepped forward to speak. Pisander's appearance surprised me. He was a small man in both stature and build. His bulging eyes and white, pointed beard gave him the appearance of a goat that had been transformed into a man. When he extended his arms and began to speak, it was with a surprisingly deep and sonorous voice that filled the air rather than with the bleating one expected.

"As you know, fellow citizens, at the last assembly, the people voted to appoint a commission to revise the constitution of our great polis." He paused for effect and looked about solemnly at the faces staring back at him. "Therefore, on this appointed day and at this appointed place, before gods and men, I will present the recommendations of the commission for debate. To this end, I now present the first motion."

"Here comes the hammer blow," Neleus muttered.

Pisander opened a roll of parchment and holding it out in front of him recited the contents. "By the authority of the council, I put forward the following motion for debate. On behalf of the commission, I move that all currently existing institutions be terminated immediately. Upon the dissolution of these institutions, the commission shall elect five men to be interim presidents. These men in turn will elect one hundred men, who in turn themselves will select three men apiece. This body of Four Hundred shall have full authority to govern in whatever matter they deem best."

This was the culmination of the manoeuvring, the plotting, the intimidation. "They are going to dissolve the assembly and install an oligarchy," my father said grimly.

Neleus pounded his fist into his other palm. "They have bigger balls than Zeus himself!"

My father put a restraining hand on his friend's arm. "This battle is lost. No matter what happens, do not get involved. Do you understand, Captain?"

"Aye, *strategos*," the old veteran said through clenched teeth.

Not everyone was privy to my father's wise counsel. At the front of the assembly, my father's friend Isobates rose to his feet and pointed at Pisander. "This is an outrage! You have gone too far if you think that we will accept this!" He turned to face the rest of us. "Will you stand with me, fellow Athenians, in defeating this motion? Will you rise to protect our democracy?"

"Don't be a fool, Iobates," my father implored in an angry whisper.

Most people were focused on the raging Iobates, but I saw Pisander give a nod to a group of soldiers that stood nearby. Three of them came forward, one with his dagger drawn, and waded into the crowd. I recognized the dagger-wielding man from the road, his scar easily visible even from my vantage point.

Iobates was still making his appeal, unaware of the threat coming up behind him. Some other assembly members pointed frantically trying to warn him, but he realized the peril too late.

Seizing Iobates' cloak with his left hand, the scarred man spun him around with a violent jerk. Iobates raised his hands in a pathetic attempt to ward off the assault as the Andrian mercenary punched five thrusts of the dagger into the old man's guts before stepping away. Iobates fell to his knees, his life flowing away through his fingers as he clutched his belly.

The killer wiped the blade on the shoulder of his still kneeling victim, leaving bright red smears on the pale cloth. Taking a position at Pisander's side, he sheathed his dagger and glared out at the audience, daring anyone to challenge him, and by extension, the motion before the assembly. There was only impotent silence.

"Father —," I whispered.

"I know. Keep silent," he warned me.

Iobates pitched forward and lay unmoving. The Andrian's companions dragged the slain man's limp form away and out of sight of the assembly.

Pisander continued as though the murder had not even occurred. "The motion is now before the assembly for debate. Are there any who wish to speak in favor of the motion?"

Pisander looked towards a man seated near the front of the gathering, who stood and turned to face the rest of us. He did not introduce himself, but I learned later that his name was Phrynichus, himself a former *strategos* and exile recently returned to Athens.

If Pisander was a goat, then Phrynichus was a hawk, with a thin face and intense eyes under a permanently furrowed brow. To his captive audience, Phrynichus bemoaned the foolishness of the democracy that had led to the wasteful, prolonged war with Sparta and her allies. The disaster of Sicily, he proclaimed, only proved that the fate of Athens could not be left to the whims of a capricious assembly. On the contrary, only under the guidance of best of men, the *aristoi*, would Athens be able to conclude the war with an honourable peace with Sparta. There were cheers and applause from supporters, but most endured the speech in gelded silence.

One speaker after another repeated the same sentiments. My father's sharp ears knew their names by voice alone. "Theramenes," he said under his breath. "Antiphon," for the next.

Eventually, those in support of the motion had their say, and Pisander addressed us again, spreading his arms wide in a gesture of invitation. "And are there," he said, "any who wish to speak against the motion?"

His appeal was met with defeated stares. But among the anguished faces, there were smiles of triumph. For the first time, the supporters of the oligarchs felt confident enough to reveal their true allegiance.

In the excitement of what had been happening, I had forgotten about Adrastos. I looked back to where he was sitting with his companions. They were grinning too. He became aware of my gaze, and his smile disappeared, replaced by the flash of a sneer. He returned his attention to the front of the assembly, for Pisander was preparing to speak again.

"If there are no more speakers for or against the motion, then let us proceed with the vote."

My father's unseeing eyes were shut, and he pinched the bridge of his nose in thought. Around me, most expressions ranged from stunned incomprehension to obvious fear to barely contained anger.

The herald stepped forward once again. "All those against the motion..." The request hung in the air, but no one dared raise their hands to oppose the measure.

"All those in favor of the motion," the herald called out. About two hundred or so hands went up immediately. The remaining citizens hung their heads or shifted uncomfortably where they sat. A few held their chins high in vain defiance.

The soldiers encircling the assembly took a step inwards. Reluctantly, more hands rose, until there was a clear majority.

"The motion is passed unanimously!" The herald announced. No one called him out on the blatant lie. "The commission will now choose its new leaders."

My father grimaced. "It is a shameful day," he said gravely.

The first democracy in the history of gods and men was dead, voted out of existence by its own members.

The rule of the Four Hundred had begun.

# CHAPTER 3

It is said that if you are not a citizen of a polis, then you are not a man. You are either a god, who has no need of such a thing, or you are less than a man — a slave or one of the *ethnoi* that live little better than animals on the edges of civilization.

Or, you are like me, neither a slave nor a god nor a barbarian, but like a shadow cursed to wander the earth, unseen but craving to be part of the life teeming around you. It is to always be on the outside looking in. It is loneliness.

On the festival of Apatouria, proud fathers introduce their newborn sons to their kinsmen. These infant boys receive their first haircut under the welcoming gaze of other members of their clan, who drink and sing and dance for the newest members of their tribe. The babes who are not citizens, like me, stay hidden away, suckling their mothers' tits as on any other day, their names not learned, their existence uncelebrated.

A child who is not born of two Athenian parents is never allowed to forget the fact. He is bullied and teased by those who have been granted citizenship as their birthright. And no matter how often he bests his tormentors with his fists or cunning, it will only make them despise him even more.

Adulthood does not free him of his invisible fetters. He is called upon to serve his polis in times of war, but he cannot own or inherit property. He has no voice in the assembly, nor can he represent himself in the law-courts without the backing of a citizen. He is trapped in a state of permanent adolescence, self-aware but powerless.

In the assembly or law-courts, a man proves his citizenship by reciting his family lineage for both his parents. My ancestry through my father would be the envy of most Athenians. My father was Nikodromos of the deme Skambonidai. Like him, my grandfather Alkimachos was also a general – a *strategos*. My great-grandfather Nikandros stood shoulder-to-shoulder with the general Miltiades at Marathon as they drove the Persians back into the sea. His father before him helped break the power of the aristocracy, helping the great Cleisthenes midwife Athens' frail democracy into this world.

But my mother was a freed slave. She did not even know the name of the Thracian village where she was captured as a child, let alone the deeds of her forebears.

She was kind and beautiful, with the fiery red hair that is so common among her people and one of her legacies to me and my sister. She was also quick-witted and mischievous, refusing to play the part of a proper Greek woman, and my father loved her.

I loved her, too.

But she was not a citizen, and I resented her for it.


MY FATHER AND I WERE going on a journey.

A month after the coup at Kolonos, a messenger from the port of Piraeus arrived at our home. The young man moved and spoke with a confidence that belied his youth and brought forth a pang of jealousy in my chest. He threw me a smile as I stared at him from the side of the courtyard.

The man delivered his message to my father in the privacy of the salon. When the visitor had left, my father summoned me. He was pacing in agitation. No, I was mistaken. It was excitement, something so rare in my father that I had not recognized it. "You will accompany me to Piraeus, Daimon," he stated. "We will set out once the heat of the day has passed. Help Neleus in the smithy until it is time to leave. I need to think," he said, dismissing me.

For the rest of the afternoon, I could not focus on my work, much to the annoyance of Neleus. "If you keep grinding that spear-point, there will be nothing left to stick in the Spartans," he observed.

"Sorry, *lochagos*," I said, addressing him by his military rank. "I'll be more careful." I could not stop thinking about the impending trek to Piraeus. I struggled to master my impatience as the sun plodded across the sky with agonizing slowness.

After an age, my father appeared at the door of the smithy. "Go and bid your mother farewell while I speak with Neleus," he instructed me. "And fetch my things. Your mother will have prepared them for me."

"Yes, Father," I replied obediently.

Neleus was not about to let me escape my duties so easily. He pointed to the pile of unpolished spear-points. "Whatever you don't do today will be waiting for you when you return," the old warrior warned.

"Yes, lochagos," I said before spinning away and hurrying off through the passage that connected the smithy to our own house.

Despite my father's status, our home differed little from hundreds of other such houses in the city. From the street, a heavy wooden door set into the high plastered wall admitted visitors to the pillared courtyard through which I now strode.

At the stone altar in the centre of the courtyard I paused, running my fingers over its worn surface. The original sharp edges of the great limestone block had been worn smooth by time. The carved figure of a god decorated the front panel, but countless years of rain and sun and cold had nearly obliterated the deity so that even my father was hesitant to guess which of the divinities was actually portrayed there. The altar radiated a silent power, and I was in awe of it. Each morning I stood beside my father as he made a sacrifice to Zeus and poured a libation of wine over the ancient stone. Now I whispered a quick prayer and moved on.

Several rooms lined the courtyard, including the kitchen and salon, as well as the storeroom that also served as a sleeping chamber for Tibetos and me. A doorway in the kitchen led to the property next door where Neleus lived and kept his smithy. I smiled to think of the toil I would escape that day. A walk to Piraeus! The gods had blessed me!

Still buoyant with this thought, I ascended the stairs to the upper level containing the women's quarters and my parents' bed-chamber. I glanced at Adrastos' room at the top of the stairs, and my mood darkened, though I knew my brother was not at home. He rarely was. The Four Hundred used gangs of aristocratic youth to harass and intimidate anyone foolish enough to openly criticize the regime. It was not hard to guess whose company Adrastos was keeping.

Almost unconsciously, I trod softly, avoiding the boards that would creak and betray my presence. It was a childhood game that had since become an ingrained habit. I padded along the landing, coming to a halt outside the doorway to where my mother was working. My breathing shallow, I cocked my ear towards the room.

My mother was humming, as she often did when she was working. It was her favourite, and mine too, the tale of a shepherd and a Thracian princess and their doomed love. It was one of the rare things that she had brought with her from Thrace besides her language and her gods. It was also something she had given to me, as she had sung it to me almost every day when I was a child.

As if she had heard me smile, my mother suddenly stopped humming. "Daimon, is that you?"

My weight shifted slightly, causing the floor to groan. A patter of light footsteps fluttered towards the doorway. My sister Melitta barrelled into me, driving the air from my lungs. "Dammo!" she cried out joyfully, pinning my arms to my sides as she hugged me. "Take me with you today! I promise to be good!" she begged.

With an exaggerated roar, I flexed my arms outward and broke my sister's embrace. I grimaced menacingly. Meli giggled, her emerald eyes flashing. Her perpetually unkempt hair blazed like fire.

"I'm sorry, Amazon, but I can't. It's only me and Father this time." I often called my sister my Amazon, which she liked immensely. But now she pouted, making her look younger than her thirteen years. She chafed at being restricted to the house and looked forward to any chance of escape beyond its walls. "I'll take you out when we get back. I promise," I said.

The concession seemed to mollify her. She grinned and led me by the hand into the room where my mother was spinning wool.

My mother held a short rod with a weighted mass of wool on its end. The weight of the turning spindle teased out a lengthening thread, which she was watching intently. But I knew her sharp mind was considering other things.

"Will you be departing soon?" My mother asked in Thracian, her eyes not leaving her work.

I answered her in Greek as I always did. "Yes, Father is eager to set out."

"It is good that he is taking you with him. He sees that you are growing up. He needs your help." I did not respond. I was looking forward to seeing Piraeus, but was less enthusiastic about being in my father's stern company for such a long period.

The spindle reached the ground, and my mother bent over to retrieve it. She wound the fresh span of thread about the spindle before placing the implements on a table. She turned and walked over, stopping in front of me. Like most Thracians, she was tall, the top of her head almost reaching my nose, even though I was almost full-grown.

Taking my hands, she tilted her chin to look at me. "These are dangerous times, Daimon. You must promise me to take care of your father. And yourself."

"I promise, Mother," I said dutifully. She smiled at her small victory, for I had spoken in Thracian.

She stretched up to kiss my cheek. "Go *pasha!*" she said, laughing. Wool-head. It was her favorite nickname for me, sometimes when she was angry, but more often than not it was said with affection. "Your father's things are in his room, and there is a satchel of bread and cheese for the trip in the kitchen. Remember what I said, Daimon. Now go!"

She presented her cheek and I returned the kiss. As I leaned in close to her, I caught the light scent of perfume. It was one of the few Greek habits she had adopted. With the herbal scent still lingering in my nostrils, I hurried to my parents' room. Meli followed closely on my heels, her light steps shadowing my heavy ones.

On the bed lay my father's cloak and broad-rimmed straw hat along with other supplies my mother had prepared. I picked them up and turned to find Meli looking at me expectantly.

"I told you that you can't come," I said. But I had mistaken her intentions.

"It's not that," she said. "I had a dream last night, Dammo."

I arched one eyebrow. My sister was prone to vivid dreams that she insisted were visions from the gods. I often teased her about her wild claims, but she persisted in her beliefs. I humored her now by letting her speak.

"I saw an acorn fall to the ground, Dammo. It was you, I think," she said, looking at me so earnestly that it was difficult to suppress my smile. "The rain came and a tree began to sprout. It was young and strong. Then I woke up."

"That doesn't sound so bad," I said.

"It means change is coming."

"Change is always coming, Meli! You can't stop it!" I said with a shrug. "Now go back and help Mother!"

My sister hugged me one more time, burying her face into my tunic. "Just take care, Dammo," she said before scurrying away.

I let out a sigh. As I moved to pick up the satchel of supplies, my gaze fell upon my father's great shield. The *aspis* hung on the wall opposite the olive-wood bed. The burnished bronze rim framed the image of a Pegasus, battered and faded, but still clear. For reasons lost to time, the winged horse had been the symbol of my family since the time of Solon. I revered that shield, for it radiated the glory and honour of its past.

Beside the hoplite shield, my father's breastplate and helm hung on a stand. The disembodied armour floated in the air as though worn by a ghost. The bronze helmet stared back at me, faceless and silent. The breast-plate was a thing of beauty, the hammered musculature the work of some long-forgotten master craftsman. Even in the low light it glistened under a coating of protective oil. I let my finger trace the incised scroll-work that coiled and looped about the cool metal. My fingertip came to a stop on a roughly-mended tear under the left breast.

Far from being a defect, the damage was a scar of pride for my father. A cup or three of wine might make my normally sombre father recall how the rent in the armour had come to be, courtesy of a Megarian spear-blow. He pointed out with pride that though he was a *strategos*, he had stood in the front ranks with his men, taking his wounds to the front of his body like a true warrior.

My father called impatiently from the courtyard. I hastily cleaned my fingers of oil by wiping them on the floorboards before hurrying downstairs.

In the courtyard, my father stood before the ancient altar. He was eager to be off. We would be fortunate to reach Piraeus before sunset. "Daimon, bring me a cup of wine."

I did as I was bidden, fetching a bowl from the salon and placing the vessel in my father's waiting palm. He turned towards the altar, holding the offering of wine at chest height with both hands. Beside him, I bowed my head and raised my palms upward. My piety was genuine, for my father had raised me so. As a child the only thing I feared more than a beating from my father or Neleus was the wrath of the gods.

My father invoked the name of Zeus the Protector, beseeching him to see us safely to Piraeus. I echoed the words in a whisper. A simple prayer, but my father would have considered it inauspicious to set forth without it.

The invocation complete, he tipped the cup and the wine came out in a stream, splattering on the top of the altar. Rivulets meandered to and fro over the surface of the stone before dribbling over the edges in tiny waterfalls. At the base, the dry earth drank the wine greedily, each drop vanishing as soon as it struck the ground.

We made our final good-byes. My mother had come down to see us off. My father touched her cheek gently and whispered something to her, and her eyes lifted towards me. Her smile did not completely mask her unease.

Meli was less circumspect, hugging my father unabashedly. He returned the embrace, for he loved my sister greatly and was unashamed in his affection for her.

Outside, Tibetos was holding our donkey's halter. He looked depressed. I too was disappointed that he would not accompany us. But my father had been insistent that I be his sole companion on this journey.

The lock of the heavy wooden door clicked behind us. "Piraeus awaits, Daimon," my father said. But the purpose of our journey was still a mystery to me.

INSIDE THE CITY, MY FATHER rode our long-suffering donkey. The impassive beast bore its burden patiently, seemingly more disturbed by the flies that pestered it than by the load on its back.

The mercenaries employed by the Four Hundred made their presence felt in all parts of the city, cowing the population into fearful obedience. More than a few citizens had vanished, dragged away to prison or worse. But to anyone who saw us that day, my father and I would have seemed nothing more than a blind old man and his slave. The mercenaries let us pass through the Piraeus Gate on the south side of the city wall without incident.

Once past the gate, my father slid from the donkey's back, touching the ground with a satisfied sigh. "I believe I shall walk for a spell. The road is straight enough, anyway. Even for a blind man!" Letting out the odd grunt, he stretched out the kinks in his body.

To the southwest extended the road of which my father spoke. Two high stone walls, the aptly named Long Walls, shielded the connection between Athens and the port of Piraeus seven miles away. The protected roadway was the lifeline of the city, the artery that was vital to the survival of Athens. Food and supplies from the hundreds of poleis of the empire could come into the port at Piraeus and be transported to Athens, completely safe from the enemy. The Spartans could raid and burn all the lands of Attica and shout outside the city walls until they were hoarse, but it would do them no good. Athens was in effect an island.

It was close to sunset when we finally reached Piraeus. The mixed aroma of sea air, sewage, smoke and pitch for sealing the hulls of ships had been growing ever more pungent for the last part of our journey until we finally passed through the city gate.

"Where are we going, father?" I asked. So far, my father had not revealed our final destination.

"I will direct you, lad. I could find it with my eyes closed." He chuckled at the irony of his own joke. My father guided us confidently, through the broad, straight streets of the port. He came to a halt. "We are here," he said.

Unlike the other shops and warehouses that lined the streets, the compound now before us was enormous, occupying an entire block of the town. A pair of guards stood at attention at the lone entrance along the southern wall. "What place is this?" I asked in wonder.

"The headquarters of the *peripoli*. Come. We are expected."

The *peripoli*. My fatigue from the journey vanished. I had heard tales of these hard men many times, but even in Athens they were something of a mystery, spoken of in whispers that were equal parts scorn and grudging awe. Many older men disdained the *peripoli* for eschewing the traditional hoplite ethos and phalanx battles of our forefathers. Instead, these lightly-armed fighters ranged about the countryside, relying on stealth and ambush to fall upon unwary enemies. The unorthodox general Demosthenes had used them with great success to carry out attacks deep in Spartan-controlled territory. They were said to worship Hades and the creatures of the underworld.

As I pondered this, my father addressed one of the guards. "My name is Nikodromos and this is my son –"

"Welcome, strategos," the young sentry cut him off enthusiastically. "Commander Hermon is eager to see you." He nodded to the other soldier. "Zenthanos will see to your beast. Please follow me."

Beyond the massive double door, a covered passage led deep into the compound until at last we emerged into a large courtyard at the heart of the complex. Each wall framed a wide gate that led to other parts of the enclosed community.

I gaped in awe. Around me, the courtyard bustled with activity. Two armoured men were sparring in one corner, the clanging of iron and bronze ringing in the enclosed space as swords and shields clashed. One of the combatants deftly avoided a stab before soundly rapping his opponent's helmet with the flat of his blade. The dozen or so rugged spectators roared in admiration for the blow. As his dazed counterpart recovered, the victor removed his helmet. His black hair was matted with sweat and he was grinning broadly. His gaze met mine and for an instant his wolf-like eyes narrowed, but then he turned back towards his fellows.

A voice pulled my attention away from the rangers. "This way, *strategos*," our guide said to my father, indicating the gateway at the east side of the courtyard. "Commander Hermon is waiting."

My eyes still wide with wonder, I tried to take everything in as we were led to the commander's headquarters. "Commander," the guard said smartly, "*Strategos* Nikodromos has arrived."

Hermon leaned over a large table covered with documents, his hands spread wide. He pulled himself up. The commander was nearly as large as Neleus but uglier in every way, and that is saying quite a lot. Though he had a thick, grey beard, Hermon's head was completely bare, and the lines etched in his face and head seemed to dance with every gravelly word. He may have been handsome once, but it was impossible to say, for his original features were obscured by a twisted nose and the scars of a long life of violent encounters.

"It is good to see you, *strategos*." The commander's eyes flicked over my way before returning to my father, but he said nothing to me.

"Likewise, Hermon. It has been too long," my father said.

Hermon grunted. "Aye, it has. I wish it could have been over a cup of wine, but the gods don't want to give old men like us the rest we deserve, it seems."

My father shrugged. "We can only accept the will of the gods. They may grant us that cup of wine later, old friend. But let us meet your guest."

"Of course, *strategos*. Peiros here will take your son for some food," Hermon said beckoning the young guard. I was surprised that Hermon knew my identity.

"My son will accompany us," my father said simply. It was a statement of fact, not a request.

Hermon raised a bushy eyebrow but did not protest. "As you wish, *strategos*."

The commander led us through a warren of buildings, workshops, and courtyards. It was more akin to a village than a compound. Men, women, and children went about their business, sparing us little more than a curious glance as we passed. By the time we reached our destination, I was completely disoriented. A guard at the doorway stepped aside to let us enter.

"This is who you have come to see," Hermon said with a sweep of his hand.

The object of our expedition sat slumped over the table in front of a cup of wine. Upon our entry, he straightened up but did not rise. One eye was bloodshot and ringed with a purple bruise. The other just registered fatigue.

Yet he smiled weakly when he saw my father. "*Strategos*, my name is Chaereas. I have come a long way to see you."

## CHAPTER 4

Chaereas told us his tale.

He had sailed from the island of Samos on the other side of the Aegean where the bulk of the Athenian fleet was stationed. Prior to the coup at Kolonos, the Four Hundred had sent agents to convince sympathetic generals and captains — and there were many — to seize control of the Athenian forces and kill the leaders of any democratic factions.

And they had failed.

As he continued his story, Chaereas became more impassioned. The fighting had been fierce at times, but the democrats had prevailed. The generals who had sided with the Four Hundred were either dead or had fled into exile. The victors had held elections and chosen new generals to lead them. I sat in thrall as I listened to the tale.

My father, for the most part, had listened attentively while Chaereas related the events across the sea, only interrupting occasionally to get clarification on some point or to ask the name of a particular individual. "Who is in overall command now?" he asked at one point.

"Thrasybulus, *strategos*," Chaereas answered without hesitation.

My father nodded. "I knew his father, Lykos. A good man. If the son is anything like the father, then the fleet is in good hands."

"Thrasybulus united us, *strategos*," Chaereas said, eager to say more.

"What do you mean?" my father asked.

"After the fighting," Chaereas began, "the men's blood was up. Many of our comrades had died and we wanted to punish those responsible. The leaders may have been killed, but most of those who fought for them were still among us. We wanted blood for blood. But the *strategos* wouldn't allow it. On the night after the fighting, we were ready to attack the traitors. But the *strategos* visited every camp and told us that they weren't the enemy. If we took revenge, it would be a victory for Sparta, not for Athens. He said that united we could beat the Spartans, but divided, we had already lost. And he went to the camp of the defeated enemies and said the same thing."

The soldier paused, considering his words. "It was strange, but I really believed what he was saying. And not only me. Everyone believed it. After a few days, the *strategos* brought us together, those from both sides I mean, and made us swear an oath to defend the democracies of Samos and Athens. By the gods, I was clasping the hands of men who a few days earlier had been trying to kill me!" Chaereas shook his head in wonder.

"Why did you come back to Athens?" my father asked.

"To report to the assembly, of course!" Chaereas said, suddenly sitting upright. "But we didn't know there was no assembly to report to! The news of the coup hadn't reached us when we departed for Athens. We came on the *Paralus*," he said, referring to the Athenian flagship. "It's still moored in the harbour. As soon as we arrived, the entire crew was arrested. I managed to escape. If Hermon's men hadn't found me and hidden me here, I'd be captured or dead!"

"Indeed," my father said, stroking his beard. "The Four Hundred does not want word of their failure to seize the fleet to spread. Your report from Samos has given us hope, Chaereas. But you are no doubt exhausted. Rest your weary bones! We will speak more of this tomorrow with full bellies and clearer heads."

Chaereas rose to his feet. "It would be my honour, *strategos*."

Outside the building, Hermon spoke to my father in a low voice. "What do you think, *strategos*?"

"That the fleet remains out of reach of the Four Hundred is welcome news, but gives us much to consider."

"What will the bastards do now?"

"Without the ships, they will not have enough soldiers to back their regime and no money to pay their mercenaries. They will look elsewhere for the spears and swords to intimidate the people, I think."

"Sparta?" Hermon asked, incredulous.

"Who else is there?" my father asked.

"But that is treason! We must strike soon, while they are weak!"

"Perhaps, but the beast is most dangerous when it is cornered and fighting for its very life," my father responded. "We must be cautious." The commander of the *peripoli* scowled at this but did not challenge my father.

Later, after we had been given lodgings and food, I was sent to the commander to express gratitude for the accommodation. Entering the headquarters, I nearly collided with someone coming out.

"Watch it, lad!" the man said in an easy manner. It was the black-haired ranger I had seen sparring earlier.

My eyes widened. "I saw you fighting in the yard!" I exclaimed, immediately feeling foolish.

The man winked. "Seeing the commander?" he asked. I nodded. "Better make it quick. He's liable to eat you in the mood he's in." He patted my shoulder sympathetically and strode off.

With more trepidation, I went into the headquarters and delivered my father's thanks to the commander of the *peripoli*.

"For the *strategos,* anything. It is nothing to speak of," Hermon said gruffly with a wave of his hand. He put his head down and went back to the document that he had been reading when I entered. I was clearly dismissed, but I did not leave.

My father's former rank of general had always afforded him a certain degree of respect, but I was increasingly confused by the deference he commanded among men like Hermon. Mustering some courage, I cleared my throat.

Hermon looked up with an irritated frown. "What is it, boy?" he growled.

Nervous under the commander's hard stare, I asked my question. "Why was my father called to speak to Chaereas?"

An amused grin appeared on Hermon's face. It was like a wolf baring its teeth. "Don't you know, boy?" he laughed. "Your father leads the resistance to the Four Hundred! Once a *strategos,* always a *strategos!*" He rose to show me to the door. Still chuckling, he slapped my back with a meaty hand, but I was still in too much shock to notice.

THE FLICKERING LIGHT FROM two lamps illuminated the storeroom that I would share with my father that night. Sealed amphorae filled one corner, and stacked high against the opposite wall were bales of wool, ready for spinning. They reminded me of my mother. A bed had been scavenged from somewhere in the compound for my father. I would make do with a canvas sack stuffed with straw.

My father was going through his night-time ritual of twists and stretches before he took to bed. I looked on, statue-like, still shaken from Hermon's revelation that the old man before me was a revolutionary.

At last, he made a final stretch. Yawning, he felt about for the edge of the bed and sat down, exhaling wearily. "Why do you stare at me so, Daimon? I can hear your eyes upon me."

In the dim lamp-light, his clouded eyes appeared dark, as though the gods had granted him sight once more. I squirmed under his unseeing gaze, knowing that he could see me well enough, blind or not.

"Hermon told me that you lead the fight against the Four Hundred!" It came out as more of an accusation.

My father did not deny the charge. "Evil men have taken control of our polis. Good men must stand up and thwart their ambitions," he said. My father ever saw things in such simple terms.

I was not so sure. In the streets I had seen only fearful people, cowed into subservience by the Four Hundred's army of brutal mercenaries. "The people are afraid," I said doubtfully.

My father sighed. "Sometimes courage is slow to wake in men's hearts. They will follow whoever is strongest if they can get on with their lives. But the people have seen the evil of the Four Hundred, how they offend both gods and men with their deeds. The citizens of Athens only need a push before they turn on their new masters."

"And Chaereas is that push?" I said, trying to understand.

"The oligarchs are losing their grip. They needed the fleet, but it has sided against them. The grain and tribute will dry up and the mercenaries will leave."

It sounded too easy for me. "So the Four Hundred are finished?" I asked.

"No," my father said. "Now is the most dangerous time. They will move to betray Athens. They will appeal to Sparta for aid."

"But Sparta is our enemy!" I exclaimed.

"The aristocrats have waited one hundred years to overthrow democracy. Do not underestimate what they will do to cling to power now that they finally have it in their grasp. Betraying Athens to Sparta means nothing to them as long as it helps them to achieve their aims. But if the people discover this, they will rise up and restore our democracy."

"It isn't my democracy, Father," I said, a festering resentment building inside me. "I am not even a citizen. Mother, Melitta, me... We are nothing. I am the son of a *strategos*, but when others look at me, they only see the son of a slave. A barbarian."

"I understand your frustration, but if the Four Hundred succeed, they will make slaves of us all. And what will that mean to you? And your sister? And your mother? Be patient! I will get you your citizenship and then —"

"Why should I believe you? You have always failed before," I said bitterly, cutting him off. I suddenly feared I had gone too far in my insolence.

But my father sighed, massaging his forehead. "You are so like your mother in many ways: a good heart but uncontrollable. Like a storm! I do not know if you got the best part of her or the worst!" he laughed, shaking his head in wonder.

His hand moved to a scar on his cheek. It was one of many such blemishes on his body. "Your mother saved me, Daimon, and not only from the *nosos*." The plague. His voice had dropped almost to a whisper, as though the very mention of the illness might summon the dead back to haunt us.

At the beginning of the war, when every farmer and slave and old woman in Attica had huddled behind the walls of Athens, the great sickness came, sweeping through the city as a scythe cuts through so many stalks of wheat. The walls could protect the inhabitants from Spartan blades, but not from the invisible killer. Rich or poor, the plague did not discriminate. Entire households were wiped out, men and women, young and old, master and slave. Some, like my mother, were untouched, spared by the gods or fate.

"Your mother could have fled," my father continued, his voice wavering. "The other slaves did. My wife was dead, and your brothers and I lay dying in our own filth and blood, covered in black sores. But your mother did not leave. She cleaned our soiled clothes and fed us gruel like we were infants. She prayed to that Thracian goddess of hers to heal us. She nursed us back to health. Is she less noble for having been born a slave, Daimon?" he asked me and I felt ashamed. "Judge people by their actions, not by their birth. That is the promise of democracy."

He composed himself once again. "Daimon, when this war is over, Athens will need citizens to become strong again. When the democracy is restored, you and your sister and your mother will receive the special dispensations to become citizens. I will fight to make it so." His resolute tone ignited a tiny flame of hope in my chest.

"Remember," my father continued. "It was only recently that citizens were barred from having mixed blood. It was not so in the past. Even your great-grandmother was a barbarian from the north! After all these years, I can still remember the old woman's green eyes. Did you know that even the great Themistokles' mother was Thracian, like your mother? Maybe you will be the next Themistokles!"

I scoffed lightly, and there was a moment of silence, filled only by the rippling shadows cast by the lamplight.

"Why do you think I insisted you accompany me here, Daimon?"

"I don't know." It was true. My father was a *strategos*, a serious man, but he was an enigma to me, stern and distant.

"You are grown, Daimon. It is time for you to move beyond childish things. Neleus tells me that you are clever and a hard worker in the smithy, and that in your training exercises you are fast and strong. Your mother says you have a kind heart and you are loyal. Melitta adores you more than anyone." My heart swelled at this rare praise. But the feeling was short-lived.

"But Neleus tells me you can be disobedient and pig-headed. You do not listen to the advice of those who know better. Your mother worries about your temper. You are willful and impulsive, and it has ever been so, Daimon. Is this what you wish to be?"

I thought of the boys who taunted me. I thought of Adrastos. "I want to be feared," I said truthfully, as though by voicing my desire the gods would grant me my wish. I was a simple boy.

But my father laughed, and I felt foolish. "It is good to be feared by your enemies!" he admitted. "But it is better to be a good man, to be a bold man, to fight for those who cannot. Your brother Heliodoros was such a man, as are Neleus and Commander Hermon. Men who would stand in the front rank of the phalanx, risking themselves for the sake of others. Do you not want to be like them?"

"I do, Father," I said.

My father grasped my hand. "It is difficult to stand among the bold, Daimon. Among the just. Will you stand with me, or would you count yourself among men of lesser worth and submit yourself to the tyranny of cruel men like the Four Hundred?" He leaned forward. "What kind of man do you want to be, my son?"

"I want to be like Heliodoros," I said earnestly.

My father smiled. "That is a worthy goal. But remember: it is the hottest flames that forge the strongest blade! The way forward is not for fearful men!"

"I am not afraid, Father," I said with more confidence than I felt.

My father squeezed my hand. "Then I am happy. But it is late, and my age haunts me. We will speak more of this tomorrow."

But I had one more question for my father. "And Adrastos?" I asked softly. My father's face fell as if he had aged ten years in a heartbeat, and I immediately regretted my words.

"He has chosen what kind of man he wants to be," he said sorrowfully. My father lay down with his back to me and said no more. I blew out the lamp and settled in on the straw mattress on the floor. In the darkness, my father's breathing became deeper and more regular. I lay on my bed, unable to fall asleep as thoughts of the day's events ran through my mind like the torrents of a winter river. My sister's words from that morning accompanied me as I slipped into unconsciousness.

*Change is coming.*

# CHAPTER 5

I became my father's *kataskopos*. A spy. His eyes and ears on the streets and in the alleys of Athens. I carried out my missions zealously, eager to vindicate the trust my father had placed in me.

It was not difficult work, for I appeared to others as no more than a lowly slave going about his master's business. I shadowed members of the Four Hundred, noting their comings and goings and reporting back to my father. My knowledge of the narrow, winding laneways of Athens allowed me to observe my targets without being seen myself. Mostly, though, I waited.

On some days, such as this one, my sister and Tibetos accompanied me. It made the trudging hours pass more quickly. Today I regretted it.

"Why can't we go to the agora?" Meli pestered me. It was a market day, but we had been idling in the vicinity of the southern gate of the city for the entire morning, watching the traffic to and from Piraeus. The bread and cheese we had brought were long gone. Tibetos kicked at a rock absent-mindedly.

"We will stay a little longer," I said brusquely. "You didn't have to come, you know." Meli pouted at me.

In fact, my father had instructed me to watch the gate that day, but I did not know what I was looking for. I did not want to return from my mission empty-handed, so we had suffered the growing heat of the day at my insistence.

Yet as time passed, I began to lose hope, for I could see nothing out of the ordinary. The mercenaries manning the gate were checking everyone coming and going from the city. There was grumbling from the queue of traders, slaves, and carts, but no one dared raise their voices to the grim-faced soldiers.

My stomach rumbled insistently. We could go buy something to eat in the agora, I thought, and return. I was about to give in to my sister's demands.

"Clear the way! Make way!" A squad of mercenaries was bearing down on me, pushing and shouting their way through the crowd.

"Out of the way!" the leader growled. I was shocked to find myself staring into the scarred face of the Andrian mercenary who had slain Iobates. But he looked through me and shoved me aside.

Recovering from my surprise, I craned my neck to see past the cordon of soldiers and the crowd of bystanders, trying to catch a glimpse of who the mercenaries were escorting. My heart beat harder when I laid eyes on the man in their midst.

It was the hawk-faced Phrynichus, the former general who had spoken so adamantly for the installation of the Four Hundred. The oligarch kept his unblinking eyes focused straight ahead as he walked, only adding to his raptor-like appearance.

Trailing behind the ring of guards was a cart laden with chests and sacks, as well as slaves bearing loads on wooded frames. They were provisions for a long journey, and I knew their destination. Phrynichus was going to Sparta.

The procession pushed its way past the queue and through the gate. Once the last of the porters had vanished through the opening, I beckoned to Tibetos and Meli.

"We have to get back home!" I said impatiently. I was eager to deliver the news to my father.

"What about the agora?" Meli said petulantly.

"Later!" I snapped. I dashed away, leaving Tibetos and my sister to stare at my rapidly shrinking figure.

MELI AND TIBETOS TRIED TO keep up with me, but I was too fast. I weaved through the throngs, careening around corners and taking short-cuts. I avoided the hustle and bustle of the agora, opting instead to run along one of the streets that ran parallel to it.

As I ran I cast a quick glance back over my shoulder. Meli and Tibetos were dodging past the same startled pedestrians that I had left in my wake. My sister was beaming, thrilled by the excitement of it all.

And I ran headlong into a man coming around a corner.

The impact of the collision knocked my breath from my lungs. I fell down, the gravel on the road surface embedding itself in the skin of my elbows. The man I had barrelled into was now flat on his back in the dirt. As I scrabbled to rise, the man's three companions bent over and hoisted him to his feet.

They were young men of wealth and standing. Their hair and beards were cropped fashionably short. Necklaces, bracelets, and rings of silver and gold accented their finely-made white tunics, a sharp contrast to the coarse dun cloth that I wore.

I groaned inwardly. The man I had bowled over was unknown to me, but I knew one of his friends. It was my brother, Adrastos.

My brother's companion stared down at the dirty streaks that sullied his clothing. With a look of disbelief and rage, he looked up at me. "What in the name of Hades have you done, you fucking slave?" he screamed. The corded tendons of his neck were taut like bowstrings and his fury marred his handsome features. His hand reached for the hilt of knife hanging on the belt of his tunic. I raised my fists instinctively.

"Stop!" Adrastos stepped forward, his outstretched hand preventing his enraged friend from moving forward. "It is my brother," Adrastos explained with a sneer. His baleful eyes never left mine. I glowered back at him.

Suddenly there was the patter of feet as Tibetos and Meli finally caught up and skidded to a stop behind me. Meli let out a low hiss at the sight of our brother.

Adrastos' companion sized me up contemptuously. "So this is the little Thracian whore-spawn bastard you keep telling us about. Filthy animal running around the streets, just like you said," he said, taunting me. I gritted my teeth and bore the insult. I was strong for my age after years of working at the forge with Neleus, but four grown men against a youth, a slave, and a girl were not odds in my favour. Adrastos smirked and his other two friends laughed at my impotent silence.

The lane was wide enough so that we could pass. "Come on," I called over my shoulder to Meli and Tibetos. As I stepped forward, my brother's friend moved to block our way.

"Not even an apology, *pai*?" he said mockingly, drawing out the final word.

My fist tightened. *Pai*. From a parent's lips, it means "child." Even as an adult, a man may be called *pai* in affection by a grandparent or kindly uncle. But from a master, it is the term of address for a slave or servant. There was no ambiguity in the man's tone. He grinned maliciously, awaiting my reaction. My breathing deepened, like a bellows. But I refused to let him goad me. Meli edged closer to me.

The man's eyes slid over to Meli, appraising her. "The barbarians are good for something at least," he said, his lascivious gaze not leaving my sister. "I've heard the Thracian whores are the best, especially the young ones. A drachma for a roll with this one and all is forgiven." He reached out and groped at Meli's young breasts through her tunic and she recoiled in disgust.

My rage exploded and I lunged at him. My fist smashed into the side of his face, sending him sprawling back into the two other men behind him. I spun towards my brother with my fists raised. Adrastos glared at me with pure hatred. I drove a punch towards his head with a snarl.

My brother side-stepped my wild attack with ease, following up with a vicious hook that caught me neatly in the cheek. I stumbled past him in a daze, barely bringing my arms up in time to stop my face from grinding into the wall. Shaking off the blow, I turned and launched myself at him again, tackling him around the waist, but he was ready, bracing himself for the impact, and he trapped me in a suffocating headlock under his arm. His knee pounded up into my gut, and with a roar he heaved me into the air, tossing me towards Tibetos and Meli. I landed hard on my back and the impact drove the wind from my lungs.

Tibetos, his teeth bared in anger, stepped between me and my brother. Adrastos scoffed. "Do it, slave!" he sneered. He spread his arms wide, daring Tibetos to attack. "See what happens to slaves who dare strike their masters!" Tibetos' clenched fists quivered, but he was restrained by the invisible chains of his status.

I rolled over onto my hands and knees, gasping for air and trying to get to my feet, but the sandaled foot of my brother's companion buried itself in my ribs.

"You whore's bastard!" he screamed at me, kicking me again. He stomped on my back and I was flattened to the ground. "You fucking barbarian slave!" I curled instinctively to protect my head and chest from the onslaught, but no blow came. Instead, there was a surprised yelp of pain.

I ventured a glimpse from my protective shell and was startled to see Meli standing between me and my attacker. I scrabbled to my feet.

My brother's friend clutched his forearm, blood dripping from between his fingers onto the dusty ground. A spray of red spots on his tunic had only added to the dishonor done to his fine garment that day. He stared wide-eyed at my sister. His jaw moved soundlessly as he searched for more insults to hurl, but he found none.

Meli stood in a low crouch, a sailor's knife held firmly in her hand. My Amazon. The blade swayed lightly before her, like a serpent poised to strike at its next victim.

The stolen knife had passed into my sister's keeping, and she treasured it above all things. My father knew it was in her possession but said nothing, for he loved Meli and could not help indulging her. In the courtyard of our home she would practice slashes and stabs and lunges with savage intensity. "Mother says that the women of Thrace can fight like men!" she would proclaim proudly as she whipped the blade to and fro in slicing arcs. It was always on her person, tucked away in a hidden pocket in her tunic.

Now, the vicious little knife danced like a scorpion's sting. Adrastos' eyes narrowed as he sized up the new threat and considered the best way to deal with it. He could surely overwhelm my sister, but the familiarity with which she wielded the weapon gave him pause.

Distant shouts distracted my brother from the stand-off with his half-sister. His eyes flicked up, looking over my shoulder. The shouting was drawing nearer. Adrastos growled in frustration. I hazarded a quick glance behind me.

The Skythians were coming.

The Skythians are barbarian slaves from the great plains north of the Euxine Sea. Unsympathetic and efficient, they are selected for their brawn, lack of intelligence, and willingness to use their clubs and staves on anyone who disturbs the peace, regardless of wealth or status. Just the sight of the fair-haired warriors is enough to send street brawlers scurrying for safety, their own quarrels suddenly forgotten.

Adrastos had made the same calculation. "It is time to leave," he called out. His companions, only now seeing the approaching Skythians, reached a similar conclusion and turned to flee. Adrastos snarled once at Meli, who was still crouched and watching him warily. Then, he shifted his icy gaze onto me. "Next time, when you don't have this little girl and a slave to save you, watch out, *brother*." He pulled at his friend's shoulder. "Let's go," he said.

Meli's victim, still staunching his bleeding arm, found his tongue once more. "You are a dead man, slave!" he hissed. The two of them turned and trotted up the street before vanishing around a corner.

The four Skythian guards bounded up just as Meli and Tibetos were helping me to my feet. With blank expressions, they watched my brother disappear but made no effort to pursue. The peace kept, they were satisfied.

Their leader cast a wry look in my direction as I held my aching ribs. "Next time, let girl fight," the man said in plodding, heavily-accented Greek. He translated for the other Skythians, who laughed heartily at the jibe. I felt myself flush red in embarrassment, but for once I had the sense to keep my mouth shut. With Meli and Tibetos on either side, I walked painfully away from the patrol, who watched our departure with amusement.

"Let girl fight!" the Skythian called out again and the guards' mocking laughter echoed in my mind long after they were out of earshot.

ONCE HOME, I FOUND MY FATHER ENGAGED in a discussion with Neleus in the salon over wine and figs. I reported the departure of Phrynichus, omitting any mention of my encounter with Adrastos and his friends. The shame of the defeat still burned inside me, but if my father detected the humiliation that tainted my voice, he said nothing of it. He was very interested in what I had seen, though.

"It was Phrynichus? You are certain?" he asked and I confirmed what I had seen. "On his way to betray our city to Sparta," he said solemnly. "We must work to prevent that from coming to pass."

My father's sightless eyes could not see the angry bruise on my cheek or the scrapes on my arms and legs. Neleus suffered no such blindness. "What happened to you, boy?" the old warrior asked, looking me up and down.

"One of Phrynichus' guards hit me when they cleared a path," I said evasively. Neleus raised a sceptical eyebrow but did not push further.

"Neleus," my father said "Daimon has neglected his training on account of the errands I have had him doing. Perhaps you should work with him today?" I had not fooled my father after all.

Neleus took the hint. The corners of his mouth rose, but his eyes were hard. I knew trouble was coming. "My thoughts exactly. In the courtyard in an hour, lad."

I let out a low groan and accepted that I was in for an exhausting afternoon. "Yes, *lochagos*."

Besides teaching me his trade, Neleus was also my *hoplimachetes* — my arms-master. He had little time for the athletics of the gymnasium. "What use is vaulting or wrestling in a battle?" he would say. "If you want to get better with a shield and spear, then train with a shield and spear." A simple philosophy that he put into practice. But he was a good teacher, demanding but patient, and skilled in the warrior's trade.

At the appointed time, Neleus appraised me as I prepared for that day's training. "You seem unfocused today, boy," he said casually.

"Just tired, *lochagos*," I lied, continuing to don my gear.

Neleus always made me practice in the full panoply of breastplate, helmet, and greaves. The bronze carapace weighed half as much as an average man and was as hot as a kiln. Neleus insisted I get used to the discomfort and thicken the skin where the metal chafed my flesh.

I clasped the greaves onto my lower legs and tied the leather cords to hold them firmly in place. There was wool padding between the bronze and my shins, but they still rubbed uncomfortably against my skin. Neleus helped me shrug on the timeworn breastplate that he kept for my training. It was a plain, functional piece, slightly molded to follow the contours of a man's body. The armour bore the scars of many battles but was still polished and usable, for Neleus had beaten into me the need to maintain one's gear. I lowered my battered helmet over my head. The helm was of the old style, enclosing my face so completely that I could barely see or hear anything except for my own huffing breaths and the ringing clangs when Neleus struck me with the rod he liked to carry when he was instructing me. Lastly, I slipped my arm through the straps of the bulky *aspis* shield that protected me from knee to chin. I hefted the shield and nestled my shoulder into its concave recess to support some of the weight.

Neleus tossed the spear and I snatched it out of the air. With the butt on the ground, the long ash-wood spear towered an arm's length again above me. A wicked blade three hands in length topped the ash shaft, which was weighted on the other end by a spiked iron cap. I adjusted my grip to find the perfect balance point and awaited Neleus' command.

The veteran gave me a slight nod and I dropped into a crouch, shifting the spear into an underhand grip and cradling it in the crook of my arm. "One hundred," Neleus said. I was reading his lips as much as hearing the muffled words through the helmet.

"Yes, *lochagos!*" I pressed my left shoulder into my *aspis* as if pushing against an imaginary enemy and rammed my spear up under my shield.

"You're lifting too high again!" Neleus barked. "Do you want to die gloriously with your balls skewered on an enemy spear in your first battle?" he bellowed into my face.

"No, *lochagos!*"

"Then keep your shield lower!"

"Yes, *lochagos!*" I stepped back and snapped out another thrust.

Neleus grimaced and looked at the sky in exasperation. "By the gods, what was that?"

"*Lochagos?*"

"Are you trying to kill your enemy or tickle his cock with your spear? Hades! Your sister could ram a spear with more power than that!"

"Yes, *lochagos!*"

"Again! And no shirking or I'll have you hauling a loaded cart to the agora and back." He meant it.

One hundred thrusts later, the sweat was flowing steadily, stinging my eyes and dripping from under my gear. My left arm was numb from the burden of the shield. Neleus motioned for me to raise my helmet. I propped it on my head and waited for his instruction.

The old soldier did not speak for a moment. Stroking his beard, he picked out a louse. He regarded it with disdain before crushing it between his thumb and forefinger and flicking the tiny carcass away. "Did you have any problems today?" he asked casually.

"No, *lochagos.*"

He snorted. "So be it. Two hundred overhand thrusts," he said.

I dropped the helm back down over my face with a jerk of my head and changed my grip so that I could stab over the top of my shield. Each attack left me weaker, but I dared not let my shield drop or let my lunges lose their focus. By the end, my breath was coming in heaving gasps, and the little food I had eaten in the morning threatened to end up splattered on the inside of my helmet.

As I stood dripping and gulping air, Neleus limped in front of me and stared me in the face. "Did anything happen today?" he asked more pointedly than before.

"No, *lochagos.*"

Neleus pursed his lips. My breathing was more controlled now. "Defensive position!" Neleus snapped suddenly. "And don't move or Ares himself couldn't protect you from the hiding I'll give you!"

"Yes, *lochagos!*" I crouched lower so that only my eyes were visible over the edge of the shield as Neleus stalked off.

It was not long before my legs started to burn. My jaw trembled from the exertion and the glaring heat of the sun beat down me like a club. The muted sound of Neleus' limping gait returning to the courtyard promised a brief respite from my training, but I was wrong. He was wearing his own helmet and carrying a shield. In his immense hand he gripped two short oaken rods that he used for sword training. He tossed one on the ground at my feet.

"Pick it up," he said.

I leaned my spear against the altar and returned for the wooden rod. My hands were slick with perspiration, so I rubbed some grit between my palms before gripping the mock sword in my hand. I had barely raised my shield when Neleus bashed it with his own shield, driving me back several steps.

"Is that the best you've got, boy?" Neleus taunted. "Meli could do better!"

I clenched my jaw and braced my shield against my shoulder before charging towards him. It was like colliding with a wall, causing me to rebound from the impact, and before I could recover, Neleus stepped forward and gave me a crack on the side of my helmet that left the world spinning.

"Again!" Neleus commanded. "Like I showed you!"

I shook off my dizziness and ran at him again, with better results, for I planted my feet in a wider stance which kept me from bouncing back, and I stabbed over my shield at Neleus' helmeted face, but the battle-hardened veteran merely flicked his shield up to deflect my attack. Another blow on my temple sent me reeling.

"Dead again!" Neleus spat. He appealed to the heavens. "Gods, what poor materials you have given me to work with! Look where you're attacking boy!"

I felt nauseous. "Yes, *lochagos*," I managed to sputter.

"Come on, turd-sniffer! Dung-eater!" Neleus spat through his faceplate. "Are you a warrior or a slave?"

Suddenly it was not Neleus I saw before me but Adrastos and his sneering friend. My fatigue evaporated in a surge of hot fury. I rushed at him.

Such was my momentum that Neleus' feet slid back when I hit him. I stabbed and slashed wildly in a frenzied assault. I do not recall if I managed to land a blow, only Neleus' frantic defence. I was in a blind rage.

Neleus took a sudden step back, and I found myself pushing against air. With nothing resisting me, I tumbled to the ground in a heavy crash of metal and wood. I scrambled to my feet, the weight of the armour and shield keeping me off balance, and spun around looking for my target. Locating Neleus through the window of my helmet, I hacked at him with a howl, but he calmly shifted to one side and let me fall on my face again. Once more I rose, my attacks becoming increasingly wild.

"Enough!" Neleus bellowed. ButI did not stop. "Enough!" He sent me sprawling on my back with a thump of his shield, my oak sword flying out of my hand. Before I could recover, he pushed me down with a foot on my chest and held me there. "Enough, boy," he said, his voice calm. I shook off my shield and tried to twist his foot, but it was anchored like a tree trunk. "Enough, *pai*," he said gently, and I stopped struggling, exhaustion finally overcoming me.

The pressure on my chest eased as Neleus removed his foot. "Do you want to tell me what happened?" he asked once more, but the stern tone was gone, and he held out his hand. My anger was spent, and after a few heartbeats I grabbed his outstretched hand.

I raised the helmet off my head and let it drop to the ground with a clang. The trickles of sweat masked my tears and my body slumped as I stared at the paving stones at my feet.

"You need some water, boy," Neleus said, and with his heavy arm on my shoulder, he took me back to his workshop.

IT WAS AN ERROR TO BELIEVE THAT I could deceive Neleus, for in truth he knew me almost better than anyone. I told him of my encounter with Adrastos. I confessed my powerlessness against my brother's superior skill. I described being saved by Meli and the mocking taunts of the Skythians. He listened silently, his eyes never leaving me.

When I was done, I just stared at the ground, not wanting to see his disappointment. But he just exhaled loudly. "There is no shame in your actions, Daimon." I looked up at him, surprised. "You defended your sister, which was the honourable thing to do. Perhaps, though, it was not the best idea to take on your brother. One against four? As for Meli, she has courage that would put most men to shame." His voice swelled when he mentioned my sister, for he adored her as if she were his own daughter. "I pity the man she marries. He will have his hands full!" He laughed, and I could not help but smile.

Neleus became serious once again. "But after you had defended your sister, you should have run."

"Run?"

"There is a time to stand and fight and die, but there are some battles you cannot win. If your phalanx collapses around you, retreating and regrouping is your only option."

"Have you run before?"

Neleus dropped his head for a moment but raised it again to look me in the eye as he spoke. "Aye, lad. I am not proud to say it, but I have been in a beaten army often enough, even with our great generals like Perikles and your father. Truth be told, every man in Athens over a certain age has fled the battlefield at one time or another."

I challenged him. "The Spartans never run."

Neleus scoffed. "Let me tell you something, boy. The Spartans don't have to run because they avoid battles that they can't win in the first place. But they are just men like you and me, and don't forget it. Mark my words, boy. There will be a day when you will see Spartan backs as they flee for their miserable lives.

"But other times you must survive. For vengeance." He gave me a sympathetic smile. "You are still just a boy. What could you have done against them? But you are a better fighter than almost anyone I have seen at your age. You have much to learn, but someday you will be fearsome. Remember your shame, and use it to make yourself stronger."

"Yes, *lochagos*," I said, but memory of the defeat still gnawed at the pit of my stomach.

"I will not tell your father what happened with Adrastos."

A wave of gratitude welled up inside me. "Thank you, *lochagos*," I said sincerely. Under his coarse exterior he was a good man.

Neleus rose with a groan. "Age gives a man no respite, Daimon. Would it be that I had peace to rest my old bones!"

And the gods laughed.

# CHAPTER 6

I awoke in darkness. Tibetos was snoring softly in the corner under his coarse blanket. I slipped on my chiton and left my friend to his dreams.

The stillness of night was disturbed by a dog barking in the distance, but silence soon reasserted itself. In the cold light of the waning moon, the stone columns around the courtyard kept vigil over my father's offering of wine and fruit on the family altar. I stopped before the ancient stone table to say a prayer before continuing to the kitchen to find some food.

Finding some leftover bread, I tore off a hunk and wolfed it down with a cup of water from the cistern. Light footsteps behind me made me turn. The kitchen doorway framed my sister's silhouette in the predawn light. With her wild hair and thin limbs, Meli's silent form took on a menacing, monstrous air.

"I thought an *empousa* had come to get me," I joked. An *empousa* was a daughter of Hekate, a creature from the underworld that roamed the night, feasting on the blood of unwary travellers. It was my other nickname for my sister, one that she loved even more than Amazon.

Meli dashed over to me and clasped me tightly about the waist. "I thought you had gone already!" She buried her face in my tunic and hugged me more tightly.

"You can't come with me," I said firmly, pushing her away. Since the run-in with Adrastos, I had carried out my excursions alone. It was not only for my convenience. The mood in the city had become taut and ready to snap like a frayed bowstring. It was dangerous.

Meli ignored my rebuke, clutching the front of my tunic and staring up at me. Even in the dim light, I could see her green eyes narrow as she peered at me.

Meli's eyes had a life of their own. Sometimes they were like emeralds, sparkling with mischief. On other days they were the green of spring shoots, bursting with growth and budding potential. But the eyes gazing at me now were deep and unfathomable, like the sea, with hidden wisdom lurking beneath the cold surface. A chill rose up the back of my neck.

"Do not go out, Dammo!" She said in Thracian, her preferred tongue with me and my mother.

"What are you talking about?" I asked, also in Thracian.

My sister spoke in a desperate whisper. "I had a dream. Something terrible will happen. Please Dammo! Stay!"

I tried to convince her that I would be safe and that nothing would happen, but to no avail. She would not reveal what she had seen in her dream, but she was insistent that I remain home.

"I have to deliver a message for father," I lied, for my father had given me no such task. "I will return as soon as I'm done!" I reassured her.

Meli sighed in a concession of defeat. She lifted her hand my cheek and I felt its surprising coolness on my skin. She closed her eyes and mumbled a stream of words that I could not make out.

"What was that?" I asked when she opened her eyes.

"I asked Bendis to protect you," she said, looking past me to a small altar that had been set up in the corner of the kitchen. It was where my mother and Meli made their offerings and prayers to the Thracian goddess. "Be careful, Dammo."

"I promise," I said solemnly.

Meli followed me to the front door. I stepped out into the street and turned to give her a reassuring smile, but her sea-green gaze made it melt away. I almost changed my mind at that instant, so intense was her expression. But I pushed my misgivings away and tousled her hair. The heavy door closed behind me, and the lock engaged with a metallic clack.

The chill of the night lingered in the morning air but would dissipate rapidly with the rising sun. I would not stay out long. I would keep my promise to Meli.

Only a fool ignores those who hear the whispers of the gods.

And I was a fool.

FOR THE PAST MONTH, at my father's direction, I had helped to fan the smoldering embers of suspicion and resentment against the Four Hundred. A word dropped here and there was all it took. The rumours of collusion with Sparta spread like a silent plague. Now the seething anger of the city simmered around me in the agora.

A clutch of mercenaries escorted three oligarchs past where I was sitting in the shade of a cloth merchant's cart. "Bastard Spartan-lovers," the grey-bearded merchant muttered. "To the crows with them!" Hostile stares followed the oligarchs and their protectors across the agora and up the stairs into the *bouleterion*, the council chamber. "Bastard Spartan-lovers," the merchant grumbled again to no one in particular.

I stood up and brushed the dirt off of my tunic. "What is happening?" I asked.

"Those bastard oligarchs are meeting again. Planning to sell us out!" The merchant spat on the ground in disgust.

"Do you think the Spartans will come?" I prodded.

"How the hell should I know, slave? Be off!" He waved me away irritably.

A vendor selling pomegranates bitterly echoed the sentiments of the cloth merchant. The fruits were heavy with ripeness and it would have been easy to palm one without the distracted vendor noticing. With a tinge of regret, I pulled on the man's tunic to get his attention and gave him my last obol for a particularly swollen pomegranate. I tucked it into my tunic with the intention of giving it to Meli when I returned home.

I weaved my way towards the steps of the council chamber. Other members of the Four Hundred were arriving, all with their own bodyguards. The soldiers blocking the stairs let the oligarchs pass, seemingly oblivious to the growing thrum of resentful murmuring around them. A sudden surge in the raucousness of the crowd made me crane my neck to see the source of the provocation.

"Phrynichus, the whore of Sparta!" someone yelled, stoking the mob into further agitation. I recognized the hawk-faced oligarch, who was peering out from behind his cordon of bodyguards. Jeers and heckles rained down on him and he berated his escort. The mercenaries, grimacing and efficient, clubbed and beat those who blocked their path but the density of the throng hindered their progress.

I shoved my way to the front row of the crowd. The lead guard turned and once again I found myself face-to-face with Iobates' killer, the scar-faced Andrian. Before I could react, the mercenary clouted me on the side of the head and I fell to my knees, stunned. "Clear the way, slave!" he snarled, pressing forward.

A strong hand gripped my upper arm and hauled me back to my feet. "Take care, boy!" A bear of a man with a thick black beard and hair grinned humorlessly at me. His skin was deeply tanned, and his arms were thick with scars. "Those bloody bastards will get theirs soon enough," he said, jerking his head towards the passing guards. He spoke with the guttural accent of Argos. "It's best you stand back, boy, you hear?" I nodded my throbbing head and he gave me a gap-toothed grin before shoving me back behind him.

Without warning, the Argive lunged forward with a roar and buried a dagger in the side of the nearest bodyguard before I even realized what was happening. The guard dropped his spear with a cry and pulled at the dagger in his ribs.

Chaos erupted. Panicked bystanders scrambled to get away from the melee, flowing past the Argive like rapids around a boulder in a river. The remaining bodyguards turned on the Argive, who scooped up the spear of his first victim. Bellowing a war-cry, he ran to meet them, plunging the spear-point into the belly of another mercenary. He ripped out the spear with a vicious twist and brandished it at the rest of the soldiers, challenging them to step forward.

As the guards converged on the ursine Argive, I suddenly saw the point of his actions. The attack had only been a feint to draw away the men around Phrynichus, who now stood alone and unprotected.

A man wielding a leaf-bladed *xiphos* sword materialized from the throng and dashed towards the exposed oligarch. The scar-faced Andrian saw him too and shouted a warning, but he was too far away. Phrynichus held out his hands in a feeble attempt to ward off the blade as the assassin pulled the oligarch in close with his free hand and plunged the sword through the older man's abdomen. Phrynichus shrieked like a crow and collapsed on the ground, his hands clutching at his ruined belly.

Hearing the scream of Phrynichus, some of the guards whirled to face the new danger. The killer stood over the dying oligarch and I saw him clearly for the first time.

I knew him. His hair was shorter and his beard gone, but there was no mistaking the predatory glare. It was the man I had seen sparring in the *peripoli* compound. The realization that my father must have had a hand in this assassination struck me like a thunderbolt.

A guard ran at assassin with his spear levelled, like a hunter trying to skewer a wild boar. The *peripoli* parried the thrust gracefully, shifting his sword up to slash across the guard's neck. There was a spray of blood and the mercenary toppled onto his face, his spear clattering on the paving stones. He thrashed helplessly as a red pool spread from the gash in his flesh.

The scar-faced Andrian, too late to save Phrynichus, barked a command and he and two other guards approached the sword-wielding *peripoli* with more caution. The three guards fanned out to surround the assassin, who dropped into a defensive crouch. The Andrian gave a feral grin, scenting blood.

I made a choice. These were the enemies of my father. I would fight the evil men and make myself worthy of my father's pride. I would live up to the values of my brother Heliodoros. It seemed so simple.

My hand slipped down to the folds in my tunic pulled out the pomegranate nestled there. With an explosion of breath, I hurled the dense sphere at the Andrian. The heavy fruit flew true, smashing into the dead centre of the mercenary's face. He stumbled back as blood poured from his crushed nose. He shook off the pain, looking about furiously for the origin of the attack. The scar-faced mercenary spotted me and spewed a torrent of curses. "You stinking little turd! I will gut you! Do you hear me?" He glared at me one more time and returned his focus to the assassin. The enraged Andrian stepped over the squirming, mewling form of Phrynichus.

One of the Andrian's men flicked his gaze my way. The *peripoli* took advantage of the distraction, dancing in and stabbing his sword into the guard's throat. The soldier dropped his weapon and fell to his knees, frantically trying to staunch the river of blood gurgling from his neck.

The Argive, his tunic splattered with gore, was still battling two soldiers off to my left. The *peripoli* assassin was still to my front, slowly backing towards me as two more mercenaries closed in from opposite sides.

Madness seized me. I dashed forward and picked up one of the fallen spears. The weapon weighed nothing in my hand. I should have been frightened. I should have run. But my blood was running high. I saw only my enemies. The *phobos*, the fear, was washed away by the euphoria of action. I pointed the iron tip at the sword-wielding guard on the right of the assassin. The guard's eye's widened in surprise as I charged.

The spearhead took the guard under the ribs, as Neleus had taught me. The weapon punched through the sheet of his abdominal muscles and emerged from his back. The momentum of the thrust brought me face to face with my victim, who stared at me in disbelief, gasping. The stink of his breath and flecks of spittle hit me in the face. My savage exultation abandoned me as fear suddenly gripped my chest. The man's eyes rolled back in his head. His body heaved spasmodically and then sagged as his spirit left him, his weight pulling stubbornly at the spear in my hands. I released the weapon and the man toppled backwards. The wooden shaft cracked beneath him so that he lay grotesquely before me.

The scarred Andrian, seeing me standing unarmed, roared and took one step in my direction, but the assassin advanced to cover me and the mercenary checked himself, not willing to face the *peripoli* single-handed.

"Time to run, boy!" the assassin hissed, his eyes never leaving the Andrian.

A great bellow drew my attention, and I caught a final glimpse of the Argive as he vanished under the stabbing spears and swords of a clutch of soldiers. At that moment, only the Andrian faced us, but that would soon change. Phrynichus had finally stopped struggling. He lay on his face, the stones and sand around him stained dark by his blood. Many of the crowd had fled, but many others formed a kind of perimeter around the combat, screaming for more blood. I glanced back over my shoulder. More soldiers were streaming from the door of the *bouleterion*.

"Go now!" the assassin shouted.

I ducked into the pandemonium around me. The *peripoli* was at my heels, and we sprinted past the stoa at the south side of the agora and into the dense maze of houses and workshops beyond. Only when we were well away from the agora did we risk a halt, both of us panting to catch our breaths.

I looked down and saw that my right hand was covered in blood. The warm tackiness of it made me sick. I knelt down and wiped my hand on the ground, trying in vain to get rid of the stain.

When I stood, I saw my hands were trembling. I clenched my fists so that the *peripoli* would not see my cowardice.

If he noticed my fear, he did not mention it. Putting his hands on my shoulders, he spoke. "Look at me, boy." It took all of my effort to hold his gaze and I looked at him closely for the first time. The blood of Phrynichus and the other men he had killed had seeped into his tunic and darkened to the color of wine. "We must go our separate ways. The Four Hundred will be searching for me."

At last I found my voice. "I know you!"

He smiled at that. "I am in your debt, Daimon, son of Nikodromos. Someday I may be able to repay you for what you did today. But now return to your home. It is safe there. And you must tell your father what has happened. He will know what to do. Now go!" I nodded and with a last glance at the *peripoli* I began to run.

He was correct that he would repay his debt to me, many times over.

But he was wrong in his first prediction.

I would not be safe.

# CHAPTER 7

I had to double back, for my home was to the north of the Acropolis, not the south where I now found myself. I raced through a maze of lanes and alleys, avoiding the larger roadways and giving the agora a wide berth. But this doubled the length of my journey, and my lungs were burning as I made the last familiar turn towards my home.

The door was ajar. The muffled sound of Adrastos' raised voice carried out to the street. I swallowed hard and slipped through the gap left by the open door, stepping through the narrow vestibule and into the courtyard.

My brother was in a rage. My stone-faced father let the gale of abuse wash over him. Neleus stood behind my father frowning grimly, his thick arms crossed in front of his chest. The commotion had even brought my mother down, her features betraying the helplessness she felt as she bore witness to the confrontation. Meli crouched on the stairs, like a harpy perched on a rock.

"A leader of the assembly killed in the street like a dog!" Adrastos cried out.

"You will lower your voice," my father said through clenched teeth.

Neleus was the first to notice me standing dumbly at the entrance to the courtyard. His frown deepened. His change in expression was not lost on Adrastos, and my brother suddenly spun to turn his fury on me.

"I saw you there!" he hissed, pointing an accusing finger. "You aided the assassin!" A wave of nauseous fear washed over me, for only then did I realize the danger I had placed my family in because of my foolhardy actions in the agora.

My mother, seeing me for the first time, gasped. I glanced down at the dark stains on my tunic. Everyone had turned their eyes towards me. I opened my mouth, but no words came forth.

"Who was the man who you were with?" my brother demanded. I stood gaping like an idiot. My apparent refusal to answer only enraged Adrastos further. "Who was he?" he repeated, taking a step towards me. "I'll have it beaten out of you, barbarian!"

My father suddenly reached out and seized Adrastos by the tunic. "You will do no such thing!" The order was like a thunderclap, the power of it momentarily stunning Adrastos to silence.

My brother recovered his wits and slapped my father's hand away. "I am not a child to be scolded." His voice was ice. My father stared at him through clouded eyes but said nothing.

Adrastos felt our eyes on him. He glanced about, his face a mix of anger and uncertainty. He took our disapproving silence as license to speak. "When the council discovers that you are sheltering the murderer of Phrynichus, our property will be confiscated and you will be tried as a traitor! And for what, father? To fight for the restoration of democracy? Those days are gone forever, and it is no great loss! The Council of Four Hundred is the best thing to happen to Athens in one hundred years, and they will finally lead us out of this never-ending war and —"

"And deliver Athens into the hands of Sparta!" my father cut him off.

My brother did not deny this. "We would do well to look to the Spartans!" he said raising his voice. "We must restore the proper order of things! Rule by the worthy, and not," he said casting a look my way, "by lowborn rabble. What would you have us do, father?" Adrastos demanded, sweeping his arm towards my mother and Meli. "Return Athens to the rule of an ignorant mob and the children of whores and —"

My father struck my brother hard across his face. Adrastos staggered back from the blow and fell unceremoniously on the hard flagstones. He struggled to get to his feet, but my father stepped forward and hit him again, knocking him back to the ground in a heap.

The voice of a *strategos* filled the courtyard, a voice of authority and command. "You have forgotten your place, Adrastos. You forget the debt you owe to the woman who saved both of us when we lay dying from the *vosos*. Without her, we too would have been taken by the plague."

Adrastos put his hand to the welt on his face and looked up in stunned disbelief at my father, who was still looming above him.

"You cannot do this to me —"

"I can," my father cut him off. "If you only disagreed with me, then I would forgive you. But you have done more than that. I know of your activities in the past months. You have thrown your lot in with murderers and tyrants. Before the sight of gods and men, I name you a traitor to your polis and your family. The Four Hundred will fall, within days if not a month, and democracy will be restored to Athens."

"Father —" Adrastos tried to speak.

"I disinherit you."

My mother's hand rushed to stifle a gasp. Even Neleus looked shocked, so unexpected was my father's declaration. It was a rare thing for a father to disown his son. Possible, but seldom seen. With just three words, my father had taken away Adrastos' future as a leading citizen of Athens.

Adrastos rose unsteadily to his feet, his composure utterly deserting him. If he thought about retaliating against my father, the muscular figure of Neleus dissuaded him. He cast his gaze about the courtyard but was only met by mute stares. His bewilderment metamorphosed into a mask of hatred before he turned and fled out to the street.

How many heartbeats passed before my father spoke I cannot say, but it seemed like an age. "Daimon, come tell me what happened in the agora. Erta," he said, calling my mother by name, "prepare our things. We must leave immediately."

My mother cast a worried glance at my bruised cheek and blood-spattered tunic before hurrying upstairs, shooing a reluctant Meli ahead of her.

Stuttering and gushing in turns, I related the assassination of Phrynichus and my role in the chaos that had ensued, omitting nothing. Neleus' gaze bore into me, and I shuffled uncomfortably under the weight of his stare. My father let me speak until my tale was done.

He put a hand over his face and massaged the fatigue from his sightless eyes. I waited for the hammer to fall, but my father just sighed. "What's done is done," he said. "But there is danger if we remain here."

"Where will we go?" I asked.

"Iasos can hide us until the storm blows over." The name of my old tutor surprised me. "Hermon and the *peripoli* will offer us refuge if we can get to Piraeus," my father said. I thought of the gruff commander and wondered if he would be as enthusiastic as my father believed. "Tibetos!" my father suddenly hollered. "Get yourself out here, boy!"

My friend suddenly popped out from the storeroom where he had been hiding discreetly and scurried over to stand in front of my father.

"Master," he said.

"Go and prepare some food and water-skins for the journey."

"Yes, Master," he said. He shot a quick look at my bruised and bloodied figure before darting back to the storeroom.

My father turned to me, his hand resting on the edge of the altar. "Daimon!"

"Yes, Father."

"Help Neleus make his preparations."

"Yes, Father."

As I turned to follow Neleus, my eyes fell on the heavy door to the street. In the confusion, no one had bothered to shut it completely and lower the bar. I trotted over to remedy the situation.

My hands had just begun to press on the time-worn planks when the door burst back towards me as though animated by my touch. The massive gate knocked me hard on my forehead, throwing me heavily onto my backside.

Shaking off the blow, I looked up at the figure in the doorway.

Adrastos loomed over me.

And he was not alone.

HOSTAGES AND CAPTORS CROWDED the courtyard. A ring of guards had herded us to where we now stood in front of the altar. My mother clutched Meli close to her. Beside her, Tibetos glanced about nervously. Neleus stood expressionless and unblinking, but rage was radiating from him like heat from a fire. I hazarded a glance at my father beside me. An angry welt flared on his cheek where he had been struck, but he said nothing, his jaw clenched.

The brooding Adrastos paced restlessly behind the altar. The scarred face of the Andrian stared at me through eyes ringed with purple bruises, his teeth bared in a malevolent grin. But neither my brother nor the Andrian frightened me as much as the third man. I did not know his name, but he was not unknown to me. I had only met him once, but the encounter had not gone well. He had molested my sister and he had felt both my fist and my sister's knife for his trouble.

He was dressed well, draped in a white *himation*, the folds of the robe falling artfully about him. He alone seemed free of tension, yet the calm he projected was an illusion, belied by the icy gaze that was locked on me. My hackles rose.

The man beckoned. "Come closer, *pai*. Let me see you."

I made no move. My guard prodded me forward so that I stood before my brother's friend. The man circled me slowly as though inspecting me. I kept staring forward. With each step, his sandals ground the grit on the flagstones. He leaned in close. "Do you wish to hit me now, barbarian?" he said softly. His breath stank of wine.

My father could not suppress his anger. "You have no shame Adrastos! You will —"

My interrogator made a slight gesture and a mercenary short-punched my father hard in the side. He gasped in pain but did not fall.

The man turned back towards me and smiled apologetically. "There is no need for this. Just tell me who the assassin is, and we'll be gone. I'm sure that you were just in the wrong place at the wrong time." I glanced at my father, but his grim expression told me to expect no mercy from the man before me. My silence stretched out.

The aristocrat sighed. "Orchus!"

The scar-faced Andrian casually spat on the ground. With slow, measured steps, the Andrian approached, his purple-ringed eyes never leaving mine. "You will not get away this time, boy."

I tightened my muscles in anticipation of the blow to come, yet I crumpled easily as the mercenary's fist drove into my belly. My mother gasped and attempted to step to my aid, but one of her captors jerked her back roughly by the arm. My own guard grabbed my hair and yanked me upright.

"Who was the assassin?" The control in the aristocrat's voice was beginning to waver. I held my tongue. My intransigence was rewarded with a solid punch to my cheekbone. Flashing lights filled my vision and my ears rang with the sound of crashing waves.

A cacophony of voices greeted me as I regained my senses. My mother was crying and begging them to stop. My father was in a shouting match with my brother and his companion. Alone in the chaos Meli was silent, her face unreadable except for the green fire blazing in her eyes.

"Enough!" my brother's friend snapped. Order was restored, but his authority had been broken. The façade of restraint had shattered, and his true nature came to the fore. Enraged by my defiance, he slapped me across the face. "Why do you defy me, slave?" he yelled, and the wine-breath washed over me.

Slave.

Pride and shame. These are the two things that drive men, even to their deaths. Pride makes a man run into the spears of an enemy phalanx, for death is preferable to the shame of being called a coward by his fellows. Pride and shame guide the hands of the Sisters as they weave our fates. It was pride that made me speak. It was pride that cost me everything.

"I am not a slave," I whispered back to him.

My tormentor blinked in surprise. "What did you say?"

"I am not a slave," I repeated more clearly.

The aristocrat's eyes widened at my insolence, but then his handsome features contorted in anger, the same crazed face I had seen in our first encounter. "Hold him fast!" he commanded my guard, and I was suddenly immobilized by an iron forearm crushing my throat. The enraged man came close and spat his words in my face once again. "You are the son of a slave and that makes you a slave!" he spat. "Your life is worth nothing except the silver you would fetch at the slave market. You – "

"I am an Athenian," I rasped hoarsely.

He exploded. "You are a slave! I will show you what the life of a slave is worth! Bring the woman here!" He pointed at my mother and one of the guards grabbed her roughly, but she tore herself from him and scrabbled onto the altar.

Kneeling atop the stone block, my mother cried, "I supplicate myself to Zeus the Saviour!"

The proclamation caused the guards to hesitate, for she had invoked the ancient right of divine protection. The wrath of the gods would fall on anyone who violated the sanctity of a supplicant's plea. A mercenary looked over to my brother in mute appeal, but Adrastos was frozen by indecision.

The aristocrat's face tightened in frustration. "She is a barbarian!" he shouted at the reluctant guard. "She cannot claim the protection of our gods! Seize her!"

Yet still the mercenary hesitated, as did my brother, who stood behind the altar.

"Orchus, bring her." The scar-faced Andrian had no qualms about offending Zeus and dragged my mother off the altar with emotionless efficiency. She struggled to escape his grip but was no match for his soldier's strength.

"Mother!" Meli screamed, suddenly coming to life. The strong arm of a soldier restrained her, but her cries did not stop.

Orchus planted my mother a pace in front of where I stood immobilized, pinning her arms from behind so that she could not move. Her terrified eyes were locked on mine.

My brother's friend stood beside her. "A slave is property," he said. He drew the back of his hand downwards, caressing my mother's red hair down to her shoulder. "A slave is nothing." He bit each word. "Watch and see what you have wrought, slave!"

In a fluid motion, he drew a dagger from the belt of Orchus and smoothly drew it across my mother's throat. Her eyes widened in shock as the spray of her blood speckled my face. I screamed out. Orchus opened his arms. My mother fell in a heap and her lifeblood flowed out onto the ground, seeping into cracks between the stones. She shuddered once and was still.

All the will to move or speak had left my body as I stared down at my mother's crumpled form. A moan of anguish poured out from my father, and Meli sobbed. It took three men to hold Neleus. Even Adrastos had paled at the murder of his stepmother.

I struggled in vain to tear myself from the arms that bound me. My father was mad in his grief. My eyes fell on Neleus, and he shook his head almost imperceptibly. His eyes flicked over my shoulder to the front door behind me.

"Slave!" My brother's friend struck my face again, but in my shock I hardly felt the blow. "Do you need to see another die before you tell me what you know?"

A fresh wave of fear and helplessness pounded me as he motioned for the soldier with Meli to come forward. The soldier hauled her to the aristocrat's side. "Tell me what you know, slave, or she dies. Now." His dagger floated impatiently in front of my sister's neck. She had stopped squirming. I felt the weight of her sea-deep eyes upon me, but her face was strangely calm.

I loved my sister more than life. My life. My father's life. And certainly more than the life of an assassin to whom I owed nothing. I was Meli's protector. I would have broken any oath to men or gods to save her. My shoulders slumped and my chin dropped, and the corners of the aristocrat's mouth curled upwards.

But we were both fools. For we had both forgotten about Meli. There was a yelp as my sister bit down hard on the forearm of the mercenary holding her, and she tore herself from his grasp. In a flash, her knife was out. With an inhuman shriek, she drove it deep into the aristocrat's armpit and he squealed in pain.

It was all the distraction Neleus needed. Now the raw power in those arms forged by countless hours with hammer and anvil unleashed death.

With a roar of rage, the old veteran lunged at the guard who held me. Neleus took hold of my captor's head in his huge hands and twisted it around with a sickening snap, and suddenly I was free. Almost before the dead man had struck the ground, Neleus had scooped up his sword and driven it through another guard as though he were made of straw. He yanked the blade free and bellowed a challenge to the remaining guards.

Orchus lunged at my sister, but she evaded his grasp and bolted towards me, her bloody knife clutched in her tiny fist. The Andrian leapt for her, but he was stopped short as my father tackled him about the waist, heaving him to the ground.

"Run, Daimon!" my father shouted as Orchus struggled to free himself from my father's tight hold.

The way to the door was clear. Meli pulled at my hand.

Yet I hesitated. The body of my mother still lay face down, her copper hair flowing into the pool of darker blood. Beside her, Orchus writhed to free himself from my father's grip. The aristocrat was cursing as he tried to staunch the flow of blood from his chest, but no one paid him any heed. Three guards lay dead at Neleus' feet. The remaining soldiers converged on him. I looked on in horror as Neleus was stabbed by spear and sword from three sides. His eyes met mine one last time, imploring me to run, before he vanished under a flurry of blades.

Then my brother strode forward, a sword in his hand. He plunged it into my father's back. My father spasmed and went limp without a sound. As the Andrian shook off my father's corpse, Adrastos looked up at me with hatred in his eyes.

"Daimon! The door is opening!" Meli yelled. I spun away to face the new threat.

The mercenary posted outside had come to investigate the commotion within. With a desperate howl, I charged, using my shoulder like a battering ram, and we tumbled onto the street outside in a tangled mass.

Grappling with the struggling guard, I yelled at Meli to flee, but she did not obey. As swift as a weasel, she was beside me, sawing her vicious little knife in the guard's throat, and he released me to clutch at the gushing, gaping tear in his neck.

I scrambled to my feet and grabbed Meli's hand.

And we ran.

# CHAPTER 8

The two of us, a bloodied youth and a wild-haired, knife-wielding girl, plunged through the warren of lanes and alleys that made up the district, dodging past anyone in our way. The slapping of my sandals echoed off the looming walls. Meli cried out and stumbled. I caught her hand and we slid to a halt, ducking into a recess between two buildings to catch our breath.

"Are you hurt?" I asked between gasps.

Meli said nothing but pointed at her feet. The big toe on her left foot was a mess of blood and dirt.

"Can you run?"

She gave a quick nod. The clap of running feet halted my response. A bolt of fear ran through me. I crouched down, preparing to tackle whoever appeared. I would be captured or killed, but it would give Meli the opportunity to flee.

"Dammo! Are you there?" Relief washed over me at the sound of Tibetos' familiar voice.

I poked my head out from the behind the wall and beckoned my friend into the sheltered nook, I looked at him in amazement. "How did you escape?"

"They forgot about me. I'm just a slave," he said. "I saw you get away with Meli. I slipped out through the smithy."

"Were you followed?"

"I don't think so." We peered out into the empty lane. "Where should we go?"

Loss, helplessness, rage, and shame threatened to overwhelm me. I was scared.

Meli pulled on my tunic. "Dammo?" Her voice was small and frightened. Tibetos looked at me expectantly.

I did not want them to see my fear. I tried to infuse my voice with a confidence that I did not feel. "There is someone who can help us."

*

MY FORMER TUTOR'S EYES WIDENED at the sight of us, which I had not thought possible, for Iasos had the bulging eyes of a frog. He was also bald as an egg, and when I was younger, I had mocked him for his amphibious appearance in the cruel way that boys do, but I regret it now, for he was a good man. My father had known this and insisted on the devout but sharp-tongued follower of Pythagoras as my teacher.

I was not a good student. My letters I learned well enough, but for all other tasks I had neither the aptitude nor the patience. Reciting poetry and playing the lyre were a torture, more for the listener than for me, I reckon. The only talent I had was for fighting. The other boys would taunt me with whispers of slave and barbarian, and it was a rare day that I returned home without either a bloody nose or bruises on my backside because of a thrashing from Iasos.

But it was my teacher whom I sought out now, for it was the refuge my father had mentioned earlier. Seeing our bloodied, dishevelled forms, Iasos did not hesitate. "Off the street!" He practically dragged us into his home and slammed the door shut with great haste. "Come, children!"

He hustled us through the courtyard to one of the rooms he used as a classroom. A great pile of clay sherds lay in one corner, just like the ones upon which I had scratched out my letters as a child. Iasos ordered his slave Xanthias to fetch some water and bread.

The blue-eyed Skythian was almost as old as his master and had been his servant since before I was born. He was in a state of perpetual discontent, and I had never seen him smile. "Trouble! Trouble!" the slave grumbled as he shuffled off to do as he had been bidden.

Iasos sat us down on stools and pulled up the small bench that he was accustomed to using when he conducted his lessons. "What has happened, child? Tell me!" Staring at the ground, I began in a low voice. "Don't hang your head, boy! Speak clearly! And omit nothing!" Iasos said reprovingly.

I once more felt like a child under his gaze. I cleared my throat and began again. Listening intently, Iasos leaned forward and pulled idly at his beard as I recounted the ill-fated events that had led us to his door.

When I had finished, he leaned back on his bench and said nothing, regarding us through narrowed eyes. "It is not safe for you here," he said. "We must get you out of the city."

"But the soldiers manning the city gates will be on the lookout for us," I said.

"Leave that matter to me, boy!" Iasos said, arching an eyebrow. "In the meantime, you will need a place to hide."

Now that we were out of immediate danger, I had been considering that very problem. "I think I know of just such a place," I said.

THE ABANDONED POTTER'S WORKSHOP was one of those hidden places children seek out almost instinctively. At various times it had been my base of operations, my cache, or just a quiet place to whittle away idle hours. That night it would be our refuge.

The slave Xanthias, his face as inscrutable as ever, held up a finger. "You will remain here until I return," he ordered flatly before shuffling off into the dusk.

The three of us clambered through a collapsed section of wall where thieves had burrowed through in search of treasure. Any such burglar would have been disappointed. Roof tiles and potsherds littered the floor, and the roof was gone, the timbers salvaged long ago for fuel or other building projects.

The three of us cleared out a corner as best we could and sat down. Evening was coming fast. In the shadows of the workshop it was already becoming cool but the heat of the day still emanated from the walls, providing a little warmth. We huddled together against the encroaching night, three children weeping softly in the darkness.

If I shut my eyes, I could only see the look of terror on my mother's face as she died. The enormity of what I had done crushed my soul. "I killed them, Meli," I said in despair. It was true. My rash actions in the agora had put those I loved the most in danger and they had paid with their lives. My mother. My father. Neleus. They had died for my impulsiveness and pride.

From where she had nestled under my arm, Mei lifted her head and looked at me. The darkness gave her eyes a serpent-like cast, and an involuntary shiver passed through me. "It was Adrastos and his friend," she said. There was no reproach in her voice. "You thought you were helping Father. He and Neleus would have done the same in your place. Heliodoros would have been proud of your bravery," she said. In my grief, it was not her voice I heard but that of my mother, as if my mother's shade was speaking through Meli. "Adrastos is an evil man," my sister finished. She put her head down on my chest and was quiet. I held her tightly, for she was all I had left, but her words did little to salve the burning shame in my heart.

Outside the potter's workshop, some voices drew near and then receded into the distance. Hints of smoky odors from the cooking fires of the people of Athens found their way into our sanctuary. Life went on.

Night came. Through the collapsed roof, the cold starlight shone down on us. I shifted against the wall, and pain shot through my ribs. During our flight, I had not noticed my injuries, but now my body protested with every movement. The swollen side of my face throbbed. Yet the soreness and discomfort were welcome, for they distracted me from my thoughts.

Tibetos had said very little, but now he gave voice to the insistent fear that dogged my thoughts. "What can we do, Dammo?"

"We can only wait," I answered weakly.

Meli looked up at me one more time. "The gods will protect us," she whispered. She wriggled in close to me and began crying once more.

I stroked her hair gently. The memory of my mother's face persisted, as did her expression when she died. But then there was something stronger. I heard her singing to me. It was a Thracian song, of love and love lost. Softly, I began to sing, the familiar words a shield against the darkness within and without. In the lonely night, I sang to my sister until I heard her breathing deepen, and I knew she was asleep.

Eventually, exhaustion overcame pain, and I fell into a troubled slumber haunted by the spirits of my parents and Neleus. They bemoaned the cruel fate that had befallen them and I cowered before them. Over and over they asked one thing of me.

They demanded justice.

XANTHIAS DID NOT RETURN in the morning. Sometimes we spoke in hushed voices, but mostly we kept our silence. Whenever voices or footsteps approached, we would remain motionless, like leverets hiding in the tall grass. Day slid into night, and we were once again enveloped in darkness.

"Daimon!" The voice came as a shock after so many hours of waiting. It was not Xanthias. The familiar voice called out again, softly. "Daimon, son of Nikodromos. I come at the bidding of Iasos!"

I motioned for Meli and Tibetos to stay out of sight. "We are here!" I responded.

"Come! We must leave immediately!"

I took a deep breath and stepped out over the rubble of the collapsed section of wall. And I gasped.

The assassin of Phrynichus stood beside Xanthias, who bore an expression of patient indifference. "Lykos will help you leave the city," the Skythian said with a yawn, indicating the cloaked *peripoli*.

"Did they come looking for us?" I did not need to elaborate.

"Some ill-behaved men showed up, but they were disappointed in their search," Xanthias said simply. "My master bids you well. I am tired. I have had a long journey today. To Piraeus and back!" he shook his head, and my heart surged in appreciation of the risk Iasos and his long-suffering slave had taken on our behalf. "Too much trouble," the slave added, and then trudged off into the night.

"Come!" the assassin whispered. Xanthias has called him Lykos, which means *wolf*. It was an apt name for a man who moved with such predatory grace and confidence. "There is little time!"

I called for Meli and Tibetos. Under the glow of the waning moon. The man Lykos led us wordlessly through the streets, gesturing to us to indicate when it was safe to move. Once a patrol of mercenaries passed by as we crouched in the shadows, but we were otherwise unmolested on our journey.

As we came around a corner, the torches of the Aetionian Gate came into view. It was the smallest gate of the city, but it would still be well guarded. The gatehouse towered some forty feet high, forming a square arch over the massive barred gates below. Atop the structure I could see two guards peering over the wall, regarding our procession with interest. From the sides of the gatehouse the city walls ran in either direction, though I could see no more soldiers.

There was no saying how many guards were in the building itself. I had put my faith in this man called Lykos, but I could not imagine under what circumstances we would be allowed to leave the city.

Two guards flanked the gatehouse. One of them approached, one arm holding his spear upright and the other hand resting lightly on the hilt of his sword. He came to a stop before us. Lykos stepped forward and pulled back his hood. My heart was pounding.

"Telekles," Lykos addressed the man. "There were no problems, I take it?"

"Nothing that we couldn't handle, *lochagos*," the guard answered with a curt nod. My jaw dropped as I recognized him as the messenger who had visited my father a few months earlier. He noticed my wide-eyed stare and winked at me. He then turned and waved at the tower. After a moment, the heavy timber barring the inner doors began to rise, the cranking of the mechanism disturbing the silence of the night. Once the bar was vertical, the second soldier pushed the gates, and they swung inwards with a groan. The outer doors already lay open. Beyond them, the road disappeared into the blackness.

"Come with me," Lykos ordered.

Hurrying after him, we ducked into the guardroom. In the dim light of the lamp, I nearly tripped on a body. Three more dead mercenaries had been heaped ingloriously in the corner. I pointed to the corpses. "Who are they?" I asked in a hushed voice. Lykos ignored me as three more men appeared from guardhouse stairwell.

"Where is Meges?" Lykos asked.

"Still on top of the wall," one of the newcomers responded. "He'll leave once we're gone."

Lykos grunted. "Let us depart, then."

With that we were gone. Swallowed by the night, our odd party of assassins, a slave, a youth, and a girl abandoned the gate that was now guarded only by corpses.

# CHAPTER 9

The eyes of Hermon, commander of the *peripoli* in Piraeus, bore into me as though he were trying to see into my very soul. It did not seem possible, but he was even more intimidating than he had been at our first meeting months earlier. To my great relief, the commander turned his glare on the man Lykos. "You were forbidden to leave the compound." The commander's voice was ice.

Lykos stood at attention and spoke matter-of-factly. "Commander, I swore to the *strategos* that I would take responsibility for the boy should anything befall him. I felt my oath superseded other considerations." I glanced at Lykos in surprise, for I had known of no such agreement.

Hermon ignored him. "Several guards at the Aetionian gates were killed last night. Enlighten me." The commander was very well informed indeed.

"I have no knowledge of this event. This is the first I have heard of it, Commander," Lykos lied blatantly.

"I would be most upset if I were to find that you had involved others under my command in this mission," Hermon said in a low voice, like a dog growling a warning. Lykos stared straight ahead.

Hermon suddenly spun on me. "How did you leave the city, boy?" he demanded.

I was ready. "Through the Diochares Gate, Commander," I said with a straight face.

The commander narrowed his eyes, watching me intently, but I did not flinch. "How did you pass through?"

"Lykos bribed the guards, Commander."

Hermon snorted. "A likely tale."

The statement hung in the air for a moment. Hermon sighed, apparently giving up on this line of enquiry. He turned and walked over to a wooden table, picked up a jug, and poured himself a generous cup of wine. "I don't believe either of you," Hermon said, regarding us coolly. He drained his cup in one gulp and continued. "But I have bigger problems to deal with than you two lying sacks of dung."

"What has happened, Commander?" Lykos inquired.

"The entire city is sinking into the dung-heap that it made for itself, that's what is happening," he said in exasperation. He refilled his cup to the brim. "The Four Hundred are finished. It's no secret that they invited the Spartans to take the city. Those black-braided turd-sniffers are already on their way. Probably smacking their lips at the prospect of ending the war without a fight." Hermon spat on the floor in disgust. "All the hoplites in Piraeus will march on Athens tomorrow and take back the city."

"Are the Four Hundred preparing to fight, Commander?" Lykos asked.

"Not if they know what's good for them. All they have now are their mercenaries, and they can hardly count on them. If the bastards are smart, they'll be packing their carts as we speak. It will be better if we don't need to fight."

I did not want the oligarchs to slip away. *Let them fight*, I beseeched the gods. I thought of my brother Adrastos and his aristocratic companion. *Let them die.*


THE GODS WERE KIND TO HERMON.

A complete lack of resistance marked the rebel army's journey from Piraeus to the gates of Athens.

Hermon and Lykos had permitted us to follow behind the hoplites where Lykos and three hundred *peripoli* were acting as a rearguard. If fighting broke out, we were under strict orders to return to the *peripoli* compound in Piraeus.

Trudging towards the city, it was a battle between the insistent ache of my injuries and my eagerness to see justice done. A jerk on my sleeve from the sharp-eyed Tibetos pulled me out of my meditation on pain. He pointed off to our left.

I pulled up abruptly. Meli was some twenty-five paces away, skirting the edge of the road like a wary red fox. Her knife was backward in her right hand so that the blade lay parallel to her wiry forearm. I cursed out loud, for I had forbidden her to come, despite her crying and pleading. I shouted out her name. Before I could call out again, the little harpy had dashed off ahead and vanished into the forest of men that filled the road.

As we passed through the undefended city gate, there was still no sight of her. It was one more thing to worry about, but it would have to wait.

Deserted streets greeted us at every turn. As the hoplites filed into the agora, we trod over the ground where Phrynichus had been assassinated only a few days earlier. It seemed to have been a lifetime ago.

Shouting from up ahead brought me back to the moment. A ripple of tension flowed through the ranks. Helmets that had been casually pulled back were suddenly lowered, and lines tightened so that each man was protected by his comrade beside him.

Lykos ordered the *peripoli* to position themselves to the side of the main body of hoplites. "Find some cover," he advised, and Tibetos and I scrambled to the top step of the *bouleterion*, which afforded a better view of the agora. Hermon, easily distinguished in his white cloak, was conferring with a group of ten or so unarmed men who had come into the agora in the path of the advancing hoplites. A murmur of voices surged through the masses of ranked soldiers. Some of the hoplites began shaking their spears and cheering.

Lykos peeled away from the circle of excitement and trotted back to the *peripoli*. I gestured to Tibetos and we hurried back down to see what news he brought. Lykos was flushed, but he was grinning broadly.

"They're gone!" he laughed.

"Who? Who's gone?" one of the *peripoli* pressed.

"Pisander! Antiarchus! All of them! The leaders of the Four Hundred have fled the city!"

A cheer rose from the thousands gathered in the agora.

The rule of the Four Hundred was over.

THE DOOR OF OUR ABANDONED HOME hung open. Lykos nodded and bade me enter, but I hesitated. A miasma of pollution clung to the place, holding me back like a barrier.

Pollution. The invisible stain that emanates from death and illness and childbirth. Even brave men fear it, for it is insidious, like a plague, inflicting ill-fortune on all who are tainted by it. A place polluted by murder must be purified with salt-water or the blood of a pig. I felt the filth of death on my skin.

Lykos did not share my aversion. "There is nothing to fear," he said softly. I did not wish to shame myself in front of the *peripoli* captain, though I hardly knew him. I entered my home.

The flagstones still bore the evidence of my brother's treachery. I fell to my knees and placed my palm on the dark stains of my mother's blood. My tears came forth and sobs wracked my body. I did not know what Adrastos had done with the bodies of my parents and Neleus. If they had not received proper burial, their shades would wander between worlds, never finding the numb oblivion of the underworld.

I felt a hand on my shoulder. "I am truly sorry, Daimon," Lykos said quietly. He extended a hand to help me to my feet. I was surprised to see tears in his eyes.

"Dammo." We both turned quickly toward Meli's voice, startled by her sudden appearance.

She stood in the doorway, her dagger still clutched in her hand. She had tailed us through the streets undetected. Lykos pursed his lips in a silent whistle of admiration, and for a heartbeat it seemed as though my brother Heliodoros had come back from the land of the dead.

My anger at Meli's disobedience was dulled by a hollow sense of failure. "Adrastos is gone," I said forlornly.

"The gods will grant you the vengeance you seek," she said, but her eyes were red, too.

Everything of value or use had been taken. My father's armour and weapons were gone, stolen by my patricidal brother. Adrastos had also plundered all but one of the caches of gold and silver my father had concealed about the house. Neleus' smithy had been stripped of weapons and even the kitchen was stripped bare. Weapons, money, and food. All the things that my brother would need to sustain him on his flight from the city.

Neleus' quarters had also been scavenged. The room would have made a Spartan proud, containing just a bed and a chest. My presence in Neleus' private chamber made me uneasy. It was strange to be sitting in that room, for in all my years, I had never seen it. Though we had never been explicitly forbidden from entering, it was somehow off-limits, a trust that I had never violated.

At the bottom of the chest was a small cloth bundle tied with a single cord of twine. Opening it revealed a small wooden horse — child's toy— and a thin gold necklace. Neleus never spoke of his wife and children, taken from him by the plague that had killed my father's first wife. My parents had pushed him to find a new wife, and he had borne their chiding with good humour, claiming that he enjoyed his freedom as a bachelor. But I saw in those objects that he simply could not let go of those he had lost before.

Clutching the bundle, I returned to the courtyard Lykos was waiting with Meli and Tibetos. "What will happen now?" I asked.

A look of disgust flashed across the *peripoli* captain's face. "Some moderate members of the Four Hundred are trying to hold on to power until a new council can be chosen. I don't like it, but there's no choice right now. With a Spartan force on its way, we must unite for the time being to defend the city walls. But once the threat has passed, they will have to bow to the will of the people. Democracy will be restored."

But Lykos had misunderstood my question. "What will happen to *us*?" I said, glancing at Meli and Tibetos. Not being citizens, we had no rights to the welfare provided to orphans by the polis. I had no legal claim to my father's house. Except for the small bag of coins I had found, we had nothing.

Lykos took a deep breath. "Your father was a wise man, Daimon. He foresaw much of what has occurred, and he made plans for all possible eventualities, even the possibility of his own death. He was a *strategos* to the very end. Your father bade me swear an oath to take care of you and your sister should anything befall him. I swore to him in all sincerity that I would, though I never imagined that I would be called on to fulfil that oath in such a manner as we see before us." He let these words sink in, awaiting my response. Meli and Tibetos listened anxiously, aware that their own fate was being decided alongside mine.

I straightened my back and looked Lykos in the eye. "And what will we be?" I said sweeping my arm towards Meli and Tibetos. "Will we be *servants*?" The word tasted bitter in my throat.

Lykos raised his eyebrows in genuine surprise. "No, of course not. You will train as one of the *peripoli,* should you wish it. But it is a hard and thankless life."

It was more than I could ever have expected, but I was not speaking only for myself. I glanced at Tibetos. As a slave, my friend's fate was even more tenuous than mine. I looked back to Lykos and made my demand. "I accept your offer, provided you take on Tibetos as well."

Lykos laughed. It was open and without guile. "You are indeed your father's son, Daimon! I accept your conditions." Tibetos' mouth had fallen open.

Lykos and I clasped hands in affirmation of our new relationship. Once we had disengaged, Lykos offered his hand to Tibetos, who stood with his eyes wide. Recovering himself, he stepped over the threshold from his life as a slave to being something more. He shook hands with Lykos, and I could see in my friend's face that Lykos had won an eternal ally that day.

Then, to everyone's surprise, Meli stepped forward with her right hand extended and it was Lykos who was struck speechless. For a girl to offer her hand thus to a man was so far from proper behaviour that I had never seen such a thing before, nor have I seen any such thing since. But Meli waited patiently for Lykos to accept the oath of friendship. The *peripoli* captain blinked as if waking from a dream. He hesitated for a moment, giving a small laugh of disbelief as he reached out and clasped my sister's thin hand. Meli's lips creased slightly in an enigmatic smile.

But before anyone else could speak, Tibetos surprised me one more time by venturing a question. "*Lochagos,*" he said addressing Lykos by his rank. "Will we become hoplites?" My friend was still unsure what his sudden change in status meant.

Lykos became serious once again. "We are not hoplites. We are the *peripoli.*"

"But what are the *peripoli?*" I asked, for like most I knew little of the secretive band of warriors

"We are wolves in the night," Lykos said, his voice infused with pride. "We are the shadows in Spartans' nightmares."

Tyranny

# Part Two

# Crucible

# CHAPTER 10

The *peripoli*.

A miscellany of three hundred rogues and outcasts. The *peripoli* compound was a place where a man was judged by his skill rather than his birth. Some members were leftover sons from aristocratic Athenian families. But thieves and cutthroats also figured prominently among their number, as well as sundry exiles from dozens of poleis, all united by their unquenchable thirst for Spartan blood.

The *peripoli* did not fight as hoplites, the way Neleus had been training me. Instead, lightly-armed bands of *peripoli* haunted the hills and passes around the borders of Attica and beyond, harassing invaders and laying ambushes at critical passes. In enemy camps, men would wake to find their comrades dead, victims of ghosts that came in the night. The *peripoli* were feared.

And they took no prisoners. Peloponnesian and Theban corpses were left for scavengers and served as a warning for those invaders who followed. It was said that the Spartans had offered a bounty of fifty drachmas for any *peripoli* corpse. It was a bounty that was never collected. This was the fearsome reputation I had heard whispered of since I was a boy.

Now Lykos strode through the compound with Tibetos and me stumbling behind him, gawping at the hard-looking men appraising us as we passed by. Meli was not intimidated at all, keeping pace with Lykos with her chin held high.

Commander Hermon had little use for us. "Ares' balls, man!" Hermon barked, looking up from a table covered with papyri and wax tablets. "What in the name of Hades makes you think I have time to deal with trivial nonsense like this right now?" Hermon's irritation was not unfounded. The Four Hundred were gone, but the Spartan army they had invited was still bearing down on Athens, a point that the commander of the *peripoli* pointed out to us in no uncertain terms. "We might be eating Spartan black soup by tomorrow morning, and you bring me two boys and a girl?" He waved us away impatiently. "Take care of them and make sure they stay out of the way. Then come back here immediately. I have orders for you."

"Yes Commander," Lykos answered with a stiff nod of his head."

"Yes Commander," Tibetos and I said in unison, parroting Lykos.

Hermon raised his eyes from the document he had been reading. "Why are you still here?" he bellowed at us. Taking the cue, we scurried after Lykos. My sister had the presence of mind not to offer Hermon her hand.

Out in the large courtyard and beyond Hermon's wrath, it was Meli whom Lykos addressed first. "You will stay with the women, of course," he said in a tone that left no room for argument. He learned fast.

Lykos strode purposefully through the various areas of the vast compound, acknowledging numerous greetings from armed men with a nod or quick wave. Everyone seemed to be in a rush to get somewhere else, just as we were.

Passing through a wide double gate, we were hit by the sights and aromas of a busy kitchen. All about us, women and girls toiled at their tasks. Some were grinding grain for bread, others hunched over large cooking pots or heavy domed ovens. A young girl's legs hung out of a cistern as she leaned in to scoop out the water near the bottom. Along one wall there was a chicken coop, atop which stood a brilliant cock supervising the numerous hens that scratched and pecked for fallen grains of wheat and barley in the dirt.

A wizened crone stopped kneading the dough she had been making, slapped the flour off her hands, and shot towards us like an arrow. The tiny woman could have passed for one of the three Moirai who weave our fates, so deep were the ancient grooves on her face. There was no lack of vigour in her step and the corded muscles in her wiry forearms looked like the entwined ropes from a ship. Her obvious energy was matched by her boldness. She came to a stop before Lykos and stared up at the captain of the *peripoli* with black eyes, strands of grey hair stubbornly refusing to stay tied in the bun at the back of her head.

"No handouts! You know the rules!" She thrust her chin out, daring Lykos to tell her otherwise.

Lykos took no offense at her tone, instead smiling warmly at her. "I would never think of it, Lampita."

She eyed him suspiciously, searching for any hint of mockery in his voice. Finding none, she gave a disdainful sniff.

"But I do have a new girl for you," Lykos said, indicating Meli with one hand.

Lampita squinted at Meli, raising an eyebrow at my sister's flaming red hair. "Is she a slave? I don't have time to wring some work out of a lazy slave." I flinched at the question, but Meli calmly held the old woman's hard stare. It was like watching two cats encountering each other on the street, the battle won in the eyes before they ever resorted to claws and teeth.

Lykos interrupted the battle of wills. "She is Greek-born, Lampita. Daughter of a *strategos*."

"Hmmph!" the old woman snorted derisively. "Chickens don't care whether it be a queen or whore's brat that chops their heads off!"

Before Lykos could say anything, Meli gave a gentle bob of her head. "*O* Lampita, I will set my hand to any task you assign me. I will let your wisdom and experience be my guide." Her voice and words struck just the right balance between strength and deference.

Lampita inhaled deeply through her nose, keeping her inky eyes locked on Meli's green ones. Apparently, she found nothing to criticize, and some of the tension left her face. "You might regret those words, *pai*," she said with an arched eyebrow. "But mark my words. Any trouble from you, and you'll be out on the street sucking cocks for a crust of bread, *strategos'* daughter or no, do you hear?"

I was shocked to hear these words from a woman. Tibetos looked at the ground, suddenly finding something fascinating in the dirt by his feet. Lykos merely smiled patiently.

Meli, too, maintained her poise. "Of course, O Lampita," she said politely.

If the old woman had been trying to rattle her, she had failed. "There may be hope for you, *pai*," she conceded with a hint of grudging respect in her voice. "Come with me and I will see if you are more than just pretty words."

"Then I see that the child will be well cared for!" Lykos said clapping his hands together. "But I have kept you from your work, and we both have our duties to attend to!"

Lampita gave a non-committal grunt before taking Meli by the arm and leading her back toward the kitchen fires. As he watched them go, Lykos let out a long, quiet breath. He turned back to Tibetos and me. "We need to get you outfitted and settled," he said, and we followed him back to the main barracks.

The unusually loquacious Tibetos gave voice to my own thoughts. "Who are all those women?" he asked.

"The orphans of war," Lykos answered over his shoulder. "A few of them are wives of my comrades, but mostly they are the widows. Some are the wives of the *peripoli* who have fallen, or our sisters whose husbands were killed, or wives of our brothers. In return for a roof over their heads, they labour for the *peripoli*. It is not the life of leisure, but in any case, it is a better fate for them to end up here than in one of the brothels."

"Why haven't they remarried?" I asked.

Lykos shrugged. "Who would they wed? The war had made many heroes, but even more dead men. There aren't enough men left anymore."

"And who was the old woman?" Tibetos interjected, continuing to surprise me.

"Lampita? She keeps order among the women. It would take a brave man to cross her. Even Hermon watches his step when he deals with her. There is still debate among the men as to whether she is a harpy or one of the Furies incarnate." Lykos seemed to consider the question before returning to the present. "But now for you two."

Lykos took us to a man named Heirax, a Skythian, responsible for training younger recruits. The northerner's face was like leather, with deep lines accentuating every grimace as his blue eyes appraised us coldly.

"More pups to feed!" Heirax said disapprovingly in a clipped Skythian accent.

"They can earn their keep," Lykos responded.

"They'll end up as someone's bum-boys, by the look of them," the Skythian said doubtfully.

"They have smithy experience. Timonax will make use of them at his forge. There are always weapons needing repairs."

"Not completely useless, then," Heirax conceded.

"You will take them?" Lykos asked the arms-master.

"The Mede is too small," Heirax said dismissively of Tibetos. "Better to make him a slinger or javelineer. Send him to Sabas."

"And the other?" Lykos nodded in my direction.

Heirax grabbed my shoulder, squeezing the muscle hard like he was buying a horse. "The Thracian is big enough, but can he fight?" I bristled at the word 'Thracian' but held my tongue.

"He has potential," Lykos vouched.

Heirax snorted. "I'll be the judge of that, boy!" The Skythian regarded us for a long while before finally exhaling loudly. "*Papaios*," he said, invoking the name of his Skythian god. "What poor materials you give me! Very well, leave them with me."

Tibetos and I exchanged glances. Neither of us knew what awaited us, but there was no choice but to accept the opportunity fate had granted us.

Our metamorphosis had begun.


WITHOUT THE FOUR HUNDRED IN POWER, the Spartans had no allies to admit them into the city. They turned their army around and marched back to Sparta. Athens had survived.

Lykos had attempted to determine the identity of my brother's friend but to no avail. "One of the oligarchs' sons, no doubt. Whoever he was, he must have fled with your brother and the rest of the Four Hundred to join their Spartan masters," he told me with palpable frustration in his voice.

"I will find them," I said. "And give my parents and Neleus justice."

"And I will help you," Lykos said. "But you and Tibetos must train hard to become one of the *peripoli*."

"It is my only purpose now," I said.

Tibetos and I threw ourselves into our new lives. My friend spent most of his days hurling missiles at various targets. At first he had been disappointed not to be training full-time with spear and sword. But he soon began to appreciate the deadly accuracy of his adopted weapons. His teacher was Sabas, a mad Cretan who was master of anything shot, hurled or slung. "Sabas hit a crow in mid-flight!" Tibetos reported to me in awe. "It must have been fifty paces away at least!"

"The boy has some aptitude," Sabas said after some months. Tibetos beamed at the praise.

I rarely saw Lykos. Instead, I trained with twenty or so other youths under the watchful eye of Heirax. His lean, soldier's body was like a taut snare that could suddenly snap with a whip-fast lunge or strike. Even the smallest lapse of attention would earn the unwary victim a bruise from the stick of olive wood that never left the Skythian's hand. On the odd occasion when Lykos checked in on us, he was more nostalgic than sympathetic. "I see that Heirax has not changed since I was your age. He is the best arms-master in Athens. Count yourself lucky!"

My days were filled with one-on-one contests with blunted swords or spears, interspersed with severe punishments when I did not live up to Heirax's high standards. Autumn and winter were a blur of endless drills that were only broken up by meals, labour, and exhausted sleep in which the ghosts of my parents and Neleus haunted me.

Other members of the *peripoli* were eager spectators of our training sessions, shouting advice and encouragement and betting on the outcomes of individual contests. They would jeer the loser, or erupt in cheers for a well-executed move. My name was never used. Instead, I was called "Thrax" or "Pommo," for Lykos had shared the tale of my pomegranate-throwing exploits in the agora.

The regimen of drills and sparring left me forever bruised and drained of energy.

But I was good.

I was taller than most, and years of assisting Neleus at his forge had packed me with lean muscle. But it was the blacksmith's strict training that served me best. In my cohort of young recruits, I was soon unbeatable with sword or spear. Heirax began to put me against two or three opponents at the same time. On the day when I first blocked one of the arms-master's random attacks, he gave a grunt of grudging respect, the highest praise that he would give. My skill brought me my first taste of *kleos* — fame and reputation — and it swelled my pride in equal measure.

And so, I deserved the thrashing that Lykos gave me.

He had been watching with some of the other veterans. I wanted to display my prowess to him, for I yearned for his praise above all others. The veteran spectators gave loud voice to their approval, yet Lykos remained silent, his brow creased in a frown as he took in the contest between me and Mnasyllus, a youth three years my senior and closest to me in skill. Mnasyllus was built like a bull but quick for his size. But I was faster. It was a hard contest, but the result was never in doubt. I wore my opponent down with blow after blow, and soon Mnasyllus was puffing and swinging more and more wildly, leaving himself exposed to my attacks. Whenever I landed a particularly devastating hit, I opened my arms to accept the acknowledgement of the audience, basking in their cheers. When Heirax called an end to the match and declared me the victor, I raised my helmet and beamed at Lykos.

A look of barely-restrained anger filled Lyko's face. I stood frozen in his glare like an idiotic statue caught by the sculptor in mid-smile. Others became aware of the awkward tension between us, and eyes darted repeatedly from the stunned Thrax back to the brooding captain.

At last, hands on knees, Lykos pushed himself to his feet. He addressed Heirax. "With your permission," he said coldly. The arms-master acceded to his request with a shallow nod and stepped back a few steps to give the captain room. The veteran soldiers witnessing all this were quick to catch onto what was to come. They elbowed each other in gleeful anticipation of the upcoming clash.

Lykos strode towards Mnasyllus, who was still grimacing from the blows I had landed. He took the training sword from the youth's hand. Mnasyllus dumbly offered the buckler as well, but Lykos merely gave him a friendly slap on the back and waved him off. Only then did I finally realize that Lykos meant to challenge me.

He faced me with the blunted sword hanging loosely in his hand. "Come, boy. Show me what you have learned." His voice was ice.

I threw a look of silent appeal to Heirax, who just shrugged, and I knew that there was no way to extricate myself from the situation I had somehow unwittingly placed myself in. I glanced back at Lykos. He waited, expressionless, his arms slightly open as though inviting the first attack.

Word of the contest must have spread, for more spectators began crowding the courtyard. Even Hermon was leaning in the doorway. I swallowed nervously but resolved to tread the path that had been set before me. I lowered my helmet and raised my shield and weapon. My body fell naturally into my fighting stance and I advanced on my waiting opponent.

My first attack was a feeble thrust that Lykos swatted away with disdain. Some in the audience booed at the poor spectacle. "If you are the best in your group, we should surrender to the Spartans now," Lykos sneered loudly for the crowd. "I could get a better fight out of one of the slave-girls." This elicited guffaws from some of the soldiers watching. I felt my face flush behind my helmet.

The shame focused my resolve. I pressed my next attack with vigour. I slashed and feinted, lunged and jabbed, but Lykos parried and dodged with ease. In frustration, I over-extended on a downward stroke, but Lykos stepped lightly to the side and let my momentum take me past him, whereupon he snapped his blade across my shoulder-blades and I was sent stumbling away, barely avoiding falling flat on my face.

More laughing and clapping ensued as I tried to recover my dignity. Lykos waited patiently. I raised my guard once again and moved to engage him, but with more caution. I took a more defensive approach, waiting for my opponent to bring the fight to me. Lykos shrugged in acceptance and lifted his weapon. I deepened in my crouch and braced myself for his attack.

He loped towards me in a loose, side-to-side stride. His first strike was a direct stab that I blocked with my buckler and responded to with a counter-stroke that Lykos ducked with nonchalant grace. But I had expected this and used my momentum to spin and strike out with a follow-up slash.

My weapon cut through empty air with a hiss. I suddenly felt my legs being swept from under me and I landed flat on my back with a jarring, flat thump that knocked the wind out of me. As I lay looking up at the sky, a cheer erupted from the onlookers, who were clearly enjoying the show.

Lykos was toying with me. My embarrassment made my temper rise, and I scrambled to my feet, eager to salvage any scrap of honour that I could. Any trepidation that I had felt about the contest with Lykos had burned away in the heat of my anger. Catching sight of him, I did not hesitate. With a shout, I charged at him with a flurry of blows. The savagery of my attack caught him off-guard, and he yielded a few steps before the onslaught, parrying and weaving. I swept away his attacks, possessed by a fury wrought of shame.

My best was not enough. A blow came under my guard and thudded into my belly. I doubled over trying to catch my breath, stumbling away and coughing. Straightening up, I saw my enemy. Lykos was breathing more heavily, but his expression was calm. I flew at him. There was no technique. Afterwards they said I attacked like a madman but it was for naught. Lykos drove the hilt of his sword into the nose-guard between my eyes. My vision was a blur of flashing light. My sword and shield falling from my grasp, I reeled backwards and slammed to the hard-packed earth like a felled tree.

I lay there like a dead man for a moment before struggling in fits and jerks to get to my hands and knees. With a shaking hand I pulled off my helmet and it dropped with a metallic thud. I scrabbled blindly in the dirt searching for the training sword, eventually locating it. I lurched sickeningly to my feet, my eyes falling on a blurred shape in front of me. I raised my weapon weakly. I had come to my senses enough to hear the shouts and cheers of the audience. I could not move. Swaying like a drunkard on his last legs, all my concentration was focused on staying upright and holding in my vomit. I awaited the next attack.

"Enough!" The commanding voice of Hermon cut through the noise in the courtyard. "The boy has had enough for today. We have all had a lesson today!"

The rest of *peripoli* rose and applauded in appreciation for the entertaining contest. Some came to me and slapped me on the back, praising me for giving them a good show. A few of the more sympathetic men put my arms around their shoulders and half-dragged me to a wooden bench. I plopped down on the bench, and the last vestiges of strength and control drained from my body. I looked about for Lykos, but he was gone.

Dropping my head between my knees, I threw up in the dirt.

TIBETOS HELPED ME BACK TO MY BED in the barracks. "By Zeus, Dammo! You should learn when to stay down," he advised me sagely before leaving me to suffer the pain of my injuries and nurse my wounded pride. I shut my eyes against the throbbing in my head as well as my shame and confusion. I did not know why my captain had turned on me.

In the evening, soft footsteps made me open my eyes. I expected to see Tibetos, but instead it was my tormentor from a few hours earlier. I jolted upright in surprise, wincing as a lance of pain shot through my bruised ribs. "*Lochagos*," I addressed Lykos formally through clenched teeth.

"How are you feeling?" he inquired. The coldness that had been in voice was gone. It was the Lykos who I had grown to know who sat across from me once again.

My pride got the better of me. "I'll recover," I said curtly.

Lykos sighed and rubbed his face with both his hands, massaging away the exhaustion from his features. He looked at me and asked, "Do you know why I did that today?"

I glowered in the dim light but did not answer.

"This is not a contest at Olympia, boy!" he exclaimed, irritation seeping into his voice. "Watching you strut and preen, you would think that you had just been crowned with a laurel wreath! Mnasyllus is not an opponent to be mocked or humiliated! He is not your enemy! He is the person who will stand at your side and watch your back. By the gods, this is not the gymnasium where wealthy scions compete with each other for prizes and honour. We are the *peripoli*. We work together. We train to kill Spartans. Do you understand, Daimon?"

I hung my head, for I was ashamed. "Yes, *lochagos*." It was almost a whisper.

Lykos blew out a long breath. "The *peripoli* are your clan now, Daimon. We are your family. We will stand and die to protect each other. The question is, do you want to love us as brothers, or would you rather exalt in your arrogance like the great Alkibiades? The proud die alone, Daimon," he finished softly.

His words moved me. "I understand, *lochagos*."

"Then this day was not a waste." Lykos rose to leave.

But my pride was not completely vanquished, for I could not help but challenge him before he departed. "But did you need to humiliate me so?"

He responded with a laugh. "That was the second part of the lesson. You are not as good as you think you are. Underestimating your enemy will get you killed. You are young with much to learn." My pride was deflated. My defeat at his hands was proof enough of his words.

Lykos left me to ponder the wisdom of what he had said, but my heart surged at his parting words. "You have talent, young Daimon. You will do additional training with me from now on."

That night, among the snores of my comrades, I stared into the darkness. In my mind I saw the faces of my mother, my father, Neleus. They had been my family, and they had died for me. But now I was alone. Lykos had offered me the chance to become part of a new family, but until that moment something had prevented me from committing myself to the *peripoli* with all my heart. I had refused to let go of the ties that bound me to my parents and Neleus out of loyalty and grief. But now, I whispered a prayer that I hoped would reach them in the underworld, swearing that I had not forgotten them.

In that instant, in my heart, I became part of my new family. I was *peripoli* now.

Blackness came and I slept peacefully for the first time in months.

# CHAPTER 11

The winter offered no respite from our training. When I was not under the stern eye of Lykos or Heirax, I was tramping outside the walls of the city, building up my endurance. "We move fast and far," Lykos told me. "There is no place for stragglers."

I saw little of Tibetos and even less of Meli, who could not escape Lampita's watchful eye. The screeching old harpy would chase me away if I had the temerity to seek out my sister in the women's quarters. When I managed to catch a glimpse of Meli, she would flash her mischievous smile and scurry off to complete whatever errand Lampita had demanded of her.

I was oblivious of Meli's blossoming beauty. She was thirteen and approaching the age of marriage, yet I only saw the girl with a mass of tangled hair who would stick her tongue out at me when no one else was watching. But her desirability was not lost on the other men of the *peripoli*. They soon learned to be wary, however.

On that day, I was sparring with the imposing but soft-spoken Mnasyllus, who was attempting to shatter my bones with a wooden sword. Heirax and Lykos stood to one side shouting instructions. Veteran soldiers occupied their usual places on the benches, chipping in with their own advice and wagering on the outcome.

Mnasyllus suddenly halted his attack. He stepped back and raised his helmet, looking past me in surprise. I turned to see what had drawn his attention. Meli was striding across the courtyard. One of the veteran *peripoli*, a Plataean named Epimenes, blocked my sister's path.

Epimenes grinned lasciviously. "Where do you think you're going, beautiful girl? Come, I have some wine. Let us drink together! Maybe more!" He looked back at his comrades for approval. They slapped their knees and guffawed as though this was a witty line worthy of Aristophanes.

An audible grumble rose in my throat. For the honour of my sister, I stepped towards Epimenes, but before my foot had fallen, I felt the restraining hand of Mnasyllus. "Wait," he hissed. It was a good thing he did so.

Epimenes was called *Bos* — Ox — by his comrades for good reason. His neck was almost invisible, so thick were the muscles of his shoulders and back. He was crude in manners and overly fond of wine, but had a reputation for unstoppable ferocity in battle. For all my youthful vigour, I was not his match.

Epimenes, playing to his audience, leered cheerfully at my sister. Meli spat loudly into the dust at his feet, never taking her eyes from the hulking figure before her. Epimenes shifted awkwardly beneath her unflinching stare, causing the other *peripoli* to howl with laughter at his apparent discomfort. Even from across the courtyard I could see his face redden in embarrassment.

Meli made to step past him, but Epimenes, goaded on by the others, was not yet giving up on his loutish attempt at seduction. He seized her delicate shoulder in his rough hand.

"You don't know what you're missing —"

There was a flash of movement. Epimenes froze in mid-sentence. His fingers gently released their grip on my sister and with exaggerated care he slowly raised his hands in a gesture of surrender. A confused murmur washed over the courtyard as all present strained to see what had caused Epimenes' sudden act of supplication.

The truth of the matter became clear. Meli's hand lay hidden under the big man's tunic between his trunk-like legs. Her eyes were locked on his, daring him to move. He was as still as a statue.

The tension was broken by a shout from the audience. "She's taken hostages!" The entire courtyard erupted into laughter, and though it did not seem possible, Epimenes turned an even darker hue of red.

Meli nodded slowly and Epimenes stepped gingerly away. The cause of his extreme trepidation was revealed, for in Meli's tight fist was the knife I had given to her so long ago. Upon seeing the blade, the *peripoli* who were present broke into applause. To his credit, Epimenes smiled sheepishly and removed himself graciously from my sister's path.

As quickly as it had appeared, the knife vanished into the folds of Meli's tunic. I gaped in further amazement as my sister strode right up to the other men who had been egging Epimenes on. She stood before them, hands on hips, staring them down with her terrible emerald eyes. The hard men withered under her glare. She cursed them in Thracian and spat one more time. The men looked like whipped puppies. Meli turned on one heel and marched out of the courtyard, throwing a secret wink my way as she did so.

The *peripoli* exploded into cheers and applause at my sister's audacity. Beside me, Lykos laughed in admiration. Even Epimenes was grinning like a fool and clapping his hands.

I cast a glance towards the gate. Lampita stood there with her arms folded across her chest and a knowing smile on her face. She barked a satisfied laugh and disappeared.

MY STANDING AMONG THE MEN ROSE. The fierce Thracian siblings. That is what we were known as. I could do little to stop it, even if I tried. The truth is that I enjoyed my modest reputation. All my life I had striven to shed my Thracian roots, but now I played them up, wearing the name '*Thrax*' with pride.

In the spring, Lykos deemed me fit to join my first long-range scouting mission. "You're coming with us. Sword, spear, and javelins only. Meet us at the altar when you are ready."

In a state of nervous eagerness, I scrambled to my quarters. As I gathered my gear, a familiar voice came from behind me. "Dammo!" No sooner had I turned around than my sister crashed into me and embraced me tightly around my chest in her accustomed way. After a moment, she gave a final squeeze before releasing her grip and taking a step back to regard me wordlessly.

"I'm going out on a patrol with Lykos," I said, breaking the silence. I waited for the protest and warnings that I was sure would come, but the expected words did not come.

"I know. You will be safe," she said matter-of-factly.

Meli's declaration bolstered my confidence. "I don't know how long we'll be gone. Lampita didn't give me much food," I said, picking up the smallish sack of provisions the old woman had given me.

"Lampita is wiser than you think. And she cares for you silly men like you are her children," my sister said reprovingly. She bit her lip, hesitating. "But you must do something for me," she added.

"Anything."

"Tell Epimenes to be... to be careful." She sucked in her lips as if that had been difficult to say.

"I thought you despised Epimenes."

"He is a great lout but not a bad man. I would see him return safely," she said softly.

The back of my neck tingled uncomfortably. "Why?"

Meli looked at her feet for a moment before answering. "A dream came to me last night. I didn't understand it. I saw Epimenes covered by a myriad of ants."

I did not want my sister to be upset. "I will tell him," I said solemnly. I leaned over and she hugged me around the neck once more before scampering off. Her words unnerved me, but I pushed them to the back of my mind. The *peripoli* awaited me.

IN THE CENTRAL COURTYARD, Lykos and fifty or so other *peripoli* had gathered around the altar, preparing to offer a sacrifice for the success of the mission. I scanned the knot of men and my heart fell when I saw Tibetos was not among our number. My gaze fell upon Epimenes and our eyes locked for a heartbeat longer than was comfortable. The hefty veteran misinterpreted the concern on my face.

"Young Thrax looks frightened!" Epimenes joked. "His sister is the braver of the two, I think!" This brought forth a round of laughter from the men, and I flushed in embarrassment.

One man, Meges, had not joined in the others' mirth. He just stared at me with unconcealed contempt. Of all the *peripoli*, Meges was the only man I feared instinctively.

It was rumoured among the younger recruits that Meges had been a cut-throat or an assassin before joining the rangers. He was short and thin, but like Lampita in the kitchen, his corded muscles looked like iron under his skin. He was perhaps forty years of age, with thinning hair that hung lankly from his scalp. His clean-shaven face set him apart from the others and served to make his perpetually intimidating gaze seem even more baleful. Now his deep-set eyes regarded me menacingly. He spat casually to one side before finally breaking eye contact with me to watch Lykos perform the sacrifices.

Lykos invoked the names of Zeus the Saviour and Athena the Protector, and I echoed the words with most of the other men, hoping that Zeus would take note of my piety. Meges looked bored and scratched his balls lazily. Sabas the Cretan archer knelt, whispering in the ears of his wolf-like hound Argos. With a final appeal to the gods, Lykos poured the libation until the cup on the altar overflowed with the wine.

"A waste of good wine, that," Meges grumbled.

The ceremony completed, Lykos gave the order to move out. Soon we had passed through the northern gates of Piraeus and into the countryside. With our hats and cloaks and packs of food, we looked more like a band of travellers than a group of soldiers. We headed west along the road to Eleusis but soon veered north onto rougher terrain. I trudged on in silence, taking in the unfamiliar landscape.

The cold rains of winter were already a memory, and the fields and hills were dotted with spring blossoms. Green shoots pushed through the tired growth from the previous year, and a whiff of pine resin floated in the air, carried by the light breeze flowing from the mountains in the west. Midges swarmed in great clouds and humming bees went about their business, oblivious of the invaders trespassing on their land. Songbirds punctuated the air with their trills and flashes of color. The hound Argos ranged freely, occasionally flushing out a hare or partridge. Sabas loosed an arrow at one hare as it bounded out of the brush, and the shaft caught it cleanly through the neck, drawing a cheer from the rest of the men. Sabas gave a mock bow to his appreciative audience as Argos returned with the limp prize dangling from his mouth.

But of men, we saw none. The seasonal ravaging of the countryside by the Spartans and their allies had not yet begun, but evidence of their previous trespass was everywhere the eye fell. Plots of farmland lay abandoned and reclaimed by brush and thistle after having lain untended for so long. The ruins of homes and outbuildings were always within view for the first part of our journey. But for the rest of the day we were the lone mortals in the world, neither molested by enemies nor greeted by friends.

We Greeks call our lands Hellas and think it vast and bountiful, but we are mistaken. It is a tiny, dusty scab on the skin of the world. By dusk, we were not far from the borders of Attica, but a few weeks' hard marching could have taken us to any corner of Hellas. Three months is needed to reach the capital of the Persians, and they control even more land beyond that. It is said that the Euxine Sea could swallow our lands whole a dozen times over, and that the grasslands of Skythian horsemen are endless. To the west, they say the world ends at the gap Herakles left when he went to the great western sea, but I have heard men speak of lands beyond in the north inhabited by giants. And our land is not lush like the lands around the sacred river of the Egyptians. Hellas is mostly rocks and mountains, parched and desiccated. And we Greeks fight endlessly amongst ourselves over rocks and hardscrabble farmland.

That is what I know now, but on that day I was only taking my first steps into a larger world. As twilight fell, the landscape became increasingly rugged. As we picked our way along a stony goat path high on a crest, I lost my footing several times in the fading light, scrabbling to prevent myself from tumbling down into the valley below. Telekles was behind me and more than once he clutched my tunic to haul me back to my feet.

"We are men, not goats!" he said unconcernedly. "But you will grow your hooves soon enough!"

Just when I thought I would surely perish, not at the hands of a Spartan spear, but as a shattered mass of flesh and bone at the bottom of a cliff, we began to descend.

About halfway down the slope, Telekles spoke, much to my relief. "We will bivouac here tonight."

Amidst the trees and brush was an abandoned hunting lodge. Inside, a kneeling Meges was already starting a fire. A tiny kernel of light brightened and faded with each coaxing breath, until suddenly the kindling ignited into rippling life, illuminating the interior of our shelter for the night.

The lodge must have been built by someone of considerable wealth, for now I could see the dimensions were substantial enough to house our fifty men for the night. Debris from the collapsed roof littered the ground.

My appraisal of the lodge was interrupted by Meges' voice. I could hear the sneer on his face. "I think the youngest member should be responsible for gathering wood. Don't you agree, brothers?" The other men happily assented to this suggestion and began to unload their packs and weapons onto the floor, stretching and groaning from the day's exertions.

Lykos did not contradict Meges. "Sabas, go help the lad, or else he'll get lost in the dark and never be seen again."

"We can only hope," Meges muttered, but if Lykos heard the comment, he ignored it.

After Sabas and I made a dozen trips, there was enough firewood to satisfy Lykos, and even Meges grudgingly conceded that there was no more that needed to be done. The five hares that Sabas had shot were spitted over the fire and lovingly tended to by Kirphis, a man whose company I came to enjoy, for he was quick to laugh and generous to others. The meat glistened, and drops of fat sizzled and snapped as they dripped into the flames below, filling the lodge with a mouth-watering aroma.

Away from the fire, I chewed on a hunk of heavy, coarse bread from my pack, trying to ignore the maddening aroma of the cooking meat. The others were also fixated on the poor beasts over the fire, and when Kirphis finally lifted the spits away, they leaned forward with ravenous stares. Kirphis carved off hunks of meat with his dagger and distributed them to the eagerly waiting men.

It was meager fare for so many men and the carcasses rapidly dwindled in size. Just when I thought there was no more flesh to be found, Kirphis managed to dig some out and offered it to me on the end of his dagger. It hung temptingly before my eyes, but I held back.

"It is the last of the meat," I said regretfully to Kirphis. "There is none left for you." That earned me some comments of approval from the other men.

Kirphis winked at me. "Don't worry, boyo. I snuck a piece while it was cooking. Take it." He poked the steaming meat even closer to me. I gratefully accepted the hunk of hare meat, closing my eyes in pleasure as the salty juices danced in my mouth.

"And I offer this piece of flesh to Zeus the Saviour," Lykos said loudly, tossing his portion into the fire. "May he offer his protection to us." The rest of the *peripoli* repeated the prayer, save for Meges, who picked at his teeth with a twig.

Soon, wineskins were being passed around the fire, each man taking a swig when it was his turn. The sour wine tasted of leather but was delicious nonetheless. There was laughing and joking as the men exchanged stories and good-natured jibes, but I did not join in, content to merely listen.

As night deepened, the mirth subsided, and the men's minds turned inwards as they contemplated the hypnotic motions of the fire. I thought of what my sister had said about Epimenes, and my eyes fell upon him where he sat opposite me. As though sensing my stare, his eyes flicked up at me. I dropped my gaze. Too obviously, for he snorted loudly and challenged me to explain myself.

"What is it, boy? You've been watching me like a hawk all day! Spit it out!" I froze as the conversation stopped and all eyes turned towards me. Even Lykos watched me with a curious expression on his face.

At first I tried to deflect his accusation, but the denial fell flat, and Epimenes persisted in his interrogation. Eventually, I saw no way out but to tell the truth. I explained what Meli had told me before we had set out.

Epimenes stared at me in disbelief. Then he burst into laughter. "Ants? It will take more than ants to kill me, lad! I'm not worried about a little girl's dreams!" The rest of the men joined him in his laughter, and I was embarrassed by my foolishness.

Meges' sour voice cut across the laughter. "Taking advice from a little girl! What would you expect from a whelp? Probably still needs his mother's kiss before he goes to bed to keep away the bad dreams," he needled. His black eyes bore into me from where he leaned against a wall away from the others.

The stinging barb was deliberate. Meges was well aware of what fate that had befallen my family. My bile rose and I was emboldened by the wine. Past advice from Neleus and my father about keeping my temper was swept aside as I leapt to my feet and pointed an accusing finger at the seated thief.

"What is the reason for your dislike of me, Meges? What harm have I done you?" The words came through clenched teeth.

The rest of the men leaned forward, eagerly anticipating Meges' response, but he merely shrugged. "You're a Thracian. I dislike Thracians."

"I am an Athenian!" I shouted, stabbing my chest with my finger. I made to step towards Meges, but the firm hand of Kirphis held me back.

Meges' disdainful tone never wavered. "You look like a Thracian to me, and if there's one thing I know, it's that you can't trust a Thracian. Little better than animals, if you ask me."

"That comes from a man who cuts people's throats as they sleep!" I spat back.

The arrow struck a nerve, for an edge of anger crept into Meges' voice, and he shifted so that he was facing me directly. "Only Spartans, boy. Only Spartans. But for you, I'll make an exception." The words dripped venom.

"Enough!" Lykos exploded. The silence was broken by the snap and hiss of the fire. He glared at Meges "There is no place for petty sniping! Or," Lykos said pointing an accusing finger at me, "for flying into a fury at every drunken jibe that comes your way!" I began to protest, but the anger in Lykos' eyes made me hold my tongue. He lifted his hands to the heavens in exasperation. "By the gods, we are the *peripoli*, not a gaggle of boys in the gymnasium squabbling about who has the biggest cock! Tomorrow, Meges, Epimenes, Daimon: you march together. See if you can get through the day without killing each other, or else I'll send you all to Hades myself." Meges and I looked at each other with mutual loathing. Epimenes appealed with a confused expression to his comrades, but no support was forthcoming. "As for the rest of you," Lykos said to the rest of the men, "we set out early. Get some sleep." He scowled, daring anyone to protest.

Amidst some muted grumbling, the men found a place to lie down on the packed earth of the lodge floor. Kirphis gave me a pat on the shoulder and a what-can-you-do shrug before he settled down and closed his eyes.

The fire died down to embers, suffusing the lodge in the dimmest of red light. With my head resting on a makeshift pillow made from my pack, I stared at the exposed sky above to the sounds of men snoring or scratching themselves. Hypnotized by the stars, my anger subsided, overcome by the exhaustion of the day's journey.

Epimenes made one last protest into the darkness. "*I* have the biggest cock, though," he muttered. There was laughter from the other *peripoli*, and I smiled in spite of myself as sleep took me.

CHAPTER 12

At dawn we set out, staying in the mountains that ringed the flat plain below. To the southwest the sacred town of Eleusis was visible in the morning light. "We'll cross the mountains," Telekles informed me. "With luck, we'll find some prey coming from Boeotia."

During the trek, Meges and I stubbornly ignored each other, but the good-natured Epimenes spoke enough for the both of us, happily sharing his views on all subjects from the best brothels in Piraeus to every battle or skirmish he had ever been involved in. When he spoke of the former, Meges chipped in with his own opinion, and when he spoke of the latter, I could not help pestering him with questions, which he answered cheerfully. The banter was a welcome distraction, and we were soon overlooking the plains of Boeotia.

For three days, Lykos sent out scouting missions from our base in the mountains. I accompanied Telekles, who instructed me in the basic points of the rangers' craft, showing me how to remain concealed and how to use the land to my advantage. He was a good teacher and I listened raptly to all that he said, but Telekles downplayed his own talents. "If you want to learn from the best, you must go with Meges. He could sneak so close to an enemy that he could hold their dicks while they were taking a piss and they wouldn't even know it."

I grunted non-committedly, for I was unwilling to concede any respect for the ill-tempered Meges. But it was Meges who returned on the fourth day with valuable intelligence, and all gathered round to hear his words.

A troop of approximately sixty soldiers was skirting the northern edge of the mountains. Meges had crept close enough to their camp to hear them speak. "Megarians, by the sound of them." There were grumbles from among the men, for the Megarians were regarded bitterly as the most traitorous of Athens' many enemies. But Meges had saved the best for last. "There was a Spartan with them. I heard the bastard ordering the rest of them around." The men chuckled as Meges proceeded with an exaggerated imitation of a Spartan accent.

"Do you know where they are now?" Lykos asked.

Meges cleared his nose before answering. "Aye, they'll be coming through the valley below, heading for the pass at Leipsydrion."

The men exchanged glances and looked expectantly to Lykos. "Then we must be there before them," he said firmly. "*Peripoli*, we move out immediately. Bring water and weapons only. We travel light."

THE PASS WAS AN IDEAL LOCATION for an ambush.

Hedged in by steep, uneven slopes on both sides, the path was broad enough for a dozen to walk abreast, but not much more. There were enough boulders and wallows to hide an army, let alone the fifty or so men that made up our number.

"Are you certain they will come here?" Telekles asked to Meges doubtfully. The wiry *peripoli* waved him away with a hiss.

But the hours passed, and there was still no sign of the enemy. Lykos came to where I sat in the shelter of a hollow up the slope. In a low voice, I asked him about what would happen.

"We will leave thirty men there under Telekles," he explained pointing up the valley. "He will let them pass, and then give the order to attack with missiles and stones."

"That will kill them all?" It seemed unlikely to me.

"No. Some will be killed, and more wounded. If they're smart, they'll form a phalanx. But they're unlikely to be wearing their armour, so it would be weak. They will most likely flee up the valley.

"And we'll be waiting for them?"

Lykos raised an eyebrow. "*You* will be watching today, Daimon. You will not move from this position," he said unequivocally. My heart sank, for I had a young man's insatiable yearning for honour. Lykos chuckled at my crestfallen expression. "Today you will learn how we fight." He patted my shoulder and left me to stew in my disappointment.

It was late afternoon when Sabas reappeared. From the reaction of the men with Telekles farther up the valley, I knew that the

Megarians were not far behind. From my lonely perch, I could see Lykos and the remaining men a shout away from me as they waited to spring their secondary ambush. I watched in simmering resentment, bitter that Lykos had deemed me unready for the engagement to come.

My vexation was soon displaced by the arrival of the Megarians. It was a whisper at first, but the steep walls of the pass focused the sound of the approaching enemy into a steadily growing hum. A loose mass of men appeared with pack mules and slaves bearing heavy loads. I crouched low, my breath deepening in anticipation.

From my vantage point, I watched as the trap closed with alarming ferocity. A wicked hail of javelins rained down on the hapless victims below, and many of them fell in the first barrage. Their shouts and screams filled the confined space of the pass.

It played out much as Lykos had predicted. Panic set in as a few of the enemy foolishly abandoned their comrades and made a mad dash up the valley. The isolated men were soon cut down by missiles or butchered by teams of *peripoli* descending from the slopes with spears and swords.

Forty or so survivors had managed to get hold of shields and weapons, forming a circular wall. They advanced away from the first attack, but with their focus on the *peripoli* behind them, the Megarians were unprepared for the hammer blow of the second ambush. Javelins and arrows punched into the exposed flanks of the disorganized mass of men.

More of the *peripoli* came down from the slopes. Like a pack of wolves converging on a wounded but still dangerous animal, the rangers warily formed a loose perimeter around the doomed men, still pelting their hapless quarry mercilessly.

A shout came from within the circle of survivors. "Forward!" Under the jeers of the *peripoli*, the stump of a phalanx began its shuffling retreat. The two groups of *peripoli* herded the hapless Megarians up the valley like a shepherd and his dog corralling sheep. The odd javelin found a gap in the enemy shields. Rocks were more effective, falling in the centre of the circle and crushing flesh and bone. The dwindling mass continued to inch forward.

From within the phalanx came a shout, the command crisp and clear above the din. "Now!"

In an instant, the circle of men unfolded to form a two-line phalanx six men in breadth. The suddenness of their desperate counter-attack caught the smaller group of *peripoli* by surprise. Before anyone could react, the diminutive Megarian shield-wall broke out into a full-speed run, the enemy intending to batter their way through the thin line of *peripoli* that blocked their escape route through the pass.

There were a dozen *peripoli* to hold the line. Not enough.

I bolted from my observation point, propelled by an equal measure of fear and frantic eagerness to aid my comrades. Only my momentum kept me from slipping and tumbling down the slope. But I could see that I would be too late.

The *peripoli* had not had time to form a proper line, but the veteran fighters threw themselves into the charging enemy with sufficient force to slow them down. I was on the flat part of the pass now, racing towards the raging battle, but I was still an arrow shot away.

Two *peripoli* fell, and suddenly two of the enemy burst through the line and came sprinting down the pass towards me, tossing away their cumbersome shields. One of the men had long plaited hair that flapped wildly as he ran. I knew what he was.

It was a Spartiate. An elite warrior of Sparta.

All Greeks knew the tales. The hoplites who calmly combed and oiled their long hair before battle, when other men's bowels were turning to water. If I had had sense, I would have felt fear. I craved honour and prestige and the respect of my fellows, yet there was more than desire for these things. For the first time, I felt the *aristeia* fill my being.

How can one describe *aristeia* to one who has not experienced it? It is like trying to describe the sun to a blind man. It is strength and speed and blood-lust, a taste of divine power made manifest in mortal flesh. Now the *aristeia* surged within me and I found myself screaming a mad challenge as I hurled myself towards enemy sprinting towards me.

I could see them like pieces on a game-board. It was so clear. When engaging two enemies, do not get caught between them. Kill the weaker opponent first, and then focus on the more skilled fighter.

The Spartan immediately ascertained my goal and veered to cut me off, but I had caught them both off guard and the Spartan's momentum took me out of reach of his slashing sword.

The second man, suddenly facing the prospect of colliding with a howling madman, attempted to pull up. It was his mistake. I did not slow down, though I had no sense of speed. There was a look of terror as he desperately hacked at me. It was nothing to me. It was as though he was moving in water while I was still on dry land. I ducked beneath the weak blow and slashed my *xiphos* across his belly as I went past him. I felt the iron edge rip deeply through clothing and flesh, and the man shrieked, trying to hold his guts in as he collapsed to the ground.

I skidded to a halt and spun to face the Spartan. The Spartan did not hesitate and tried to turn my own trick against me. He barrelled towards me, his war-cry filling the air.

An instinct honed by the countless hours of training took over. I stepped to one side in order to limit the Spartan's options. He adjusted to my defense, feinting a stab at my chest before shifting to a backhand blow that would have sliced into my neck. But it was a trick Lykos had drilled into me, and the Spartan's blade hissed through empty air. I was grinning like a madman.

The Spartan had seen a youth with a sword and underestimated me twice. Now he eyed me warily, circling me lightly with his blade in a low grip. With a growl he came at me again.

Iron sang as our swords clashed in a flurry of strokes, parries, and counterattacks. Despite my battle-madness, the Spartan's experience came to the fore and a kick to the chest sent me sprawling onto my back. The Spartan roared and tensed his body to leap towards me.

Before the Spartiate could spring, he suddenly jolted himself erect, his body rigid. His face was a rictus of pain. I looked on in confusion and scrambled to my feet. There was a thwack of an arrow biting flesh and the Spartan spun. Two shafts protruded from his back. His sword fell from his grasp and he fell to his hands and knees. A third feathered shaft struck him in the side, and he collapsed.

Lykos and the other *peripoli* were running towards me. Sabas had another arrow nocked in his bow. The *peripoli* converged on the spot where I stood over the Spartan, who struggled in the dirt, groping for his sword on the rocky ground. Spreading red splotches stained his tunic where Sabas' arrows had pierced him.

The *aristeia* deserted me as quickly as it had come on. Wide-eyed, I watched my vanquished foe writhe on the ground before me. I could hear the pain in his short quick breaths. I did nothing.

The Spartan shifted onto his side, and his eyes met mine. There was no fear. Only fury. Rage at the ignominy of his defeat. He grimaced as he rolled onto his back, the arrows bending and snapping under his weight. Not once did he cry out.

"You are without honour," he rasped at me through clenched teeth. "You are all without honour," the Spartan cried at us.

A gentle nudge on my shoulder woke me from my trance. Telekles was holding a spear out to me. I looked at him incomprehensibly for a heartbeat. He glanced down at the Spartan and then proffered the spear to me once again. At last, knowing my duty, I took it. My hand was trembling.

The Spartan was still glaring at me. Blood now trickled from the corner of his mouth. I handed my sword to Telekles and raised the spear with both hands.

"Without honour," the Spartan sputtered one more time.

The spear-point drove down through the Spartan's chest. His body tensed one last time and his eyes rolled back in his head. Then his spirit left him. To my shame, my cheeks were wet with tears. But there were hands on my back accompanied by murmurs of praise. A gentle hand gripped my arm, pulling me away from the scene.

I looked up and was surprised to see it was Meges. His customary scowl was gone, replaced by an expression that was both sad and wise. "You did good, boy," he said. I nodded dumbly and let him lead me away from the first Spartan I had ever killed.

I have heard tales told of how the Demon slew his first Spartiate single-handed when he was but a boy, but it was never so. I was almost beaten by my better until he was shot in the back with arrows and then I drove a spear through his heart while he lay helpless on the ground. That is the truth of it.

LYKOS CURSED SOFTLY AS HE GAZED down at the *peripoli* corpses awaiting burial. The bodies had been laid side by side away from the enemy dead. Scenting death, flies already crowded about their closed eyes and open wounds. More than fifty dead Megarians and a Spartiate on top of that, all for three of our own. Yet Lykos saw it as a failure.

With great relief I saw that the imposing Epimenes was not among the dead. He had been wounded in the thigh in the final clash but dismissed the injury with a laugh. "It just nicked me! I've had worse in a tavern brawl!" he kept saying. Indeed, the gash had gummed up and he was hardly hampered in his movement. He gave me a tremendous slap on the back and left me to look at our prisoners.

The enemy soldiers had been slain to a man, but there had been almost twenty slaves with them to bear the burden of armour and supplies. Most turned out to be prisoners taken from the allies of Athens. The others swore oaths to return peacefully to the city with us. There was always a need for rowers for the triremes of the Athenian fleet, and it was a better life than being a slave.

One of the freed men was a helot named Iollas. His skin was like tanned leather and his back hunched from his years of labour serving his Spartan masters. He had never known a day of freedom in his life. I had a question for him.

"Who is the Spartiate, Iollas?" I said, pointing to the dead Spartan warrior.

"Not a Spartiate, Master," Iollas corrected me. "A *mothax*. Kalchas." A wave of sympathy washed through my chest, for the Spartan's lot in life was not dissimilar from my own. A Spartiate was a member of the elite class in Sparta, born of a Spartiate father and Spartan mother. A *mothax* was a half-breed, usually the offspring of a Spartiate father and a helot woman. To be a *mothax* in Sparta was to forever be denied respect and honour, no matter how great one's deeds or bravery. In Sparta, as in Athens, birth was everything.

The enemy dead were stripped of weapons and valuables and were left where they had fallen, food for the crows.

Save for one.

A sturdy wooden frame made of spears propped up the corpse of Kalchas the Spartan. His great lambda-emblazoned shield leaned against his lifeless legs and his helmeted head hung down as if in shame. The gruesome trophy was a warning to those who dared invade our land. My father would not have approved, for he despised the desecration of the dead by the victors. Neleus, on the other hand, would have shrugged and said that one could not expect men to control their beastly natures in times of war. But as I gazed upon the lolling head of the Spartan, I felt no hatred for him, though he was my enemy.

We left Kalchas to his silent vigil. Despite the mules and freed slaves, every man was weighed down by the plunder of weapons and armour. Rivulets of sweat trickled from under the cuirass and helmet I was now wearing. I glanced over at Iollas, helot no more. He seemed more goat than man. He carried as heavy a burden as anyone, but uttered not a single complaint and seemed no worse for wear when we arrived at the abandoned lodge soon after sunset.

Epimenes stood in stark contrast to the freed slave. The burly fighter had started the return journey strongly but ended it cursing and limping. The wound in his thigh had opened up, and the cloth we had used to bind it was stained with dark blood. Epimenes sat down heavily and leaned against a wall, removing the rag to examine the injury.

"Just let it rest for the evening." Epimenes winced as he shifted slightly to make himself more comfortable. "I've had worse from sharp-toothed whores!" he joked, but his grimace belied his easy manner.

But by the morning, Epimenes' condition had deteriorated. A pallor had set in, and a sheen of sweat glistened on his forehead. Sabas, who had some knowledge of the healing arts, examined the wound on Epimenes' leg. From over the Cretan's shoulder, I could see that the area around where the spear had pierced the thigh was an angry red. It was only because of the mules that we were able to get the bulky warrior back to the compound in Piraeus.

Epimenes, delirious with fever, was laid in his bed. The sallowness of his skin had deepened, and his eyes were sunken and dark. He sweated profusely but sputtered and choked on any water that was put to his lips. Lampita was summoned to tend to him. When she pressed on the wound, a foul liquid gushed forth, assaulting the nostrils of those who stood by. Through the night, we stayed with him. He slept fitfully, groaning and trembling. Occasionally he called out to someone only he could see. Many of the other men peeked in the door to look in on their comrade, for he was well-loved among the *peripoli*, but the fear of being polluted by his illness stopped them from entering. Hermon ignored the taint of sickness and sat by the bed for what seemed to be an age, silently staring at his fallen soldier.

Following three lingering days and nights of moaning and confused rambling, Epimenes entered a period of relative lucidity. He asked that Lampita purify the room with the blood of a young pig, and it was done. Their fear assuaged by the ritual, the men gathered to hear the dying man's words. It must have surprised everyone when he called me to his side. "Thrax," he said weakly, "bring your sister to me. I would have words with her."

I ran to fetch my sister from the women's quarters and returned hastily. Furrowed brows greeted her arrival. Hands moved to touch iron or grasp their genitals as protection against the evil eye. I knew what they feared, for I had heard their furtive whispers. *Tombas.* Witch. They believed that Meli had cursed Epimenes and called down this evil upon him.

Meli stood meekly beside me, her hands clasped lightly in front of her.

"Girl, come here." Epimenes rasped.

Meli stepped forward and knelt beside the bed. "What is it, O Epimenes?" She asked in a tone so gentle that it could have made grown men cry.

"I itch everywhere. It feels like ants crawling under my skin. They are eating me from the inside, I think, as you said they would. Why have you cursed me thus, *pai?*" There was no malice or accusation in his voice, just curiosity.

Meli laid her tiny hand on the sick man's cheek. "I did not curse you, brave man." It came out as a plea rather than a declaration of innocence. "I told only what the gods showed me. I wished you no ill." Tears ran down her face.

Epimenes strained to smile and a feeble chuckle rattled in his throat. With great effort, it was he who now moved his hand to cup my sister's face gently in his great hand. "Worry not, *pai*, for it was I who brought the gods' wrath down upon me when I offended you. Woe to the man who seeks to harm you, for the gods will surely bring him low!" The uncharacteristic string of eloquence exhausted him, and he broke out in a fit of coughing. When he recovered, he spoke not to Meli, but to all those assembled about him. "Know this," he said more loudly. "This child is to be protected and cherished, for she is no witch, but an oracle favored by the gods. Brothers, swear to me that you will heed her words! Swear to me now this thing."

Everyone in the room spoke their pledge. Epimenes seemed satisfied, for he closed his eyes and settled back onto the bed with a peaceful expression on his face.

And he died.

## CHAPTER 13

Meges became my tutor in the art of stealth. I discovered he was not a bad man, though he was almost permanently in a foul temper. And as Lykos had predicted, Meges had much to teach me.

The Spartans and their allies provided ample opportunity for practice. With Meges in the lead, we would shadow enemy patrols over mountains and plains. When the enemy was not near, Meges would show me ideal locations to set up an ambush and how to carry one out.

"People are just like sheep," he explained, "and you're the dog. If you bark at them right, they'll run wherever you want them to run. Then it's time to slaughter the lambs." When Meges spoke of killing the enemy, it was inevitably accompanied by a menacing grin of jagged teeth.

"Look over there." He pointed at a point in the ravine ahead of us. Steep, rock-strewn slopes rose from either side. "You could hide fifty men in those rocks without anyone the wiser." Indeed there were countless boulders or shrubs that would easily conceal a man. "Anyone who wants to cross these hills needs to come through here, or else go a half day's march north for the next easy route. Now, if you wait 'til you're behind them and start pouring javelins and rocks and arrows on them like it's Zeus himself pissing lightning on them, what are they going to do, boy?"

"Run?"

"Hera's tits, boy! Of course they're going to run! Right up that ravine there," he said, jerking his head in the other direction. "And that's where the rest of your men are waiting. Lined up right across the ravine and more men up the sides. And they're caught." Meges punched his open palm. "Advance on them before they have a chance to form up. First team attacks from behind. Between hammer and anvil. Dead sheep. The lot of them."

Scouting and ambush tactics were not the only skills Meges imparted to me. He was also teaching me to be a shadow.

The most dangerous and thrilling task was to creep close to an enemy camp at night. When passing through Attica, the enemy would arrogantly camp in the open, knowing that Athens would not challenge them. But they had to be reminded to fear the darkness.

Cooking fires blinded those within the camp. Looking out they could only see the blackness of night. Sometimes Meges and I would edge so close that we would listen to conversations. Drunken boasts and lewd stories. Fights and arguments. Singing and laughing. They were soldiers after all. But more than that. Worries about the fidelity of wives back home. News of a child that had fallen ill. The eagerness to return home to till fields that still lay fallow. The concerns of men. One could sympathize with them. But they were the enemy.

Wine and fatigue make a man careless. Guards were posted, for trespassers in Attica had learned to beware the *peripoli*. But sooner or later, a man going for a piss would wander too far away from the safety of the camp, or a guard at the perimeter would turn his back for a moment too long. Meges would strike. There was never a sound. Just a cold body to be found in the morning, the killer long gone.

"When can I try?" I asked.

"When I say you're ready, boy," Meges always replied.

And we talked of other things.

If we made a fire, which was rare, I would throw in a portion of my food and offer a prayer to the gods. This never failed to elicit a scoff or some eye-rolling from Meges. In the beginning, I did not let his impiety provoke me. But as I grew to know him, my fear of the man diminished.

"Why do you not sacrifice to the gods," I challenged him one night. I had just thrown a portion of sausage into the flames, causing the fire to crackle and flare while Meges bemoaned my actions. "Why do you mock them?"

Meges laughed out loud at my offended dignity. "I don't mock the gods, boy. It's just that I don't believe in wasting perfectly good sausage."

"It's not wasted," I protested.

"The gods don't care for your piece of sausage, boy. Or the thigh of an ox. Or the wine that Hermon and Lykos pour at the altar every day. Zeus and the lot of them don't give a godly shit what we do."

"Do you not fear their punishment?"

In response, Meges stood and lifted his face to the sky. He held his hands held out to either side. "O Zeus, O Saviour, O Father, O Protector!" he intoned solemnly. "Come down from your throne in Olympus and suck my mortal cock!" Whereupon he hoisted his tunic, grabbed his balls and shook his member about at the heavens above.

My eyes widened in shock at his blasphemy. My heart was racing and I instinctively held my breath in fear of the wrath that would surely befall us.

Meges ceased his crude gestures and stood as still as a statue. Still clutching himself tightly, he gazed expectantly at the heavens. A pocket of resin in the fire exploded with a sharp crack and I jumped at the sound. Meges merely shrugged and let his tunic fall back down once again.

He sat down and looked at me from across the fire. "You see, boy? The gods don't care."

"But you will surely bring some misfortune upon yourself!" I countered, but there was less conviction in my voice than before.

Through the shimmering air above the flames, I saw Meges' expression change. It was sad and hard at the same time. His voice changed too. More resigned, his normal arrogance gone. It reminded me of my father more than anyone else. "Hear me now, Daimon." It was the only time he ever used my name in all the time I knew him. "The gods care not for the prayers and offerings of men. A man can make his offerings every day with fear and reverence, but it makes no difference. His wife and daughters will still be taken by the plague, while the children of impious men may live on untouched by sickness." He gazed into the fire before raising his eyes to mine once more. "Or perhaps it is the other way round and it is the pious man whose children live. It makes no difference. The gods only ever give something so that they can take it away." He spat into the fire and then tilted his head slightly, regarding me coolly. "Your father was a pious man, I have heard," he said.

"Yes." My shoulders sank.

"Did he make offerings to the gods?"

"Yes."

"Every day?"

I nodded.

"Did it help him?"

"No," I admitted softly and slumped even further.

"So save your sausage and wine, boy. The gods won't miss them. Look at me! Not a day goes by that I don't insult the gods one way or another, yet I am alive as any man! We are ants to them. The just and the unjust. The pious and the impious. It does not matter. There is only one goddess that governs their mortal lives – Luck. And she does not listen to prayers.

"But there is only one way to win Luck's favour," Meges continued. His normal voice had returned, and the dancing flame made his eyes glint with his characteristic menace. "It is *tekne* – skill. This is what I am teaching you, boy. If your skill is good, you will enjoy Luck's tender caresses. Listen to me, and Luck will be better than any woman, boy! Well, perhaps not that good!"

He laughed out loud at his own joke, and despite myself I found myself laughing with him. It was contagious and soon we were both nearly in tears.

Finally, Meges regained some control of himself, taking deep breaths. He pointed at me accusingly. "Lykos was right, boy. You might be a dirty Thracian, but I can't help liking you anyway. That is something, for I don't like anyone!" He shook his head in wonder. "Maybe you don't need more luck from me at all," he chuckled.

We stared silently into the fire until it had died down to embers and then lay down to sleep. My companion was soon asleep, the air whistling softly through his pinched nose with each deep breath. I soon followed, but my slumber was fitful and restless, for Meges' words echoed incessantly in my dreams, all while my father's ashen face stared at me accusingly from the dreaming mist.

LUCK AND SKILL. I thought much about Meges' words. For the fickle goddess of luck had once again given her favour to Athens.

Across the sea at a place called Cyzicus, the *strategos* Thrasybulus smashed a Spartan fleet. It irritated me to learn the renegade Alkibiades had been present at the battle as well, returning from exile to rejoin the Athenian cause. I had inherited my father's dislike of the demagogue, whom I stilled blamed for the death of my brother Heliodoros, but the silver-tongued aristocrat still had many supporters in the city.

The victory of Thrasybulus was not the only welcome news. Outside the walls of Athens, another *strategos,* Thrasyllus, had routed an unprepared Spartan army and pursued the fleeing enemy all the way back to their fort at Dekeleia, north of the city. The tides of war had turned. Food and tribute began pouring into Athens once again.

The Spartans, seeing the futility of besieging Athens, abandoned their useless fort. And for the next month, the *peripoli* wolf-pack became fat as we preyed on the columns of soldiers streaming out of Attica. With our knowledge of the terrain, we could strike and disappear before any organized defence could be mounted. Such was the fear among the enemy that they took to marching in full armour, the heat and discomfort be damned to Hades.

And like Meges, I became a shadow, a wolf in the night.

No camp was safe. The enemy would wake up in the morning to find one or more of their number with their throats cut. The guards they posted were of no use, for a patient killer can find the opportunity if he waits long enough. Spartans, Boeotians, Megarians, Corinthians. They all fell victim to our silent daggers.

Tibetos joined the patrols, his proficiency with slings and javelins growing along with his own confidence. A year ago our lives had been stolen from us, but our new incarnations had arisen from the ashes. The past was almost a dream.

I was reborn. Bolder. More aggressive. I delighted in the thrill of the hunt. I felt invulnerable.

But I was not.

The gods will never let us escape our pasts. The gods are cruel.


I HAD NOT RETURNED TO ATHENS since joining the *peripoli*. My memories had spawned an aversion to the city whose people I now protected.

My sister had no such qualms and had been begging me to take her to the city, I had always put her off with weak excuses. In the end, my reluctance did not matter. My sister had gone to a higher authority.

"Take your sister to the city," Hermon ordered me. I began to protest, but the stern look in the commander's eyes told me that it was an argument I would not win.

It was a festival day, the Niketeria. On this day, the people commemorate the victory of the goddess Athena over Poseidon to become the patron of our city. Though sacrifices are made to the goddess, the sea-god also receives honours so that he will not be offended. But once the gods have been appeased with offerings, the people of the city gather on the streets and in the agora to celebrate in their own way, with wine and singing and contests.

On the day of her festival, the goddess blessed the city with a cool breeze that blew across my skin as I walked with Meli and Tibetos. A small coin-purse filled with twenty obols was tucked inside my tunic, a gift from Lykos. It was more than a rower might earn in three or four days. "It is not a great amount, but enough to enjoy yourselves. Don't lose it to the hucksters in the agora!" he said with a grin. I smiled as I thought of it, and the dense mass of coins bounced reassuringly on my skin with every step.

The fine breeze dispelled my reservations and I found myself in a good mood. Meli was talkative and cheerful in a way I had not seen her for a long time. She prattled on about the gossip from the barracks, about which she was surprisingly well-informed. At times I felt my face turning red as she spoke openly about things that were not right for a young girl to mention, but Tibetos and I could not help laughing as she described in great detail the romantic goings-on among the *peripoli* and the women. Tibetos was happy, too. He strode through the city not as a slave but as a freedman. If any of us had thoughts of the events that had befallen our family, we did not give voice to them.

It was like slipping on an old boot that conformed to every swell and bump on one's foot. The familiar smells of the city assaulted my nostrils, that combination of refuse, sweat, and dung baking in the mid-morning sun, mixed with incense and sweet fruit and the tantalizing smoke from the vendors grilling their sausages and salted fish. In the agora, the noise of thousands of voices filled my ears. It was raucous with arguments, haggling, the shouts of vendors hawking their wares, children's shrieks, exotic accents, low voices discussing secret agreements. It was the sound of life. It was the sound of Athens. I had not realized how much I missed it.

Drums and trilling flutes heralded the arrival of the procession. We craned our necks with the rest of the crowds to catch a glimpse of the pomp as it passed by. The courtesans danced with refined abandon. Slaves bearing baskets laden with a bounty of grapes and figs were followed by a dozen oxen garlanded in myrtle boughs that tramped resignedly to the ululating chants of priests. The parade disappeared at the other end of the agora on its way to the acropolis where the sacrifices would be performed. The elated throngs took up the rear, eager for the precious chunk of meat that would be their portion of the sacrifice.

We remained in the agora to peruse the wares of the hawkers who had set up stalls. I parted with a few obols to buy a grand meal of bread, sausages, wine, oil, and grilled fish. As we sat on the steps of the south stoa, the activity of the market-place provided us with entertainment for our feast.

Men well-sated with wine and meat are careless with their coins, and today bulging purses offered tempting targets for a light touch, but a glare of warning from Meli convinced me not to try my luck. Gazing longingly at the easy marks, I sighed and stood up from the steps. "Come on," I said gesturing to Tibetos and Meli. "The walk back to Piraeus will do us good."

Tibetos belched loudly and smiled contentedly. "I think I'll stay a bit longer," he said pushing himself to his feet. My eyes followed his line of sight to a troupe of musicians and acrobats, among them a particularly lithe olive-skinned girl who leapt and twirled with seductive grace.

I grinned broadly at my friend. "I don't think she'd be interested in a silent stone like you, but good luck!" I handed him a few coins from the purse. "Don't let her get your money without at least a kiss!" I joked.

It was hard for a person of Tibetos' complexion to blush, but I believe he did. But he did not refuse the coins, and weighing them in his hand, he flashed a smile and then strode off towards the performers.

Meli and I glanced at each other and started to laugh. Shaking our heads, we turned to set out for the walk back to Piraeus. Meli held my hand as we weaved our way through the revelers along the south stoa and turned onto the road leading back to the Piraeus Gate.

A girl's shriek made me glance to my right. A knot of men stood with their backs to me, blocking my view of whoever had yelled. The men's fine tunics and sandals marked them as wealthy, as did the ornate dagger-sheathes strapped to their belts.

"Any girl out on her own is no proper lady! Three obols for a quick hump. I can afford to be generous," one said, causing a round of loutish laughter among his companions.

The joy of the day vanished in an instant. Meli's fingernails dug into the back of my hand. I spun towards the direction of the voice and stepped closer to get a better look.

A handsome aristocrat gripped a girl's forearm with his left hand and held up a coin in his right. Apples and figs had spilled to the ground from an overturned basket at the girl's feet "So what do you say?" the man said, leering at the girl. His words were slightly slurred. It was my brother's friend. The man who had murdered my family.

The thin girl slapped the man smartly across his cheek with her free hand. He twisted her arm viciously in response, forcing her to double over. "Let me go!" the girl half shrieked, half pleaded, her dark eyes wide with terror. She was a maiden, perhaps the same age as Meli, or a little older. Old enough to be married off. Her raven-black hair was tied back in the manner of a child, but the bumps of young breasts pressed against the fabric of her dress. It was her misfortune to be pretty.

An older woman, evidently the girl's mother, stepped forward spitting curses and tore at the tunic of the man holding her daughter. One of the man's friends pulled the mother away and shoved her with such force that she stumbled backwards and landed heavily on her backside.

Another of the man's companions, younger than the others but thick-necked and broad across the shoulders, put his hand on the shoulder of the aggressor. "Let's go, cousin. You're going to attract the Skythians."

The girl's tormentor shook him off angrily. "Fuck off, *Plato*." He stressed the name mockingly. "It's just a bit of fun. It's —"

The girl saw me first. Her eyes darted to look over the man's shoulder and locked onto mine. "Help me!" she cried imploringly.

Realizing that he was not alone, the man's head snapped around to find out who was interrupting his amusement. "Be off to the fucking crows!" he spat. He was about to say something more, but he halted before the words came out. His eyes flew wide in recognition. "You —"

He didn't get the words out. In two lunging strides, I was upon him. His face shattered under my fist and he reeled backwards holding his crushed nose, colliding with the girl and knocking her to one side.

His companions now whirled to face the unexpected attack, but I was driven by savage fury, punching the man closest to me in the side of his jaw, and he spun away from me with the force of the blow to land heavily on the ground. I pivoted to face the remaining three, my fists raised.

Too late, two of them whipped out their daggers and brandished them at me. Like me, the young man named Plato was unarmed. He crouched low with open hands raised in a wrestling stance. It was three against one, but they hesitated. Their leader was still moaning and rolling on his back cupping his bloody face in his hands. Behind the supine man, the older woman was pulling the girl to her feet, but the maiden was still dazed from her fall.

A rock struck the head of the tallest of the three men, leaving a dripping gash. Meli had started picking up stones and hurling them at the men. This snapped them out of their indecision and they advanced on me, making the choice to deal with the more dangerous threat rather than stand still to be pelted with stones.

It was too easy. After the strict tutelage of Lykos and Heirax, it was like taking on three raw recruits. They came at me one at a time. A mistake. The bloody-faced man thrust his blade clumsily at my chest. I stepped inside his defenses so that the dagger stabbed the air beside me. Grabbing his extended arm, I smashed my forehead into his face with a sickening crunch and I heard the dagger skitter away on the ground behind me. I swung his unconscious form into the two other men to my left, knocking them away from me.

The second dagger-wielding aristocrat tried his luck with similar results, and I was left staring at the youth named Plato. He stood between me and his cousin, who was struggling to his feet behind him. Plato licked his lips and was breathing quickly, the terror plain on his face, aware of his position between me and my quarry. Then, like a coward, he bolted past me just out of my reach, abandoning his cousin to my rage.

The older woman had finally helped her daughter to her feet, jerking at the girl's arm and urging her to flee. The girl seemed anchored to the earth, looking about in astonishment at the groaning and unconscious men lying about on the ground. Our eyes met and for a heartbeat she stared at me, her mouth open as if to say something.

The girl's eyes widened in fear. I can only imagine what a terrifying spectacle I was for her to behold. A ferocious, red-haired barbarian, teeth bared like an animal, my tunic flecked with the blood of the men I had just pummelled with my bare hands. Her mother found the strength to drag the girl away, but she craned her neck to get one last glimpse of the carnage.

My eyes left hers and fixed upon the agent of my misery. He had recovered somewhat from the initial blow I had dealt him, but he was still unsteady on his feet. He noticed too late that I was bearing down on him and scrabbled feebly at the dagger on his belt. The blade had barely left its sheath when I swatted it out of his hand and followed through with a hammer to his guts that made him spew out an explosion of air and crimson saliva. I clutched bunches of his tunic as he doubled over and hauled him up once again, his bloodied face smearing my front red.

I jerked him towards me so that his face was only a finger's breadth from mine. "What is your name?" I shouted. The question seemed to confuse him so I punched him again in the belly, but I did not let him bend over to catch his breath. "Your name!" I yelled again.

He gasped for breath, and the hot reek of wine washed over my face. "Menekrates," he finally rasped, though I could barely understand because of his pulped nose.

It did not matter, but I had wanted to know before I killed him.

I grunted and entwined my fingers in the hair at the back of the head and pulled his face down into my rising knee. I felt his broken teeth bite into my skin as his body snapped back with the force of the blow and he thudded hard onto his back. I let him writhe on the ground as I stood over him and felt his suffering.

Something was drawing me out of my hot rage. Something gentle. It was my sister's voice. "Brother." I heard it through the pounding blood in my ears, a whisper in the storm. I turned and she was standing with one hand extended towards me. Her sailor's knife rested lightly on her palm.

I was vaguely aware of people behind her. The commotion had attracted some passers-by, gawking at the scene, but no one dared interfere. I reached out to take the blade from my sister's palm. Her wide eyes were the dark green of a raging sea, relentless and unforgiving. The dagger pulsed in my hand, as if sensing the blood-debt about to be repaid.

Menekrates had managed to lift himself to his hands and knees. Sticky blood and drool dripped down to form a small pool in the dust. I stepped around him and kicked him in the ribs to flip him on to his back. Stepping over him, I knelt down, straddling him and pinning his arms to either side.

"This is for my mother," For some reason I had spoken in Thracian and Menekrates blinked in confusion.

I brought the knife to his throat, and his eyes widened in terror.

A scream from my sister stayed my hand. Before I could turn, something crashed into the back of my head and my world went black.

# CHAPTER 14

I opened my eyes and immediately regretted the decision. The stabbing light from the sky above intensified the pounding ache in my head and I clamped my eyes shut once more. I remained still and breathed deeply to quell the urge to vomit that was rising in my gut. One by one, my senses refocused. Flashes of the fight with Menekrates and his companions pushed their way into my mind. The sound of his voice. The girl's look of terror. My sister's knife in my palm. And then nothing.

The gritty stone on which I lay was still radiating the leftover heat of the day, filling my nostrils with a warm odor like baked clay. My mouth had the rank, dry taste that comes with extreme thirst. But I was alive. I let my eyes open just a crack, taking in the odd geometry from my uncomfortable vantage point.

I was lying in the courtyard of a house. Attempting to shift my weight, I also discovered that my hands were bound. My eyes gradually adjusted to the light and I realized that it was later in the day than I had initially imagined.

The house was not unlike my father's in size, but whereas my family's house was conservatively drab and utilitarian, this residence betrayed the owner's taste for luxury. Fine, fluted pillars with painted bases and capitals lined both storeys of the courtyard, the corners of which were decorated with potted plants that stood taller than a man. The wooden doors and railings bore delicate patterns of sharp-cornered whorls. The emptiness also struck me, for there was no clutter of tools or stores to be seen. It was as if I were in a temple, save for the fact that there was no altar. And no people as far as I could tell.

I tried to sit up. A foot in my back shoved me to the flagstones and then pinned me to the ground, the abrasive leather sole grinding into the side of my throat. Only when I stopped struggling did the force ease up so that I could breathe once again.

"Tell your masters that their guest has awoken," a gruff voice barked. Unseen feet padded away in a prompt response to the command.

A whispered thought struggled to reach me through my addled brain. "Where is my sister?" I exclaimed hoarsely.

"Shut your mouth or I'll cut your throat right now, boy," my watcher said. The way he said the word 'boy' caused another faint spark of recognition. I was in no state to resist in any case, and so lay still on the ground in silence, tormented by my ignorance of what had befallen Meli.

A few moments later, footsteps and voices drew near. The foot in my neck gave a sharp, painful twist, then the pressure disappeared. My captor jerked me up on to my knees and I found myself staring at the scarred face of Orchus.

A yellow-toothed grin split the Andrian mercenary's face. "It's been a long time, boy," Before I could respond, he hawked a gob of phlegm onto my face before joining the men assembling in the courtyard.

Menekrates was there, as were his bruised and bloodied companions. His change of clothing could not hide the trauma of the beating I had inflicted upon him. His broken nose was a twisted mass of purple and blue, crusted with dried blood around his nostrils. His breaths came in raspy huffs through exposed broken teeth and grossly swollen lips. From behind deep rings of black, boar-like eyes peered out at me malevolently.

In stark contrast to his cousin, the coward Plato stood unscathed and unbloodied. He was also the only one who was not glaring at me with murderous intent. Instead, he studied the ground, the sky, the pillars. Anything but me.

But it was the older man who stood calmly beside Menekrates who naturally drew my attention.

He radiated a combination of power, detachment, and authoritative menace. His silver hair was starting to thin, but his beard was thick with well-tended curls. A pale red robe was draped around him so perfectly that it looked to be cut from stone. Pursing his lips slightly, he appraised me, his cold blue eyes revealing little of what he was thinking. I tried to swallow as I waited for him to speak, but there was no spit left in me.

He smiled a politician's smile. "Welcome to my home, Daimon, son of Nikodromos," he said spreading his hands slightly. "I am Kritias. I –"

I cut him off. "Where is my sister?"

The man Kritias shrugged apologetically. "Alas, she abandoned you to your fate, young man. But you will be reunited soon, I assure you."

The ice in his voice made me tremble despite the heat. "If you harm her, I will kill you," I said flatly.

Orchus guffawed at my empty threat. Kritias simply ignored my outburst. "It is a wonder that no one was killed. If it were not for my nephew Aristokles," he said, indicating the youth who Menekrates had called Plato, "my son and his companions would surely have met a foul end at your hand!"

"He is a coward! He ran away!" I shot a disdainful glance towards Plato.

Kritias raised his finger to make a point. "Ah! Indeed, cowards may run, but not all men who run are cowards. Cunning can triumph over brute strength, and young Aristokles is proving to be a most cunning young man!" Kritias placed his hand affectionately on his nephew's shoulder. "How could he have defeated you? You had already taken down three men! Had he fought you, he would have fallen to your mad rage as well and my son would be dead, slaughtered like a sheep. Much better to fetch a detachment of the Skythian guard from the agora, no? They are very good with their clubs, I understand. They can render a man senseless, but not strike so strongly as to break his skull. You are fortunate to be alive. My son would have killed you right then and there in the street. Again, Aristokles had better sense. He convinced the Skythians that you were just a house slave driven mad by too much drink, which was plausible enough. You Thracians have a deserved reputation for being somewhat unpredictable. The guards were even kind enough to deliver you here to recover in the privacy of my home."

Kritias then frowned slightly and came forward to stand before me. He studied my face and features as one might examine livestock before purchase. I bore his scrutiny in sullen silence, my eyes never leaving him as he conducted his inspection. "I have heard of you, Daimon, son of Nikodromos," he said at last. "Athens is not so large that the family matters of a former *strategos* go unnoticed by others, I'm afraid. I can see him in you, though. And his obstinacy." A flash of hardness in his voice was quickly masked by a more conciliatory tone. "I'm sorry that we are not meeting under better circumstances.

I was a great —" he paused, " — *admirer* of your father's. I was most distressed when I learned of his death."

"Your son is a murderer!" My voice was now spent, and it came out like a dry cough.

"Menekrates," Kritias said through a thin smile, "was carrying out his duties given to him by the ruling council. If he faced any resistance or provocation during the course of those duties, any violence was legal and justified."

A thought occurred to me. "Were you a member of the Four Hundred?" I whispered.

"*Pai*," he said, feigning shock. "Had I known about your father's predicament, I surely would have done all that I could to have intervened on his behalf. Your father and I had our differences, but we both wanted the same thing: what was best for Athens." His icy stare gave lie to the warmth of his tone.

My hands still bound behind me, I drew myself up and took one shuffling step towards Kritias. Orchus drew his sword a fraction in warning and I stopped. "Your family is polluted with blood-guilt," I said hoarsely, "Your son murdered my family." I glared at Menekrates, who parted his swollen lips to reveal a broken-toothed sneer."

"A task that he failed to complete," Kritias shrugged. Orchus was grinning broadly. Plato fidgeted uncomfortably. Menekrates gloated in eager anticipation. And I knew the time for my execution had come. It would not be swift.

Words were the only weapon that remained to me. "The son of Kritias is a coward," I sneered. The insult was as much to buttress my courage as to play for time.

Menekrates' piggy eyes flared. Heretofore content to let his father do the speaking, he could no longer restrain himself. "We'll see who's a coward when you are begging for your life, slave!" he howled through his ruined face.

I kept flinging insults. "A bound prisoner might be too much of a challenge for you. Perhaps you should find some more unarmed women to practice on," I taunted him. Orchus snorted in amusement at my comment, further infuriating Menekrates.

"I will kill you slowly in the Persian fashion! You will beg me for death!" Menekrates continued screaming insults. He lunged towards me, but Kritias barred his way with an extended arm.

"Step back!" Kritias' mask of calm morphed into one of barely controlled fury. Menekrates was on the verge of protesting, but his father's sudden wrath made him hold his tongue. "Control!" Kritias bit the word. "Always maintain control!" Menekrates stepped back, chastened. Plato continued to stare at the ground. Orchus made no effort to hide his enjoyment of the unexpected entertainment.

"Orchus will see to it that you are well taken care of. Farewell, Daimon, son of Nikodromos." Kritias turned to leave.

Flames of triumph danced in the eyes of Menekrates. Orchus' hands clenched and unclenched, as if he were savoring the prospect of setting my soul free. My body would be dumped somewhere outside the city walls, left to be eaten by birds. I wondered if my shade would find its way to the underworld, or whether it would wander the Earth, forever lost. In a silent prayer, I asked Athena to protect Meli and beseeched Nemesis to bring retribution to the house of Kritias.

Fear fought to consume me, but as ever my pride was stronger. "The gods will punish you, Kritias," I said with false calmness to the retreating figure in the red robes.

Kritias stopped at my words. And laughed. He turned and approached me, stopping a few strides away. "The gods will not punish me, Daimon," he said. He leaned forward slightly, as if he were sharing a secret and did not want the others to hear. "For there are no gods," he whispered conspiratorially.

Now I am an old man. I know that there are as many gods as there are villages, some benevolent, some fearsome, but most unconcerned about the world of men. The Persians believe that there is only one great creator, whom they call Ahura, who will vanquish the forces of darkness at the end of time. The Egyptians seem to have as many gods as there are stars in the sky. I have also heard men express their doubts about the existence of the gods at all, but they do so in private, for they are afraid of retribution from the superstitious masses. But at that time, even with my death imminent, Kritias' declaration shocked me to my soul. It was one thing to disdain the gods as Meges did. But to deny their very existence? So bold was the assertion of Kritias that I shuddered involuntarily.

"Don't you see, Daimon," Kritias pressed on, "the truth of it?" His hands were held out palms upward as if he were offering me an invisible loaf of bread. It was plain that he was expecting an answer from me, but I merely glowered at him. Preparing himself, he closed his eyes and savoured the moment the way a man might enjoy a particularly fine cup of wine.

"The gods," he began, "are but a tool created by man, no different from a hammer or sword." Kritias paused, locking eyes with me. "The gods are a tool to be used by the best men, the *aristoi*, to keep their inferiors afraid and obedient."

"And you are one of the *aristoi*?" I challenged him, knowing that my life would last only as long as he spewed his sophistry.

Kritias smiled coyly. "Every man," he continued, "is born into his own class, each to be kept pure and isolated from the others, each group essential to the success of society, each with its assigned role to play. There are golden guardians, men with the self-restraint necessary to be entrusted with the decisions that will guide a city to stability and prosperity. There are soldiers of silver who protect a society from enemies within and without. There are craftsmen, those with bronze and iron in their veins. And there are slaves," he said, dipping his slightly in my direction.

"My father believed that men ought to be judged by their deeds, not their birth, and he was a better man than you," I prodded.

Kritias' eyes flashed angrily. "Men like your father cause society to rot! Democrats! They let pure blood become sullied with that of lesser men! Democracy is chaos," he hissed, letting his vaunted self-restraint slip, and I smiled at my small victory, ephemeral as it was.

Kritias remembered his audience and regained control of his emotions. He reached out and grabbed my chin, gripping it with surprising strength. "And what does that make you, *pai*? The spawn of an aristocrat and a barbarian slave woman?" He turned my head to get a better look, narrowing his eyes. "It makes you an abomination. Your existence is an affront to order," he said, releasing me.

The fire in Kritias' eyes abated, and the edge in his voice lost some of its sharpness. "You wish the gods to punish me, young Daimon?" he asked spreading his hands in mock helplessness. "I cannot be punished by gods that do not even exist. No, I will continue to be master of my own destiny. The fate that awaits the virtuous and the evil is the same, *pai*. It is just that some of us will suffer it sooner than others. Farewell, Daimon, son of Nikodromos."

"The gods will punish you," I spat out. But doubt had entered my heart and I did not have faith in my own words.

Kritias regarded me curiously. "You are so like your father," he said finally. He shrugged and once again turned his back on me and walked away.

Orchus hit the back of my legs so that I fell to my knees. His hand clutched my hair and pulled my head back. Menekrates drew his dagger with eager speed. His other companions looked on, grim-faced, except for Plato, who turned away.

Then, as if to spite Kritias, the gods saved me.

# CHAPTER 15

A crack like the snapping of an enormous bone reverberated through the courtyard, halting Kritias mid-step. Another splintering snap came and the main gate quivered, dust shaking loose with the impact. Kritias blinked in surprise, his expression quickly turning to one of irritation. The door was being hacked with an axe.

"Daimon! Are you there?" Lykos muffled voice came over the wall.

I yelled frantically in response. The voices outside demanded that the gates be opened. Kritias regarded me calmly as he considered his options. This contrasted sharply with the look of panic on the face of Menekrates, who saw his prize about to be snatched away. He strode towards me with murder in his eyes but was brought up short by an angry growl from his father.

"You would kill us all, fool!" Kritias snapped. Menekrates' gaze darted back and forth between me and his father in agonized frustration, struggling to break free of his father's will. But in the end he was bound too tightly. He lowered the quivering knife.

Kritias pointed at two slaves. "Open the gate!" he ordered.

The slaves ran to the gates and lifted the heavy bar into its upright position. The massive wooden doors flew apart as they were pushed open from the street.

Mnasyllus stood clutching a massive woodsman's axe. A band of twenty armed *peripoli* poured into the courtyard around him. Relief washed over me. I stumbled towards them.

"Dammo!" My sister burst through the mass of men. I wanted nothing more than to hug her, but my hands were still bound behind me. As she sawed through my bonds, Tibetos also stepped forward, and I nodded to him in thanks, for I knew he and Meli were my saviours.

Lykos stood before Kritias, sword in hand. "You have abducted one of my men!" he said pointing at me. There was fury in his face.

If Kritias felt any fear, he did not show it. A soulless smile crept up his face. "And you are?" he asked calmly.

"I am Lykos, son of Lykos!"

Kritias narrowed his eyes. "It was you in the agora when Phrynichus was slain. The *peripoli* should mind their own affairs." He glanced over at me.

Lykos gritted his teeth. "We will take our man."

"Without provocation, he assaulted my son and his companions in the street. He is a menace."

"Your son is a murderer!" I shouted in a rage. Freed from my bonds, I lunged forward but was held back by the firm hand of Telekles.

Kritias ignored my outburst. "If you take him now, I will bring the matter before the law-courts. Surely we will find justice there."

It was no idle threat. The law-courts were notoriously fickle in their judgments. A jury of politics-mad Athenians could be as relentless as a Spartan phalanx. In cases brought by wealthy citizens against those like me, the verdicts rarely turned out in the defendant's favour. And the punishments could be harsh.

Lykos knew it too. He sheathed his sword and turned. He jerked his head towards the gate, indicating we should leave.

The others turned to do so, but Meli made no move to follow. Her hand slowly rose to point towards Menekrates. "I curse you." Kritias scoffed, but the men of the *peripoli* fell into a hushed and fearful deference.

She drew her knife across her palm. She clenched her fist and blood dripped from between her fingers onto the ground. "You will find no haven from those you have sent to the underworld. They will come for you." Meli turned her back on the speechless Menekrates, taking the hand of Lykos. "Come," she told him, and he did.

Shielded by a wall of my comrades, I walked away from my execution ground and out into the street where a crowd had gathered.

Menekrates found his voice and ran out onto the street to rage at our receding backs. "You are a dead man, slave!" I turned and took a step towards him, but Telekles pulled at my arm.

His father was more subdued but no less threatening. Kritias stood framed by the damaged doorway of his home, watching us depart. "Our business is not yet done, Daimon, son of Nikodromos," he called out, his false smile unwavering.

And I felt fear.

KRITIAS MADE GOOD ON HIS THREAT. Soldiers from the law-courts came to arrest me for the unprovoked assault on Menekrates and three other upstanding citizens of Athens.

Hermon sent them away, claiming that I had fled the city. In prison, I was unlikely to survive a day before finding a knife in my ribs, and even if I did, a jury of citizens was unlikely to be merciful to the son of a slave, no matter who his father was. "They will come again," Hermon said wearily. In vain he tried to rub the exhaustion from his tired features.

I rose in anger. "Menekrates is a murderer" I protested. I kicked over the stool I had been sitting on in frustration.

"The only thing that matters," Hermon's said slapping the top of the table, "is that four men from wealthy Athenian families have been set upon by a non-citizen member of the *peripoli*. That is all the jury will see."

This provoked a flurry of enraged shouts from the *peripoli* gathered at the meeting called by Hermon and Lykos. Hermon lifted his hands in an appeal for calm and the discontent in the courtyard settled down to a low grumble.

"The question is," Hermon said, extending his arm towards me, "what is to be done about our comrade?"

"They tried to kill one of ours, so we should return the favor to Kritias and his goat-lover of a son," came a voice. It was Meges, and there were murmurs of approval from the assembled men. "I volunteer for the task."

Hermon sighed and scratched at his bald head. Lykos answered for the commander. "Don't think we haven't considered it. But Kritias has a small army about him. It would be messy. And even if we were to succeed, the *peripoli* would be blamed."

"We will never turn our brother over to the courts!" someone yelled, and the rest of the men shouted in support. Hermon and Lykos had lost control again. I grimaced as the debate raged around me, but I had nothing to say. Tibetos gazed at me grimly, and I shrugged despondently.

My sister was present too, standing close to Lykos and watching the proceedings with cold detachment. Our eyes met and she gave me a sad smile. Her expression unlocked something inside me. I had been grappling with the possibility, but now my path was clear. I knew what I needed to do.

"Brothers!" I raised my hands. "Brothers!" The din of voices fell, and the eyes of my comrades turned to me. "I will go into exile."

I had said it. There was no other way. I would follow the many others who had fled into exile to evade the rulings of the law-courts or the decisions of the assembly. It was almost a tradition in Athens.

Lykos spoke above the angry shouts of the other *peripoli*. "But where, Daimon? You have nowhere to go. You have no allies outside of this room. Better to stay here with us." But I suspect he knew how I would answer.

"I will join the expedition of Thrasyllus," I declared. Lykos let his shoulders slump almost imperceptibly. Meli moved to his side and placed her hand softly on his arm, and he put his own hand on top of hers. Meli's eyes were impenetrable.

Some of the *peripoli* protested, but others nodded at the soundness of my plan. The assembly had recently voted to equip an expedition to Ionia under the *strategos* Thrasyllus. The ships were due to set sail in a matter of days. One more soldier would not be noticed.

I addressed Hermon. "Commander, can you equip me and get me on the rolls?"

"Aye, I can do that, lad," he said stroking his beard. "I can do that." Hermon looked torn, but I would be relieving him of a burden. My presence would only cause problems for the *peripoli* from within and without.

I glanced over at Tibetos, but my friend was watching Meli and Lykos. Pain etched his features as he struggled with something. He sensed my eyes on him and looked over to me.

"I will go with you!" he blurted out. Hermon raised his eyebrows in surprise. "With your permission, Commander," Tibetos added, and Hermon nodded his assent. I stepped forward and embraced Tibetos, to the cheers of those watching.

"The matter is settled, then," Hermon declared. "Our brother Daimon will sail to Ionia to slay Spartans and bring honour to the *peripoli*." This brought another rousing cry from the comrades who had become my family.

I scanned for Lykos amidst the press of men that crowded us, but he was already gone.

\*

THERE WAS A FEAST in the peripoli compound that night, and the raucous sounds of celebration filled the courtyard. Someone had paid for musicians and dancers. Laughter, music, and the occasional squeal permeated the space. Hermon had opened up the stores of wine, and coin was spent to procure enough mutton to feed a small army. A charred thigh-bone that had been wrapped in fat smouldered in a brazier, a sacrifice to Zeus the Protector.

"A damn waste," Meges muttered to me as we watched Hermon make the sacrifice. His complaint lacked its usual bite, and he slapped my back lightly before going to find some more wine.

Others had found their cups as well. I have never had a head for wine, but it was an effective distraction from our impending departure. The room spun lazily about me, for there had been too many toasts and the wine had not been cut with as much water as it should have.

My wandering thoughts were interrupted by a hand on my shoulder. It was Hermon. I almost did not recognize him because of his smiling visage. "How are you enjoying this spontaneous festival, lad?"

"Very much, Commander," I replied, nearly sputtering wine down my chest, but I recovered. "Everyone —" I paused while a pair of flute girls passed with a trail of dancers in their wake. The sight of the lithe forms of the women nearly made me forget to complete my sentence. "Everyone is enjoying themselves."

Hermon laughed. "It's good for morale. The gods know we needed it."

"Yes, sir." I was trying in vain to see the dancing girls, but they were obscured by a wall of men who were clapping and shouting encouragement and lewd comments.

Hermon sat down heavily beside me. The wine had loosened his tongue. "I've grown used to having you here. You remind me of your father." He cocked his head slightly and squinted, as though trying to see my father in my face.

"My father?" I exclaimed in surprise.

"You have your mother's colors, to be sure, and not a bit of her temper. But when I see you watching — that concentration — I see your father before me." He stood up from the bench. "Come join us when you're finished ogling the girls, hmm?" He winked at me and went off to check on more of the men.

Beside me, Tibetos rose and invited me to go watch the performers. Tempted as I was, I waved him off. He shrugged. "More for the rest of us!" he said with a huge, drunken grin, and disappeared into the crowd. Watching him go, I shook my head in wonder. In the past six months, slave no more, my quiet friend had thrived. The men called him "*Lithos*," – "Stone" – for when he had come, he had been as silent as a stone. I thought that the nickname now had a different significance, one of hidden strength. I valued his friendship in the coming journey.

Chuckling to myself, I staggered off to seek Lykos. I found him with his usual company. I plopped down beside them and was greeted by a chorus of cheers.

"It is the young Achilles!" shouted Telekles. "Get this man a cup!"

Someone handed me a cup filled to the rim so that the wine sloshed onto my hand. "To the Spartan-slayer!" Telekles shouted. The tale of my single combat with the Spartan had been told and retold around the barracks, and the battle grew in scale and drama with each telling. There was little truth left in the story, but my reputation had been established, if nothing else. Everyone at the table raised their cups and drained the wine in one gulp. The room rolled.

Cups were refilled and the men went back to their animated discussion. They had been speaking of the great naval victory the previous autumn.

"Thrasybulus lured the Spartans into a trap," Telekles said excitedly, clearly thrilled to have the opportunity to describe the battle once again. He cleared the table in front of him, using cups and plates to explain the course of the battle.

"The *strategos* brought our fleet up the Hellespont here to Proconnesus," Telekles explained pointing to one cup on the table "It was at night, so the Spartans didn't know they were there. The Spartan fleet led by Mindarus was moored here at Cyzicus," he said pointing at a plate that represented the mainland. "The *strategos* sent out a squad of twenty ships to lure the Spartans out, and they took the bait. Those dung-eaters sent out their whole fleet!" Telekles exclaimed. His expression suggested a disbelief that anyone could be so stupid. "When the Spartans chased them out to sea, the trap closed. *Strategos* hit them from both sides with the rest of the fleet."

"What happened next?" I asked, enjoying the story.

"Buggers ran is what happened next, boyo!" said the good-humored Kirphis, taking up the story. I noticed that Hermon had joined the table and was delighting in the tale as much as anyone. "They tried to land their ships, but the *strategos* had already landed his troops. Mindarus and the rest of the Spartans were cut to pieces right there on the beach." Kirphis made exaggerated chopping and slicing gestures with his hand, generating another round of cheers.

"And don't forget the message!" Lykos shouted over the din. The Athenian forces had intercepted a message from the demoralized remnants of the Spartan force. Lykos extended his hand towards Telekles, who bowed with mock seriousness, like an actor towards his audience, clearing his throat repeatedly. Everyone grinned at him in wide-eyed anticipation.

In his best Spartan accent, Telekles repeated the content of the intercepted message in a deep, tremulous voice, his lower lip quivering with sadness. "'Ships sunk. Mindarus dead. Men starving. Don't know what to do.'" It was probably the tenth time the men had heard it that evening, but they laughed so hard that tears rolled down their cheeks and they held their sides in pain. I was laughing too.

When the mirth had subsided somewhat, Hermon raised his cup, and in his booming voice he bellowed, "To the *strategos*! To Thrasybulus!"

"To Thrasybulus! To Thrasybulus!" we all shouted in drunken unison. Soon the cheer had been taken up by all those at the celebration, and the *strategos'* name echoed into the night.

The name of Thrasybulus had barely ceased being chanted when a new name was shouted out.

"To Alkibiades! To Alkibiades!"

The toast was taken up by the rest of the *peripoli*, but many of the cheers were half-hearted at best. Amidst the sea of acclamations for Alkibiades, our table was an island of silence. I glanced over at

Lykos, who was glowering into his wine. He rose suddenly and somewhat unsteadily, knocking a half-full cup to the ground in the process. Without a word, he marched away and disappeared through the gates of the courtyard.

I blinked in drunken confusion. "What was that about?" I asked Telekles.

Hermon answered for him. "He hates it that someone else gets praise that rightfully belongs to his brother."

"His brother?" I responded, even more confused.

"Thrasybulus," Hermon said simply. I looked at him dumbly, my wine-addled brain not following the path he was showing me. "Thrasybulus, son of Lykos."

I shook my head, still not comprehending.

"The *strategos*. Thrasybulus. He is Lykos' older brother."

If I had been less numbed by wine, I might have sensed the thread of my life altering its course under the nimble hands of the Weaver, moving slowly but surely towards the bright golden yarn of Thrasybulus.


THE ORDERED CHAOS OF THE HARBOUR surrounded us. Everywhere there was the noise of an expedition getting underway. On the ships that crowded the pier, captains and steersmen barked commands at the sailors to tighten a rope or check a mooring as if the fate of the entire mission depended on it. Slaves bearing sacks of grain and other provisions marched up and down the gangplanks, cursing those who carelessly blocked their way, whatever the person's rank or station. The gamblers, as always, had scented each other out and had gathered in clutches here and there as they wagered their coin on a throw of the dice. Old comrades, recognizing one another in the crowds, called out enthusiastic greetings. Except for Tibetos, I knew no one.

Lykos and my sister had come to see us off. I cast an uneasy glance at the transport that would take us to Ionia. The barley and onion stew I had eaten in the morning weighed down my stomach like a lump of lead. The fear of battle was something I had grown to embrace, for I trusted my own skill and I knew of the euphoria that came with it. But the sea was another matter. Being a child of the city, I had never set foot in a boat, and not once in my life had I offered a sacrifice to Poseidon. The prospect was quietly terrifying.

Lykos must have sensed my discomfort. "You will be able to link up with my brother in Chios or Samos sooner or later," he said in an attempt to distract me. "Give him the letter of introduction I wrote for you."

"Yes, *lochagos*." The letter was well protected in an oiled leather packet in my kit, and my hand automatically sought the reassuring presence of the satchel hanging on my back.

"He is the finest commander of Athens. You will learn much from him." Under the pride, there was something left unsaid. When I had asked about Thrasyllus, the commander of our present expedition, Lykos had been less forthcoming in his praise. He regarded him as courageous and bold, but too direct and traditional. It was dangerous in a war that had grown to require cunning and flexibility instead of brute force.

My sister and I embraced. No longer a child, she was tall enough that my face was buried in her thick hair. A whiff of perfume tickled my nose and I recognized it as my mother's favorite scent. We separated, holding hands.

"Bendis will protect you. You are going back to her lands where she is strongest," Meli said, and I trusted her. She let go of my hands and placed herself in front of Tibetos. Before he could say anything, she kissed him warmly on the cheek. He blinked in surprise, and a look of joy slowly spread across his face. "You are brave and kind, Tibetos. The gods of your ancestors will welcome you home."

A holler came from the ship, the last call to board. Tibetos and I marched up the gangplank with the other men in our company. Behind us was Iollas, the freed helot, hauling the bulk of my gear. He had insisted that a proper hoplite needed an attendant and that he would gladly fill the role.

The boat lurched as its massive bulk pushed away from the pier. The trireme's deck had been broadened to give more space for troops. Like every other man on deck, I sat huddled motionless, for movement would cause the finely-balanced ship to tilt, throwing off the precisely measured strokes of the one-hundred and seventy oarsmen below. There we would stay until we made landfall for the night.

I shifted to stare back at the receding wharf. My sister held on lightly to Lykos' arm. It was not the proper behaviour for a Greek woman, but my sister was never one for obeying anyone's customs but her own. That is why Lykos loved her. The two of them grew smaller until we could no longer make them out among the restless activity of the waterfront.

The ship threaded through the narrow channel formed by the gap in the moles and then the open sea loomed before us. The salt air washed away the odor of the city. I whispered a belated prayer to Poseidon and tossed a drachma coin into the sea as an offering. I wished only to find the *strategos* Thrasybulus as quickly as possible.

Watching the oars bite into the sea, I recalled Lykos' words from the previous evening. Lykos had told me more of his brother over a farewell cup of wine. "Do not underestimate him, as others have. He may appear stiff and overly pious, but there is none braver or more cunning in battle." Lykos hesitated, before adding, "And ruthless when he needs to be. Woe to the man who stands between Thrasybulus and victory, for he is surely doomed."

# CHAPTER 16

Our lives are threads in a great cloth woven by the *Moirai*, the three sisters of fate, Clotho, Lachesis, and Atropos. Clotho spins us into being, Lachesis allots us our measure of life, and Atropos' shears cut our thread when our time on this earth is done. But when the *Moirai* weave our fates, I am uncertain whether we are forced to follow the weft and warp they choose, or whether their timeless hands only spin the pattern that we mortals impose upon them. But whether it was the hand of immortals or that of man, my enemies had compelled me to choose exile as a hoplite in the Athenian expedition to Asia under the *strategos* Thrasyllus.

Athens was desperate for fighting men. I was a mere eighteen and not even a citizen at that, but with Hermon's influence and bribes quietly paid, it was no difficult matter for me to become enrolled in the expedition under the assumed name Gelon, son of Hippasus.

In truth, the expedition was little more than an army of bandits, sacking and plundering enemy-held towns up and down the coast of Ionia just to survive, for Athens was nearly bankrupt and could not afford regular pay for her ships and soldiers.

As raiders, we had been moderately successful. Since landing in Asia, there had been no opposition worthy of the name as we made our way down the coast of Ionia. At the town of Pygela we had easily bested the combined force of Pygelaians and Miletans. The city of Colophon, seeing the futility of resistance, came over to the Athenian cause without a fight. From that place our forces launched raids against villages in Lydia, taking much plunder in the form of grain and captives and gear abandoned by routed enemies, though there was little in the way of silver or gold. Yet we did well enough for ourselves.

Until Ephesus.

THE OMENS HAD BEEN PROPITIOUS.
No general will lead his men into battle without first offering a sacrifice and reading the secret signs that reveal the will of the gods. Accordingly, Thrasyllus had his trusted seer, Barates, slaughter a

sheep before dawn. I disliked the soothsayer instinctively, for he struck me as an obsequious pile of dung. The entrails promised success that day. As men gathered in the dawn light, the *mantis* Barates pointed at an eagle flying in the direction of Ephesus. The auspicious signs gave men courage, and the hoplites set out confident that victory would be forthcoming.

Yet as we marched, doubt gnawed at my guts.

My father and Neleus had always told me that the strength of the phalanx came from the bonds of family and friendship between the men that made up the ranks. Kinsmen and lifelong friends stood shoulder to shoulder. Men you would die to protect and who would throw themselves in front of a spear-thrust for you.

But this was an army of strangers, made up of merchants, mercenaries, and a hundred different accents from around the empire. I was young. I feared disgracing myself more than my doubts, and so I trudged on in silence.

Tibetos was not at my side. He was with a secondary force of slingers, javelineers, and cavalry concealed north of the city walls. Thrasyllus wished to draw out the enemy hoplites from the safety of the city walls and surprise them with a second force mid-battle. Until that time, our infantry force would be exposed.

A spear rapped on the side of my helmet. I looked over to my squad leader, Podaroes, who was marching beside me. "It looks like it's going to be a right fight!" The veteran had to shout to be heard over the low, thunderous rumble of five thousand armoured men tramping through the dust. He had reason to be optimistic. Ephesus was reckoned to have two to three thousand men, only half of them hoplites. We would outnumber them two to one. If they refused battle and stayed hidden behind their walls, all the better. We could plunder the surrounding villages with impunity.

A trumpet's peal pierced the air and the column came to a halt outside the western wall of Ephesus. The order to prepare arms rippled through the column. Shields were unslung. Swords were loosened in their scabbards. Helms dropped down into place. My sweat ran freely under the battered, stifling armour given to me by Hermon. I shifted uncomfortably and bounced the butt of my spear in the dirt. After what seemed an age, two more trumpet blasts came, the signal to form the phalanx.

The marching columns broke apart to form the battle line. There was much jostling and cursing as men rushed to occupy the front ranks where a man wins honour and reputation. I was shoving my way to the front as well, for I had found myself well back of the action in previous skirmishes. I craved the honour that my father and Neleus had earned. The young are foolishly courageous. And I was young.

A hand grasped the neckline of my cuirass and jerked me back. I whirled in anger only to see that it was Podaroes who had stopped me. "Not today, boy," he yelled. "Today, you watch, you learn, you survive." Before I could react, he hauled me over to his side and held me there as the rest of the formation coalesced around us. "You have my flank, Gelo," he shouted with one final punch to my shoulder.

We grounded our shields, relieving ourselves of their burden, for bearing the weighty *aspis* will quickly tire even the strongest man. I cursed aloud, realizing we were in the fourth rank on the right side of our battle-line, not in the place of honour on the left. Hardly a place for glory.

"There'll be plenty of plunder for all," Podaroes yelled. He pivoted and glanced towards the rear of the phalanx. "As long as those sailor scum at the back keep pushing."

Podaroes had given voice to my misgivings. A phalanx follows a certain pattern. The soldiers in the first rows are experienced but still young and strong, young bulls who would bear the brunt of the impact when the two armies crashed together. In the middle are the younger fighters like me who would push and support the front lines, and fill the gaps should anyone fall. Shoulder to shoulder, each hoplite holds a spear in his right hand and his shield in his left, locking shields with the man beside him and forming a nearly impenetrable wall from behind which soldiers could stab and hack at the enemy. The back rows are filled by older veterans who would hold the line and prevent the inexperienced soldiers from fleeing once the terror of battle took hold. And then it was a contest of wills, the two armies pushing against each other until one side broke and fled.

But Thrasyllus, wanting a wider front so that we would not be outflanked, had spread his hoplites more thinly. To compensate, the general had equipped a thousand rowers with shields and spears to add mass to the phalanx, replacing the veteran soldiers who traditionally filled the back rows. My father would not have approved.

Under a sky the colour of weathered bone, the city walls of Ephesus loomed before us. Unseen by mortals, Phobos, the god of fear, walked among our ranks, whispering in men's ears and planting the seeds of terror in their minds. Before a battle, bowels churn and piss runs down men's legs, for they know that the *Moirai*'s shears hover ready to sever their thread if that is their fate that day.

And the *Keres*, the daughters of Night, are drawn to fear like flies to rotting flesh. The foul death-spirits circle and swoop above the battlefield, eager to feast on bodies ripped and pierced by spear and sword. Some claim to have seen them, misty streaks glimpsed from the corner of the eye as their talons raked and tore across the plain. I glanced up at the sky, half expecting to see them, but they were hidden from me. I reached down to touch the iron of my sword-blade to protect me from their ravenous gaze. But the soul-eaters were there at Ephesus, for they knew what was to come, even if we did not.

A trumpet rang from within the city, pulling my nervous gaze from the sky. The west gates opened wide, and a column of troops emerged at a trot. We hurled abuses at them, calling their mothers whores and their fathers whore-masters. We shouted for their blood.

But the enemy kept pouring from the city. Hoplites and missile-throwers of every kind. The garrison had been massively reinforced. Our zeal withered as we beheld disaster before us and I felt the icy finger of Phobos stroke my neck.

Soon, the line opposite us was as wide as our own, yet it kept growing as more soldiers streamed out of the gates. They would soon outflank us on both sides. Even then, had we charged while the enemy lines were disordered and porous, Thrasyllus' plan might have worked.

But the ringing of horns from the north blew that hope away like a wisp of smoke. The tone was odd, foreign. Thousands of heads turned northwards simultaneously and a collective moan of despair filled the air. It was the sound of doomed men.

I had never seen real Persians before, but I knew them on sight from the tales I had heard as a child. The colorful uniforms of the

Persian riders danced, flashes of red and yellow and purple, accompanied by a low rumble of hooves like a distant storm on the horizon. A formation of hundreds of cavalry streamed out from behind the north wall of the city. It was not a rabble, but a beautiful column of charging beasts, row upon row of horsemen four abreast riding out to crush our hidden reserve force.

The shock of seeing the Persian horseman had not yet set in when the Ephesians and their allies struck up their paean and began their advance. The power of thousands of men chanting their ancient battle hymn in unison resonated across the plain. It froze the soul.

The war-song of our enemy jolted us out of our stunned reverie. Up and down the lines infantrymen scrambled to insert their arms through the inner loops of their shields. I hefted my own concave shield up to rest on my shoulder just in time to deflect an incoming arrow. To my right a man too slow in his reaction toppled with a javelin run through his throat. Blood spurted onto the back of the hoplite in front of him as he collapsed and disappeared at the feet of his comrades.

Like the sudden deluge of rain after the first drop of a storm, enemy missiles pelted our formation mercilessly as we cowered behind the protective curve of our shields. The discordant clatter of javelins, arrows, and slingers' lead bullets ricocheting off wood and bronze filled the air, pierced by screams as projectiles found exposed flesh. Something careened off the top of my helm, and I hunched down even more.

"Brace! Brace!" Shouts from the front ranks filtered through to the soldiers in the rear. The collision was coming. I pushed my shield into the back of the hoplite in front of me, putting my full weight behind it. My heaving breaths echoed in my ears. Men started to yell, cursing the charging enemy that most of them could not even see. There was no paean for us, just screams of defiance. I screamed too.

In the fourth rank where I was standing, the impact was merely a shudder, but my feet dug into the dust as I slid back a hand's breadth or more, and the phalanx groaned like a great beam of timber bending under a great weight.

Suddenly bellows of rage and the screams of the dying filled the air. Missiles continued to rain down as blurred streaks flickering through the air, the sound of their impact washed out by the grinding sea of bronze-clad men beneath the leaden skies of Ephesus. The pulsing imperative to push forward and meet the enemy shield to shield obliterated my fear. And by the gods, I embraced it.

I groaned as I pushed with all my strength, my jaw clenched so tightly it was if my teeth would shatter. I stumbled forward as the man in front of me suddenly lurched forward and I nearly fell on the hard ground, barely managing to prop myself up with my spear and regain my balance. Slipping and falling in a phalanx is as sure a way to die as a spear in the throat, for a fallen man will be trampled by his fellows as they move forward to fill the gap. It was the fate of many hoplites and very nearly my own on that day.

The hoplite in front of me stepped forward to plug a hole in the line and I, in turn, advanced to the third line. Above the edge of my shield I could catch glimpses of the enemy just within range of my spear. Grasping my spear far down the shaft, I stabbed furiously over above the shoulders of my comrades into the faces of the enemy, but the awkward grip robbed my thrusts of accuracy and power. Some blows found only air, while others deflected off helmets and shields, but one at last struck flesh, piercing under a man's eye all the to the back of his skull. I wrestled to free the spear-point, but it stuck fast and the weight of the dead man pulled the shaft down, bending it until the tip was torn from the weapon.

Into the breach left by the dead man stepped a colossus. I gasped, for I had never seen a man so large. The living mountain roared as he moved, bashing his shield into the hoplite in the front rank and shoving him back. The titan bellowed into the face of his opponent, challenging him to come forward. The hoplite refused, choosing instead to thrust ineffectually at the giant's face with his spear-point. The massive fighter disdainfully swatted the spear away and clove through the man's helmet with a forward-curving sword that matched its wielder in size and ferocity. It was a *kopis*, a hacking butcher's weapon favored by the Spartans.

Wrenching his sword free with casual savagery, the giant waded into our phalanx, seeking to further widen the gap in our lines. I let go of my broken spear and drew my sword. It seemed but a dagger next to the *kopis* wielded by the enormous brute. I howled a mad challenge.

His eyes locked on me, though we were still separated by a rank of soldiers. He flashed a cruel grin, indicating that he had seen me and accepted my challenge. He refocused his attention on the men immediately before him, decapitating one soldier in a great sweeping cut of his weapon. My muscles were taut like a set snare, ready to propel a foolish boy to an ignominious death in another forgotten battle.

A whisper called to me, something sensed through the clamour of arms and the screams of dying men and I realized what was wrong. The pressure on my back had vanished.

A sharp jerk pulled me backwards and I heard Podaroes screaming at me. "Run, boy!" I ventured a glance behind me only to see the backs of my fellows as they fled the field. "Run!" Podaroes shouted one more time. Then he threw his burdensome shield to the ground and took off after the rest of the fleeing hoplites.

Our phalanx was collapsing. Our rearmost ranks of the sailors and rowers were abandoning their comrades and deserting the field. The ground behind me was littered with shields, helmets, and spears. I glanced one more time to the last stand of the front ranks of Thrasyllus' force, which continued to fight and die. The monster was beset by three men, but they seemed as hounds pestering a great boar. Phobos gripped my heart and icy fear ran through my veins.

Around me the rout was nearly complete, and even now all these years later, I feel the bile in my throat as I recall my actions, but I wish to give an honest account of what occurred.

I did what I swore I would never do. I shook off my shield and turned my back to the enemy.

I fled for my life.

CHAPTER 17

There is no greater shame than that which settles over the camp
of a defeated army. It pollutes the air like poison, robbing men of
the ability to speak or even look one another in the eye, those who
have left the corpses of their comrades on the field of battle to be
plundered by a rapacious enemy.

The Ephesians and their allies harried us all the way back to the
sea, only giving up the chase when the men left guarding our
beached ships threw up a hasty defensive phalanx. It was more
trouble than it was worth, especially when there were easier
pickings among the stragglers who had become separated from the
main pack of fleeing men.

Our camp on the shore was haunted by those demeaned and
belittled by defeat. Some paced about aimlessly, while others sat on
the ground, holding their heads in their hands. Tears marked the
faces of many, though whether they were from the shame of defeat
or for the miracle of their own survival, I could not say. The
*strategos* Thrasyllus had taken refuge in his tent, shielded from the
stares of the men he had led to a crushing rout.

I sat on a hill overlooking the camp with Podaroes, grimly
watching late survivors stumble into camp. Perhaps two hundred
hoplites had not returned. I strained for any view of the javelineers
and slingers, but there were none. Tibetos had been with them.

Podaroes broke the silence. "I'm going to kill that goat-humping
seer," he grumbled. "If he's not already dead, that is." I stared ahead
without answering. Podaroes sighed. "We need to send a herald."

The word herald snapped me out of my silence. "Herald?"

"Who knows how long the *strategos* will sulk in his tent?
Meanwhile, our dead are lying out in the sun being picked at by
crows. The sooner we remove them from the battlefield, the sooner
we can get away from this cursed place." At the mention of the
dead, he spat superstitiously over his shoulder.

"Who is the herald?" I asked. It was little more than a croak
from my parched throat.

He laid a hand on my shoulder. "It might as well be us. Better
than sitting around here. Maybe we'll meet up with your friend and

the others." He knew what I had been thinking. If Tibetos was there, I needed to be the one to find him.

I nodded in helpless agreement. Podaroes rose and offered me his hand, hauling me to my feet. He turned to head down to the camp, but I stopped him.

"Thank you," I said.

Podaroes frowned. "For what?"

"For saving my life."

The veteran let out a small laugh. "I told you that you wouldn't die today, didn't I, boy? And you learned something, I reckon."

"Too much."

"And you're too good of a lad to end up as just another notch on the spear of Akras." He shuddered involuntarily.

"Akras?"

"That great brute who was cutting men down like so many stalks of wheat."

The hair on my neck rose as I recalled the malevolent stare of the giant. "How do you know him?"

Podaroes' eyebrows rose in disbelief. "You do not know Akras?" Seeing my blank expression, he explained. "He is a Syracusan, a mercenary. Even the Spartans are afraid of him, so I've heard. And he loves killing Athenians. They say he slew more than one hundred men in Sicily alone." The mention of Sicily made me think of my brother Heliodoros, and I could not help wondering if he had been one of those felled by the mighty Akras. "The gods favour you today, Gelon. There are few men who have stood so close to Akras and lived to tell of it. But that is the past, and this is now. Let us go volunteer to be the heralds. Somebody has to do it."

"Daimon," I said.

Podaroes stopped and turned. "What?"

"My name is Daimon."

Podaroes pursed his lips and regarded me with narrowed eyes. "And I would wager there's a tale to be told as to why you are Gelon on the rolls?"

"It's a long story," I said.

Podaroes gave a mirthless laugh. "Don't worry about that, Daimon, my young friend. We'll have plenty of time walking back to Ephesus."

THE EPHESIANS HAD ERECTED A TROPHY on their field of victory, marking the point where our phalanx had broken and fled. The trophy was shaped like a man. From atop a spear lodged in the dirt, the sightless eyes of the helmet observed our approach. A horizontal spear-shaft that looked like an extended pair of arms supported a breastplate. A pile of overlapping shields had been placed around the base of the post to mimic the appearance of an armoured skirt. As we drew closer, we could see the dried blood on the cuirass, lapped at greedily by a swarm of flies that hummed and buzzed.

The rank stench of death hung in the air like fog. Corpses littered the plain and baked under the midday sun. The dead had been stripped of their armour and weapons, and anything else of value, even their tunics if they were of high enough quality. Some bore ghastly wounds, their entrails spilled out where they lay, or limbs partly amputated. Yet others, bloody as they might be, appeared unmarked and lay as if sleeping, undisturbed by the scavenging birds that hopped among them and picked at their slain comrades.

The dead were not the only ones who greeted us. Five horsemen came at us at a gallop, spears lowered as though to skewer us where we stood.

"Stand your ground. Do not let them provoke you. I will speak for us," Podaroes said stepping forward. He bore a herald's staff, though its true owner lay dead somewhere on the field before us.

But the riders pulled up at the last moment, laughing at the fear on our faces. Their mirth subsided and the men edged their mounts closer so that their spear-points hovered at our throats.

"Are you eager to join your brothers in Hades, Athenians? We would be glad to send you there!" the cavalryman in the middle said loudly. This provoked laughter from his men, but I could see the murder in their eyes.

"We come on behalf of the *strategos* Thrasyllus to beg a truce so that we may gather our dead," Podaroes intoned clearly.

The leader gave a small kick and his horse began a lazy circle around us. "You Athenian turd-sniffers invade our land and expect our mercy? Why should we not just gather our men and attack the band of pirates cowering at your camp?" We remained silent and unmoving.

A kick in my back sent me tumbling and I scrambled to my feet amid the jeers of the horsemen. Podaroes gave a tiny shake of his head and I straightened up, my fists balled at my side. I took a deep breath and stared ahead.

"Bah! I do not kill cowards or children," the horseman sneered, looking at me as he spoke. "At least those lying on this plain had the courage to die as men. Come beg before our *strategos*. Perhaps he is in a good mood. It is difficult to tell with him." He gave a shout, and the five horsemen took off towards the city, leaving us to follow in dishonour.

The victors were gathered before the city gate, still celebrating their triumph. The spoils of the victory had been heaped beside the gates in a great pile of plundered weapons and armour. Somewhere in the mess was the shield that Lykos had presented to me before I had set out, and the shame welled up in me once more.

Our arrival prompted an extended round of insults and shouting. The giant Akras was not difficult to pick out among his fellows. He was cyclopean in stature, only differing from the monster in that he regarded us with two hateful eyes rather than one.

One comes across giants from time to time, men a head taller and a body heavier than their fellows. They almost inevitably spring from the earth on remote farmsteads or lonely islands. The poet Hesiod tells us that in both stature and strength we are but degraded reflections of men from the age of heroes. Perhaps the blood of the old ones still trickles through to our age from time to time. Such a thing was not beyond disbelief when one laid eyes on Akras. Even though I was a head taller than the average man, my crown would have barely reached the giant's shoulders. In girth and weight, even the ox-like Epimenes would have seemed but a child were he still alive to stand beside the Syracusan giant. Akras grimaced at us, revealing yellow, spade-like teeth as large as those found in a horse's mouth.

Yet imposing as he was, Akras was not the only person who drew my attention. Beside the enormous Syracusan stood another man who gazed at us with predatory intelligence. His breastplate gleamed beneath a scarlet cloak, his dark braids dangling over his breast.

A Spartan.

At first glance, he was beautiful to behold. But closer inspection produced a feeling of unease. It was as though the gods, jealous of his beauty, had just accentuated or lessened his features to mar the composition as a whole, his lips too thin, the angles of his face too severe, all making him appear cruel rather than strong, his cunning eyes the most fearsome at all.

Those eyes regarded us as a cat might contemplate a mouse, a plaything at his mercy. The Spartan raised his hands and the din of Ephesians and their allies died down to a hum.

"I am Lysander, guest-friend of the Ephesians." He called himself *xenos,* guest-friend, but it was false modesty. This man Lysander was their commander, though he did not use the word. When allies called to Sparta for reinforcements, the Spartans often responded by sending a single general in the arrogant belief that one Spartan was sufficient to turn a weak army into a victorious one. More often than not, they were proven correct. The Spartan's voice was filled with authority, but not hostility. "Why do you return here, Athenians?"

Podaroes stepped forward and played his part, requesting a truce so that we could collect and bury our dead. It was the ancient way to concede defeat to those who held the field after a battle.

"Granted," Lysander said, his voice raised so that all present could hear. "But any Athenians remaining in Ephesus at sunset tomorrow will never leave these lands alive." A mocking cheer erupted around us. We could do nothing while the noise continued. I turned my gaze northward, still ignorant of what had befallen Tibetos.

Lysander noticed this and made a motion for silence. "You will have to work hard to fulfill your task," he said with the hint of a smirk. "For the dead we have left north of the city outnumber those here three to one!" he said with a flourish. This prompted another burst of victorious shouting from the assembled soldiers. My heart sank. "Now be gone. You shall not be harmed while you collect your dead. But only until sunset tomorrow." We turned to start the return journey to our camp.

"Wait!" a booming voice commanded.

It was Akras the Syracusan. He left Lysander's side, striding directly towards me. He seized the collar of my tunic, hauling me up so that only my toes scraped the dirt. His voice was like an earthquake. "I know this one. I saw you on the battlefield," he said, his eyes narrowing. Still clutching me, Akras turned and appealed to Lysander. "This one owes me a death!" The gathered soldiers howled for my blood, anticipating a show. Lysander pursed his lips as he considered the request.

It was Podaroes who saved me, striding before Lysander, his hands motioning for silence. The mob ignored him but became quiet with a single wave from Lysander.

"Your commander," Podaroes shouted, "has given his oath before the gods guaranteeing our safety. It is a crime to violate the person of a herald," he admonished the crowd. There were angry shouts at his words. I sucked in my breath, for Podaroes was provoking the Ephesians by reminding them that the Spartan *strategos* was their master and not their guest, despite what Lysander had said earlier.

Lysander himself frowned at Podaroes for a moment, but then smiled magnanimously. "Akras, release him."

With a growl, the Syracusan dropped me to the ground. "My sword awaits you, boy," he said in a low voice before returning to the side of the Spartan.

"Remember," Lysander called out as we departed. "You have until sunset tomorrow!"

For the second time in a day, the Ephesians cheered at the sight of our backs.


"DAMMO!"

My heart leapt. "Tibo? Tibo!" I hurtled towards Tibetos, the darkness of the day vanishing in a ray of relieved joy. We grasped one another by the shoulders in joyful reunion, hardly believing our eyes.

His clothes and face were smeared with dirt and dried blood, but there was light in my friend's exhausted eyes.

"What happened?" I asked.

His face darkened. "It was a massacre," he said quietly. He explained that our meagre cavalry had been driven off by the vastly superior Persian forces, leaving the remaining light troops defenceless. More than three hundred of them lay dead to the north of the city. "We were hiding from their cavalry patrols. That's why it took so long to get back."

I related the slaughter that had transpired before the western gates of the city. I shuddered at the memory of the mighty Akras.

"But Meli was right," Tibetos said. "The gods have protected us!" His faith in my sister was unshakeable. But I wondered what Meges would have said about the benevolence of the gods.

The entire army was mobilized to collect our dead. Night had fallen before all of the corpses were hauled back to our camp. Thrasyllus worked as hard as any man loading the bodies onto ships through the night. My bitterness towards him abated somewhat, and I saw him for what he was. A fine hoplite and a brave man, able to inspire men by his example. But not cunning. Not like Lysander.

With the sun rising over the hills to the west, our ships departed from the shores of Ephesus for the short journey to the city of Notion where we would bury our dead. The Ephesians and their allies left us unmolested. The Spartan Lysander had kept his word.

OUR FLEET LIMPED NORTH, slowly making our way to the city of Lampsacus on the eastern shore of the Hellespont. The army would winter there, linking up with the army of the erstwhile traitor Alkibiades, who would take command of the joint forces.

Despite my doubts about the leadership of Thrasyllus, the prospect of serving under the man who had persuaded Athens to invade Sicily sickened me. My mind had been poisoned against him, for I blamed Alkibiades for the death of my brother Heliodoros. But as it came to pass, I never laid eyes on the man while I was in Lampsacus.

A grey-haired quarter-master was barking orders as we disembarked. The arrival of so many ships threatened to overwhelm the small port in a sea of weary soldiers, all impatiently seeking a hot meal and a bed to collapse on.

The quarter-master rubbed his forehead in exhaustion. "What have I done to offend the gods to land myself in such a dung-heap?" he muttered to himself.

"Having a good day then, are we?" Podaroes said good-naturedly.

The quarter-master responded with a look of frustrated exhaustion. "There are too many men in the city, with the meeting of all of the generals and such. It's my job to see you all quartered and fed. I pray to Zeus daily to strike me down, but here I am."

"*All* of the generals?" I asked. "Who else is here?"

The quarter-master did not look up from his roll-lists. "First Alkibiades, then Thrasybulus, and now Thrasyllus and you lot. That leaves you with the worst of the accommodation."

I was instantly awake. "Thrasybulus is here?" I asked, hardly believing my luck.

"Arrived here five days ago with thirty ships. Word is he's not staying long."

I let out a whoop. "Do you know where the *strategos* is?" I asked impatiently.

"In the north part of the city. More than that, I cannot say."

Revived, I could barely contain myself as the quarter-master recorded our names with frustrating slowness. He handed each of us a pottery sherd with four lines scratched on it. "Present this at the camp on the east side of the city and they'll set you up. Tents for the lot of you," he said brusquely.

But I was not going east. "Tibo, we need to find Thrasybulus," I declared.

Leaving Podaroes to find his billet, I set off with Tibetos and the freed helot Iollas in tow, stopping occasionally to ask where we could find Thrasybulus. A soldier directed us to the home of Stratolas. "Just keep your ears open. You'll hear him long before you see him!" Not understanding his jest, we hurried on our way.

A lone soldier stood leaning on his spear in front of the door. "Is this the home of Stratolas?" I asked.

The soldier cleared his throat loudly and hawked a gob of phlegm onto the road. "What if it is?"

"We seek Thrasybulus. I must speak with him."

The soldier regarded us sceptically. "What? Two boys and a slave? To the crows with you!" He turned his gaze away from us.

"I bring an urgent message from his brother in Athens, Lykos, son of Lykos." I insisted. The soldier narrowed his eyes, weighing my words. At last, he exhaled loudly and rapped on the door. In a moment the door opened slightly to reveal the thin face of a man with a black beard that jutted sharply from his chin. The soldier whispered something to the man, who eyed us suspiciously.

"My master is engaged in serious business. He has no time to deal with messengers. Give the message to me and I will pass it on."

"The message is to be delivered by me in person," I said.

"Then it will not be delivered at all!" The servant began to shut the door.

"Wait!" I yelled. The servant peeked his head out. He said nothing, but his hungry expression was enough to tell me what he wanted. With a sigh, I fished out the small leather pouch that hung by a cord around my neck. I shook out the last drachma coin to my name and placed it in the outstretched hand of the attendant.

"Perhaps my master needs a short rest," said the slave, suddenly agreeable, and the door opened more widely to admit our party.

The servant led us to what would have been the salon in normal times, but it had been converted into a headquarters, a war-room. A large wooden table was covered by parchments and rolls of papyrus. The room was unoccupied save for one man who stood with his back to us as he perused a document. The servant coughed, and the man turned. I knew him at once, though I had never laid eyes on him.

Thrasybulus, son of Lykos.

He was older than Lykos, being perhaps forty years of age. Grey touched the dense black curls of his hair at the temples and in his thick beard. Where Lykos was lithe, Thrasybulus was noticeably thicker in his chest and limbs. One would not have guessed them to be brothers except for the similarity in their faces. In both of them, a heavy brow and long straight nose framed intelligent eyes that missed nothing.

"What is it?" he asked the slave, glancing at me and Tibetos. I now understood the soldier's joke, for the general's deep, resonant voice almost caused the walls to vibrate.

"A message from your brother Lykos, O *strategos*," I answered before the greedy slave could respond. The servant glowered at me as I dug the letter out of my kit bag. I gingerly removed the folded papyrus from its pouch and extended it towards the general.

His eyes on me, he took the letter and unfolded it. His eyes flicked up at us occasionally as he read. I watched nervously, wondering what pattern the Moirai were weaving now. At last he refolded the papyrus and addressed us. "My brother speaks highly of both of you. He also explains how you came to be with him and why you were compelled to leave Athens." Thrasybulus smiled gently. "I served under your father, Daimon, when I was not much older than you are now." I blinked in surprise, for I had not been aware of the direct connection between my father and the general standing before me now.

Thrasybulus searched for a memory. "He was a fine general, always standing in the front ranks with the soldiers he led." His tone hardened. "I was angered when I heard news of the manner of his death."

"Yes, *strategos*," I said.

Thrasybulus shook his head in disgust. He narrowed his eyes at me, glancing at my copper hair. "Your mother was a Thracian, no?"

The question caught me off-guard. "Yes, *strategos*," I answered, and I felt my hackles rising in anticipation of a slight against me.

But the general's inquiry was a practical one, for he was a practical man above all else. "Do you speak the language?"

"Yes, *strategos*," I responded, confused.

Thrasybulus nodded approvingly. "Then I have need of your skills. Fate favors you, Daimon, son of Nikodromos, to have found me in Lampsacus. If you had been much later we would not have crossed paths."

"You are departing soon, *strategos*?" I asked in surprise. I had assumed that the general would winter his troops in Lampsacus with those of Alkibiades and Thrasyllus.

"We head for Thrace in two days. You will join us." It was his first command to me, but not his last.

My destiny became entwined with that of Thrasybulus. And the three Fates smiled at their work.

## CHAPTER 18

My mother's ghost haunted my dreams.

I thought that I would be able to feel something of her in her homeland, something that would resonate inside me. Instead, I just felt cold.

In Athens, traces of summer linger in the air until late autumn. It is not so in Thrace. Where I stood, a few miles inland, the damp chill of early winter presses deeper and deeper into your body until it eats its way down to your very bones.

"By Apollo's shining balls, I'd hate to be here when it really gets cold," the man beside me said in a puff of mist. It was Perimander, my captain.

I pulled my cloak around me more tightly in a vain attempt to keep warm. Beside me, the *strategos* Thrasybulus was silent, seemingly unaffected by the cold. I shivered and peered into the wind coming down from the north.

The tiniest ripple appeared on the horizon. "They are coming, *strategos*," I said.

Beside me, Perimander squinted and scoffed. "There is nothing there, boy! You're seeing ghosts!" But a moment later, another soldier shouted out. Perimander frowned.

"By Zeus, you have sharp eyes, boy!" Thrasybulus shook his head in amazement. I accepted his praise in silence, staring ahead as the tremoring line began to resolve itself into individual horsemen. Hundreds of them.

Even on the barren plain, the booming voice of Thrasybulus filled the plain like rolling thunder. "Hoplites! Advance arms!" Behind us, five hundred hoplites hoisted their shields and tightened their lines.

The Thracians were coming.

THE HORSEMEN CAME TO A HALT a bowshot away, their number some five hundred riders. A moment passed as Greeks and Thracians stared at each other across the windswept plain.

"What are they waiting for?" muttered Perimander.

"Patience, *lochagos*," Thrasybulus said.

I was broadly aware of the Thrasybulus' overall plan. The *strategos* had landed on the coast of Thrace with his squadron of thirty triremes and five transports. Now we would attempt to bring rebellious cities along the Thracian coast back under Athenian authority.

The priority was the city of Abdera. It was a valuable port on the north coast of the Aegean, laying on the land route between Hellas and the Hellespont. If the city could be taken before winter, it would be an ideal base of operations for the campaign against the rebellious island of Thasos the following spring. But to reclaim Abdera, we would need good fortune. Or the cooperation of the natives. To this effect, Thrasybulus had sent a messenger to the Thracian king Medokos proposing an alliance. There had been only silence until a messenger from Medokos had arrived at Thrasybulus' base in the city of Xantheia demanding a meeting on the spot we were now standing with our spears lowered.

Perimander was unconvinced by the reassurances of his general. "This could turn into a dung-storm fast," he said suspiciously.

"We'll soon find out," I said, nodding towards a contingent of ten Thracian riders that began to approach us at a leisurely pace. They stopped twenty paces away.

The Thracians were rough but impressive. "They all look like you," Podaroes told me later. The comparison was not unfair. The Thracians were tall like me and of similar complexion but differed greatly from Greeks in their dress and grooming. Their thick-spun woolen cloaks bore bold, maze-like patterns and crudely rendered figures and animals. Coarsely-stitched leather caps with high peaks and long ear-flaps covered their reddish or brown tangles of long, unkempt hair. Scrolling, winding patterns of ink traced their way over the exposed skin of their forearms and necks. In short, they were what every Greek imagined Thracian barbarians to be.

There was no mistaking King Medokos. He was an enormous man of noble bearing with a heavy fur cloak that flowed over his shoulders and over the rump of his midnight-black steed. He was armoured much in the Greek manner, with a fine breastplate polished to a high sheen. His helmet was a bronze version of the Thracian leather head coverings, with a knob of metal sweeping forward where a Greek helm would bear a crest.

Beside the king on a white stallion was a flame-haired warrior clad in an odd corselet of shiny black plates. Slung over his back was a blade the likes of which I had never set eyes on, though I had heard Neleus and other men speak of it: a Thracian *rhomphaia*. It was a great, gently-curving blade three fingers in width and nearly four feet in length. The hilt alone was as long as a man's forearm. I had no idea how such an unwieldy weapon would be used. In any case, I had no time to consider the matter.

"Come with me, lad," Thrasybulus ordered me, and I strode with my general towards the waiting king, coming to a stop before the king's honour guard.

It was the flame-haired warrior who spoke first. "I am Prince Zyraxes," he said in Thracian. "My father wishes to know," he said flicking his head towards the defensive phalanx behind us, "why you would greet a potential ally as though he were an enemy?" Medokos sat expressionless, his eyes locked on Thrasybulus.

In fact the five hundred hoplites were only half of our total number. Like any force of significant size, we were more akin to a moving village than an army. Slaves, attendants, and pack animals hauled weapons, armour, and the supplies that would sustain the soldiers. There were women, too. Even in our short stay in Xantheia, widows and abandoned women had attached themselves to men under the command of Thrasybulus, for this gave them better prospects for surviving the winter than fending for themselves. Now they followed us, cooking and taking care of other needs. All of these camp-followers now huddled in the center of a bronze square that bristled on every side with spear-points.

They were sure to hear the booming voice of Thrasybulus as he replied to the challenge of Zyraxes. "And I would ask why the king looks down on us from his horse as though we are subjects instead of friends?" I translated the *strategos'* question.

Medokos pursed his lips, and then with a casual wave of his hand motioned for his men to dismount. The king himself alighted from the back of his black horse with surprising agility and grace. Handing his reins to one of his guards, he removed his helmet and bearskin cloak and handed them to another warrior who had appeared at his side. Having rid himself of these burdens of authority, a grinning Medokos came and stood before us, Zyraxes a step behind him.

On level ground, Medokos was still imposing. The chief was half a head taller than me, and towered over Thrasybulus. He must have had more than fifty years, but he did not look it. His copper hair had dulled with the years and was shot through with grey, radiating authority rather than age. His emerald eyes betrayed a latent cunning that his smiling face could not hide.

Medokos rested a broad hand on Thrasybulus' shoulder. "Ha! I hate all Greeks, but I hate Athenians the least. Better than those arrogant Spartan boy-lovers. Athenians know how to deal, but Spartans only know how to dictate terms. And fight. I'll give the idiots that." His Greek was heavily accented but well-spoken.

"King Medokos," Thrasybulus grinned back, placing his own hand on Medokos' shoulder. Some men simply get along, and this was one of those instances.

Medokos turned towards me unexpectedly. "And what of you, boy?" the king asked in Thracian. "How does a Thracian come to serve as a hoplite in Athens?"

"My mother was a Thracian," I responded in his language. "King Medokos," I added hastily.

A corner of the king's mouth curled in amusement to my hasty recovery. "She was a slave, then?" he inquired.

"A freed slave, O King."

"And your father?"

"My father was Nikodromos, son of Alkimachos, O King."

"What is your name, son of Nikodromos?"

"Daimon, O King."

"Then do you consider yourself Greek or Thracian, Daimon?" he pressed.

Caught off-guard, I hesitated. I wished to say Greek but felt there was a trap. Thrasybulus had been watching the exchange with interest and he raised a curious eyebrow at my evident discomfort. Prince Zyraxes was also regarding my conversation with his father with a keen eye.

In the end, I avoided the question the best I could. "I was raised in Athens, O King. It is all I know."

The king looked at me narrowly then laughed in concession. "You speak like an Athenian, that's for certain! I've never met an Athenian who could give a straight answer! But," he said leaning forward slightly, "you look like a Thracian. We'll see how Greek you still feel in a few days." He winked at me. I liked him, too.

"*Strategos*," the king addressed Thrasybulus. "Let us march north as allies. The Kikones think to rebel against their king. We will put them back in their place. When the traitors are dealt with, we will be free to assist you in your own war."

Oaths were exchanged and both Thracians and Greeks made sacrifices to their gods for the success of the campaign. The formalities completed, the Thracians galloped off to the north, leaving us with their guides. The Thracian prince Zyraxes regarded me curiously. He gave a nod of farewell before digging his heels into the flanks of his horse and taking off in pursuit of the rest of the red-haired warriors.

"The king and his son have taken a liking to you, lad," Thrasybulus said thoughtfully while watching the receding horsemen. "You have shown your value, as my brother predicted, though not in the way he might have expected." With that, the general turned and bellowed at his men to prepare for the march.

We were heading north.

To war.

FOR THE NEXT MONTH WE RAIDED Kikone villages in the mountains. For the most part, the people fled before our coming, leaving much of their winter stores to be plundered by our ravenous horde. After we sheltered in the abandoned huts and buildings for the night, we would set them ablaze and move on to the next village.

The Kikones attempted to ambush us in the narrow passes, raining down rocks and arrows. But we kept our formations tight and let our Thracian escorts chase the defenders away, leaving us a clear path to the villages. If the men resisted, they died, for this is where we hoplites surpassed our Thracian allies. Under the cover of our heavy shields and armour, we could hack and batter our way through the palisades that surrounded the villages. Once a breach was opened, we would pour in through the gap and slaughter would ensue.

I remember the first Kikone I killed. I was in a small company with Podaroes when dozens of warriors fell upon us, screaming their battle cries and calling for our blood. But against our locked shields, the Kikones' charge broke like waves crashing upon rocks. The green-eyed man facing me howled as he chopped down with his hooked sword, but I dropped down, raising my shield to deflect the blow harmlessly. My underhanded spear-thrust was just as Neleus had drilled into me a thousand times before, taking the frenzied warrior in the groin below his leather cuirass. He collapsed when I ripped the spear from him, disappearing from my sight forever but never from memory. With a cry we pushed forward over the first line of wounded and dead, crushing their bones under our trampling feet and sharpened spear-butts.

In every village it was much the same. The Kikones would defend their homes in a frenzied onslaught only to be crushed by formations of bronze and iron. We would lose a few men to javelins and rocks, but the losses were more than compensated for by the plunder left for the rest of us. My reputation grew too, despite my youth, for I was fearless in battle almost to the point of recklessness. My fellow soldiers took to calling me 'Thrax,' – the Thracian.

The women and children in defeated villages were rounded up like sheep. The slavers would appear as if by some magic. These traders of flesh and misery attached themselves to any expedition of consequence. Several of the vultures now shadowed us, ever ready to buy any captives that might be taken.

It was a buyers' market, for soldiers would gladly barter the lives of their captives away for a few coins just to get the burdensome human chattel off their hands. Each life was cheap, but there were always more in the next hovel that we razed to oblivion.

Some women would take their own lives and those of their children rather than be taken captive. But many more resigned themselves to capture. I felt pity for them, but fate had no mercy for the weak or young. In one village, I stood frozen as I gazed upon a woman who could have been my mother's sister, so alike did they appear. My mother had been captured in such a raid long ago, taken and sold like an animal. A young boy and girl huddled close to her in fear, clutching at her legs. The woman sensed my eyes on her and turned her head suddenly towards me. Her stare hit me with a mix of fear and defiance. I turned away in a flush of shame.

Any men captured in battle were subjected to taunts and abuse by their Thracian countrymen before being slain outright with an almost joyous brutality. Sometimes a near-naked captive was given a sword and the opportunity to fight for his life, much to the amusement of the other Thracians and many Greeks who gathered to watch the spectacle, often making bets on how long the outmatched victim would last.

Thrasybulus disapproved but was powerless to interfere in the settling of scores by his Thracian allies. I confess to watching these uneven contests, though not for amusement. It was the grim-faced determination with which the prisoners fought and inevitably died that filled me with fascination.

Not all the prisoners went to the Underworld alone. One skilled combatant killed two of his better-armed tormentors in quick succession. The Kikone was finally brought down by one of Medokos' captains, a veteran wielding two swords against the prisoner's single blade, but even then it was a close thing. When the Kikone fell, the cheers from our Thracian allies were half-hearted at best, dulled by their admiration for a worthy foe.

Soon, villages did not resist at all, throwing open their gates to Medokos and his dreaded Greek mercenaries. The tide had turned and they knew where to cast their lots.

The Kikone capital did not yield willingly. The Kikone chief, Mucapor, knew he would find no mercy from Medokos. His village was as large as many Greek poleis, nestled in a valley and well-defended with stone walls. Our attack came just as evening fell. The Thracians and our missile throwers kept the defenders on the walls occupied while the forces of Thrasybulus attacked the gates.

Too sturdy for axes, the wooden barrier was no match for fire. Hurling pots of pitch, we coated the massive doors and set them ablaze. The flames illuminated the floodplain as the fire did its work, the silhouettes of men dancing like shades before the brilliant wall of light as they fed the conflagration's insatiable appetite with more fuel. Just after dawn, the left gate groaned before falling forward with a crack, revealing a fiery path into the village. Our column poured through the breach. Thrasybulus stood in the front ranks, his booming voice rising above all others. I was behind him.

The desperation of their last stand brought out the best of the Kikone warriors, who outnumbered us two to one. They threw themselves on our spears, calling for their god Ziberthiurdos to smite us down. But the god did not answer their pleas.

As our phalanx advanced over the Kikone dead, Thrasybulus stumbled over the corpse of a slain tribesman and he fell forward onto his shield. A tremendous red-bearded warrior wearing a fox-skin head-covering leapt towards the defenceless general. With a keening howl, the Kikone raised his spear to dispatch the gift his gods had laid at his feet.

I vaulted over the sprawling Thrasybulus to meet the Kikone. Podaroes told me later that my leap would have won a laurel at the games of Olympia, though I recall very little of it. "You were screaming like a madman," he said, shaking his head in wonder.

My spear thrust took the Kikone directly through his open mouth, punching out the back of his neck. The man toppled sideways, taking my spear with him. I tore my sword from its scabbard and roared at the Kikone line opposite us. My comrades reformed the front rank around me, their screams adding to mine.

It was too much for the Kikones. Their line broke and fled among the huts of the village. In our blood-rage we made to pursue our vanquished foes.

"Hold!" The command of Thrasybulus penetrated through the metal of our helmets and the pounding of blood in our ears. "Hold!" With agonizing reluctance, we broke off our pursuit. As the enemy disappeared, so too did the madness of battle begin to recede from our minds. Thrasybulus was correct to halt us, for there is danger in pursuing a routed foe. Like the Spartans, the northern tribes will often flee to lure their pursuers into a trap.

The *aristeia* that had filled me with battle-rage drained away, I raised my helmet and stood panting in exhaustion. I turned towards Thrasybulus and grinned sheepishly between gasps.

The *strategos* removed his own helmet and glanced down at the body of the warrior with the fox-skin head-covering. "By Zeus, it was fortunate that my brother sent you to me!"

The carnage of the assault surrounded us. The corpses of Mucapor's men lay strewn about. Greeks were stripping the dead of anything of value, which was not much. One Kikone moaned pitifully as he tried in vain to prevent his guts from spilling out from beneath his cuirass. Podaroes ended the man's misery by slashing his throat. Fumbling at the fastenings of the Kikone's bloody breastplate, he noticed me watching and shrugged before attacking the stubborn prize with renewed vigour.

A horn sounded. Thrasybulus cocked his ear. Three short blasts, a pause, and then the signal repeated again. "It is victory, then," he said simply.

The Kikone uprising was no more.

## CHAPTER 19

In the central square of the village, a dozen Kikone prisoners knelt in the cold dirt, their hands bound behind them. Not one was without wounds of some sort, but it was apparent from their expressions that the greatest injury was to their honour. Their chins were held high, but the defiant gesture could not hide the shame in their eyes as they suffered the insults and jeers in both Thracian and Greek.

Medokos conferred with Thrasybulus. The Thracian warlord's breast-plate bore the dark stains of Kikone blood. Like Thrasybulus, he led from the front.

Zyraxes caught sight of me. He strode towards me, beaming. "Daimon! Tales of your prowess have reached my ears! It is said that you slew Komozoi in single combat!" I blinked at him dumbly. "Mucapor's son," Zyraxes said, seeing my confusion.

"I think he's talking about the brute who ate your spear," Podaroes added helpfully.

The warrior with the fox-skin cap, I realized. "It was a lucky blow," I confessed.

Zyraxes laughed. "Then the victory belongs to whatever god guided your spear. But luck is seldom given to those who don't deserve it." Medokos' son became more serious. "Mucapor is dead. The Kikones will have no choice but to accept my father's rule." With the victory, Medokos had now extended his authority over a wide swath of Thracian territory.

A voice cut me off before I could respond. "Zyraxes! You are a coward!" We turned as one towards the source. It was one of the bound prisoners. An angry bruise marred the left side of his face. "You are afraid to face me!" the man bellowed from his knees. One of Medokos' men snapped a vicious kick to the prisoner's gut and the man doubled over from the blow, coughing. But he straightened himself, his defiant eyes locking on Zyraxes. "Zyraxes, killer of women and children," the man said mockingly. "But you shit yourself in fear before true warriors." He spat on the ground in disgust.

A hush fell as all eyes turned to Zyraxes. A cold rage darkened the prince's features. The Thracian beside the prisoner had drawn his hooked sword and raised it to hack down on the kneeling man's neck, but Zyraxes raised his hand to stay the killing blow. The king's son walked over and stopped in front of the defiant prisoner.

"Your father and brother both lie dead in the street, Sinna, cut down like the dogs they were." The prisoner was one of the rebellious chief's sons, then. Zyraxes spoke loudly so that everyone present could hear him. "But at least they fell fighting. Better to die fighting like a dog than to be taken prisoner like a stray lamb!" The Thracians voiced their agreement with jeers and insults. I translated for Podaroes beside me, who snorted in derision. The Greek soldiers nearby leaned close to hear what I was saying.

The prisoner grimaced in shame but then turned the insult to his advantage. "Let all those present remember that the coward Zyraxes hid in fear rather than face a lamb!"

Before all present, the man had questioned Zyraxes' honour. The prince could not back down. "Let the lamb have his weapons then!" Zyraxes proclaimed with a disdainful wave. "And he will see how a wolf feeds!"

A cheer erupted from the Thracians. The Greeks, knowing something significant had just occurred, joined in. Even the prisoners bobbed their heads grimly at the chance to salvage some honour from their ignominious defeat.

Over the babble of excited voices, Podaroes shouted in my ear. "The gods smile on you, lad! We are about to witness a Thracian duel." There was a bloodthirsty edge to his voice as the prisoner was freed.

I was surprised. "Zyraxes will fight him?"

"He doesn't have a choice. His honour has been challenged," Podaroes replied as though it was self-evident.

Released from his bonds, the prisoner Sinna chose two of the hooked Thracian *sica* swords for the contest. The blue patterns of ink on his bare arms rippled with coiled energy as he twirled the blades idly, testing the heft of the weapons. Across the clearing, Zyraxes paced impatiently, glaring at his opponent. His black-plated cuirass had lost its sheen under the dust and blood of the day. The tip of the long-bladed *rhomphaia* sword scratched the earth behind him with a grating sound. Around the perimeter, Greeks and

Thracians thrummed in anticipation of the duel to come. King Medokos, apparently unconcerned for his son, leaned over to say something into the ear of Thrasybulus, who stared out impassively at the spectacle.

As if by mutual consent, the contest began. A cheer erupted from the spectators. The opponents circled each other slowly, each taking the measure of the other. Zyraxes held the *rhomphaia* high in a two-handed grip, while the Kikone Sinna spun his dual blades in lazy arcs. The space separating them narrowed.

Sinna pounced. The blades moved so quickly I could not see them. Zyraxes moved deftly, dancing away from the spinning swords. A stab from the *rhomphaia* forced the Kikone backwards, and the two Thracians were apart once again.

Zyraxes gave a slight bow towards Sinna. The crowd showed no such respect, hurling insults at the Kikone captive. Now it was the Thracian prince's turn to press the attack.

The *rhomphaia* was a blur of constant motion. Like a spear, thrusts and lunges drove at Sinna high and low, probing for a gap in the whirling defense of his swords. My sword-craft had grown in leaps and bounds under the strict tutelage of Lykos, but I could only stare in awe as the two men fought. Unlike the straight thrusts and cuts I had been learning, the Thracians moved as though they were dancing. I was entranced.

The *rhomphaia* kept Sinna at a distance, flicking him with cuts to his shoulders and arms. With a roar of frustration, the Kikone dashed towards Zyraxes, launching into a spinning leap at the last moment. At the end of the spin, the two swords were at different heights, each a killing blow.

The blades scythed through empty air.

Zyraxes had dropped into a roll towards his attacker. As he pulled out of the roll, the slashing *rhomphaia* cut into Sinna's midsection, the honed edge biting deeply as Zyraxes let his momentum draw the blade across Sinna's abdomen like a saw through a log. The Kikone sprawled face first in a wet thud, his two swords tumbling from his grasp. If he was still alive, it was not for long, for Zyraxes had pivoted, and reversing the *rhomphaia* in a downward two-handed grip, he drove the tip through his prone opponent's back.

My ears rang with the cheers of the Thracians and Greeks who ringed the space. I must have shouted as well, though I cannot remember. I only recall Zyraxes.

In his triumph, Zyraxes raged as though he was possessed by a beast. The sinews of his neck were taut strings as he screamed and strode about like a madman. He shouted at the remaining prisoners, challenging them, taunting them, but they were broken men, their defiance gone. He turned his back on them and paraded about, daring any of those present to contest his victory. In the centre of his contorted features, his eyes burned with rage. I shuddered when they fell on me, for there was no trace of recognition. Only a predator remained.

Medokos grinned with pride at his son's prowess. Thrasybulus could not quite hide his distaste.

In time, Zyraxes ceased his display. "Zia!" he shouted. "Zia! It is your time!"

The Thracians craned their necks, looking about. There was some activity across from me, and the crowd parted, clearing a path. An ancient woman emerged, bringing an air of coldness with her.

"Who is that?" Podaroes asked me in a low voice.

"I don't know," I said. "A priestess, I think." The Thracian and Greek camps had not mingled. In my duties as translator, I had seen the mass of slaves and women that accompanied the Thracian warriors, but I had little interaction with them.

A hush enveloped those assembled. The aged woman moved with coiled vigour. Whorls of ink covered her face. From beneath her pure white, unbound hair, her hard eyes scanned the crowd. The Thracians bowed their heads rather than meet her stare, and even the Greeks averted their eyes, many of them touching iron or clutching their manhoods to ward off the evil eye. For an instant, the crone's gaze met mine, her eyes narrowing. A shudder passed through me. Mercifully, she turned her gaze on Zyraxes, freeing me.

The Thracian prince bowed. Without a word, he indicated the kneeling prisoners with a sweep of his hand. The priestess turned her gaze on the condemned men. Under her wordless stare, their courage began to waver, fear creeping into their faces. The crone paced silently in front of them, stopping in front of the last prisoner, a boy. The youth was quavering visibly as terror overcame him.

With surprising tenderness, the priestess placed her hand on the boy's head. She stroked his red hair as a mother might do with her child. Leaning forward, she whispered something, her words inaudible to all save the boy who was kneeling before her. Whatever she said, it calmed the young Kikone. His shaking ceased and his expression changed, a weak smile pushing through the fear. I knew the look. It was hope.

Without warning, the priestess clutched the boy's hair. A dagger materialized in her hand and flashed across his throat in a single swift motion. Oblivious to the crimson that sprayed her front, the old woman held the boy up by his hair. "This sacrifice is for you, O Pleystor, who has brought us victory today!" she shouted to the skies. A shout rose from the assembled Thracians as they acknowledged their god of war. The crone released the boy's hair from her grasp and he toppled forward, the surprise of death still frozen on his face.

The rest of the men received no soft words from the priestess. Held fast and their heads pulled back by their guards, they met their end one by one, a payment to the blood-thirsty god.

When it was done, the blood-soaked priestess exchanged bows with King Medokos and stood by his side.

Medokos raised his hands, motioning for silence. In his accented Greek, he spoke. "Achaeans," he said, using the ancient word for Greeks. "Pleystor, whom you call Ares, has brought us victory today over our enemies. But it was only with your aid, Achaeans, that we achieved this. Pleystor we honour with sacrifice. And we honour you, Achaeans, with booty. This village is yours for plunder!"

A cheer went up from the Greeks, their shock from the sacrifices erased by greed as they considered the rich booty that awaited them.

Medokos beamed as he basked in their adulation. He indicated that he wished to speak again with a raised hand. "Tomorrow, with the consent of your *strategos*," he said placing a hand on the shoulder of Thrasybulus, "we shall have games and a feast to honour the gods." Another cheer went up, and the names of Medokos and Thrasybulus echoed through the village. Beside the king, Thrasybulus stood stiffly. With visible effort, he smiled as the praise rained down.

"Now go!" Medokos commanded.

Suddenly unleashed, the soldiers scrambled to get back to the village, each man fearing to be left behind as the proper looting began. My father's voice echoed in my mind. I could hear his disgust at the frenzied pillaging that was taking place. I turned away, only wanting to undo my sweltering armour.

A hand seized my wrist. My breathing stopped as I saw that it was the wizened priestess. Her narrowed eyes danced over me as if she were searching for something. Instinctively, I pulled my arm away, but her bony fingers gripped as tightly as an eagle's talons.

She cackled at me. "You are of two worlds, boy!"

"My father was Greek," I stammered.

"What gods do you worship?" she demanded.

"I pray to the gods of my father," I answered truthfully.

"Bah! They do not listen to your prayers! You are not one of them!"

"I should pray to the Thracian gods?"

"You are not one of us! They will not recognize you." She crinkled her face. I thought she would spit on me, but instead she released my arm. "You are cursed, boy. By the gods or the Fates, I do not know, but you are cursed."

I swallowed hard at her words. "How am I cursed?" I whispered.

"The worst of all things," the crone said in her throaty rasp. "To walk alone."

CHAPTER 20

The games, if not of the calibre one would witness at Olympia, had the desired effect. For the first time, the Thracians and their Greek allies moved beyond the suspicious stares and the mumbled slurs that had governed their interactions thus far.

Laughter and cheering echoed through the valley just outside the village where the contests took place. The camaraderie and competition helped me push aside the chilling words of the old priestess.

Both sides acquitted themselves well. No honour was lost, but mutual respect was gained. Dominant in the horse races, the Thracians were no match for the swift-footed Greeks in the running contests. The Thracians slung their javelins with enviable accuracy, but all were surprised when a titch of an Athenian by the name of Agasias managed to hurl his javelin ten paces farther than any other competitor. Thrasybulus' men erupted into joyous celebration as Agasias was carried about the field on the shoulders of a squad of copper-haired Thracians.

At the urging of Podaroes, I joined the sword contests. Fighters were armed with dulled blades and a smaller, Thracian-style shield. "Earn me some coin, Dammo, and you'll get your share," Podaroes said slapping my back.

My helmet was open-faced, and the Thracians jeered at my youthful appearance. Their mocking was soon silenced as I left my first two opponents dazed on their backs in quick order. Podaroes beamed from the sidelines, having profited handsomely from a few well-placed bets.

The third Thracian was more cautious. He circled warily, probing for an opening. Eventually I gave him one as I pretended to slip on a lunging attack. He took the bait and ended up on the ground with a dented helmet for his trouble. A cheer went up from the Greeks, while the Thracians sulked once again upon seeing their man beaten. Podaroes' broad smile threatened to split his head in two.

A voice rang out. "O Greeks! Would you permit me the chance to salvage some honour for my men?" It was the prince, Zyraxes. I had no say, as my comrades accepted the challenge with a shout of approval.

I gave a nod to Zyraxes to indicate my consent. The Thracians awoke from their depressed state, confident now that the upstart would get the thrashing due to him.

The prince was dressed simply, his fine black cuirass replaced by a simple leather breastplate. The swirling lines of his tattoos snaked up his arms. He spun his sword with an easygoing flourish.

Zyraxes waved me over, draping an arm over my shoulder and leaning so close that our helmets were touching. The buzz of the crowd hummed around us, and only I could hear what he said. "You are a skilled swordsman, Daimon, son of Nikodromos," he complimented me. "A fair fight, but let us give them a good show so that honour is satisfied on both sides. Let us show Greeks and Thracians that we are stronger together." Before I could say anything, he thumped my shoulder and we separated.

It was indeed a show.

What followed was a flurry of swords, a dance of stabs and slashes and parried iron. It was a long contest, as these things go. I was not his equal, but nor was I far his inferior. The roar of the crowd infused me with vigour, and I fought above my ability. The prince's brow was knitted with concentration as I pressed my attack. A feint made him dodge, and he barely recovered from his error as I came down with a leaping, downward thrust that grazed the prince's shoulder, and the Greeks cheered at his desperation.

But that was my high point. Zyraxes pressed his attack. It was my turn to make a mistake, and the flat of Zyraxes' sword clanged solidly against the side of my head.

Rolling with the blow, I came up in a crouch behind my shield, my weapon recoiled and ready to strike out. A deafening hum filled my ears. I blinked hard, trying to focus on the blurry shapes around me. The largest shape resolved itself. It was Zyraxes, grinning, with his arms held out widespread. I growled and readied myself to pounce. Then I checked myself, the realization that I had lost the contest coming at last through my battered senses.

My shoulders slumped. I stood erect and looked to the sky as the noise of the cheering Thracians penetrated through the ringing of my ears. Zyraxes tossed aside his shield and weapon. He strode towards me, still grinning, and embraced me. The Greeks, I noticed, were cheering, too.

"Your Thracian blood shows through," he barked in my ear. We separated, Zyraxes holding me by the shoulders at arm's length. "You will sit with me at the feast." I nodded, still despondent and half-dazed. "Now let us take off our helmets and stand as brothers."

We stood there at the centre of the fighting circle, the adulation raining down on us. King Medokos was applauding heartily. Beside him, even the normally sombre Thrasybulus was beaming.

Zyraxes motioned for silence and the noise abated somewhat. "The contest was not fairly won," he declared in Greek and then in Thracian. "For your man fought four battles, while I fought only one." I shifted uncomfortably, knowing I had been beaten fair and square. "We are friends, O Greeks. Allies! Let us celebrate together as such. Gather yourselves for a feast and let us treat you to our hospitality!" He raised my hand high, and the new allies were united in their jubilant response.

"HERE IS YOUR SHARE," Podaroes said happily, dropping a small satchel of coins in my hand.

The weight of the coins sat heavily in my palm. It was a not insubstantial sum. "You bet against me in the last match, then?" I said with some resentment.

Podaroes laughed. "Don't take it hard, lad. I did bet on you to last as long as you did, though. Everyone else thought you'd be finished within the first five attacks. But I knew better." He winked at me, and I grinned despite myself. The veteran sniffed at the air. "The feast begins, it seems," he said, changing the subject.

The smell of cooking meat wafted through the air to the part of the village that we had claimed with the other Greeks. We left Iollas to stay with our gear, and as if under the spell of the Sirens' call, we let ourselves be led by our hosts to the source of the maddening aroma.

Beyond the village walls a spacious clearing was dotted with cooking fires. Spitted sheep and goats roasted over gentle flames tended to by women of the Thracian camp followers, their long braided hair coiled around their necks like copper torcs.

The men sat on the bare earth around the fires. Already some of our own soldiers had been enlisted into drinking bouts with the Thracians, the imbibed liquids doing much to ease the obstacle of language. Children ran about or stayed clinging to their mothers' tunics as the women laboured at the fires. One young girl of ten or so years caught my attention. She was stirring one of the many pots that bubbled with stew, her brow furrowed in concentration. I stopped to watch her at her task and my chest tightened, for she bore a striking resemblance to Meli. Before I could reflect further on the thought, the sound of my name awakened me to the present once again.

"Daimon!" Zyraxes' voice cut through the din of the celebrants' chatter. "Come and join me, my brother!" he shouted in Thracian. Rough-hewn tables ringed a large central fire. Thrasybulus was there with Medokos and some of the other Thracian nobles. Zyraxes beckoned, his other hand holding a cup towards me.

Podaroes arched an eyebrow. "You'd better hop to it, Dammo. It's not wise to keep kings and generals waiting." A shapely Thracian woman strode by, carrying a large basket of bread. Her eyes flashed at him. Podaroes eyes followed her hungrily. "Don't worry about me, lad. I can explore the limits of Thracian hospitality without an interpreter!" He disappeared after the woman in some haste.

Zyraxes greeted me warmly. "Sit! Sit!" He was speaking Thracian, and in an exuberant mood. He beckoned to a girl standing nearby and a cup was brought to me. "Let us drink!" We raised our cups and I took a deep pull of the beverage within. My throat tingled with the warmth of the oddly spicy and sour drink. Zyraxes noticed my expression. "Have you never tasted *rappa*? It is the drink of your ancestors. You will have your fill tonight!"

Around me, the *rappa* flowed in copious amounts. Greeks, Thracians, men and women alike, all partook in the Thracian beer freely and loudly. The *rappa* loosened my tongue as well, and I let the curious Zyraxes interrogate me regarding my own life. Something I said drew a wry grin from the prince.

"Why do you smile?" I asked.

"It is your accent. I think your mother was one of the Thynoi."

"The Thynoi?"

"They live far to the north, along the coast of the Euxine. They are a wild lot. Uncontrollable. They follow no king. Not even the Great King of Persia could tame them!"

"You sound almost Greek when you say that," I poked back at Zyraxes.

'It is true!" His face broke into a broad, disarming grin. He tapped me in the chest. "I have spent too much time with your kind!"

I seized on his words. "I am Greek to you then?"

"Do you want to be Thracian?" he turned it around quickly with a sly smile. "You would be accepted here," he pushed, seeing what lay in my heart.

"I am Greek," I said firmly.

"It is as you say then," Zyraxes conceded with a bow, yet I felt that somehow I had lost the debate.

I had no time to dwell on it. Zyraxes called to a passing girl for more *rappa*. The flowing patterns of dark ink on her arms were not the only thing I noticed as she leaned in to fill our bowls. I suppose my mouth was open, and our eyes met for the briefest of instants. I stared at her swaying hips as she left to tend to other guests, my lust inflamed.

"Perhaps you are Thracian after all," Zyraxes winked mischievously.

I laughed at being caught out. I raised my bowl. "To Dionysus!"

"To Sabazios!" Zyraxes laughed, and we drained our bowls.

There was entertainment as well. A dance by six Thracian girls was first. To the steady beat of the drums and haunting, reedy flutes, the dancers' synchronized, flowing movements held the audience in thrall. The girls' silhouetted forms cast eerie, beautiful shadows that crept and flickered on the faces of the men who watched, transfixed. The tempo picked up, and the dancers spun with ever more intensity, their braided hair whipping in furious arcs with each turn, until the drumming abruptly ceased and with one final leap the girls landed liked crouched beasts, their sweat-sheened bodies panting from the exertion.

The audience, inflamed by *rappa*, exploded in appreciation and lust. Zyraxes saw my own wide-eyed expression and slapped me on the back. "The next time we fight Greeks, perhaps we should send in a troupe of dancing girls! You seem powerless before them!" I grinned sheepishly, enjoying the Thracian prince's company

A flourish of drumbeats heralded the next performance. A hush fell over the assembled Thracians, and we Greeks took our cue from them, not knowing what spectacle awaited us.

"What is happening?" I whispered to Zyraxes, who just smiled coyly. I looked to Thrasybulus, who merely shrugged.

A low heartbeat of drums pulsed in the air. From the shadows of opposite sides of the clearing emerged two performers with weapons drawn, each of their steps falling in time with the deep pulse of the drums.

One man wielded a hooked Thracian short-sword in each hand, the blades pulled back around his bare-chested body, coiled and ready to lash out. With a flourish, he bowed to the audience and was rewarded with a flurry of drunken insults.

But it was the second warrior that drew my gawking stare, along with those of every other Greek present. It was the beauty who had brought us the *rappa* earlier. The Thracian spectators broke into clamorous acclaim as she made her own deep bow.

"Her name is Nea," Zyraxes said, reading my thoughts.

"But she is a woman!" I exclaimed stupidly.

"We do not lock our women away as do you Athenians," the prince sniffed. "Those worthy of it fight alongside their men. Amazons, you call them!" I stared at her, transfixed.

She was clad in a black cuirass and brandished a wickedly long *rhomphaia*, her hands in a wide grip on the hilt, the long graceful blade angled upwards to one side. In time with the slow thump of the drum, she began to advance in a deliberate back-and-forth stride. The Thracians shouted their approval, and only then did I realize that the girl Nea was meant to be Zyraxes. It was a recreation of his duel with the Kikone Sinna the previous day.

I looked on, entranced, as the synchronized steps drew the performers closer to each other in an ever-tightening spiral. The distance between the fighters closed until they were within striking distance. Nea made the first attack, thrusting the *rhomphaia* like a spear towards the chest of her counterpart, who spun to parry the long blade with both his swords. They moved slowly, as if they were immersed in water, pushing and yielding against some invisible resistance.

As the hypnotic drumming grew in speed and intensity, so too did the mock battle playing out before our eyes. I marvelled at the style that differed so greatly from the efficient linear cuts I had learned from Lykos. The Thracians' movements were circular, the momentum of one action flowing seamlessly into the next, blades and bodies always in continuous motion. A defensive block metamorphosed into a graceful attack in a single movement. An unsuccessful lunge carried through to a natural parry of the inevitable counter-thrust. The opponents leapt, twisted, and spun in their dance, the pace and urgency ever growing until the combatants were just a blur of flesh and metal. It was beautiful.

With a final percussive crash, the dance of combat halted abruptly. Nea was frozen in a crouch, the *rhomphaia* extended in a two-handed lunge. The swordsman stretched out his arms to either side. From where I sat, the man looked to be impaled, and for an instant I thought that it must be so until the Thracians burst out in cheers and applause.

Nea's huddled form uncurled and rose to the adulation of her appreciative audience. Her eyes met mine and I was trapped in her gaze. When she turned away to tightly embrace her fellow performer, my heart sank.

Zyraxes pretended not to notice my crestfallen expression. "So what do you think, Athenian?" he shouted over the raucous din of the appreciative audience.

I swallowed my infatuation. There had been something else I lusted after besides the girl. The *rhomphaia* called to me. I turned to Zyraxes. "The *rhomphaia*. Will you teach me?"

Zyraxes shrugged disdainfully. "Only a Thracian may wield a *rhomphaia*." He sipped at his *rappa*, but watched me over the edge of the cup. "Are you Thracian, Daimon son of Nikodromos?" He grinned mischievously, but his eyes watched me intently.

All my life I had fought to be accepted as an Athenian. It was in my bones. But my desire to prove my worth as a warrior ran just as deep, and I was in love with the deadly beauty of the Thracian weapon. "I am Greek," I said a little miserably. Zyraxes shrugged as though it did not matter to him.

My mood suddenly brought low, I watched the continuing entertainment in sullen silence. The formal performances completed, ordinary people, emboldened by drink and the occasion, made their own contributions to the night's entertainment. Songs drifted into the starry sky above, and every performer received a thunderous roar of appreciation from the gathered mass of people. Even a group of our Greek soldiers were pressed into performance, and they drunkenly belted out a ribald soldiers' song with great gusto.

The sound of my name pulled me out of my stupor. "Daimon!" It was Zyraxes. "It was not fair of me to ask you to deny your father. Forgive me for that, for a man, even a prince, should not demand such things of a friend."

There was sincerity in his words. "There is nothing to forgive. You have treated me better than I deserve." I said, raising my cup to him.

The prince gripped my forearm. "But prove to me that you have not forsaken your mother's forefathers. Do this, and I will teach you the *rhomphaia*."

"But how can I do this?" I asked, puzzled.

Zyraxes flashed a wicked smile. "I do not doubt your courage in arms. I would expect no less from the son of a *strategos*. But there are different kinds of valour." I looked back at him in confusion.

Zyraxes suddenly rose to his feet beside me. "Good people! Good people!" he bellowed holding out his arms. The assembly fell into hushed anticipation. "This has been a great feast, and shows the friendship between our two peoples, Achaeans and Thracians!" he shouted in both languages. Both Thracians and Greeks erupted in approval and Zyraxes waited for them to settle down. "What better symbol of our common cause than my new friend and brother, son of an Athenian father and Thracian mother?" Another cheer.

My face went slack with shock. I did not know where Zyraxes was taking this. Everyone was staring at me now, including a joyful Medokos and a bemused Thrasybulus. The general's raised eyebrow told me that I was on my own.

"Perhaps," Zyraxes continued, "our lost son could be persuaded to perform a song for us?" I was mortified. The assembled mass of Thracians and Greeks shouted gleeful encouragement. Even Thrasybulus was laughing. I swallowed deeply and stood up. Zyraxes grinned wickedly and took his seat. I was trapped.

A terror engulfed me as hundreds of expectant eyes fell on me. It differed from the churning fear that assaults the guts before a battle, yet was no less intense.

And then my mother's spirit found me at last. Her whispers from the Underworld filled my mind with the music I needed, the Thracian ballad she had always sung for me and Meli. With a new calm, I started to sing.

I began the tale of the slave and the princess, and smiles of recognition appeared among the Thracians, spurring my confidence forward. My voice rose as I sang of the ill-fated love of the couple and their courage and defiance of gods and men. Thracian voices joined mine. The chorus rose and fell with the vicissitudes of the lovers, building to a crescendo. But when I sang of how the tragedy ended, I was unaccompanied once again. The slave and the princess frozen in a final embrace, exiled, alone, defying the cruelty of the gods in death. The final words tumbled from my lips.

The pops and hissing of the bonfires filled the silence. Astonished faces, Greek and Thracian alike, stared back at me. Shameless tears streamed unabashedly down the faces of Thracian warriors, hardened men who only a day earlier had charged their enemies howling for blood. I was frozen before them.

Somebody coughed and the spell was broken. Shouts of praise poured down from all sides. King Medokos himself rose and came to embrace me. He grasped my shoulders in his massive hands. "It is an old tale, and one well-chosen, lad!" he beamed. He turned and held my hand aloft, and I could only brace myself against the wave of adulation that crashed over me. Zyraxes bowed to me with exaggerated pomp, provoking a roar of laughter.

The moment passed, as all do, and people returned to their own feasting and drinking. Thrasybulus, once again deep in conversation with Medokos, glanced my way. He raised his cup to me and I returned the gesture.

When I looked back at Zyraxes, he was regarding me seriously. "Daimon," he said putting his hand on my shoulder, "You have shown me that your soul is still Thracian. From this day forth, you are my brother, wherever you may wander."

"I am your brother," I said. In the low light, I could have mistaken him for Lykos, and I felt a pang of homesickness.

It must have shown in my face. "You miss your home," Zyraxes said.

"My sister and my comrades of the *peripoli*," I said.

"I would like to meet them," Zyraxes said with a laugh. "They sound more Thracian than Greek!"

I did not deny the truth of it. Our cups were filled with *rappa* once more, and I told Zyraxes more of the *peripoli* and Meli.

Upon hearing of my sister's dreams, Zyraxes was duly impressed. "She has the sight of the gods, like Zia. Bring her to us, Daimon, and let her learn the ways of a wise-woman from one such as Zia."

I shuddered at the memory of the white-haired Thracian priestess. I made a weak promise of sorts that I would try to bring Meli to Thrace, but the thought that she might be likened to Zia one day brought fear to my heart.

The fires were dying down, though not the festivities. The celebration had fallen to the level of the most debauched symposium. Drunken songs in both Thracian and Greek did little to hide the grunts and moans of men and women coupling in the darkness. The disapproving voice of my father rang in my ears, but I was but a young man infused with *rappa*, and lust rose within me.

A hand on my shoulder made me turn my eyes away from the blackness beyond the fires. It was Thrasybulus.

"Our kind host has given me leave to retire from the festivities," he said. The upright general, a paragon of moderation, could not completely hide the disapproval in his voice as he spoke the last word. "I would not mind some company as I walk off the drink."

He sounded stone sober, and I knew an order when I heard one. "Yes *strategos*." I rose none too steadily to my feet.

Zyraxes stood to greet the general. He swayed slightly, but his voice was clear. "Do you leave so soon, O *strategos*?" he asked innocently.

"It has been a long campaign, Prince Zyraxes."

"Indeed, it has. And we will take Abdera soon," Zyraxes said, recalling the walled city on the coast. "I would suggest a strategy, but we can speak of that tomorrow. Your men will need a few days to recover, I expect," he said.

Thrasybulus smiled curtly. "I expect you are correct in this, Prince Zyraxes."

We bid our farewells with pledges of friendship and duty. The general begged off the escort offered by Medokos.

"O *strategos*," Zyraxes called out as we departed. The general and I both looked back. "Daimon, son of Nikodromos, has played no small part in bringing our two sides together. Keep him close."

Thrasybulus shrugged. "Now that I know the power of his voice, I will have him sing before every battle to bring the enemy to tears." Zyraxes and I blinked at each other for a moment before we realized the stiff general had made a joke, and we laughed more in surprise than from the humor of the jest.

"A wise strategy worth considering!" Zyraxes conceded.

As the *strategos* and I left the light of the banquet behind us, I glanced back one more time. Zyraxes had retrieved his cup and raised it in the air. I waved back.

At my Thracian brother.

# CHAPTER 21

Thrasybulus and I walked unspeaking for a time. We were not unlike master and servant returning home through the streets of Athens in the dead of night after a night of revelry, except that the road illuminated by my torch was a goat-path in Thrace.

With only the crunch of the stones beneath our feet, we walked in silence, my own mind absorbed in a *rappa*-fueled haze of lustful frustration. Thrasybulus' question brought me back to the present.

"Pardon, *strategos*?" I asked.

"Do you like them?" he repeated. "Prince Zyraxes and the Thracians."

I was wary, but I answered honestly. "I do, *strategos*."

"Why?"

I considered my words before speaking, as my father had taught me. "I am an Athenian," I said at last. "But in others' eyes, I have always been something else. A Thracian. The son of a slave. Anything but an Athenian." A long-nursed bitterness crept into my voice. "But Zyraxes and Medokos do not care about that. To them, I am what I am: A Greek with a Thracian mother, nothing more, nothing less. I do not think I could live in the manner of these people, but from what I have seen in the last few days, I must say that yes, I like them, *strategos*." I feared that I had revealed too much, but the *rappa* had loosened my tongue

The general glanced over at me. "And do you trust them, Daimon?"

I weighed my words. "One of the *peripoli*, Meges —" there was a grunt of disapproval from Thrasybulus "— told me that Thracians could not be trusted. I took offense at his words, but I have learned that he is anything but a stupid man. I value his judgment, *strategos*. I have enjoyed the hospitality of Medokos and his Thracians, but I know that it is because the king needs our strength."

"Then perhaps you have learned something useful after all, Daimon, and that is not to let your personal feelings cloud your judgment. Especially in war," he added.

"Do you trust them, *strategos*?"

If he was surprised by my boldness, he did not show it. "It is a foolish commander whose strategy depends on good faith in others, Daimon."

"Then why do you ally yourself with Medokos?"

Thrasybulus was not offended. "I do not place my faith in men, but in necessity."

"What do you mean?"

"Medokos needs us."

"He does?"

"I have been in communication with him for quite some time."

It was a revelation to me. "But why does Medokos need us?"

"King Seuthes died last year. He was strong enough to hold the various tribes together. But now the Thracians have fractured into regional powers once again. Medokos is the most powerful among the chieftains vying to be the new king, but cannot overcome the combined strength of the other tribes himself. The Spartans have unwisely spurned his overtures, so he has come to us for aid."

"He is using us, then?"

"And we will use him," Thrasybulus shrugged. "And we will both continue to do so as long as it is beneficial to our own goals."

For some reason, this logic disappointed me, as sound as it was. "Do you like the Thracians, *strategos*?" I asked, turning his own questions back at him.

Thrasybulus sighed. "It is not a matter of liking or disliking. You don't need to like someone for them to be your ally. Indeed, I have often found myself allied with those I have a profound distaste for, but the goal of defeating Sparta must come before personal enmity. Or personal ambition," he added more softly.

I was curious as to what he meant, but I did not press the issue. "But you haven't answered my question."

"Ha! There aren't many eighteen-year-olds who would challenge their *strategos* so directly! I see now why Lykos is fond of you. He has always lacked respect for authority, much to the displeasure of our father."

"I apologize, *strategos*," I said, chastened by his rebuke.

"No, no. It is no matter," he said, waving off my concern. "To answer your question, yes, I like Medokos. He is a shrewd leader who sees beyond the next sunset. I can work with him. His people – your mother's people – they are brave and skilled in war, like

Achilles and the heroes of old. But they are wild and unpredictable, Daimon. Their gods are ancient and bloodthirsty. I think you have seen that."

I nodded, recalling with a shudder how the priestess had slaughtered the prisoners.

"I fear them sometimes, too," Thrasybulus confessed after a moment of reflection.

"The Thracians?"

"The Thracians, the Skythians, the Makedonians… It doesn't matter. You have seen the skill of their warriors. How many Greeks could defeat their best in single combat? Even Lykos would be challenged, I think. But they fight only for honour and individual glory. That is their weakness. They squabble amongst themselves, stealing each other's livestock, raiding each other's villages. Gods help us if they ever learn discipline, lad, for on that day the wave that comes crashing down on Hellas will make the Spartans look like a group of boys training at the gymnasium."

We had arrived at the incinerated remains of the village gate. The odor of charred timbers and burnt pitch still hung heavy in the air. As if to prove Thrasybulus' point about the discipline of the Thracian regulars, a yawning, drunken guard watched us enter the village with bored interest, but made no attempt to question us. I thought that the *peripoli* would have made short work of such careless defenses.

I accompanied Thrasybulus to his hut.

"I enjoyed talking with you, Daimon. Sometimes I need a fresh perspective, and you have given me some things to think about."

"*Strategos*," I said with a slight bow.

Thrasybulus cocked an eyebrow at me. "Our Thracian friends have taken a special interest in you. I will make sure you work closely with Zyraxes."

"Yes, *strategos*," I said trying not to sound too eager. In fact, I was hoping to spend more time with Medokos' son.

Thrasybulus extended his hand. I looked at it dumbly for a heartbeat before belatedly reaching out myself. We clasped hands, general and common soldier.

"Get some sleep! We have much to do tomorrow," he said. He did not look tired at all.

"Yes, *strategos*." I was suddenly exhausted.

I found my way back to my hut easily enough. The steady light of a lamp pushed through tiny holes in the cloth draped over the low doorway. I ducked my head as I entered, wondering who might be within.

Nea rose from where she had been sitting. The flame of the oil-lamp flickered with the rush of incoming air, casting her rippling shadow on the wall behind her, like a shade from the underworld. The lambent light accentuated every hill and valley of her body, the curve of her breasts, the flare of her hips. The sinuous tattoos that ran up her arms seemed to writhe with a life of their own.

Only her eyes were unmoving, holding me as tightly as any bonds. Even in the dim half-light, I could see the green of her irises, dark like the sea in winter, calling me to fall into their depths. I did not resist their summons.

For the first time, but by no means the last, I disobeyed my general's order.

For I did not sleep much that night.


OUR CARTS GROANED UNDER THEIR LOADS of the grain. At the gates of Abdera, a delegation challenged us from atop the walls. "Why aren't you selling to the Athenians?" someone shouted down.

"They have neither gold nor silver nor wine nor oil. They are freezing and starving. We do not do business with beggars. But I hear you might pay better! " Zyraxes shouted in reply.

The men of the delegation were delighted to hear of the deprivations of Thrasybulus and his men. The constant poverty of the Athenian forces was well-known, so the lie was readily accepted. "We will gladly do better than their best offer, Thracian," the leader called down with a laugh.

The men vanished from their perch. Zyraxes winked at me. A moment later the gates swung open. The enemy had just let us into their city.

By all appearances, our party of twenty men and women were Thracian traders. We surrendered any weapons on our persons, but not those hidden among the carts.

Zyraxes, playing the part of a Thracian grain-seller, haggled hard and obtained a good price for his goods. He complained that he was being robbed by the hard-nosed Greeks of Abdera, but reluctantly accepted their offer. It was a performance that would have won a prize at the drama festival in Athens. Despite my anxiety, it was only with great effort that I stifled my laughter. I cast a glance at Nea, and her eyes flashed mischievously.

Nea turned away, watching with an eagle's intensity as the Abderan traders unloaded the sacks of grain. Her profile was strong and clean, her nose sharp and narrow. Her hand moved unconsciously to where a sword normally hung at her side, and her fingers fumbled absent-mindedly at the empty loop on her belt. I called Meli my Amazon, but their true descendant stood before me. She was fearless and tough, and her quiet focus only made her all the more alluring. I loved her with the passion and fascination that overwhelms all sense in a youthful heart; though much of her own heart remained hidden to me.

"We have been given permission to stay within the walls tonight," Zyraxes announced to our group in a matter-of-fact tone. "We will leave tomorrow."

Knowing looks were exchanged, but we kept up the ruse. We stabled our donkeys near the city gate, attended all the while by two guards posted to keep an eye on us. Our Abderan minders were happy to share the heated wine and sausage stew we purchased from a nearby tavern, for the chill of winter was upon us.

With a belly full of warm stew, I nestled with Nea in the straw in one corner of the stable. We held each other close under the patterned wool cloak, and I could smell the lingering scent of the stew on her breath. Nea burrowed in close but said nothing, as was her habit. She would go for days without saying a word, content to observe the world with a warrior's eye.

Sleep would not come to me. Nea's body expanded and contracted in my arms in the hypnotic rhythm of sleep. The snores of the other Thracians in our party reverberated through the stable. Zyraxes lay in a mound of straw with his eyes closed. Once his eyes cracked open and he saw me watching him. He smiled languidly and shut them once more. In this way we passed the slow night, waiting for the reluctant winter dawn to come.

The lamp had long since gone out when the first grayness of day crept into the sky. Two low whistles cut through the darkness, and shadowy figures rose from where they lay, seeking out their concealed blades.

And we struck.

Our guards, sleeping off their wine, awoke long enough only to realize that their lifeblood was draining from their slashed throats. Like a pack of wolves come down from the mountains, we moved silently and purposefully towards our prey in the gatehouse. The guards had not barred the inner door, concerned more about an attack from outside than enemies within. They paid for their laxity with their lives and the tally of dead men rose from two to four and then six.

Our good fortune could only last so long. A sleepy-looking sentry with a conical helmet appeared down a stairway leading to the top of the city wall. His eyes widened and his jaw dropped at the site of the dozen armed Thracians in the gatehouse. With a gasp, he spun and dashed back up the stairs, shouting a warning as he did so.

"Daimon!" Zyraxes shouted, but I was already after the fleeing guard. At the top of the stairs, the guard spun to face me. He scrabbled desperately at his sword, but it caught in the scabbard, and I hurled myself into him, thrusting my dagger under his leather chest-piece and into his belly. With the last of his strength, the man threw his arms around me and tried to mash my face with a headbutt, but I jerked to one side so that his forehead only glanced off my cheekbone. I twisted the blade up into his guts and his grip suddenly slackened as his final breath sighed in my ear.

I was still in the guard's limp embrace when something hissed past my ear. I turned just in time and a second arrow thwacked into the back of my corpse-shield. Four of my comrades sprinted past me towards the gray shape of an archer farther along the wall. I shook the dead guard off just as Zyraxes emerged at the top of the wall.

"The gate is open!" he shouted upon seeing me.

"We have to help them," I yelled, pointing in the direction of the archer.

But the matter was out of our hands. To his credit, the Abderan bowman held his ground, firing his shaft after shaft as his attackers rapidly cut the distance between them. Two Thracians were felled by the missiles before they reached their man. The last two cut the archer down.

But Zyraxes was busy peering over the wall. "Look, Daimon!" Laughing, Zyraxes clutched my heavy tunic and pulled me to the edge of the wall.

Below us, hundreds, thousands of hoplites were pouring into Abdera through the now open gate.

The *strategos* Thrasybulus and his army had arrived.

WE DELIGHTED IN THE SIGHT, shouting for victory, for it was a vindication of the plan born of the cunning of Zyraxes and the initiative of Thrasybulus.

Thrasybulus. *Keraunos*, his men had taken to calling him — the Thunderbolt — for his ability to appear anywhere and strike without warning. He had not yet lost a battle on land or sea. Abdera was just his latest victory.

The plan had been bold. To row a ship at night was extremely risky. To do so in winter was madness. But that is what Thrasybulus had done, bringing his army swiftly from Xantheira and disembarking a mile or so from the gates of Abdera. Gates that we had just opened for him. Victory now in hand, I marvelled at the sheer audacity of it.

The Thracians who had slain the archer trotted up to where Zyraxes and I were taking in the grand sight.

"It is beautiful, is it not?" Zyraxes exclaimed to the new arrivals.

One of the men, Dotos, looked at me uneasily, opening his mouth as though to say something, but nothing came out. He spoke to Zyraxes instead. "My Prince, we have suffered casualties." There was defeat in his voice.

I looked over Dotos' shoulder. In the growing light of the morning, the unmoving shapes of the men dropped by the archer's arrow lay where they had fallen.

It was one of those sickening realizations that is like the shock of plunging into cold water. My heart lurched in my chest, and with a cry I sprinted to the nearer of the two forms. The smaller one.

Nea's lifeless eyes stared up at me. The arrow had taken her cleanly through the throat. Moaning, I dropped to my knees beside her. I cradled her head in my lap. Her blood was tacky on my palms and fingers.

I whispered her name again and again, as though a gentle voice might wake her. I stroked her cheek, but it only marred her beauty with a crimson smear. Tears streamed down my face.

A quiet voice penetrated the tiny world of sorrow that had enveloped me. "Daimon." A hand lay on my shoulder. "Daimon," the voice repeated.

I looked up mutely. Zyraxes and the two other Thracians stood in a circle around us. An expression of pure heartbreak was etched on the prince's face. He held out a hand. Through eyes blurred by tears, I stared at him dumbly. Like statues, the scene was frozen there until the moment passed and I reached out to the extended hand.

Zyraxes pulled me to my feet. My legs were weak. "Come, my brother," he said. "Dotos and Basti will see to her. Let us go and find your *strategos*."

He led me away from where Nea lay. The taste of victory had lost its sweetness.

It did not matter. Abdera was only the first victory of many in the next year at which I would play my part.

Victories led by the Thunderbolt.

Thrasybulus.

CHAPTER 22

The campaign in Thrace was bitter and brutal. Almost single-handedly Thrasybulus was turning the tide in Athens' favour. With every rebellious polis brought to heel, more tribute, the lifeblood of war, trickled back into the treasury of the mother city.

After Abdera, I threw myself into the life of soldiering with almost fanatical fervour. War was my shield against the sorrow of losing Nea.

"You do not smile enough, my friend," Zyraxes said during a break from a sparring session. The prince often accompanied his father as the king moved to consolidate his power over the Thracian tribes, but whenever Thrasybulus and the king joined forces, Zyraxes kept his promise to teach me to fight like a Thracian.

"I will smile when I put you on your backside," I responded irritably, beckoning Zyraxes for another round. My hands tightened around the extended hilt of the *rhomphaia*. Zyraxes shrugged, brushed off some dust from his shoulder and picked up his own weapon.

To the side, Podaroes was taking bets from the gathered onlookers on how long I would last this time. I was pushing Zyraxes harder and harder, but no one ever wagered that I would be victorious except Tibetos, and I loved him for it.

My aptitude for battle had not gone unnoticed. After I passed my twentieth year, I was promoted to squad leader and then again to *pentekonteres,* in charge of fifty men. There were some grumblings, for I was young for such a position. I challenged anyone to a contest of arms if they doubted whether I deserved this honour. No one accepted.

By the time I was twenty-one, I was already a hardened veteran. The life of a soldier suited me, whether it was on the field of battle or swapping stories with Podaroes and Tibetos and the other men of the camp. There was a rhythm to it. It helped me forget.

Then the world shifted beneath my feet once more. Does the ground not tremor when gods walk the earth?

Alkibiades had come to Thrace.

*

WHAT CAN I SAY ABOUT ALKIBIADES? Everything that you may have heard about him is true.

His vanity was not without merit. He was as fine-looking as a statue of Apollo, every one of his features somehow finding the golden mean of perfection. Like that god, he kept his face clean-shaven, perhaps so as to better show off the even line of his jaw and his infectious smile. At an age when most people were gap-toothed, he had a full mouth of straight, white teeth. Even though his years were beginning to overtake him, the grey in his hair enhanced his presence rather than diminishing it. By appearance alone, this man could have seduced whomever he wished, whether it be the fickle mobs of Athens or the wives of kings.

Yet it was not by good-looks alone that Alkibiades achieved his success. Whenever he was present, all ears bent to hear his sonorous voice and flowing words until you inevitably found yourself aligned with his position. A witty comment or humorous tale was always at hand, and he could bring a smile to the most stolid of characters. In battle, he showed personal courage, the first to attack and the last to retreat. In the camps, he was not above sharing a cup of wine or meal with the common soldiers amidst cheers and laughter, and they loved him for it.

Alkibiades was brave, charismatic, and beautiful to behold. I deny none of these things.

I hated him.

I was not alone in my enmity. Those of us loyal to Thrasybulus grumbled to each other about how Alkibiades had usurped the authority and reputation that rightly belonged to our *strategos*. "Alkibiades has never won a battle without Thrasybulus, but Thrasybulus has won many battles without Alkibiades!" Perimander liked to remind anyone who would listen. Yet to our great frustration, Thrasybulus did nothing to counter the influence of the returning hero.

But this only fed a hatred I had nursed in my breast for years. I only remembered the kind face of my brother Heliodoros and how Alkibiades had sent him to a miserable death under the hot sun of Sicily. Alkibiades should have died there too but avoided that fate by fleeing to Sparta to escape his political enemies in Athens. Now

Alkibiades had betrayed his Spartan protectors in turn, returning, he claimed, to help the Athenian cause. Rumours persisted that he fled Sparta only because he had seduced the wife of King Agis and now the angry king sought retribution.

My hatred was my shield against Alkibiades' charm. Yet I must confess something here if I am to make an honest account of things.

I am indebted to Alkibiades, whom I hated, for he gave me the truest happiness in my life.

FROM THE DECK OF THE *Paralus*, the flagship of the Athenian fleet, one could almost imagine that Athens was at peace with the world and itself. In the distance, the temples of the acropolis shone like a beacon. Two grain transports were moored at the main dock and another sat anchored in the bay. Under a confident clear sky, smaller skiffs ferried passengers to and fro, many no doubt holding spectators eager to have the best view of the day's events. The city's most famous citizen was returning to the city for the first time in eight years.

Alkibiades was home.

The breakwater that guarded the entrance to the harbor was lined with the curious, who shouted and cheered as our ship slid through the narrow gap and into the protected bay. As the slow beat of the oars took us closer to the wharf, the jumbled mass of humanity began to resolve itself into individual citizens, many of whom sat upon derricks and windlasses for a better view. The rumbling din of excited voices carried over the water, occasionally accented by the keening cries of the greedy seabirds that circled overhead.

Alkibiades, standing with Thrasybulus at the front of the deck, leaned to say something to the general. Concern marred his beautiful face.

The returning demi-god was right to be nervous. Not all those who had come to greet him were supporters. The charges of blasphemy that had forced him into exile still hung over him. There was a very real possibility he would be arrested as soon as he stepped onto land. Or assassinated. I smiled at the thought.

Adjusting his robes yet again, the great man glanced back in my direction. I grinned wickedly at him. He looked away, turning back to reassess the mood of the throngs that awaited him, perhaps a little less certain of their intent than he had been a moment earlier. I laughed out loud at his discomfort.

"By the gods, you can't stand him, can you?" Perimander said beside me. Behind me, Tibetos snorted at the foolishness of the question.

Alkibiades did not know what to make of me. My relationship with Thrasybulus brought us into contact more than either of us would have liked. In front of the general, I spoke to him with polite hostility, but if Thrasybulus was not present, I returned Alkibiades' attempts to win me over with sullen silence or undisguised distaste. Evidently he had mentioned my lack of respect to Thrasybulus, for the *strategos* had ordered me to treat Alkibiades with the consideration his rank was due. I promised to do so but never kept my word.

My outward antipathy masked my own gnawing fears. Athens' favorite son was not the only person with threats of violence or prosecution in the law-courts hanging over his head. On the rolls I was still Gelon, son of Hippasus, but Piraeus was a small place, making it easy enough to be recognized if I was careless.

Thrasybulus had requested I accompany him back to Athens. "It does a man no good to be away from home and family for so long, Daimon," he said. It was the one argument that could have swayed me, for only the thought of seeing Meli and Lykos once again could draw me out of the refuge I had found in Thrace. In war.

"You are certain that you wish to return?" Zyraxes had pressed me before we left Thrace. He had arrived in Abdera only a day before the fleet set out. "You have a home here, should you wish it."

I resisted the temptation to accept his offer. "I cannot," I said, "abandon my *strategos*." Disappointment at my response showed on the prince's face. It had taken effort for me to say those words, for I loved him like a true brother. But there was truth in my loyalty to Thrasybulus. "Or my sister."

This seemed more acceptable to Zyraxes. His disappointment morphed into resignation and he forced a smile. "Then bring her back here, to her homeland! If she is your sister, she is also mine! I would lay down my life for her." I knew that he meant it.

"I see that your decision is made," he continued. "But you will take some of Thrace with you, Brother." He turned and called out. Two slaves appeared, each bearing a princely gift.

I could not help inhaling sharply. Lying across the outstretched hands of the first slave was a *rhomphaia*, its graceful arc sheathed in a patterned scabbard. Gingerly, I picked up the weapon. The oiled blade hissed as it slid from the protection of the wool-lined leather. A pattern of fine, ghostly ripples played across the polished, blue-tinged metal. It was a far cry from the battered weapon I had been training with. The beauty of its craftsmanship left me breathless.

Zyraxes was obviously pleased by the awe with which I held the weapon. "There is a Persian smith in our capital. He is quite mad, but his blades are both stronger and lighter than any I have ever seen. I have questioned him on his techniques, but he refuses to part with his secrets."

"I have no words," I said. It was true.

"But you must name her if she is to be yours!" Zyraxes said. The Thracians and other barbarians have an odd custom of naming their weapons. They believe that the name ensouls the blade, tying it to the person who wields it.

I rose. The balance of the weapon was perfect. I snapped a downward cut and the air parted with a susurrating sigh. And I knew what her name was.

"Whisper," I said, staring at the blade in my hands. I felt her pulse in my palms.

"She is well-named!" Zyraxes proclaimed.

"You honour me, O Prince," I said gratefully, and I bowed to him. Normally Zyraxes would have chided me for such formality, but now he was enjoying his role of a magnanimous prince bestowing gifts.

"And I would not have you clad in that battered breastplate like all those Greek farmers who pretend to be warriors!" He clapped and the second slave came forward carrying a leather-wrapped bundle. With a tip of his head, Zyraxes indicated that I should open it. My breath caught in my throat as I peeled back the folded leather.

I looked up at Zyraxes. "I do not deserve this," I said, staring longingly at the second gift.

"Promise me that you will return someday and it is yours," Zyraxes said.

It was an oath I agreed to eagerly. "I swear it."

"Then try it on," Zyraxes said grinning.

The night-black plates of the horse-hoof armour seemed to absorb all light. I moved about experimentally, astounded by how little the corselet weighed. "It will turn away the sharpest blade. The Sarmatians treat the hooves with some magic, but they guard their craft jealously," Zyraxes said admiringly. The prince became serious. "Remember, Daimon, when you are among your Greeks, that your ancestors are here."

But in my mind, the spirits of my father and Neleus whispered. "And in Athens," I added softly.

Zyraxes put his hands on my shoulders. "Then honour all your ancestors, Brother." At his parting, I wondered if I would ever lay eyes on him again, despite my promise to return.

On the *Paralus*, the shout of the helmsman pulled me back into the present. "Reverse oars! Reverse oars!"

The rowers responded instantly, beating the water into a churning mass of foamy whirlpools. The massive trireme's momentum kept it gliding towards the wharf, but it gradually slid to a halt not a stone's throw from the waiting crowds.

Alkibiades scanned the wharf anxiously, still uncertain of the fate that lay in store for him once he set foot in Athens again. The crowd grew more restless. There was a loud splash as an unfortunate spectator was jostled off the edge of the pier, momentarily distracting the impatient masses. I edged closer to hear what Alkibiades was saying to Thrasybulus.

"I do not see any that I would count as friend!" he said, waving his arm at the throngs before him. "The guards could arrest me!" Indeed armed men stood at regular intervals along the edge of the water.

"They are just to control the crowds. They will provide you with an escort. I will accompany you in any case," Thrasybulus said, trying to reassure him.

A man waving furiously from the front of the crowd caught the attention of Alkibiades. "Wait! It is my cousin Euryptolemos!" he said, his voice rising. "Yes! And some of his family and friends!" The presence of those he trusted had an immediate effect on Alkibiades. Confidence reasserted itself and he strode to the front of the deck to raise his arm to the crowd. He was rewarded with a chorus of cheers.

Sailors on the *Paralus* tossed ropes to eagerly waiting hands on the wharf. The lines tautened as the Athenian flagship was hauled flush to the landing.

Resentment filled me as I watched Alkibiades disembark into jubilant crowds. Thrasybulus walked behind him, eclipsed by the bright sun that was Alkibiades. The people cheered for the wrong man.

Alkibiades embraced his cousin. I turned my head and spat on the deck. When I looked up again, an icy hand gripped my heart, and I stepped back among the others on deck to be less conspicuous.

Among the well-wishers for Alkibiades was a man I recognized easily. The way he held himself would have made it possible for me to identify him even at a great distance.

The silver-haired Kritias grasped the hand of Alkibiades warmly, and the gesture was reciprocated. Was Menekrates there? I squinted, but I could not find him. I cursed aloud, drawing a curious glance from those around me.

My low spirits sank to new depths as Kritias and other supporters formed a protective ring around Alkibiades and escorted him through the cheering crowds until the entire lot of them disappeared from view. The majority of the raucous mob followed, leaving the wharf occupied mostly by dockworkers and slaves. Thrasybulus had gone, too.

We were among the last to go to shore. Podaroes wished me well and disembarked soon after Alkibiades. I hardly remember stepping onto the wharf with Tibetos and Iollas. The familiar odor of the docks filled my lungs, a mix of sea, wood, sweat and piss, all overlain by the queer sweetness of grain and wine. Feeling more tired than my youth should have allowed, I slung my *rhomphaia* over my shoulder along with a bulky, leather kit-bag.

I turned to Tibetos and Iollas to say something, but Tibetos was staring at something beyond me, his eyes as round as shields.

"Dammo?" The small voice behind me startled me as though I had been struck by a thunderbolt. I spun towards the source. Before I could react, Meli had barreled into me and buried her head in my chest. "Dammo!" she squealed.

My kit-bag fell to the ground, instantly forgotten. I clutched my sister tightly. In front of me, Lykos stood with a wide grin. The melancholy, uncertainty, and simmering anger vanished like so much flotsam, washed away by a wave of joy.

I was home.

## CHAPTER 23

"Ares' balls, boy! I didn't think it was possible, but you've grown!" Telekles said as he punched me hard in the shoulder. He turned to the others. "He's grown, hasn't he?"

Telekles had seen us first upon our arrival at the compound and had called for my other *peripoli* brothers, who now surrounded me and Tibetos, laughing and slapping our backs. Even Meges cracked a broken-toothed smile as we grasped each other's hands in greeting. They pelted me with questions, my horse-hoof corselet and the *rhomphaia* drawing the most attention.

"Daimon, son of Nikodromos!" Hermon strode through the rangers and grasped my shoulders. He stared into my eyes as though he was looking for something. "Yes, I would say that he has grown!" he said after an age and embraced me tightly. Hermon turned to Tibetos and subjected him to a similar examination. To a great cheer, the commander declared us both worthy to rejoin the *peripoli*.

Meli was radiant. The change in her was striking. My sister was no longer a girl. She was almost as tall as my mother had been, and she only needed to raise her chin a little to look me in the face. Her emerald eyes were as intense and hypnotic as ever, though they were now red with tears. The lines of her face were longer and sharper, giving her a fox-like grace to match her cunning gaze. Her boyish figure was gone too, something that was made more apparent by the rugged, brutish appearance of the grinning men that stood about us in the courtyard. But it was still Meli.

She broke her eyes away from me to beam at Lykos, and she placed her hand lightly on his shoulder. "I told you they were coming back! Did I not say it?"

"I have learned not to doubt your word," he said shaking his head in disbelief."

There was an impromptu feast of sorts that night. A few sheep were conjured out of nowhere and were soon reduced to well-gnawed bones strewn about the ground. Hermon had also opened the wine-stores, and the *peripoli* were happy to indulge themselves.

I had less time to drink, for I was busy telling the tales of our adventures, with Tibetos chipping in when I had forgotten something. There was a bit of the rhapsode in me that night. My voice rose and fell, drawing out the characters and exaggerating deeds in the nature of good stories. Meli sat close to Lykos as they both listened in rapt attention, and no one thought it odd that she should be there. Even Hermon leaned forward, as enthralled as the rest of them.

I told them of the rout at Ephesus and how I had barely escaped the scything blade of the fearsome Akras. There were nods among the *peripoli*, for the name of Akras was known even here. Meges surprised me by speaking up at this point. "We feared for you both when news reached us," he said solemnly. Hermon and Lykos exchanged a knowing look as I described the Spartan Lysander, but it slipped my mind as I continued.

The story moved to Thrace. The duel between Zyraxes and the Kikone I described in minute detail, moving about as I did so. I was proud to praise the prince's skill.

"And he has passed on that skill to you?" Lykos asked with interest.

"I look forward to showing you what I have learned," I responded with a bow, and the men clapped in anticipation of the battle they would witness in the next few days.

The smith Timonax was present as well. Whisper fascinated him. His finger ran gently back and forth along the blade, caressing the metal as though it were a woman's skin. "How does it get that color?" he kept repeating to himself. I thought he was in love.

The *peripoli* appreciated the ruse in Abdera, Meges in particular. I did not mention Nea's role in it, but from across the fire, Meli's eyes caught mine and I knew she had sensed the sadness I had buried deep within me.

Between ample gulps of wine, my *peripoli* brothers peppered me with questions about Thrasybulus' campaign through Thrace. My imitation of the bellowing voice of the *strategos* brought much laughter, and Lykos nodded in acknowledgement of the accuracy of it.

"So my brother led you well, then?" he asked.

"He is the best *strategos* in Athens," I declared sincerely.

"That he is," Lykos agreed, but softly.

Words exhausted themselves as they do, and men stumbled away into the darkness to find their beds. With a final embrace, Lykos departed, leaving only my sister sitting beside me to contemplate the dying fire.

"Prince Zyraxes told me I should bring you to Thrace. You would be welcome there," I told her.

Meli looked up with a smile, for I had spoken in Thracian. "Someday, perhaps," she answered in kind. "But for now I have a place here," she finished in Greek.

"You are happy with Lykos?" I asked directly.

"He is a good man."

"I know it."

Meli turned to me and put her hand to my cheek. "Do not worry about what you have lost, brother." I knew she spoke of Nea, though I had said nothing to my sister of what had happened. "The gods favour you. I have seen it," she said, nestling in close as she had done as a child.

We watched the last licks of flame play over the embers. As I thought about her words, something tremored in my heart, but I could not tell if it was hope or fear.

THRASYBULUS CAME TO THE *peripoli* compound some ten days after our return to Athens.

His presence caused a great deal of excitement among the men, for there was no one who did not wish to glimpse the renowned older brother of their captain Lykos. The *strategos* bore the tide of greetings and introductions gracefully and patiently.

At last he was led away by Hermon and Lykos to a location more suitable for a private debriefing. With a jerk of his head, Lykos indicated that I should join them.

Hermon's office served as a makeshift salon. The commander poured generous cups of uncut wine for each of us. Hermon made a curt toast befitting a soldier and we raised our cups. The commander, never one of limited appetites, drained his cup in a huge gulp. The abstemious Thrasybulus barely touched his own wine.

"And what of Thrace?" Hermon demanded of his guest. "We have heard from the lad," he said waving a hand in my direction, "but I would hear it from you, old friend."

Methodically, Thrasybulus gave his account of the campaign. Lykos listened intently as his elder brother spoke, giving me the opportunity to consider the contrast they presented. In profile, they shared the same long nose and slightly jutting jaw, though the *strategos* wore a thick beard in contrast to his clean-shaven sibling. But where Lykos was lithe like his namesake, the wolf, Thrasybulus was broad and barrel-chested, though not as much as Hermon.

In manner, too, Lykos was more akin to a wolf, disciplined in the hunt and comfortable in a pack, but driven by a hungry impatience and an untameable spirit. Thrasybulus was an ox, powerful and steadfast, with the patient temperament to pull a plough, but nearly unstoppable if roused to anger.

"And Daimon was of use to you, I presume?" Lykos asked, shooting a glance my way.

Thrasybulus let out a laugh. Lykos and I both raised our eyebrows at the novelty of such a rare display of genuine humor. "Indeed he was! I thank you, brother, for sending him my way," he said with a bow. Still addressing Lykos and Hermon, the general regarded me appraisingly. "Daimon is headstrong and rash, but fearless and skilled in war beyond his years. Did he tell you how he saved me from the spear of a crazed Thracian?" I had not, and Thrasybulus proceeded to relate the tale with ample embellishment. I confess that I swelled with some pride upon hearing my general's praise.

With some glee, Lykos then related my lone suicidal rush towards the Spartan warrior years earlier until everyone was almost in tears. The moment passed and everyone collected themselves once again.

Thrasybulus took a deep breath and pursed his lips, considering his next words. "But I bring important news." Thrasybulus frowned and placed his clasped hands on the table, leaning forward as he spoke. "Alkibiades will be named Supreme General of the Athenian forces."

The stunned silence that followed was shattered by the cursing of Lykos. Hermon scowled fearsomely at the news. In my own anger, I began to rise, but Hermon shot me a look to put me in my place and I sat down with gritted teeth.

Lykos leapt up and banged the table with such force that the near-empty ewer toppled over, dribbling the last dregs of the wine over the wooden surface. "How is that possible? Even Perikles at the height of his power was just one general among ten! The Assembly will surely reject the motion?" he cried.

Thrasybulus let his brother's furious incredulity wash over him. "I think the Assembly will grant him his wish," he said, taking an uncharacteristically large mouthful of wine.

Lykos turned on his brother in frustration. "You could speak against the motion. Every success of Alkibiades was gained by your victories. Your words will sway the Assembly so that they do not commit this folly!"

"Alas," responded Thrasybulus, "the gods have given me a voice like thunder, but not the rhetoric to match it. But if I recall, brother, the gods have blessed you with the gift of words to match that of Alkibiades. Yet you have always chosen to remain in the shadows, out of the public eye. A better assassin than politician."

"I have no standing with the Assembly. You have the power to do so now!"

Thrasybulus contemplated something at the bottom of his cup. "So you say, Brother. But it is a simple thing to ask others to do what you yourself are not willing to attempt, is it not?"

Still standing, Lykos glared at his brother. I shifted uncomfortably. An ancient argument was playing itself out again before my eyes, that was evident, but I could not fathom its origins.

The commander of the *peripoli* cleared his throat. "You said that you had need of the services of the *peripoli*, *strategos*."

Thrasybulus turned away from Lykos. "It is Alkibiades who has made the request, commander." The camaraderie of a few moments earlier had evaporated, replaced by polite formality.

"If it is in my power, *strategos*," Hermon replied.

"Alkibiades wishes to lead the procession to Eleusis for the Mysteries. The *peripoli* would be of great aid in ensuring that the road is safe."

Hermon pursed his lips. "He will open the road to Eleusis?"

"That is correct," Thrasybulus said, and patiently waited for Hermon's response.

Lykos was shaking his head. "It is too risky. The pilgrims will be completely vulnerable," he protested.

Hermon held up a hand to silence his captain. "No, I think not. But Alkibiades is a clever one, isn't he?" the commander said appreciatively. "There hasn't been a procession for six years. If the people are permitted to make the pilgrimage, then Athens will love him even more, won't they?"

"I cannot say what his motivations are," Thrasybulus replied noncommittally.

Lykos scoffed and folded his arms across his chest, scowling. I frowned in solidarity with him, but even I knew that Hermon was correct in his assessment of Alkibiades' intended course of action.

The procession to Eleusis was the most revered festival of the year, a pilgrimage west along the road from Athens to the holy city of Eleusis, open to any man, woman, citizen or slave. Only pilgrims were permitted in the sacred precinct, where they were initiated into the Mysteries through a ritual that lasted a day and a night. Initiates were sworn to secrecy as to what they had experienced, but no one came out unchanged by the experience.

My father had been initiated into the deepest Mysteries, but he never spoke of it. As children, Meli and I would pester him to tell us what occurred in that holy place, but he revealed very little. My stern father spoke with such hushed awe that it had frightened me: "The gods spoke to me."

But Spartan incursions meant the road to Eleusis was unsafe. Many believed that the temple had to be approached on foot, and the denial of salvation was a gaping wound in the spiritual heart of Athens. A wound that Alkibiades now sought to heal.

"The Spartans have been mostly quiet since they decamped most of the garrison from Dekeleia," Hermon mused, stroking his beard. "Even the Thebans haven't been sending in cavalry patrols recently. Alkibiades has chosen his time well. I suppose the Supreme Leader wants us to go on patrol and watch out for the enemy, lest they suddenly appear to spoil his grand gesture?"

Thrasybulus nodded in acknowledgement.

Lykos leapt to his feet, unable to restrain himself. "Surely you are not considering this?" he protested vehemently. "There is too much risk —"

"Captain!" Hermon cut him off with a bark. "Know your place! The *peripoli* serve Athens, not your own petty grievances! Not another word!" His baleful expression challenged Lykos to do otherwise. Lykos' trembling hands slowly balled into fists. Glowering, he took his seat once again, silenced by his commander's rebuke.

"You may tell Alkibiades," Hermon growled to Thrasybulus, "that the *peripoli* are ready to do their duty. *All* of us," he jabbed a finger at Lykos and me.

And under the *Moirai*'s busy hands, a new thread turned towards mine.

PILGRIMS CLAD IN THEIR SIMPLE ROBES and with satchels of provisions slung over their shoulders tramped past us in their hundreds. Men, women, the young, the old, crippled veterans, the wealthy and the poor, citizens and slaves of every station, all were equal in the eyes of the gods on this day.

The pent-up desire to receive the blessing of the gods had come out in a flood once Alkibiades had shrewdly declared his intention to lead the procession. Now many citizens, particularly the poorer classes, regarded him as only a little less exalted than the deities themselves.

The great man himself was at the head of the line of pilgrims snaking along the road. I glared at him from where I stood with Meges on the lookout for phantom Spartans and Boeotians. Alkibiades glanced over at us as he trod by in triumph, flashing a smile as he recognized me. I wanted to smash his white teeth down his throat.

Behind Alkibiades, the river of chanting initiates seemed never-ending. Occasionally, some of the pilgrims would cry out fervently to the gods, so overpowering was the divine presence within them.

Beside me, Meges rolled his eyes. "They always call to the gods, but you never hear the gods answer back, do you, boy?"

I shook my head.

"It is nothing but a trick by those Eleusinian whore-mongers," Meges sneered. I gave a what-can-you-do shrug, but the wiry killer was not put off. I was a captive audience and Meges was not about to let the opportunity to lecture me slip by.

"Those turd-sniffing priests stuff them all in the temple and let them stew there until dark,' Meges said with a toss of his head towards the initiates. "Then the priests make them all drink some bad wine that makes them all go off their heads so that they think they are talking to the gods when all they're doing is blathering to the raving fool next to them. By the gods, I've had some wine like that in my time! The next morning when they sober up, they think they've had a conversation with Zeus or Athena!" He shook his head in disgust before spitting on the ground. "Dung-eating Eleusians," he muttered for good measure.

Out of boredom and irritation, I challenged him to explain how he knew these things to be true, since he himself had never participated in the Mysteries, and initiates swore oaths never to reveal what they had witnessed. Meges spluttered and evaded, claiming that he heard it was so, but he could not remember who it was that had told him. When I pressed him, he cursed me for my insolence and stomped off to sulk on a boulder where he glowered at me and the pilgrims in equal measure.

I waved a dismissive hand at him and snorted at his stubbornness, though I was secretly pleased with myself for having won the argument. Savoring the small victory, I leaned on my spear and turned my gaze towards the flow of humanity before me.

And my eyes fell on her.

She was certainly beautiful. A delicate face, but with a nose and a determined chin that projected a little too much, giving her a proud strength. One cheek was streaked with dirt, perhaps where she had wiped her face with a sweaty hand, but it had the effect of endowing her features with even greater resolve.

A pilgrim's crown of white myrtle flowers sat so lightly upon her head that it seemed to float there, held by some invisible force. Tresses of her raven-black hair had come free, defiantly refusing to stay in the tight bun at the back of her head. A gust of breeze set her tunic fluttering so that she could have been a dryad caught away from its tree. And like a mortal in the presence of the divine, I watched, enchanted.

The girl was tired, I could see that. She bit her lower lip and kept her eyes focused on the road ahead. Her sack of supplies swayed rhythmically with each step, and I found myself willing her on.

The tip of the girl's sandal caught on a stone and she stumbled. She threw her hands forward to catch her fall, dropping her sacred stick and supplies. The garland tumbled from her crown to plop unceremoniously in the dirt in front of her.

The incident drew cursory glances from other initiates trudging past her, but they were too absorbed in their own trek to salvation to come to her aid. Without thinking, I let my spear drop beside me and in a heartbeat, I was kneeling beside the girl helping her with belongings.

"I am fine, stranger," she said hurriedly. Still on her knees, she shuffled forward towards the rod of myrtle, which lay just out of her reach in front of her.

"Let me help you, O pilgrim," I said picking up the branch and extending it towards her.

She picked herself up hastily, brushing the dirt from her tunic. "No, please. I do not require your —" she came up short as her eyes fell on me for the first time.

Her brow creased slightly before her eyes opened wide in recognition. "You!" she said simply. To my amazement, she reached out and clasped my extended hand in her own. Her skin was cool.

I stood frozen as though turned to stone. I was a *peripoli*. A veteran of the phalanx. A killer. Yet there I stood, paralyzed, with a young girl grasping my hand and staring at me. My voice had abandoned me.

Seeing my stunned expression, the girl gave a gentle laugh like a cascade of cool water. "Do you not remember me?" she asked. I frowned and shook my head. There was a flash of sadness in her eyes. Her delicate fingers dug into my hand insistently. "You saved me!" she said firmly. "In the market two summers ago, from the ruffians..." Her eyes gazed at me expectantly.

The memory broke through my mind in a flood. It was the thin girl who had been with her mother. My mood darkened, but I found my voice. "From Menekrates," I said in a low growl.

Anger flashed in the girl's eyes and she spat on the ground, grinding the wet puddle under her sandal. Her eyes met mine and her features softened once again. "I never had a chance to thank you."

Her dark eyes gazed at me with such intense sincerity that I could not hold her stare. Her staff with the supplies still lay where it had fallen. I stepped away from her to pick it up and I felt my hand slide from hers. I held the staff out for her.

"What is your name?" she asked, not blinking as she spoke. I felt as if a spell had been cast on me.

"Daimon." It came out more softly than I had intended.

"Daimon," she repeated slowly, as though tasting it. Her eyes dropped to my black scaled armour. She extended her hand hesitantly and ran a finger down one of the shiny plates. "You are a hoplite?" she asked. "Your armour is odd."

I waved a hand at Meges, who had stood up from his boulder and was watching the scene with interest. "We are *peripoli*," I said, as if that explained everything.

Throughout this, initiates had continued to flow around us just as water passes a stone in the river. There was some commotion farther down the road. A man dressed as a pilgrim was pointing and shouting in our direction. He was attempting to run towards us, but his apparel was hindering his efforts. The girl saw him and turned back to me. She was nervous.

The flustered man pulled up, breathing heavily with sweat dripping down his forehead. He was older, perhaps thirty-five or forty years of age. Like the other pilgrims, he was dressed plainly for the Mysteries, but his simple robe was made of fine wool. He addressed me in the clipped manner of the upper classes.

"Who are you, *pai*?" he demanded haughtily. He lifted his chin and stuck out his lower lip. He irritated me. I was neither a slave nor a youth to be ordered about. A low rumble began to rise in the back of my throat.

"I slipped and fell," the girl interjected before I could utter the insult that was about to pass my lips. "He was guarding the road here and saw me fall. He was merely helping me gather my things. No one else stopped," she added.

I pulled myself up to my full height, a head taller than the man. A *xiphos* sword hung by my side, and my *rhomphaia* was slung over my back. I clenched my fists and my knuckles cracked.

My looming, scowling figure made the aristocrat reconsider his position. He adopted a tone of restrained impatience. "Well, that is appreciated, but now she no longer needs your assistance. Be off and continue with your duties, man!" he said, waving me off.

I did not move. The man shifted uncomfortably under my unblinking stare. He was right to do so, for I was considering what offense the gods of Eleusis might take if I pounded one of their initiates into the dirt. It would be an excellent chance to test the theories of Meges.

From where she stood behind the man, the girl gave a tiny shake of her head.

Reluctantly, I swallowed my pride and anger. "It is my duty to protect the initiates of the Mysteries in any way possible," I said woodenly through gritted teeth. I took a step back to give the man some space to pass.

The man cleared his throat as if about to say something, but thought better of it. He took the girl by the arm and pulled her away, roughly enough to make me think twice about my decision not to do any violence. The girl gave me one last look over her shoulder. There was a pang in my chest, but there was nothing I could do.

The pair of them had only gone a few steps when I noticed that the garland of flowers still lay where it had fallen a few moments earlier. By some miracle, it remained untrammelled by the numerous initiates who had passed in the meantime.

"O maiden!" I called out.

Still held by the arm, the girl stopped and turned back, forcing the man to halt as well.

I bent down and swept up the crown of white blossoms. "You have forgotten something!" I held the garland aloft.

Before her chaperone could protest, the girl had broken free from his grasp and dashed back down the road to where I stood, her sandals slapping the packed earth of the road. She pattered to a stop before me, cheeks flushed and panting. She gazed up at me expectantly.

Holding the garland in both hands, I placed it gently on top of her head, as though it were an Olympic laurel of victory. The girl rewarded me with a radiant smile, and it was all I could do not to beam back at her.

I flicked a glance over her head to the man. He was decidedly not beaming with joy. The girl took my meaning, and she put on a face of such solemn piety that my guts hurt as I prevented myself from bursting into laughter.

She turned and trotted back to the waiting man. This time she did not look back, though the man cast one last venomous glare at me. I watched them recede until their robed figures were absorbed into the meandering stream of pilgrims.

His curiosity greater than his grudge against me, Meges appeared at my side. He handed me the spear I had tossed aside when I went to aid the girl. "What was that all about?" he asked.

"About?" I said absent-mindedly, not paying attention to him. I was still trying to catch a glimpse of the girl.

I finally turned to look at my fellow *peripoli*. He regarded me with a combination of wistfulness and sadness. "I can teach you many things, but there are some dangers I cannot protect you from," he said shaking his head.

"What danger?" I asked dumbly.

Meges sighed and slapped my shoulder. "Come. I don't think the Spartans will bother us today. Let us get back to camp." He turned and trod away, muttering something to himself.

Shielding my eyes from the sun with my hand, I strained to catch sight of the girl one more time, but it was pure folly.

With the realization that I would not see her again, I cursed my foolishness.

I had forgotten to ask her name.


THE NIGHT PASSED WITH AGONIZING SLOWNESS. While the secret Mysteries were being revealed to the pilgrims in Eleusis, I shifted and turned on my mat in the *peripoli* bivouac, impatient for dawn to arrive.

In the morning, I wolfed down my breakfast and gathered up my gear, eager to return to the Eleusis road to stand guard for the new initiates as they returned to Athens.

Rubbing the sleep out of his eyes, Meges could not resist needling me. "Anxious to be somewhere, boy? To watch out for *Spartans*," he said leeringly.

I did not take the bait. I just smiled at him cheerfully, which I knew was bound to irritate him more than any insult. With a look of disgust, he shook his head. "Just let me get something to fill my belly then. Wine, perhaps," he said somewhat predictably.

With no great haste, Meges prepared himself and we finally set out. At my urging, we found the same spot by the road where we had been the previous day. Resignedly, Meges plopped down on his boulder while I waited for the pilgrims as they returned to Athens.

It was afternoon when the first people appeared. The zeal shown on the previous day was replaced by a satisfied exhaustion. Dark crescents hung under their eyes, the result of their night-long vigil in the temple, but there were knowing smiles too, as if they were privy to a wonderful secret.

Alkibiades paraded by triumphantly, surrounded by his bodyguards and an entourage of animated hangers-on. If he noticed me, he did not acknowledge me as he had the day before. But even the sight of Alkibiades was enough to dampen my mood.

Yet I saw neither the girl nor the man who had accompanied her for the many hours I waited. Meges rose from his boulder only to stretch or piss, but was otherwise content to do nothing. The number of travellers began to wane. By early evening, Meges and I were left guarding a deserted road.

Walking slowly from his stone seat and working the kinks out his joints, Meges joined me where I stood. "I'd say we've done our duty, eh boy?" Meges said. I nodded dejectedly, waiting for the insult, but none came. Instead, he put his hand on my shoulder. "Some things are just not meant to be, boy."

We arrived in Piraeus as evening was falling. The streets of the port were already dark when we reached the torch-lit gates of the *peripoli* compound.

The first *peripoli* we encountered was Telekles. Upon seeing me, he chuckled. "Hermon and Lykos have been looking forward to your return, young Daimon," he said grinning. I pressed him to tell me more, but he went away on his own business, laughing and shaking his head.

Meges looked at me and shrugged. "No use delaying the inevitable, boy," he said. We made our way to the central courtyard.

Hermon was there in conversation with Lykos. Unlike Telekles, there was no trace of amusement on their faces. Scowling, the *peripoli* commander narrowed his eyes as we approached, an expression I knew usually preceded a torrent of abuse. I was baffled.

With obvious restraint, Hermon kept his voice level. "Come with me." Without another word, he turned. I looked to Lykos for help, but my friend, his forehead creased in a disapproving frown, indicated that I should follow with a sharp jerk of his head.

Still confused, I entered the main room of Hermon's headquarters. My eyes adjusted to the dim light cast by the oil lamps. My sister sat on one side of the large table in the centre of the room. I immediately wondered what trouble she had caused. But the ends of her lips bent upwards slightly in an enigmatic smile and a glint of mischief sparked in her wise eyes. Meli's view shifted away from me and I followed her gaze.

I had not noticed the person sitting there, a small girl with raven-black hair. She turned towards me, revealing her face. My breath caught in my throat.

It was the girl from the road.

Her hair was dishevelled and there were streaks of soot on her skin. Even in the low light, it was clear that her robe was filthy with dust and dirt. Yet she still shone, her face lighting up when she saw me. Behind me, Meges let out a drawn-out whistle.

Hermon waved a hand at her. "She arrived before sunset seeking refuge here. She said that you had instructed her to come. Do you know this girl?" Hermon demanded. I opened my mouth, but no words came to my lips. Exasperated by my silence, the commander turned to the girl. "What did you say your name was, girl?" he asked gruffly.

But she was not intimidated by Hermon's imposing manner. She smiled even more widely, her eyes never leaving mine.

"Phaia."

CHAPTER 24

Meli led Phaia away to the women's quarters to clean off the grime of her journey. I longed to say something but deemed it more prudent to hold my tongue. Phaia stole one more fleeting look at me before disappearing out the door, something that did not go unnoticed by the *peripoli* commander.

"Who is she?" Hermon demanded. "From the way she speaks, she is no slave, that is for sure!"

"I do not know," I said, keeping my voice flat.

Lykos snorted in disbelief. "I know you too well to swallow that load of goat turds. Answer the commander's question, Daimon!" he said, slamming the table.

I flushed with resentment at being interrogated like a boy who had been caught groping a slave-girl. Suppressing my irritation, I sparingly recounted the tale of our encounter on the Eleusis road, omitting the fact that years earlier it was Phaia whom I had rescued from that vile bucket of dung, Menekrates.

"How did she know to seek you out here?" Hermon asked suspiciously.

"I told her I was *peripoli*," I said staring at the wall.

"Why did you tell her that?" Lykos asked.

"She asked."

"Why did she wish to know?" Lykos pressed.

I had had enough. "I don't know," I growled defensively, turning to face him. "Why don't you ask her?" Lykos' eyes widened at the insolence in my voice.

"Ha!" Hermon barked a mirthless laugh. "She is the only person who can evade questions better than you, boy!" He scooped up a cup of wine on the table and drained it in a few sloshing gulps.

"She cannot stay here, Daimon," Lykos said pointing at me.

"What does it matter to you?" I sneered at him.

Lykos threw up his hands in frustration. "This is no time for your pig-headedness, Daimon! If it were some slave-girl or tavern wench, I would not care." My blood rose further and I began to speak, but Lykos cut me off. "But she speaks like an aristocrat. Whoever she is, people will be searching for her. What is to stop them from tracking her here? By Zeus, Daimon! Kritias and his depraved son would see you dead if they knew you had returned. You cannot take an aristocratic girl away from her family without their consent. It is — "

There was reason in Lykos' words, but I was deaf to it. My temper snapped the bonds that had been restraining it. "Who are you to lecture me on consent?" I hissed, jabbing my finger into Lykos' chest. "Am I not the son of an aristocrat? Did you come and seek my permission before you took my sister to your bed? Where is your respect for me as the head of my family?"

For once it was Lykos who was at a loss for words. I seized on his speechlessness to press my attack. "I do not heed the words of hypocrites like you! I did not ask the girl to come here. I did not even know her name until she uttered it just now. A man who steals girls away without their family's consent has no place accusing others of that crime!" I was shouting at him now.

A blush of anger and shame infused the face of my mentor. His hand shot out to grab my corselet, and I swatted it away fiercely. Our fists sprang up simultaneously and we would have come to blows if it had not been for Hermon.

"Stop it!" the commander bellowed, stepping between us. It took the great strength of his massive arms to shove us apart. "Cease!" Breathing heavily, Lykos and I glared at each other across the barrier of Hermon's bulk. "This matter will not be settled tonight. Tomorrow, you two can beat the living Hades out of each other for all I care, but tonight there will be peace!"

I drew myself up straight in my best soldierly fashion and turned to face Hermon. "Permission to return to quarters, Commander?"

Hermon granted my request with a backhanded wave. Ignoring Lykos, I spun on my heel and marched out of the building.

I trod across the torch-lit compound in a storm of conflicting emotions. Lykos was right in pointing out the danger, of course. But the thought of casting the girl out brought out a jealous rage in me.

*Phaia.*

I repeated the name in my mind, not daring to say it aloud lest it lose its magic by my uttering it. My heart swelled at the memory of her face, and my anger at Lykos ebbed away.

Exhaustion stalked me, but I was in no mood to return to the barracks and face another interrogation from my curious comrades.

Instead I wove through the shadowy labyrinth of the *peripoli* compound, finding refuge in a deserted workshop. The familiar smell of charcoal dust and iron and scorched clay brought forth memories of mindless hours of toil under the watchful eye of Neleus. I lifted a hammer, feeling its familiar heft. With a frustrated sigh I let the tool fall to the ground with a thud. I plopped down on a stool and rubbed the weariness from my face.

"Dammo?"

Awake in an instant, I leapt up in surprise. Meli stood in the doorway, illuminated by a lamp in her hand. I exhaled my held breath, feeling the tension leave my body. "How did you find me, Amazon?" I said wearily.

Meli laughed lightly. "I can always sense where you are, Brother."

I did not speak of my argument with Lykos. "I don't feel like talking right now, Meli."

"Even with Phaia?"

I looked up and my chest tightened. Behind my sister stood Phaia, no longer begrimed by the dust of her journey. She was wearing a fresh tunic, and her hair was brushed and braided.

"I think you two have much to talk about, Brother," Meli said with a cryptic smile. She stepped aside and Phaia came forward into the light. I glanced at my sister in a mute appeal for assistance, but she had already melted away into the darkness.

Phaia stood in the soft light of the lamp cradled in her hands. Her chin dipped slightly but her eyes were locked solidly on mine, trapping me.

What seemed like an age passed before I was able to collect myself and break the spell that bound me. "Wait," I said holding up my hand. Phaia's eyes danced with amusement as I fetched another stool from a corner of the workshop and set it on the floor across from mine. "Please, sit," I said waving to it.

With unassuming grace, she took a seat. Her proud bearing radiated a privileged upbringing. Pulling up my own stool, I was painfully aware of my own inelegance and filthy appearance. The dust of the journey and dry stickiness of three days' sweat coated my body.

"Why did you come here?" I blurted. It sounded like an accusation and I fumbled for other words. For the first time in my life I wished I had listened to my childhood teacher Iasos' lessons in rhetoric.

She rescued me from my own clumsy tongue. "The gods told me it was my destiny," she said firmly, but doubt flickered across her face.

Confused, I leaned forward. "What do you mean?"

Seeing that I did not scoff at her claim, Phaia scooted the stool slightly forward. She bent her head forward, her eyes wide. "At Eleusis. The Mysteries," she said in a conspiratorial whisper.

I shook my head in puzzlement. "I don't understand."

Her forehead creased at my perplexity. Looking away, she bit her lower lip as she appeared to debate something with herself. Presently, she came to a private decision.

"I swore an oath to keep the sacred rituals secret," she said. I recalled Meges' assertions that the initiates were given a vision-inducing concoction by the priests, but Phaia said nothing of this. She continued. "But I will tell you this: I saw the gods. They spoke to me. I was frightened, but they told me not to be afraid. They told me..." She hesitated, biting her lip once again. Hardly aware of what I was doing, I reached out and placed my hand on hers. She did not pull away. Instead, she recovered her confidence and stared at me. "They told me that you were my destiny. That I should seek you out."

My heart filled with a torrent of shock and joy and the fear that comes when one plunges into the unknown. "I have not stopped thinking of you since I saw you on the road," I said rapidly. Suddenly, I was fearful that I had erred in revealing my thoughts.

Our secrets both laid bare, we each waited for the other to say something, but when no words came for either of us, we both began to laugh. It was the purest happiness I have ever felt.

But doubt began to erode my joy almost at once. "Who was the man you were with?" Phaia's expression darkened at my question. She took a deep breath and told me her tale.

Her father was Eurylochus, son of Eurysophorus. Like my eldest brother Heliodoros, he had died in Sicily, leaving his considerable wealth and property to his widow and only daughter, Phaia. Since there was no male heir, the property itself remained in limbo until a suitable male relative could take possession of it. Part of that property was Phaia herself, and according to Athenian law, the person who took over the property had to marry Phaia to legitimize his family's claim.

"My father had many cousins," Phaia explained. "They fought in the courts for their right to claim my father's estate. My mother was a strong woman and managed our household well enough on her own. She wanted to protect me. She played the cousins off one another for as long as she could, but it was inevitable that the day would come when I would be given away like a horse," she said with bitterness in her voice.

The man I had seen with her on the Eleusis road, she continued, was named Amphidemus, the cousin who had finally won the protracted struggle.

"I was to move into his household as his wife once we returned from Eleusis." She hung her head, considering her next words carefully. "I wish only to speak honest words to you, Daimon. In truth, he is not a bad man. I could have done worse, and I accepted my fate as a kind one."

She raised her head, and there were tears in her eyes. "Until I saw you on the road. Until the gods spoke to me." She buried her face in her hands. "I think I am mad."

As I wondered at her words, the declaration of Lykos that she could not remain with us gnawed at me. As if hearing my thoughts, Phaia seized my hands in her own.

"Will they send me back?" she asked apprehensively.

"I will not let that happen," I declared solemnly, though I did not know how I could make it so. "And if you have been touched by madness, then I too am overcome by it."

My proclamation reassured her. She released my hands and wiped away her tears. Regaining her composure, she straightened up on the stool, smoothing out the wrinkles in her tunic with her palms. "Then the gods have willed it," she said matter-of-factly. Her bright smile reasserted itself. "But I wish to know of you, Daimon, for I have wondered after you ever since that day in the agora. How do you come to be here?"

So I narrated my own tale, omitting nothing. In truth, I spoke with some trepidation, for I was ashamed of my circumstances. I owned no property besides my weapons and armour. I was not a citizen.

But Phaia did not judge me. Like polished bronze, she reflected my own heart as I recounted my saga. She cried when I told her of the betrayal of my family by Adrastos. She listened raptly as I described how Lykos and the *peripoli* had taken us in and provided us with a new home. She wondered aloud at the campaigns with Thrasybulus in Thrace and my relationship with Zyraxes.

Speaking of Thrace, I once again became aware of my own brutish, wild appearance, for I had not even shed my horse-hoof armour. "Do I not seem a barbarian to you?" I asked.

Phaia regarded me appraisingly, her eyes finally coming to rest on my hair. She extended a curious hand and stroked the dank tresses that hung there. "You remind me of fire, warm and safe." She turned her attention to my eyes. "And your eyes are green like the sea, deep and endless. Are fire and the sea not the most beautiful things in this world?" she asked.

"Not the most beautiful," I replied, and she clapped her hands in delight at my clumsy compliment. Her simple joy was my own.

And we spoke of other things, great and small. I soon discovered that like my sister, Phaia was wise beyond her years, as sharp as a honed blade and as quick-witted as any rhetorician in the law-courts.

The darkness slipped away with the coming of dawn. Somewhere in the compound, a cock crowed. We marvelled at how the night had passed without our noticing.

A sleepy slave shuffled into the workshop to prepare for the day's work. His eyes grew round at the unexpected sight of a begrimed warrior holding the hands of a well-groomed young woman.

"I should return to your sister," Phaia said, standing up. I nodded reluctantly, rising to follow her and leaving the confused slave behind.

We stopped at a doorway. "I know how to get back from here," she said. "You must get some rest." She laid her hand on my cheek and rose up on her tiptoes to kiss me. It was light and feathery, and before I could recover from my stunned state, she had vanished, leaving me to wonder if it had all been a dream.

LYKOS WAS WAITING FOR ME in the barracks. A low rumble began building in my throat, my hands tightening into fists. If there had been doubt the night before, now there was none. I would fight anyone for Phaia.

Lykos raised his hands in appeasement. "Daimon, I do not come to —" He struggled to find his words, eventually just exhaling loudly. "Just sit down," he said, waving towards a stool.

Dark circles hung beneath his eyes, making him look older than his years. "Daimon, I should not have accused you last night. I apologize for that."

"And what of Phaia?" I responded coldly.

He gave the sigh of a defeated man. "Your sister has convinced me that it would be ... unjust to make Phaia leave, if indeed she wishes to stay." Despite my suspicion, his words elicited a twinge of sympathy in my breast. It would have been an ordeal for any man to withstand Meli's stubborn persistence.

But I was like a stray hound on the street, unwilling to back down from a fight. "Are these your words or my sister's?" I sneered. I turned my back to leave.

"By the gods, Daimon! Be reasonable for once in your life!" Lykos exploded, and I spun on him ready to strike. He leapt up from his stool, hands raised.

We glared at each other, frozen. It was Lykos who thawed first, as was his nature, for he was always a better man than me.

He sat down heavily and massaged his forehead with the heel of his hand. "Daimon," he said, "You have changed."

My mouth opened to protest, but my mentor and friend held up his hand to silence me. "Just hear me out and I will leave you in peace." With great effort, I swallowed my anger and let him speak.

"War," he began, "can twist a man. I have seen it too many times not to recognize it. I have seen the seeds of it in your eyes and manner since you returned.

"Some men come to love war and death as others love wine. Without a spear in their hands, their fingers tremble at its absence. In sleep they find only evil visions instead of restful slumber. In peace, there is only suffering, for war is for them the lotus plant that takes away the painful memories that haunt them."

"I am not that person," I mumbled.

"Are you certain?" Lykos asked. There was sadness in his voice. "I was once like you are now. Sometimes it is as if I am staring at a reflection in water. Your sister has seen it too."

I said nothing.

"Your sister told me that it is the will of the gods that Phaia is here. Who am I to argue with the gods? Or your sister?" he added, a trace of a smile on his lips.

As quickly as it had come, my anger was dissipating like morning mist. My previous harsh words towards my friend suddenly filled me with shame and I told him so.

He sighed. "There is no dishonour in fighting for those you love," he said, arching an eyebrow. I was embarrassed at his words, but did not contradict him. We embraced and parted as friends once more.

Exhaustion overcame me. I collapsed on a bed, and in moments, the torrents of thoughts rushing through my mind were replaced by a mercifully dreamless sleep.

## CHAPTER 25

The war dragged on. But I was happy. As was Phaia.

I feared that she would wilt under the strict discipline of Lampita, but she did not. She laboured with the other women of the compound, inseparable from my sister. Her bright smile flashed wide whenever I found her at her assigned tasks.

I shared my worries as she toiled with my sister over a large cooking pot. "It is more freedom than I have ever known," she said, grinning before leaning over and kissing me brazenly. Meli giggled delightedly at my shocked expression at this open display of affection. Lampita chased me away, screeching that I was disturbing the women. As I have said, I was happy.

There was no one whose heart Phaia had not won over. Hermon was wary of my sister, but for Phaia he had nothing but respect. He valued her counsel, especially in matters concerning the various alliances and enmities among the aristocratic families, of which she was particularly knowledgeable. "She has more brains than the lot of you put together," he had told me on more than one occasion

But no one approached my own love for her more than Meges. She could have been his own daughter and she loved him in return. His gruffness vanished in her presence and he did not even mock the gods when she was near, for he knew of her piety.

Phaia thought a great deal about the gods. In the darkness, when she was in that half-place between dreams and waking, she sometimes betrayed some of the secret knowledge revealed to her at Eleusis.

"Do you know what comes after this world?" she whispered airily.

"I do not know," I said, cradling her close to me. That was a lie, for I do know what comes, as much as anyone does.

It is misery. If we are buried with the proper rites, our shades find their way to the Underworld. Good and evil, rich and poor, it makes no difference. The dead crowd the bleak plain, worn out and feeble, together only in their loneliness. We carry with us the scars and anguish of life, our recollection of the light gradually dimming into a hazy, flickering memory. There we stay forever, or until the gods themselves pass into darkness.

But Phaia did not believe it so. "I will tell you, for I have seen it," she mumbled. "Ever-lasting life, with those we love. Never decaying, never aging. I will be with you forever. The goddess told me so," she said, squeezing me closer to her. She looked up at me, her eyes suddenly alert. "Do you believe me?"

"I do." That was a lie, too, but of what use would it have been to challenge her? I kissed her forehead. Satisfied, she closed her eyes once again. With an expression of pure serenity, she settled back into the slow, regular breaths of sleep.

And despite Lykos' initial misgivings, no one came in search of her.

"It is still too dangerous for her to go out," Lykos warned as we ate a meal. "As it is for you." He popped a fig into his mouth, watching me carefully to gauge my reaction. For once I did not argue the point. I had been going out on border patrols with the *peripoli*, but I stayed off the streets of Piraeus lest I be recognized. There were still those who sought to harm me.

In any case, before I could respond, Telekles ran into the hall where we took our meals. He was breathing heavily. A hush fell over the room as all eyes fell on him.

"Word has just arrived of a naval engagement in Ionia!" He took a deep breath. "Alkibiades has been defeated!" An uproar ensued. Men crowded around Telekles, clamouring for more details.

"Silence!" Hermon bellowed. "Silence! Let the man speak!" The din died down as anxious faces stared at Telekles. A major defeat could spell doom for Athens, but many also worried for kin or friends on the expedition.

"Was Alkibiades slain?" someone called out, defying Hermon's orders.

"He yet lives," Telekles responded, and the men once more broke into noisy debate. The pompous demagogue's uncanny ability to escape death had saved him again.

"Silence!" Hermon glared at the man who had shouted. "Start from the beginning, Telekles," Hermon urged, concern etched on his face.

"The fleet was at Notion blockading Ephesus across the bay," Telekles said. "The Spartans launched a surprise attack and fifteen Athenian ships were lost."

The collective tension in the room dropped palpably. Fifteen ships. A loss to be sure, but not a disaster. Had the Athenian fleet been destroyed, the war would have been over, with Athens at the mercy of Sparta.

"Where has Alkibiades gone?" Lykos asked.

"He set off for Phocaea to seek the aid of Thrasybulus." So Thrasybulus had not been at the battle. I glanced at Lykos. His face showed the relief that I felt.

"Who was the Spartan admiral?" Hermon demanded. "Kratesippidas? That fool couldn't defeat a fleet of fishing boats!" Reassured that Athens was out of immediate danger, the men laughed at Hermon's jibe at the notoriously incompetent Spartan navy.

Telekles shook his head. "No. Kratesippidas was recalled. There is a new Navarch. His name is Lysander."

I felt the hair on the back of my neck prickle, for I knew the name. Lysander. The Spartan commander with the predatory smile who had crushed Thrasyllus' army at Ephesus. Hermon glanced over to a frowning Lykos. Unease sat heavy in my chest, too, for I knew this Lysander was neither a coward nor a fool. More like a wolf, stalking his prey patiently until the ideal moment to strike presented itself.

Lykos made his way towards me through the rabble of debating *peripoli*. "Gods, I think I need a cup of wine," he said grabbing my shoulder. "I know where Hermon hides the good stuff."

It was an offer I was only too glad to accept.


ALKIBIADES WAS FINISHED.

Only his continued success had held his political enemies at bay. But the defeat at Notion was enough to destroy him. The fickle mob of Athens is quick to try and execute military leaders who have the audacity to fail. With the threat of a trial hanging over him, the god-man went into exile, fleeing to the protective arms of the Persians.

I happily prayed that he would rot there.

But my good fortune did not end with Alkibiades' spectacular fall from grace. Like a great ship, as Alkibiades sank in a storm of public fury, he took with him all those who had tied their fates to the success of his enterprise.

Like Kritias.

"He has fled the city!" Lykos told me, beaming.

"And Menekrates?"

"The snake and his spawn both!"

The news was bittersweet, for I felt my chance for vengeance slipping away. But it meant that I was free to walk the streets of Piraeus or Athens without fear of arrest and a trial. I was Daimon, son of Nikodromos once again.

Months later, I walked openly along the straight roads of Piraeus. I was on my way to the colonnaded shipsheds at the harbour of Munychia on the east side of the port. Thrasybulus had summoned me.

Thrasybulus was no longer a *strategos*. He had been deemed too close to Alkibiades and had been relieved of his position because of it. But not so close so as to have been exiled like Kritias.

I passed the ship-sheds that ringed the edge of the harbour, considering the purpose of the summons. I had some idea. A major trireme-building push was underway. Dozens of the warships were at various stages of completion. It had been decided to exhaust the treasury to build a new fleet. Much of the current armada was trapped in the harbour at Mytilene, blockaded and outnumbered by a superior Spartan fleet. A new one was needed to rescue them.

This was the reason for the frenetic activity all about me. The shouts of shipwrights and workers filled the air as they directed a cacophony of banging and hewing and sawing. The acrid smell of the pitch used to seal the hulls masked the more pleasant aroma of freshly-planed timber. I revelled in the scale of industry all about me.

All manner of men and women hurried to and fro on their business. "Get out of the way, turd-sniffer!" shouted a clean-shaven slave carrying a thick coil of rope on each shoulder, each one easily half the weight of a man. "Thracian bum-boy!" he muttered as he shoved passed me. I laughed, enjoying his impudence.

Thrasybulus saw me first. "Daimon!" His thunderous voice carried over the din of construction. He grasped my hand warmly.

"It is good to see you, *strategos*," I said, returning the gesture.
"*Strategos* no more! I am a mere trierarch now. If that is what Athens wishes me to be, then I shall accept that task gladly!" He laughed magnanimously at his new title of trireme captain but could not completely hide his bitterness at his diminished status.

"It is a great injustice, *strategos*," I proclaimed, still using his former title.

He waved my comment off but did not correct me. "We can only look to the future, lad. And that," he said pointing at the trireme sitting upon its scaffolding, "is my future."

That the warship was nearing completion was obvious. The bare wooden vessel was still not fitted with a mast. The protruding bow-ram had not received its bronze sheath, nor had any ropes or rigging been attached. But the hull and decking were done and the workers swarming over her like ants seemed to be concentrating on the finishing touches to the woodwork.

"She is called the *Kratebates*," Thrasybulus said with obvious pride.

*Kratebates*. Might-Strider. "A fine name for a ship, *strategos*," I said.

Thrasybulus snorted. "It had better be a fine name! I'm paying for her, every plank and rope and thole!" I managed to hide my surprise. It was no small thing to outfit a trireme. My familiarity with Thrasybulus made me forget that he was from one of the wealthiest families in the city.

"Epikydes!" Thrasybulus suddenly bellowed. "Epikydes! Come here for a moment."

A well-built man of middle years detached himself from the activity surrounding the trireme. His hard, intelligent eyes flashed annoyance. "What is it, Trierarch?" he asked, casting a glance my way.

"Daimon, this is the man who is spending all of my money," Thrasybulus said with a nod to the shipwright.

I did not know what to say, for I knew little of ships. "It is a fine-looking vessel, Master Epikydes."

Epikydes sized me up instantly. "Bah! What do you know of ships, boy? Couldn't tell the difference between a trireme and a donkey's fart, I reckon!" Before I could react, he turned, spreading his arms wide before the unfinished warship. "That, my boy, is my masterpiece, not a *fine-looking vessel*. She will be the finest ship in the fleet!"

Thrasybulus took up the shipwright's boast. "She is lighter with less draft than most ships, but reinforced in the bow for strength," he said pointing here and there, though it meant nothing to me.

"She will cut through the water and enemy ships with equal ease," Epikydes finished proudly.

My declarations of amazement seemed to satisfy the shipwright. He left us to shout at some of his workers.

Thrasybulus and I observed the construction for a few moments before he spoke. "A fine ship is nothing without a fine crew to man her, Daimon. I have been hiring the best rowers in Athens, but I need soldiers. The best. That is why I have summoned you: to ask you to serve as the captain of my *epibatai*."

*Epibatai*. Marines. In addition to the one hundred and seventy oarsmen, each trireme carried a complement of ten marines to repel boarders or to board enemy vessels themselves.

But I hesitated. "Would not Lykos be a better captain?" I asked.

Pain flickered across the features of the former general. "He would not serve under me," he said with a hint of loss in his voice. His normal resolve reasserted itself and he grasped me by the shoulders. "But I would have you, Daimon. You led men for me in Thrace with courage. And it takes your type of fearlessness to fight man to man on the deck of a ship. Will you serve with me once more?"

I could not honourably refuse such a direct request. "I will serve with you again, *strategos*," I declared.

Thrasybulus beamed. "Then it is done!"

I returned to the *peripoli* compound to face the consequences of my pledge to Thrasybulus. Neither Phaia nor my sister was pleased with my decision, but for different reasons.

"Poseidon is unpredictable and not easily appeased. In my dreams I see only mist and uncertainty." Meli clasped my hand in hers. Her customary assuredness quavered as she looked at me. "I am afraid, brother."

I attempted to assuage her fears. Thrasybulus was the ablest leader in the fleet, I explained, and general or not, I was fortunate to be among his marines.

Phaia remained silent throughout. Whenever I glanced her way, she looked down at the ground, her face tight with emotion.

My sister left us. Phaia assiduously avoided my gaze.

"I cannot refuse the *strategos*' request," I told her quietly. "It would be a cowardly act to do so."

Phaia raised her eyes. They were wet with tears. "I know what kind of man you are. I always pray to the gods to bring you back safely, and they have heeded my prayers."

I wiped away a tear that had trickled down her cheek. "Then what bothers you now?" I asked confused.

Her answer was barely a whisper. "I am with child."

Stunned silence became joy. Taking Phaia's wet face in my hands, I kissed her, and her contagious smile pushed its way to the surface through her tears.

"I give you my oath that I will return to see the birth of our child," I said. "Even the gods will not be able to stop me."

Phaia's smile vanished. She made a sign to ward off bad luck. "You must not challenge the gods, Daimon." She embraced me tightly, her cheek pressed against my chest. "You must not challenge the gods," she whispered.

She was right.


A MONTH LATER, I WAS ON the other side of the sea. The imminent peril of battle pushed Phaia's admonition from my mind.

From the deck of the Might-Strider, all eyes faced west. The Spartan fleet was now clearly visible, and the shouted commands of the opposing captains carried across the water as the enemy ships formed their lines to match our own. On either side of the Might-Strider, the triple banks of oars beat the water in unison to the slow pulse of the coxswain's drum, preventing the trireme from drifting out of line. The heartbeat of war.

A slight but constant breeze from the west stroked the sea into a gentle swell. The precariously-balanced trireme rolled with each sinuous wave, constantly shifting deck beneath my feet. A few paces away, Thrasybulus was gauging the strength of the Spartan ships arrayed against us.

I stifled a shudder. As before any engagement, the invisible, icy hand of the goddess Phobos wrapped itself about the heart of every man in the arena of battle, be it land or sea. I felt it too.

The spirits of death had been drawn to this place as well, circling invisibly overhead in anticipation of the feast of corpses that awaited them.

I squinted at the tiny island a mile to the north of us, a place whose existence had been unknown to me until the previous day.

Arginusae.

# CHAPTER 26

For honour and reputation, a young man will swagger and strut and taunt his enemy, even when death stalks him and his bowels are loose with terror. For there is shame in letting others see your fear, your weakness.

But the old have earned the right to speak the truth and admit their fears, so I hide nothing from you, Athenian.

The sea fills me with dread.

Poseidon is an unpredictable and arbitrary god. Some of our grandest temples are dedicated to him. How could it not be so? The sea has brought Athens her wealth and power. Yet Poseidon cares not for the sacrifices offered to him. He thirsts only for the lives and ships that he claims for himself.

I have never learned to swim. Most sailors and oarsmen can move through the water like fish, but I grew up in the winding maze of streets that is Athens. I would sink under the waves like a stone.

But whether a man can swim or not will make no difference if Poseidon comes for him. And should the Earth-Shaker claim a man, it is a fate worse than death, for being unburied, his soul will never find its way to the mindless peace of the Underworld. The sea-dead's flesh will be consumed by fish and crabs and tentacled creatures, his bones dispersed, and his spirit will drift forever in the cold depths, angry and impotent.

Sometimes I dream of pounding waves and saltwater filling my nose and throat and lungs as I am pulled down into green darkness, and I wake in terror, drenched not with seawater but with sweat.

And I tremble at the memory of Arginusae.

ARGINUSAE IS THE NAME FOR TWO ISLANDS just off the coast of Ionia. The name means 'bright-shining', which is true, for they are little more than gleaming barren rocks in the sunlight. A man could walk around the larger island in the time it takes to make a fire and cook a meal. They are nothing. But for one day they were everything.

We had beached the rescue fleet on the western island and set up camp for the night. We were making our way to Mytilene, where the *strategos* Konon's ships were besieged by the Spartan fleet of Kallikratidas. The plan was to trap the Spartans between our two fleets. It was a fair plan, as these things go, but it came to naught. The Spartans found us first.

The Spartans were now camped on the great island of Lesbos, only an hour's hard rowing from Arginusae. From the beach, the campfires of the enemy were visible across the strait as orange, star-like dots of light flickering on the horizon. The Spartans could no doubt see our fires as well.

From where we stood on the dark shore gazing out to sea, Thrasybulus regarded the distant lights curiously. "Kallikratidas is not as much a fool as I thought," he said, stroking his beard. He surmised, correctly as it turned out, that the Spartan navarch had split his fleet, sending the larger portion to seek us out and leaving just enough ships to keep Konon bottled up in the harbour at Mytilene. "The Spartans will have more than a hundred ships. The battle will come tomorrow," Thrasybulus declared.

"Can the Spartans be beaten?" I asked. I had never been in a naval engagement, but war is war. Strategy and experience win battles, and we had neither. We had one hundred and fifty ships, likely more than the Spartans would throw at us. But ours was a fleet manned by slaves, metics, freedmen, and merchants conscripted by a desperate Athens. They were lucky to make the trireme go straight. Thrasybulus and the other captains had been drilling their crews relentlessly in the month since we had departed Athens, but the fleet remained untested. In contrast, the Spartan fleet was rowed by the best oarsmen in the Aegean, attracted to the Spartan cause by the Persian gold that paid their wages.

Thrasybulus considered my question. He opened his mouth but exhaled with an air of defeat. "It is not my place to decide strategy." His outward show of modesty masked his frustration, and I knew he chafed under the command of those he considered his inferiors. It gnawed at his pride. Without another word, he turned and started back towards the fires of the camp and the crowded tent we shared with the officers of the Might-Strider.

But wisdom prevailed and two of the admirals came to sound out the thoughts of Thrasybulus, who had never suffered a defeat at sea. Lykos was there, too, conscripted under the service of the *strategos* Protomachus. I had no doubt that it was Lykos who had convinced the two admirals to swallow their pride and seek out his brother's advice. They leaned forward on their stools as Thrasybulus spoke.

"Use the islands to lengthen your lines and split the Spartans' fleet."

"And split our own forces?" asked the *strategos* Protomachus sceptically.

Thrasybulus placed a cup in the sand to represent our island. Our weak point, he explained, was a lack of skilled oarsmen. There was little doubt that ship for ship, the Spartans had the superior crews and in a straight fight would out-manoeuvre us easily. But the local geography offered some advantages to a defender. Less than a mile north of the island, the headland bulged out into the sea, which Thrasybulus indicated with a plate. Our right wing could be stationed between the north shore of the island and the headland, like a chain across the entrance to a harbour. This would thwart any flanking manoeuvres on either side, and the Spartans would have to penetrate a double defensive line of warships.

"And what about the centre and left wing? Will we place ships in front of the island?" asked the other admiral. It was Thrasyllus, Thrasybulus' old ally against the Four Hundred and the *strategos* who had led us into the trap at Ephesus. His hair had greyed, but his gruff, direct manner was the same as ever.

"The island will be our centre," Thrasybulus declared. "Our left wing will be deployed to the south of the island."

The visitors stroked their beards, looking for flaws in the plan, but they could find none. It was elegant in its simplicity. The island would effectively lengthen our lines by half a mile and protect our flanks. The Spartans would be forced to split their forces to deal with our separate fleets, for if they concentrated all their forces on one half of our ships, they would leave their flank exposed to attack by the other half. It was a strong defensive position that negated much of the experience of the veteran Spartan fleet.

The admirals rose and took their leave. "We will relay your ideas to the others," said Protomachus, shaking hands with Thrasybulus.

Thrasyllus paused as he passed me. He cocked his head. "You are Gelon, are you not?" He addressed me by the alias I had used when I had fled Athens four years earlier.

"Yes, sir," I said, surprised that he had remembered me. Despite the disaster at Ephesus, I held no grudge against him. Since Ephesus he had earned a reputation for leading his men bravely, if not imaginatively.

"And you still serve with Thrasybulus after all this time?" he asked. Thrasybulus watched the exchange with interest.

"Always, *strategos*," I responded. Thrasybulus chuckled.

"Then the gods be with you both," Thrasyllus said, and the two admirals departed up the beach to confer with their fellow commanders.

"Will they follow your brother's advice?" I asked Lykos as he made to depart.

"They are fools if they don't," he said with a shrug and followed his general up the beach.

I turned towards the surf, gazing at the flickering lights of the Spartan campfires across the strait. I thought of Phaia and our unborn child. And prayed the admirals were not fools.

AT DAWN, THE SEER OF THRASYLLUS made a sacrifice to the gods. The gathered generals and trierarchs peered anxiously at the spilled entrails of the sheep, eager to know what omens lay within.

The soothsayer held up his arms. "The signs are auspicious! Poseidon is with us!" he declared, and there was a murmur of relief among those present.

The seer was Barates, the same *mantis* whose confident proclamation had preceded the slaughter at Ephesus. Bitter experience had taught me not to put faith in soothsayers, Barates above all. I scoffed at the seer's augury, but beside me Thrasybulus paid me no heed. He was intent on the sky. "The wind," he muttered.

"What, *strategos*?" I asked.

"The wind is blowing from west to east. It is unusual." The sky was a great dome of blue over calm seas except for a few wisps of cloud drifting westwards. I shrugged, being more concerned about Barates' divination skills than the wind.

Yet it appeared that I had misjudged the soothsayer's talents. The admirals had adopted the deployment suggested by Thrasybulus. From where I knelt on the bow deck of the Might-Strider, a double line of warships stretched north towards the island where we had made camp. Somewhere to the north of the island was Lykos, deployed on the ship commanded by Protomachus. But our position was where the Spartans were most likely to attempt a breakthrough or flanking manoeuvre.

I crouched motionless on the central deck with the other marines so as not to cause the precariously-balanced vessel to rock. Most of the marines had eschewed clumsy spears for weapons more aptly suited to the narrow confines of a ship's deck. Along with a short-sword, an axe hung at my side, an inelegant weapon but brutal in close-quarters combat. A few marines had worn heavy bronze breastplates, but most, like Tibetos beside me, opted for leather or linen armour. I was clad in my black horse-hoof corselet. We used smaller, lighter shields, and each of us had a brace of javelins by his side, ready to hurl at exposed targets on enemy ships.

My helmet tipped back, I ventured a glance towards the rear of the ship. Thrasybulus was ensconced in the trierarch's seat under the arch that curved back over the stern of the warship. The structure provided little protection from missiles, but the four archers around him offered some defense. In front of Thrasybulus, the helmsman and boatswain nestled in the relative safety of the sunken central walkway that ran between the banks of oarsmen. The one-hundred and seventy rowers moved their triple banks of oars in unison to the slow pulse of the drum, holding our position as we awaited the Spartan assault.

And the Spartans came.

As Thrasybulus had predicted, Kallikratidas had been forced to split the Spartan fleet and attack our defensive position. The Spartan squadrons came at us single file, trying to penetrate our lines so that they could turn and attack from the rear. Up and down the line warships collided and became entangled in dozens of individual battles, the sounds of rupturing wood and the screams of men carrying over the water to where the Might-Strider held her position like a coiled serpent ready to strike.

The opportunity soon came. Three ships to starboard, a Spartan trireme broke through where ferocious fighting had torn open a gap in the line. With deadly grace the warship turned sharply and barrelled down on an Athenian ship trapped in combat with another Spartan vessel.

Thrasybulus reacted swiftly. At his bellowed command, the drum at the heart of the ship began to pound and the Might-Strider surged forward like a great beast setting off in pursuit of its prey. From behind my helmet, I watched in horrified fascination as the ships converged on the same point of empty sea.

If it had been any other ship, the Spartans would have out-raced us. The Spartan captain had made the same calculation. But we were on the Might-Strider, built for speed. The design of Epikydes proved its worth.

Thrasybulus had timed his attack perfectly. The bow of the enemy ship passed in front of us and I could see the men scrambling on her decks as they braced for impact. Thrasybulus shouted from the stern. "Hold!" Sucking in one last lungful of air, I bent my head forward.

The collision was devastating. The stern timbers of the enemy hull shattered with a sickening wet crack like snapping bone and our ramming beak pierced deep into the vessel's bowels, crushing in an instant a score or more of the packed rowers trapped within. The jarring impact sent me and the other marines skidding forward on the deck, knees and elbows scraped raw on the rough surface while cool water splashed over us. With a lurch our trireme recoiled as if taking a deep breath, but the two warships were still locked together, a tangled mass of wood and metal and rope and living flesh. I leapt to my feet, shield up and a javelin in my hand.

The air was a confused mass of screams. Captains and steersmen shouted orders. Marines roared their war-cries. Above all was the pitiful wailing of the trapped, the wounded, and the dying. The booming voice of Thrasybulus cut through the din, instantly recognizable. "Back water! Back water!" Oars churned the sea in a reverse stroke. The ship groaned in protest but refused to release her victim. We were stuck fast.

Their ship holed and flooding, the enemy would attempt to board the Might-Strider and massacre her crew. We would try to stop them and do the same to their ship. It would be a land battle at sea.

Pandemonium reigned on the enemy deck. Oarsmen fought each other to escape the rapidly flooding space below decks, only to be cut down by our arrow and javelin fire. The wounded blocked those below and the desperate pleas and screams of the dying rowers chilled the soul. Any who evaded our missiles plunged over the opposite edge of their ship, risking the perilous swim to shore rather than face us.

From the enemy deck, a grapnel arced through the air and landed near the stern deck of the Might-Strider, the rope becoming taut as the grapnel's teeth bit into the wooden flesh of our ship. More clawed hooks dug into our ship and tangled in the rigging. One of our own sailors leaned over the edge of the ship to hack at one of the lines, but an arrow plunged into his exposed back and with a scream he crashed into the beating oars below, throwing the finely synchronized strokes into a flailing mass of confusion. If we could not disengage the Might-Strider, we ourselves would be easy prey for another Spartan ship.

The enemy marines had been massed on the wide forward deck of their ship, but now were trapped there by their own fleeing oarsmen. Our way was clear.

"Board the enemy ship!" I yelled.

One of our marines made to say something but never had the chance as an arrow took him in the side of the neck and protruded out the other side. His eyes widened in shock as he collapsed on the ground clawing at the shaft in his throat.

"Shields up!" I roared just as a volley of arrows hissed passed me. There was a scream far behind me and I snatched a look back towards the stern. One of our bowmen lay on his side clutching the wooden shaft buried in his belly while another spun away as another arrow struck his shoulder.

Enemy archers were firing at will from the stern of their ship. From their vantage point they had a clear shot straight down the line of our own vessel. Upon loosing a shot, the archers would duck behind the shelter of leather blinds that shielded their captain. Another arrow flickered overhead, striking our last bowman in the thigh. Thrasybulus, still shouting orders, sat exposed in the captain's chair.

The madness of the *aristeia* seized me, its power infusing my being with strength and speed and the euphoria of battle. I threw down my shield and howling a war-cry, I yanked my axe from its leather belt loop and took two great strides to jump the gap to the Spartan trireme. An archer stepped out, pulled the bowstring, aimed and loosed his shot.

The arrow hit me hard under the left breast, like a punch. But the black horse-hoof armour held and I landed hard in front of the bowman. My axe came down on the base of his neck in a great hewing blow and his lifeblood sprayed across my face. Ripping the axe free, I turned on the remaining archers, screaming, and then I was among them, slaying them with sword and axe.

The grey-bearded captain roared his own challenge and tried to cleave me in two with a *kopis* sword. I do not know if he was a Spartan or not, but it did not matter for he was old and slow and I was young, battle-madness surging within me. I dodged the clumsy blow with ease before chopping him down. Splattered with gore, I spun towards the helmsman, who, eyes wide with terror, turned and hurled himself into the sea.

I whirled to face down the length of the ship. Oarsmen were still trampling each other to escape and I waded into them, butchering without mercy. They should have overwhelmed me, for a lone man is no match for a mob, but they were mad with fear, like sheep spooked by a wolf, and they died like sheep.

The others had come across now and joined me in the slaughter. Tibetos was beside me, howling like a madman. One of our men slipped on the blood and the oarsmen fell on him like a pack of wolves and we waded into the melee in turn, hacking and slashing indiscriminately. The mass of sailors parted before our blades, flinging themselves into the sea rather than face certain death on deck. We pushed towards the enemy marines, still trapped on the bow. They were not Spartans but whether they were Corinthians or Megarians or Syracusans I will never know. With their crew slain, their will to fight had vanished and fear gripped them. They threw down their weapons and begged for mercy, but we gave none, for they would have shown none had our roles been reversed.

The Might-Strider was still ensnared. I pointed at one of the taut lines that held the Might-Strider like a fish on a hook. "Cut the ropes!" We began to hack and slash, each cord snapping like a whip when severed.

There was a wet, grating moan and the deck lurched underfoot as the Might-Strider slid backwards and pulled free of us. Thrasybulus ran the length of the ship to the rapidly receding bow. He cupped his hands to his mouth. "Daimon! The battle is turning! Victory is near!"

What victory Thrasybulus was speaking of I was not certain, for I saw only chaos in the seas about me. The ordered lines of warships had degenerated into a watery field of half-submerged wrecks and individual battles. I could not tell friend from foe. Half a mile away, smoke rose from a ship that had been set alight.

"Go!" I shouted back, waving. The Spartan ship suddenly listed beneath me and I almost toppled into the sea.

"We'll come back for you!" Thrasybulus called.

I waved but did not reply, for the Might-Strider was already too far away. There was a flurry of oars and the warship came to a halt. The left bank of oars rose in the air while the right ones bit deep in the water and in a graceful arc the ship turned itself around in less than two boat-lengths. We watched in silence as Thrasybulus led the ship once more into battle.

There was nothing to do but wait.

KALLIKRATIDAS AND HIS FLEET HAD BEEN DEFEATED. That much was evident, for we witnessed the pursuit as their ships fled to the south. From our vantage point on the crippled Spartan trireme, we could not know the scale of the victory. The seabirds did not care who had vanquished whom, but only the unexpected meal provided by the corpses bobbing in the sea about us.

Some triremes passed us in the distance, heading north to Arginusae. We shouted and leapt, but they either did not hear us or ignored our call.

One of the marines, a man named Mnesus, opted to take his chances with the sea. He shed his armour and dove into the water. We were a mile or so from the mainland, but whether or not he survived the swim I do not know. For me, the boy from the streets of Athens, it was never an option. I could only await rescue.

Yet no salvation came. A pall of brooding clouds usurped the sky. The sea began to roll and the wind whipped the foam-flecked waves into a sea of angry whitecaps. My hope of rescue dimmed. I knew that captains would be reluctant to take their easily-swamped triremes out in such rough seas. We clung to the half-sunken ship amid waves that rose higher and higher.

Charcoal clouds billowed above us. The wind came in gusts and buffeted us from all sides. Poseidon was angry and I cursed the soothsayer Barates, for it was he who had boldly declared the sea-god to be our ally on this day.

Tibetos saw it first. "There!" He pointed to the north-west. A squall scarred the surface of the water, giving it a rough, scaly look. Wrecks that had been visible only a few moments earlier had been engulfed by the gale. Our despair rose as the black water raced towards us.

I seized one of the rigging lines. "We must secure ourselves!" I hurriedly made a makeshift harness for Tibetos and myself, wrapping and knotting the line through the spokes of the outrigger. The other marines, seeing what we were doing, did the same. The oarsmen still trapped below wailed and begged for the gods to save them.

The first blast hit us. I feared we would be swamped by the surging waves, but the boat fought stubbornly to stay above the churning seas around us. Salty water stabbed at open wounds and rain bit at the skin like tiny teeth. Very soon I felt nothing for the cold had numbed my skin to the point of senselessness, and only the exertion of holding on to Tibetos kept me warm. The sea about us seethed and roiled, but the boat still held. In my madness, I laughed.

And Poseidon heard me mocking him.

The full savagery of the storm came with the night. The sea god threw his full might against us, pounding the warship with ripping winds and tearing waves that threatened to flay both flesh and timber. Surging crests lifted our vessel as though it were nothing more than a child's toy, only to let it plunge into a trough, and with each descent my guts heaved and I felt we would be smashed to splinters, yet each time I thought we would surely perish, the ship shuddered but remained intact, and then we would rise up once more.

My eyes were shut tight against the wind-driven needles of rain. But when I dared to open them, it made no difference, for blackness enveloped us so completely that I thought I had been struck blind. No lightning accompanied the raging storm, and the darkness pressed all around us.

I was not deaf, though I wish I had been. The howling winds and the screams of the men clinging to the ship mingled such that they became indistinguishable from one another. There were other creatures in the darkness, sea-demons and monsters from the depths, their malevolent shrieks and calls piercing the night as they feasted on the bounty of human flesh that Poseidon had granted them.

The storm peaked in its fury, the angry roar drowning out all other voices. Tibetos' firm grip suddenly slackened and my fingers tightened around his wrist. My thews nearly snapped as the beasts and waves tried to tear him from my grip, but I held fast.

In the clawing darkness of the storm, I forgot to pray. I only shouted out to Phaia, begging her forgiveness, for I had broken my promise to her to be with her when our child was born. And I cursed Poseidon, screaming obscenities at him.

The sea god grew tired of his fit of rage. Almost as suddenly as the tempest had appeared, it subsided. The sea eased and the winds died away and the sky was full of stars. The constant roar had vanished and only the lapping of waves against the hull and my own ragged breathing remained. My fingers still clutched Tibetos' wrist. I called out to him but there was no answer. I shouted, but my throat was so swollen that it came out as a hoarse squeak.

As soft as the breeze around us, the first glimmerings of dawn came. Tibetos was alive but unconscious. There was an angry welt over his eye where something had struck him. He moaned as I shook him but did not awake. I squinted, looking for others in the half-light.

Our fellow *epibatai* had vanished, stripped away in the night, along with the front third of the trireme. The trapped oarsmen had either been sucked out of the ship or still sat entombed below. I pulled Tibetos up to a more stable position and looked about.

Another wreck floated an arrow-shot away, but it was barren of life. The other ships that had been visible the evening before had simply vanished.

The sea was not empty, however. The detritus of one hundred ships littered the water. Shredded canvas, oars, shattered timbers and every other kind of flotsam. And the dead.

In the ocean of corpses and debris, the wreck bobbed in the gentle swell, threatening to lull me to sleep, but I dared not close my eyes for I knew that it would be the death of me and Tibetos both. The sea was patient.

An age seemed to pass. A new sound touched my ears. A pulse, from the east, growing louder with each passing moment. I shielded my eyes against the morning sun. Three warships approached, their oars rising slightly ahead of the sound of the beating drum. I waved but my voice failed me. The triremes turned a shade. They had seen me.

The realization that the ships might not be our own suddenly came to me. If it were so, we would be killed. Such was the fate of marines, sailors, and rowers who found themselves at the mercy of an enemy vessel. Even if it were our own triremes, we might be mistaken for Spartans in any case and dispatched before anyone became aware of the error. It was a common occurrence. But exhaustion overwhelmed me, and I resigned myself to my fate.

The prow of the lead ship loomed closer. A half-mad laugh spilled from my lips.

It was the Might-Strider.

My shoulders still heaved with voiceless laughter as Thrasybulus' ship bumped up against the wreck. I was too weak to pull myself up. Ropes appeared and some of the seamen clambered down. Lykos was first among them.

"Tibetos!" I rasped. The men managed to get him on board and then came back for me.

Lykos kissed my forehead. "Your sister would have killed me had I let you die, you mad fool!" Tears of relief and joy rolled down his face.

"She still might," I said, smiling wanly.

Thrasybulus himself helped haul me to the deck of the Might-Strider. "I am sorry, Daimon," was the only thing he said to me. There was shame in his eyes.

I waved him off and collapsed. Darkness came as I slipped into unconsciousness. I saw Phaia's face and laughed once more. Not from happiness, but to mock the god who had tried to kill me.

Short of coming up from the abyss and smashing me with his own god-sized fist, Poseidon had done everything he could to smite me down.

And he had failed.

# CHAPTER 27

Of course it was not possible for a mortal to defeat a god. But there are ancient forces that not even the gods can defy. The three Moirai weave all of our fates, even those of Zeus and Poseidon and other immortals that rule the cosmos. My thread was still woven in the warp and weft of the world, despite Poseidon's grudge against me.

Five thousand other men had not escaped the sea-god's wrath. Only a few had died in battle, for we had routed the Spartans completely. Our men had perished in the storm that followed, clinging to damaged ships and waiting for a rescue that never came. Only a few hundred men had survived the ravages of the storm, Tibetos and I among them.

I did not blame Thrasybulus for not rescuing us sooner. What could he have done? The storm had come down as swiftly as an axe-blow.

Others did not share in my magnanimity. In Athens, someone is always to blame, even when they are not. A sacrifice must always be made. The admirals were recalled by the assembly to answer for their perceived crime of failing to rescue the survivors in a timely manner. Thrasybulus was recalled as well, and I accompanied him home on the Might-Strider.

My father had always told me that democracy was what made Athens strong. I had believed him unquestioningly, but what took place was madness born of grief and petty spite.

There was no trial. By decree of the assembly, Thrasyllus and the other admirals who had dared return to Athens were put to death, fastened to wooden posts and throttled by leather straps around their necks. This was their reward for smashing a superior Spartan fleet and rescuing the besieged Athenian ships in Mytilene. There was a motion to do the same to Thrasybulus, but in the end he only lost his title of trireme captain. The sacrifice of six *strategoi* sated the bloodlust of the people.

Thrasybulus, saved by his lowly position of captain, had avoided execution, and that was enough. The politics and machinations of the volatile mob in the assembly meant little to me.

I was an outsider to them. Let them kill their best leaders. It was not my concern.

For I was back in Piraeus.

With Phaia.


PHAIA WAS ASLEEP WHEN I RETURNED to the *peripoli* compound from my day's labour. She lay on her side, the smooth contour of her ribs rising and falling like a gentle sea swell. Gently I placed my hand on her swollen belly, feeling for the kick of the child within but there was not even a quiver of movement. I moved to leave the chamber silently so as not to disturb the serene slumbers of mother and child.

Phaia's voice stopped me at the door. "Do you think you can escape me that easily, my love?" she asked.

I smiled to myself, turning to look at my wife. "It seems I am losing my *peripoli* skills! What would Meges say if he knew I had been caught by you?"

"'By Hera's tits, boy! It's a wonder you've survived this long!'" Phaia growled in an imitation of Meges and I laughed at the accuracy of it. I had long grown accustomed to the colourful but unladylike language that Phaia had picked up gleefully from the coarser elements of my *peripoli* brothers.

"But you must rest," I said, moving back to the bed. "Now more than ever." The growing child inside her had made Phaia weak, though the draughts prepared by Meli and Lampita helped with the fatigue. Her frailty worried me.

"You worry too much," she said, but a trace of weariness pushed through the confidence in her voice. She reached out to take my hand. "Stay awhile longer and I promise you I will rest."

I was glad to do as I was bidden and slumped on the floor beside the bed. Phaia's fingers caressed my forearm lazily. "Your skin is smooth like a woman's," she chuckled.

"Arms burned bare by fire. The mark of a true blacksmith," I said. I had been spending most of my days working at the forge of Timonax in Piraeus. The smith was skilled at his craft, even better than Neleus. He was fascinated by Whisper, always examining the Thracian blade and trying to get her to give up the secret behind her strength.

Phaia's finger found a scar on my upper arm, an old battle-wound earned during a skirmish in the mountains north of Athens. She traced its familiar shape. "Will Lykos take you on patrol soon?" she asked.

"I don't know." It vexed me that since my return, Lykos and Hermon made excuses to keep me off the *peripoli* patrols. I sensed Meli's hand in this but she denied any meddling. It annoyed me to be cosseted like a child, though I was secretly happy to be close to Phaia.

"It is no matter," Phaia said, squeezing my shoulder. "I am glad you are here to protect me," she said as if reading my thoughts. We sat in comfortable silence for a while before she spoke again. "What will we do when the war is over, Daimon?"

"I don't think it will ever end," I said. I had been born in war and had never known anything else. It seemed impossible to imagine another life beyond the one we were living now.

"It will end," she insisted. "All things do."

Sparta and Athens were like two punch-drunk boxers, neither strong enough to land the blow that would finally fell their opponent. "Now that the Spartans have Persian gold to back them, they can continue the war as long as they want. And as long as we have our fleet, Athens will struggle along. It is a dream to imagine that peace is near."

Phaia let out a patient sigh. As usual she was looking beyond where I could see. "Even Spartans cannot fight forever. A treaty of some sort will be negotiated and you will not need to be a soldier anymore."

I pondered the prospect silently. It frightened me. As a warrior, I had gained *kleos* – status and reputation – among my fellow soldiers. Without war I would be once again reduced to the role of non-citizen with neither property nor prospects. Nevertheless, with Phaia, I saw hope where before I had perceived none.

"I could continue working with Timonax," I offered. "He is a worthy master to learn the craft from."

"He is a good man," Phaia conceded.

"There is another possibility," I ventured.

"Yes?" she prompted.

I hesitated. "Thrasybulus has offered me some land." I had not mentioned this to Phaia, for it seemed to be an impossible dream, more so than peace itself. Thrasybulus owned many farms throughout Attica which had lain fallow and untended for most of the war. "He will let us use the land as if it were our own. There are olive trees and a press, and good soil, he tells me."

Phaia's voice brightened. "Do you think it is possible?"

"Thrasybulus does not make promises lightly," I said. "It will be different from life in the city."

"I want the freedom," Phaia said longingly, and I remembered how much of her life had been spent as an aristocrat's daughter confined in the city.

"And the labour that comes with being a farmer's wife?" I pressed. Phaia's recent poor health concerned me.

"It is these walls that make me weak!" she countered. "Walls within walls! Outside I will be strong. As strong as you!" she said. She punched my shoulder and I gave an exaggerated cry of pain.

But doubt pulled at me. "I know how to handle a spear and shield, but a plough? I can't imagine it!" I had lived most of my life in the streets of Athens. The prospect of taking up a yeoman's life was daunting.

"You put the pointy-end of the plough in the dirt, I think," Phaia laughed.

"Mnasyllus said that farming needs more muscles than brains," I said, warming to the idea. The ox-like *peripoli* fighter had grown up in the countryside of the island of Euboea, but I suspected he had oversimplified what went into running a farm.

"Then you will be perfect!" Phaia said, cuffing me playfully on the back of my head. "Besides," she said more softly, "you will have many children to help you. And your wife."

I pressed my lips gently on the back of her hand, savouring the scent of her skin. I loved her more than ever at that moment. For as long as I could remember, anger had simmered in my heart, driving me to fight those who slighted me, to prove myself their better. But Phaia was like cool spring-water, dousing the burning loneliness within me I did not want to fight anymore. "Then I will tell Thrasybulus we accept his offer," I said, and I felt as if a burden on my soul had suddenly lifted. Phaia gave a small cry of joy. "But now you must keep your promise and rest," I admonished her.

"I am too happy to rest!" she protested.

"Then I will stay a little longer," I said and I sat by the bed stroking her hand, my heart at peace.

After a few moments, I rose reluctantly to my feet. "I will bring you some food," I said. But there was no response. Phaia had already fallen asleep.

THE HALE AND HEARTY CRY OF A NEWBORN INFANT rang throughout the compound.

Lykos grinned. "It sounds as though I am an uncle!" Meges and Tibetos knocked their very full cups together, sloshing wine over the edges. But I was already on my feet running towards the sound of the wailing child.

The wizened figure of Lampita stood in the doorway to the storeroom, barring my way. She held up a bloody hand. My heart leapt to my throat, for I feared the worst. "You cannot enter," Lampita declared sternly. "The birthing chamber is unclean. It must be purified with the proper rituals and sacrifices, but this is not for menfolk to witness, so be off, boy!" Lampita waved me off impatiently, but I did not budge from the doorway.

"Is Phaia safe? The child?" I strained to see past Lampita into the darkened chamber. The cleansing aroma of incense was already wafting from within, mingled with the sharp taint of sweat and blood.

Lampita's voice softened by a hair. "It was a difficult birth. There was more bleeding than normal. It happens sometimes. I will treat her, but she needs rest. Your presence will only make disturb her."

Chastened, I reluctantly turned away. I had only gone a few steps when a voice called me back. "Brother!" Meli had replaced Lampita in the doorway. Her hands were behind her back. "I have something for you!"

My sister showed me what she had been hiding. She held out an olive branch. It meant the baby was a boy. "You have a son!" she said proudly as I took the branch.

"But what of Phaia? Will she be well?" I asked, my resolve to obey Lampita's order to leave suddenly wavering.

"She will recover," Meli said confidently, and I knew that she had dreamt it. "Now go! I will take care of Phaia! Go!" She waved me away before scurrying back into the room. My sister's reassurance gave me the strength to turn away. The sound of my son's cries grew fainter behind me.

And I stopped. And listened. For there was another cry, distant and mournful, mirroring those of my newborn son. The wails wafted over the walls of the compound, the bleak tone of lamentation unmistakable. A death, perhaps. It was a common enough occurrence, but an inauspicious omen to greet the birth of my child. I felt a chill.

Frowning, I kept walking but halted once again. Another voice had joined the first. Then a third. All from different directions. A cold, invisible touch ran down my spine. I was running.

By the time I returned to my fellow *peripoli*, so many voices had taken up the call that it was like a chorus of droning phantoms. Lykos was standing, his hand held up to silence the others. All present were listening intently, fear and puzzlement in their faces.

"What can it be?" Tibetos asked.

So dreadful had the cries become that they could have been the souls of the damned in Tartarus. The cold hand had moved from my spine and now gripped my heart, its icy fingers ever tightening. "Let us see," I said.

Led by Hermon and Lykos, the men of the *peripoli* spilled out onto the streets of Piraeus. From every direction there was crying and moaning and voices mad with grief and fear. We looked about in confusion.

All about us were people in the throes of madness. They tore at their clothes and beat their chests viciously. An old man stumbled towards us. His face was wet with tears. Lykos seized him by the arm. "What has happened? Tell us!" The man blinked at Lykos as though he was speaking a barbarian tongue. "What has happened?" Lykos repeated.

The man regained enough of his senses to frown. Now it was he who seized Lykos by the arms. "Do you not know? We are destroyed! We are destroyed!" he cried. He released Lykos and pointed towards the Munychia harbor. "We are destroyed!" he repeated one more time before stumbling away in the opposite direction.

We sprinted east through the wide streets of Piraeus, skirting the base of the hill that blocked the view of the harbor from the *peripoli* compound. As we drew closer, the cries of sorrow grew ever louder. Many wept openly in the streets. Rounding the last corner, the harbor became visible at last.

The *Paralus*, the flagship of the Athenian fleet, was moored at the pier.

Among the distraught citizens I spotted a familiar face. "Epikydes!" I shouted, pointing at the man who had built the Might-Strider for Thrasybulus. The shipwright sat in a daze on the stone steps leading down to the ship-sheds. I ran to him and the others hurried after me. "Epikydes! What has happened? What news does the *Paralus* bring?" I asked with creeping dread.

Epikydes looked up at me. He narrowed his eyes, as though trying to recall my face. Then he spoke, his voice flat and resigned, and our worst fears were realized. "Lysander," he said dully, and my blood froze. "Lysander has captured our entire fleet at Aegospotami. The prisoners were executed to the last man. We have no more ships." He hesitated, as though he could not bring himself to believe the next words he uttered. "The war is over. Athens has been defeated."

A collective gasp came from those gathered about. Without a navy, Athens was defenceless. The treasury was empty. The city could withstand a siege for a few months at most, but no more food would come. Now there was only surrender. Our fate depended on the mercy of Lysander, the Spartan general who had just slaughtered thousands of Athenian prisoners.

Any breath of hope for the future had been smothered. Only despair remained. I looked down at my hand. I was still grasping the olive branch that Meli had given me.

# Part Three

# Forge

# CHAPTER 28

The shrill melody of the Spartan flutes was growing louder.
"So help me, I'm going to shove those pipes up Lysander's arse
if that screeching keeps up any longer!" Hermon muttered under his
breath.

The comment earned the commander a savage lash from the
Spartan overseeing our work crew. "No talking, Athenian!" The
man spoke with the harsh, guttural accent of Sparta and was just as
humorless as most of his kind.

The overseer caught me staring at him. "I said back to work,
you Athenian dung-eater!" he snarled. The whip snapped, leaving a
burning welt on my leg. With a grimace, I bent down and began
dislodging another heavy stone as the offending flute girls passed us
by, trilling and dancing to celebrate the defeat of Athens.

Athenian. I savoured the irony. My entire life I had wished to
be recognized as such, and now I had been granted the title when
being an Athenian meant little more than being a slave.

It had been so for a month.

Its navy captured, its walls besieged, and its people slowly
starving, Athens had been brought to its knees. The assembly voted
to throw itself at the feet of Sparta and beg for mercy.

If it had been up to Sparta's allies, Athens would have been
reduced to a pile of rubble and its population eradicated. Lysander,
however, saw other possibilities for Athens. And opportunities for
himself.

A vanquished and compliant Athens under the thumb of Sparta
would be a useful check against a newly assertive Thebes. As a
source of tribute and soldiers, the city would aid Lysander with his
own ambitions, or so it was whispered. Sparta may have had two
hereditary kings, but Lysander was ruler in all but name, the
hegemon of all of Greece.

And in case Athenians began to chafe under Spartan
domination, it was better to remind them of their city's utter defeat.
Every able-bodied Athenian was now engaged in the humiliating
task of tearing down the defensive walls that had thwarted Sparta

since the time of Themistokles. I toiled with the other *peripoli* atop a section of the rapidly diminishing walls that had protected the road between Athens and Piraeus.

Groaning with the effort, I pried a huge boulder loose. It toppled over the edge of the wall and crashed with a thud into the earth below. I straightened up, flexing my aching back muscles and witnessing Athens' servitude.

As far as the eye could see, the scene was much the same as on our own stretch of wall. Amidst the smell of sweat and dust, men drudged on mechanically. The chatter and laughing and singing that accompanies the labour of free men was absent. There was only the percussion of metal on stone mixed with the grunts and moans of straining backs and aching arms.

On the road below, a cluster of women passed by. Balanced on their heads were baskets of bread and water jars for the workers. Athenian women had not been excused from service to Sparta because of their sex or status. I squinted, hoping to catch a glimpse of Phaia or Meli among them, but was disappointed. I glanced over at Lykos and saw that he had been looking too.

"No shirking!" I felt the sting of the whip on my cheek before I heard the crack. I winced as my hand moved involuntarily to the wound. There was blood on my fingers.

I glared at the Spartan guard, who glowered back at me. Rage began to rise in my throat and my fists tightened at my sides. The Spartan's hand moved to the sword hanging at his side. The others nearby ceased their work, watching the confrontation. Behind the overseer, Lykos shook his head.

Swallowing my fury, I slowly bent over and started working loose another boulder in the wall. I hazarded a glance at the overseer but saw that something on the road had caught the Spartan's attention. I followed the guard's gaze to find out what could be of greater interest than tormenting his charges.

A large procession was making its way up the road, coming from Piraeus and heading towards Athens. The delegation was flanked by an honour guard of red-cloaked Spartan soldiers, their polished armour glinting in the sun. The rough column stretched down the road, a long baggage train of carts and mules trailing behind it.

Even from a distance, the hegemon Lysander stood out, not only from the way he carried himself but because of the pure white cloak that he wore. So great was his power that he could dare set himself apart from the other fiercely egalitarian Spartans.

Our work-gang had also taken advantage of the spectacle to steal a few moments rest. The overseer paid them no mind for a change, permitting a moment's respite. As the procession drew nearer, I could make out the faces of the men accompanying Lysander.

A weight like cold stone filled my guts.

Kritias, father of the loathsome Menekrates, the murderer of my family, walked alongside Lysander. His white hair was cropped short, as was his beard. Despite his age, he walked with strength and assurance.

The hegemon Lysander said something, and Kritias leaned in close to hear, revealing those trudging behind him. I sucked in a rush of air through my clenched teeth. Menekrates.

His once handsome visage was marred by the bashing I had laid upon him. His nose was twisted and flattened, his mouth permanently curled into a grotesque sneer. Only his eyes were unchanged, still full of arrogant malevolence. Beside him, the scar-faced Orchus looked calmly bored.

I turned away hastily, fearing that the hateful, searching glare of Menekrates would fall upon me where I stood atop the wall.

Beside me, Telekles felt no such urge. The *peripoli*'s jaw hung open in disbelief. "Where in Hades did that monster come from?" he said in a startled voice.

Mistakenly, I believed he was speaking of Kritias or Menekrates. But every other man on the wall was looking down with an expression every bit as awed as that of Telekles. Venturing a look, I turned my head slightly to see what had drawn the attention of my comrades. In my shock of seeing Kritias and Menekrates, I had failed to see the titan in the middle of the caravan.

Akras.

The colossus who had ravaged my phalanx on the plains of Ephesus had come to Athens. Helmetless, the Syracusan still stood taller than the crests on the helms of the Spartan hoplites beside him. An expression of indelible menace marked the mercenary's features as he marched. He stared straight ahead, immune to the attention he inevitably drew to himself.

I moved back so that I would not be visible. The footsteps from the road below began to fade as Lysander and the main body of men went past, replaced by the rhythmic clopping of mules and the creak of wooden wheels from the baggage train.

The immediate danger gone, I approached the edge of the wall and risked a look down. The Hegemon and Kritias were already well up the road, though the massive figure of Akras was still conspicuous even now.

I let out a deep breath and let my eyes linger on the thinning crowd below. My gaze fell upon one man, for he was well-dressed and carried no load, making him stand out among the porters and slaves at the rear of the procession. As though he sensed my stare, the man looked up at me. For an instant, our eyes locked. The man frowned slightly, as though he knew my face but could not quite place me.

"Hades!" I hissed, and hastily stepped away from the wall and out of view.

It was Menekrates' cousin, the one that had fled like a coward in the market. I wracked my heat-addled brains for the name. *Plato.* No. Menekrates had used this nickname, but Kritias had called his nephew Aristokles.

I cursed myself for my carelessness. Had he recognized me? It had only lasted a heartbeat. Yet it would take only a word from him to alert Menekrates and Kritias to my presence in the city.

Seeing my agitation, Lykos raised his eyebrows inquiringly. I opened my mouth to speak.

The crack of a whip cut me off. "Back to work, Athenian turd-sniffers!" the Spartan guard barked. He glared at me, daring me to resist.

With a resentful stare, I set about dislodging one more stone from the wall, willing the day to end sooner.


PHAIA GINGERLY DABBED AT THE CUT on my cheek. The sting made me wince. "Hold still!" she chastised me. "There," she said finishing. "I don't know who the bigger baby is, you or Niko." She turned so that I could see my son, Nikodromos, asleep in the sling on her back. I reached out and stroked the dark thatch of hair on his crown.

"He looks like you," Phaia said. A fit of coughing interrupted her smile, and I held her to me until the fit had passed. Phaia had never fully recovered after giving birth and the harsh conditions imposed by the Spartans since the fall of the city had only weakened her further.

"I am fine," she said, though I knew she only said it for my benefit. She shifted her weight and she winced slightly. There was no hiding her fatigue.

"Did they make you work today?" I asked anxiously. The Spartans came to the compound every morning to collect women for labour once the men had left. Phaia was not exempt despite her condition.

"I was spared today. They must have pitied me." I doubted it. The Spartans were not known for their charity. More likely they had thought her too weak to work. "Sit down and eat," she said, trying to change the subject.

We had claimed a disused storeroom in a corner of the *peripoli* compound as our chamber. On our low, rough-hewn table, I had set out my meagre rations for the day: a small loaf of coarse bread and a scant measure of oil. Phaia had added a chunk of hard cheese and some salted fish. "Where did you find this?" I asked.

"Meges brought it, but I know no more than that." The wiry Acharnian had probably stolen the food right out of a Spartan's mess kit. A month after the surrender, food was still a scarce commodity in Athens. Yet not a day went by that Meges did not somehow manage to scavenge some cheese or figs or dried fish for us. He was fiercely loyal to Phaia, and I had no doubt he would die to protect her if need be. He would wave off my gratitude as he always did.

"Meges told me that I need to eat, for Niko's sake," Phaia said.

"I agree," I said. I broke off a small hunk of cheese for myself and gave the rest of the food to Phaia. She protested but was too weak to overcome my insistence. "I ate some bread on the wall," I lied. She nodded and I made sure she ate every crumb.

I nibbled at the cheese. The memory of Kritias and Menekrates pushed itself forward in my mind, leaving me even more sullen than before. I was not the only one incapable of hiding that which plagued me.

"What has happened, husband?" Phaia's stare told me there would no evading her question.

My shoulders slumped. "It is Kritias and Menekrates. They have returned to Athens."

Phaia let out a small gasp and made a sign against the evil eye. "But why? Have they returned to be slaves like the rest of us?"

"Not slaves, I think." I sighed and told her what I had learned from the rumours flying around Piraeus. "Lysander will appoint a council of thirty citizens to rule Athens on behalf of Sparta. People are already calling them 'the Thirty Tyrants'," I said.

"And Kritias is to be a member?" Phaia asked.

"He is to be the leader," I said dejectedly. Kritias had been recalled from exile, along with many other former members of the Four Hundred. As my father had foreseen so long ago, such men would rather see themselves in power under the Spartan yoke than suffer the indignity of being governed by their fellow Athenians.

"The Thirty will rule Athens at the pleasure of Lysander. The demolition of our walls will leave us defenceless, but just in case anyone gets it into their heads to rebel, the Spartans will leave a garrison of a thousand hoplites to help the Thirty maintain order."

Phaia's eyes hardened. "What of Menekrates?" She made another sign against the evil eye after uttering that foul creature's name.

"Just accompanying his father I expect. But we are in great danger if he discovers that I am in Piraeus," I said. I had no doubts about the cruel vindictiveness that the son of Kritias was capable of.

"Did he see you?"

"If he had, I would already be dead."

"Then there is nothing to be concerned about," Phaia tried to reassure me.

"But Aristokles may have seen me."

"Who?"

"Aristokles. Plato. Kritias' nephew. That cowardly shit who ran from the marketplace and brought the Skythians."

"Will he say anything?" Phaia asked calmly. She looked down at our nursing son as she spoke, but now there was fear in her voice.

"He only saw me for an instant, and it was from a distance. If he hasn't said anything, it must mean that he didn't recognize me."

My lack of conviction must have shown, for Phaia pressed me. "Then we need not worry?"

I shook my head. "If it is not Menekrates, then I am worried about Kritias. He will remember the role the *peripoli* played in overthrowing the Four Hundred. I am afraid that we will not go unnoticed for long." This possibility had been much in discussion among Hermon and the rest of my fellow *peripoli*.

"And what of your brother?" Phaia asked.

At the mention of my half-brother, I reached instinctively to touch the iron sword that normally hung at my side, but it was not there. The Spartan occupiers had confiscated our weapons, though Hermon had caches of arms hidden throughout the compound, including my *rhomphaia* Whisper. Without iron to ward off the evil eye, though, I just spat on the ground in disgust.

But I did not answer the question, for I did not know. After the fall of the Four Hundred, Adrastos had fled to the Spartan fort at Dekeleia, but what had become of him, I had no inkling. It was possible that he had been killed, but that might have been wishful thinking. I had asked Hermon for word of my brother's return to Athens, but there was none. If he was in the city, it was one more danger that hung over me and those I loved.

A moment passed in silence. Niko detached himself from Phaia's breast and emitted a wet burp. I envied him for his freedom from responsibility and fear.

We put Niko to bed. It was a simple wooden crib, but well made and sturdy. Meges had built it himself. Atop each corner post sat a small carved owl, protectors standing vigil over the tiny occupant within.

In our own rough bed, Phaia's breathing became slow and steady as she slipped into sleep. Every time she exhaled, the warm air tickled against the hollow between my neck and collar-bone, yet I dared not shift my body for fear of waking her.

Thoughts of Menekrates and his father Kritias plagued me, denying my body the rest that it craved. Yet fatigue eventually won out. I fell into a fitful slumber, pursued throughout the night by the roars of the mighty Akras and the cleaving blade of his merciless *kopis*.

A HAND CLUTCHED MY SHOULDER. In an instant I was awake, grabbing at whoever had seized me.

"Hold, Daimon!" It was Lykos, his face illuminated in the torchlight. "Come!"

Beside me Phaia stirred. She squinted groggily. "What is it?"

"It is just Lykos!" I whispered. "Go back to sleep." I squeezed her hand. Phaia seemed uncertain. "I will be back soon! Now sleep!" Reassured, Phaia lay back down and shut her eyes. At the doorway, I cast one last look back at her. She nestled herself deeper into the blanket and was still. A pang of longing suddenly rose within me, but there was nothing to do but follow Lykos.

Wordlessly, we wended our way through the empty *peripoli* compound. Snoring floated through the occasional window or doorway, but for the most part there was only the sound of our own footsteps. After one last turn, we entered the main courtyard. The door and windows of Hermon's rooms were closed, but lamplight seeped through the cracks. The light flickered as someone moved within.

Telekles kept watch outside the door. I could not help noticing the sword hanging at his side. He nodded a silent greeting and rapped lightly on the door. Perplexed, I looked at Lykos, but his expression revealed nothing.

The door creaked open half-way. Hermon, more grim-faced than usual, ushered us inside with a jerk of his head. I slipped into the room after Lykos, and Hermon shut the door hastily behind us.

A haggard man with unkempt hair and a stained cloak was seated at the central table. He turned towards us and my eyes widened in surprise.

It was Thrasybulus.

CHAPTER 29

Thrasybulus gave a weak smile. "Platoon Leader," he said, addressing me by my former rank.

"*Strategos!*" I exclaimed.

Like all those who had endured the final siege before Athens' final surrender, he had lost weight. His face looked drawn and tired but his eyes still burned with the vigour of intelligence.

He was not alone. Beside him sat a woman. In her arms an infant slept soundly, oblivious of the tension permeating the room. Another child, a girl of two or three, stood clutching her mother's cloak. The child's wide, dark eyes regarded me with an unmasked curiosity.

"My wife, Astera," Thrasybulus said, "and my children, Thaïs and Thrasybulus."

Despite her evident fatigue, the woman sat with the straight-backed dignity of an aristocratic lady. She bowed her head demurely, but neither spoke nor met my eyes. Her hand moved to readjust the cloth covering her hair.

Hermon rescued Astera from the unwanted attention. "Vengeance has come quickly. Kritias and his henchmen are seizing the property of prominent democrats. Death-squads are executing them without trial. Some," he said tilting his head towards Thrasybulus, "have been able to escape before the long knives came for them. Kritias has not forgotten how democrats like your father worked to bring down the Four Hundred. He is making sure that any plots against the Thirty Tyrants are snuffed out like an infant throttled in its crib."

Thrasybulus spoke. "A hoplite who had served under me came to warn me at my home, a man named Podaroes. I think you know him, Daimon?" I nodded at the mention of my former comrade. "It was only because of him that we were able to escape the purge."

"How many have been killed?" Lykos asked.

Thrasybulus shrugged. "Hundreds? A thousand? I do not know."

There was a sharp intake of breath from everyone in the room. Lykos spoke for us all. "This is madness!" Lykos hissed. "The people will rise up against Kritias and the other tyrants!"

Thrasybulus' scoffed. "Who will stand up against the thousand Spartan hoplites that Lysander has garrisoned in the city? Do not be fooled. Kritias does nothing that does not have the blessing of Lysander. And the Thirty do not lack support among the aristocrats. As for the rest," Thrasybulus said, pointing back in the direction of Athens, "they have lost their courage. Anyone who speaks against the Thirty will be declared an enemy. They will be killed and their property seized. No, the people will not rise up. Better stand meekly by and wait for the storm to pass."

"Storms can be unpredictable," I said. I had not meant to speak aloud.

Thrasybulus smiled grimly. "Never has a truer word been spoken, young Daimon!" He continued to describe the violence engulfing Athens. All the while, a sense of foreboding began to build inside my head.

Lykos gave voice to my fears. "It is only a matter of time before the agents of the Thirty come for the *peripoli*. Kritias knows at least that Daimon and I were involved in the assassination of Phrynichus. We must flee while there is time."

Hermon spoke. "There are more than one hundred people here, more than half of them women and children. It will take several days to arrange even the barest provisions." Lykos made to protest, but Hermon cut him off. "The priority," he said, "is to get the *strategos* and his family to safety. At the same time," the commander said, holding up a finger to silence Lykos, "I agree that those Spartan-loving bastards are coming for us soon. The remaining *peripoli* will make preparations to leave immediately."

"And where will we flee to?" Lykos demanded. "We are surrounded by former enemies."

"Thebes."

It was Thrasybulus who had spoken, his authoritative voice bringing the room to silence.

"We will go to Thebes," Thrasybulus repeated in a lower but still sonorous tone.

Disbelief spread across Lykos' features. "What madness are you speaking of, Brother? We have fought the Thebans for thirty years!

They would have gladly seen every Athenian man executed and our women and children sold into slavery! If any Athenian exiles appear there, they will be torn limb from limb and eaten raw! Who among us can expect refuge there?"

Thrasybulus let his brother protest. In truth, Lykos only spoke the thought shared by everyone in the room. The bitter enmity between Athens and Thebes was even more ancient than that between our city and Sparta.

When Lykos had finished, Thrasybulus rose. He spoke as if he were addressing the assembly. "The Thebans will welcome us and give us shelter from both the Spartans and the Tyrants. I have received word that the Thebans have passed a decree that any and all Athenian exiles *must* be given asylum in their city." He paused as the significance of this revelation sank in.

Lykos spoke for all present, the words almost whispered. "But how is this possible? Thebes is beholden to Sparta! Why would Thebes dare defy them and risk retribution? And for the sake of Athenians, at that!"

Thrasybulus responded. "Thebes has broken with Sparta. The Thebans feel that they have been ill-treated by the Spartans. Thebes received almost nothing of the spoils of war. They have learned that Sparta has no allies, only servants. And not only Thebes! Even our ancient enemy Corinth is opening its gates for those fleeing Athens. The Spartans have gained a reluctant ally in Athens, but have lost support among their most powerful vassals."

Hermon stepped in before Lykos could speak. "Then the matter is settled. Lykos, you will take Telekles, Daimon, and Sabas and accompany your brother and his family to Thebes. You must be well away before morning. We will make our own preparations and follow you as soon as possible."

Hermon looked hard at Lykos, challenging him to argue, but the brother of Thrasybulus gave in. "Very well. Telekles! Sabas! Daimon. You heard the commander. Fetch your gear, but travel light. We meet at the storeroom gate." His speech complete, Hermon had us swear an oath to protect Thrasybulus and his family. A cup of wine was offered to the gods for the successful execution of the mission.

We hurried off like proper soldiers. As I stepped through the door back into the night, I cast a glance at Thrasybulus. The eyes of my former *strategos* were already on me. He gave a slight nod. I turned and exited, leaving the secret assembly behind.

I did not follow Lykos' orders immediately. Instead I made my way to the dormitory. I needed help.

For I had made a decision. I would keep my oath to aid Thrasybulus.

But I was not going to Thebes.

"TIBO!" I WHISPERED, SHAKING THE SLEEPING FORM of my oldest friend. "Tibo! Get up!" Tibetos groaned but was suddenly alert as I began to explain what had happened.

"I need you to pack your kit and come with us," I said flatly.

"You want me to travel to Thebes with you?" Tibetos asked confused.

"I'm not going to Thebes. Not all the way, anyway."

"What are you going to do?"

"Once the *strategos* and his family are safely on their way, I'm going to come back for Phaia, Niko, and Meli. The sooner I get them out of here, the better."

"What do you want me to do?"

I could not wait for Hermon's evacuation. I needed to get my family away from the city, for I feared the swift retribution of Kritias. But Phaia was too weak to make a long journey on foot. "I have some money. Buy a mule from a farmer. Steal one if you have to. Then wait for us at the hunting lodge." The abandoned lodge favoured by the *peripoli* patrols was the best meeting place I could think of. "I will bring the others there."

"And then we will go to Thebes?"

I revealed my decision to my friend. "There is nothing for us there. We will go to Thrace. To Zyraxes."

Tibetos did not hesitate, despite the surprise he must have been feeling. "I will not let you down."

"We are leaving through the storeroom gate. Be there as soon as possible." I left Tibetos gathering his things, for there was someone else whose help I needed to enlist.

Meges was awake when I ducked into his chamber, an oil-lamp lighting up the small space. "I suppose your being here has something to do with all the goings-on outside? Is it too much to let a man sleep?"

The misanthropic Meges had staked out his own space in one corner of the *peripoli* compound, but I had never been past the tattered leather flaps that served as a door. Despite the urgency of my visit, I could not help notice that the room was contrary to my expectations. It was spare and clean, with only a bed, a chest, and a small table to fill the space. A glazed white ewer and matching cup sat on the table, deliberately placed in balanced opposition to each other. It was almost Spartan.

"What are you gawping at, boy? If you've something to say, spit it out! Otherwise leave a man to sleep in peace!"

Meges grunted and sucked his teeth loudly as I told him of the persecutions in Athens and the imminent mission to escort Thrasybulus and his family away from the city. When I told him that Hermon needed several days to make preparations for the exodus of the remaining *peripoli* and their families, Meges shook his head. "Too long!" he rasped. "Too long!"

"That is why I need you, my friend," I said. "I will come back by sunset for Phaia and my sister. But if something should befall me and I do not return, you must take them to the hunting lodge. Tibo will meet you there." There was no one I trusted more than the fox-like Meges to elude any pursuers and protect those I loved.

Meges was too cunning to miss what I had not said. "You will not go to Thebes?"

"We will go to Thrace."

Meges inhaled a long breath and did not reply. As the air came out of him, he seemed to deflate, his shoulders dropping. When he lifted his chin to look at me, there was age there that I had not seen before. "Then I will join you, if you will have me."

I blinked uncomprehendingly before letting out a laugh. "Phaia will be pleased!"

Meges cleared his throat and his usual gruffness returned. "Those Thracians smell like dung-covered pigs, but I'll get used to it. Some of them might not be half as bad as I thought." I thought I saw a corner of his mouth turn upwards. I wished to embrace him, but he barked at me before I could do so. "By Zeus's godly cock, boy! Get a move on! The high-and-mighty Thrasybulus is not one to be left waiting by a slow-witted half-breed like you! Now go!"

At a sprint I ran back to the storeroom where I had left Phaia and Niko. Phaia was awake now, waiting for me, her eyes wide with apprehension.

"What is happening?"

A broken explanation came out as I hastily threw together my kit. I threw on my cloak, concealing the xiphos sword slung under my arm. I would have preferred Whisper, but there was no time to retrieve the Thracian long-sword from Hermon's cache of buried weapons. The ruckus woke Niko, who began to cry. Phaia scooped him up, but he only wailed more insistently.

I put my hand on Niko's tiny forehead. I slid my palm forward, covering his eyes, and his crying came to a stop. I leaned close to him and pulled my hand away, revealing my wide-eyed face and causing Niko to squeal with laughter.

I continued to play with Niko as I spoke to Phaia. "You must be ready to leave by tomorrow night. If I cannot come back for some reason, Meges will guide you. He is coming with us to Thrace," I added as an afterthought.

Phaia knitted her brow but nodded her assent.

I kissed her forehead. "My love, I will carry you if I have to, all the way to Thrace."

I took my hand from Niko's head and cupped it to Phaia's cheek. Niko burbled happily as I leaned down to kiss his mother one more time. Reluctantly, I stepped back.

Phaia gazed at me. "You will come back?"

"The gods themselves could not stop me. Poseidon tried and failed, remember? Besides, Tibo will be there to protect me," I said, eliciting a perfect smile from Phaia. I turned to leave.

"Daimon!" Phaia said.

I looked back.

"I love you," she whispered.

The words held me in the doorway, as though a great invisible hand had wrapped around my body. "I love you," I said. Only with the greatest willpower was I able to break free of the force that gripped me and go join my comrades.

CHAPTER 30

Our party gathered by the small doorway on the north-west wall of the compound. A single torch burned in its iron bracket beside the barred door.

Thrasybulus was piggy-backing his daughter, who looked at me with her black eyes as large as the moon that now shone down on us. I winked at her and she rewarded me with a smile of tiny teeth. Seeing me, Thrasybulus stepped away from the knot of people and leaned in close to me. "There is no one I would rather have with me, lad," he said in a low voice.

"I am your man, *strategos*," I said.

A quick glance confirmed that everyone was present, with a few extra bodies. Tibetos acknowledged me with a nod. Lykos and Telekles were conferring in hushed voices with Hermon. The Cretan bowman Sabas squatted by the door, patting the head of his loyal hound Argos.

Thrasybulus' wife Astera had put on a cloak and pulled up the hood, obscuring my view of her. In her arms she carried the younger Thrasybulus, who had fallen asleep with his head on her should. She turned and our eyes met for an instant. Imagining that the child must be a heavy load, I extended my arms towards her, indicating that I would relieve her of her burden. She recoiled, her eyes wide, and quickly turned away, clutching her son even more tightly.

My pondering of Astera's apparent dislike of me vanished as my attention was pulled away by the grip of small but strong fingers on my forearm.

"Meli," I said, knowing who it was before I even saw her face. Her features were hidden in shadow, but I could sense the discomfort radiating from her. "What troubles you?"

"Lykos woke me to tell me you were leaving." Her voice was distant, as though only part of her were present. "I was having a dream, but I can't remember what it was…," her voice trailed off.

Putting my hands on her shoulders, I bent low, touching my forehead to hers. "I will be back by tomorrow evening." I spoke in Thracian, for I did not want the others to understand. "I will take you and Phaia away from this place. There is nothing for us here now."

"We will go to Thebes?" she asked.

I leaned forward to whisper in her ear. "We will go to Thrace. Help Phaia prepare. She will need you."

If Meli was surprised by my plan, she gave no indication. "I will do it, brother. And I will pray to Bendis for your protection." I kissed her forehead.

As my sister and I looked at each other in the torchlight, Lykos approached. "We are ready to depart." He and Meli embraced briefly. There was a whispered exchange but I do not know what they said.

Our party emerged into the shadows of the deserted street outside the compound. The half-open doorway was a rectangle of light framing the figures of Hermon and Meli within it. The hinges creaked and the shape narrowed to a sliver and was gone. There was a muffled thud as the bar fell back into place. We all set off into the night.


WE WERE FORTUNATE IN OUR DEPARTURE. No patrols crossed our paths, and the children did not let out so much as a cough. A stiff breeze blew in off the sea, masking any noise we otherwise made. The gates on the main roads leading out of the port were manned, but it was of no matter. The demolition of the walls had left the boundary of Piraeus so porous that an entire army could have passed through unchallenged. As *peripoli*, there was no footpath or hiding place in the vicinity of Athens that was unknown to us. Unseen by man or ghost, we were soon some miles into our journey north to Thebes.

The sky grew lighter. The chirping of crickets died out with the night, supplanted by a rising chorus of birds and day insects singing to greet the sun. The human inhabitants also revealed themselves. Farmers and their slaves were already out tending to long-neglected fields, hoping to complete the most strenuous labour before the heat of the day burned away the cool morning air. From a distance, the workers stopped to regard us with the hostility and fear bred of decades of endless war. But they left us unmolested as we skirted the edges of their land, for we were a large enough group that it was better to let us pass unhindered and become someone else's problem.

At a solitary olive tree, we stopped to rest and eat. The great tree was gnarled and ancient and was already laden with half-grown fruit. Somehow it had survived the predations of ravaging Spartan armies. Perhaps it had escaped destruction exactly because it seemed to belong to no one. I suppose that it is still standing there and will still be alive when those I speak of are not even a memory.

At that time, we were thankful for the shade. I sat away from the others with Tibetos. We spoke little, gnawing on stale bread.

I passed the water-skin to Tibetos. "You should leave once we set out again," I told him.

My friend took a generous swig from the skin and wiped his chin. "And you? When will you turn back?"

"I will accompany them a little farther. I must talk with Lykos."

"Does he know what you are planning?"

I shook my head.

Tibetos looked past me. "The *strategos* is coming," he said. "It looks like you will need to speak to him first." I glanced over my shoulder. Thrasybulus was indeed making his way towards me.

Grabbing his supplies, Tibetos rose. "I will take my leave, then." I stood up and we clasped hands. Tibetos strode away to the west on his mission. He did not look back.

"Where is your friend headed?" It was Thrasybulus, who had come up behind me. "His name is Tibetos, is it not?"

"Yes." I was surprised that he had remembered. "He is helping me with a task.'

Thrasybulus considered this. "He is a loyal friend, is he not?"

"There is no one more faithful," I said truthfully.

"And I would speak to you of loyalty, Daimon," he said. "Sit with me for a moment." A long-bred and well-honed instinct made me regard him warily as I waited for him to speak his mind.

"Did you know," he said, "that it was I who asked you to accompany us on this journey?" I had not known, and I told him so, though I had wondered at my inclusion in the party. "You have proven your bravery and determination time and again. I have never seen a more fearless fighter. I trust you with the lives of my family, Daimon."

"Your wife would not say the same," I said flatly.

Far from being angry, Thrasybulus barked a laugh. "Hah! Have you seen yourself lately, lad?" he asked, genuinely amused. "With that wild hair and green eyes of yours, you have a bit of the gorgon about you! Astera has led a sheltered life." Thrasybulus held up a hand. "It is my fault, I suppose, but she has not had the chance to encounter men like you. *Fighting* men like you," he emphasized.

"I do not take your meaning, *strategos*," I said.

Thrasybulus lowered his voice, but only slightly. "Athens has been a democracy for far too long for men to give it up so easily. The rule of the Thirty Tyrants will not last. Democracy will be restored."

Democracy. That was the dream of men like Thrasybulus and my father. But not mine. Their enthusiasm once held me in its sway, but no longer.

Thrasybulus must have sensed my scepticism, but he pressed on. "I am raising an army in exile," he said. "When the time is right, we will march on Athens and overthrow the tyrants. But I need experienced warriors. Men who can lead. Men I can trust. Men like *you*, Daimon." He awaited my response.

My lack of enthusiasm aside, there seemed to me a great flaw in his plan. I almost scoffed aloud. "The Spartans will not just step aside and let you overthrow their puppets," I countered.

Thrasybulus smiled cryptically. "Not all Spartans are our enemies," he said, but did not elaborate. He returned to trying to convince me to join him. "You will be a *lochagos*, Daimon. A captain, a leader of men. I have seen that men will follow you. I have seen your father's greatness in you." Yet I was unpersuaded.

"And Lykos?" I said, glancing back to where Thrasybulus' younger brother sat with the rest of our party.

"He will be my *taxiarchos*," Thrasybulus said. A *taxiarchos* was a commander, second only to a *strategos* himself.

"He has agreed to this?" I asked, surprised.

"He will see the light," Thrasybulus said confidently. "I know my brother." And I knew then that Lykos had not yet committed himself to his elder brother's mad scheme.

But the appeal to my loyalty for him and his brother had only been the stick. Thrasybulus now revealed the carrot. "And when democracy is restored, I promise that those who help make it so will be granted Athenian citizenship. It is time for the old law of Perikles to be abolished."

I must admit I was tempted. It was something I had desired my entire life, but now it was for more than just myself. Phaia had broken the law of Athens by becoming my woman. My son was an outcast like me. Thrasybulus, should he achieve his goal, would change my destiny.

Thrasybulus saw me wavering. "The Thirty have stricken thousands from the citizen rolls. When we are victorious, they will reclaim their former status. Do you think that they will deny you, Daimon, the same honour after you have helped them throw off the yoke of tyranny?" he scoffed.

Still I hesitated. The brightness of the late morning suddenly faded. A cloud had passed in front of the sun. Thrasybulus looked up at it as though annoyed by its attempt to thwart the optimism that infused his words.

The moment passed quickly and the brilliance of day returned. But the spell that had been cast over me had been broken, and I saw Thrasybulus' scheme for what it was. A fool's dream.

How many men could Thrasybulus muster? Money is the lifeblood of any army, and Thrasybulus had almost none. Hellas was exhausted after thirty years of tearing itself apart. Where would he find support among the battle-weary cities and villages?

I could not bring myself to reject him flat out. "I will consider your offer, *strategos*," I lied. "But I cannot accompany you all the way to Thebes. I must return to Piraeus to bring my family to safety."

Thrasybulus glanced over to where Astera sat with his own children. "A man's loyalties are always divided, Daimon." He turned back and held out his hand. I grasped it firmly. "I will await you in Thebes, *lochagos*," he said, already bestowing me with the rank he had promised me.

He returned to his family. Guilt gnawed at my conscience, for I had deceived him. I knew that I would not see him again.

A shout pulled my attention away. My hand moved unconsciously towards the sword under my cloak, but it was only Sabas, back from a little reconnaissance with his faithful hound Argos. The grinning Cretan had acquired a mule, by suspect means no doubt.

From where I stood, I watched Lykos moving about, rousing the other members of our party to their feet. The resigned mule accepted her fate as packs were transferred to her back. Thrasybulus scooped up his daughter and plopped her on the mule, showing her how to grip the beast's shaggy mane. Astera let Telekles relieve her of the burden of carrying her son. The journey to Thebes was about to recommence.

I would not be going with them.

SEEING THAT I HAD NOT MOVED to join them, Lykos instead walked the fifty paces to where I stood.

"We must move, Daimon! We can reach the mountains before nightfall. Come!" He pointed towards the hazy, purple hills that lay to the north across the wide, flat valley ahead of us.

"No," I said simply.

Lykos blinked in astonishment at my refusal. "What?"

I explained that I was taking my family to Thrace and that I could not wait for them in Thebes. Lykos' eyebrows arched in disbelief as I told him that Meges had decided to accompany us.

"Tibetos will be waiting for us at the hunting lodge tonight. I will take Meli to Thebes if she wishes, and then we will head north to Thrace. I will find welcome with Zyraxes."

For once, Lykos was struck dumb. Indecisively, he looked back to Thrasybulus and the rest of our companions, who were ready to depart. When he turned back towards me, shame was on his face.

"You have reminded me where my duty lies now, Daimon. My brother and his family are safe. I think he can take care of himself." Lykos let out a tired laugh. He tilted his face towards the sun and closed his eyes, letting the late afternoon light wash over him. Presently, he opened his eyes and let out a deep breath.

Lykos put his hand on my shoulder. "I cannot abandon a brother *peripoli*. Besides, there is someone in Piraeus I love as well. I will return with you. As for Meli..." He paused, sighing. "I will follow her to Thrace, if that is where she wishes to go."

My heart filled with joy at his words. There would be a new beginning for all of my friends and family in Thrace.

With little explanation, Lykos informed the others that we were returning to Piraeus. The *peripoli* accepted this without argument, nodding as Lykos instructed them to proceed all the way to Thebes and await Hermon and their fellows there.

Thrasybulus said nothing. As the party lurched into motion, the former general paused and turned. "Remember what I said, Daimon."

"I will, *strategos*."

"And you too, Brother. I need both of you." Thrasybulus waved and turned away, never looking back, even once. Lykos and I watched them trudge down the long, shallow slope towards the valley below until they were just as ants to us, disappearing from our lives and into exile.

UNHAMPERED BY PACKS OR WOMEN OR CHILDREN, we moved at an accelerated pace. I wondered if Tibetos had succeeded in procuring a donkey or mule, but I had faith in my friend's resourcefulness.

Lykos questioned me about what Thrasybulus had said to me. He snorted. "He said much the same to me. He is already offering us promotions in an army that does not exist and spoils of a victory not yet won! The man has never lacked for audacity!"

Even unhindered, it was only after sunset that Piraeus came within sight. At a rise a mile or so outside the port, we stopped to catch our breaths. The watch-fires at the entrance of the main harbor burned brightly, as did those of the more distant harbours of Zea and Munychia.

And my heart froze. For there was another blaze of light where there should not have been one, near the center of the port. "What is that?" I said. The question nearly caught in my throat.

Lykos did not respond, nor did he need to, for I already knew the answer.

The *peripoli* compound was burning.

# CHAPTER 31

Disorder reigned in Piraeus.

The chaos on the streets brought a level of equality that democracy had never achieved, as men, women, children, rich and poor, citizen and metic joined together in an instinctive sense of self-preservation, putting distance between themselves and the orange glow in the middle of the port.

Lykos and I plunged through the streets against the human current. Harried mothers hurried with their broods, looking back in fear. Masters yelled at heavily-burdened slaves as they moved their goods and livelihoods away from the destruction. We shoved past an oil merchant who stared wild-eyed at his over-tipped cart as the gravelly earth drank his profits.

A wind from the east carried the sooty odor of death to our nostrils and lungs, and glowing embers drifted through the air like searing snowflakes.

"What is happening?" Lykos said, blocking the path of a fleeing man.

The man blinked at Lykos and then at me. "Do you not know?" he asked incredulously, as though Lykos and I were mad simpletons. "The Thirty have attacked the *peripoli*. They are lost!" He barged past us.

My guts roiled at the man's words. My sword had appeared in my hand and I dashed forward. A hand yanked me back by my cloak. It was Lykos.

"Did you not hear?" I screamed. "They are under attack! We must go!" I struggle to free myself, desperate to find Phaia.

Lykos held me even more firmly. "Daimon! We must approach cautiously if there is any hope." A trace of pleading crept into his voice. "Please!"

The wisdom of his words somehow penetrated my mind. I took a deep lungful of hot air and nodded.

'Then let us go help our brothers," Lykos said grimly.

We were approaching from the west. The extent of the fire became more apparent as we neared the compound. The east side was a mass of billowing smoke with flames leaping up into the night sky, and my guts clenched in fear, for that is where Lykos and Meli shared their quarters. The west side, where Phaia and I shared our tiny chamber, was as yet untouched, and that promise of hope drove me towards the conflagration.

The western door from which we had departed only a day earlier was sealed tight, and our cries and banging brought no response. We could not tarry. With a motion of his head, Lykos signalled that we keep moving.

The impact of the dry heat made me squint as we hazarded a glance around the southwest corner. Armed men were scattered about the street in front of the compound, mostly keeping their distance from the burning buildings. The man nearest us was a mere ten strides away, his back turned to us. We ducked back behind the cover of the wall.

"We must get past them if we are to help those within!" Lykos hissed to me. He did not need to explain of whom he spoke.

I peered around the corner once again, desperately seeking a means of getting past the milling soldiers. But there was none. If we made a dash to the gate, we would surely be cut down.

As I stood paralyzed with indecision, the hoplite nearest us turned, presenting his profile against the half-light cast by the fire. His helmet was tipped back and resting on his crown. He barked out an order to a group of hoplites milling about. I knew him instantly.

"Orchus," I whispered to myself. And I knew what I must do before the opportunity slipped out of reach. "Wait until I have him!" I said in low voice to Lykos. Before he could react, I had left our hiding spot and covered the short distance separating us from Orchus.

"Make a sound and you're a dead man!" I hissed in Orchus' ear.

The Andrian mercenary flexed in surprise, but he was held fast by my left arm around his throat. The point of my sword pressed into the small of his back under the lip of his cuirass. He grunted as I increased the pressure enough to pierce his flesh. His struggling ceased.

But my advantage was tenuous, and Orchus knew it. "I give the word, boy, and we're both dead men."

I called his bluff. I twisted my blade. Orchus growled with the pain of it but did not shout out. Unless we came under direct scrutiny, I was hidden from view. A light hand on my shoulder told me that Lykos had joined us.

"Start moving towards the gate," I ordered, applying pressure to the sword, and the three of us, hostage and captors, began to shuffle towards the front gate.

"Is that my favorite Thracian whore-son?" My silence was answer enough for him, and the Andrian kept up his taunting. "Isn't that just how it goes, eh, boy? That aristocratic prick Menekrates will be upset to learn that he missed you. Probably halfway back to Athens by now."

The mention of Menekrates struck me like a stone. For a heartbeat, my grip around my hostage's neck slackened slightly. Orchus did not waste his chance. With a jerk of his head, his precariously balanced helmet toppled to the ground with a clang.

In the midst of the confusion, it was hardly noticeable. But it was enough to draw the attention of a nearby hoplite. The man squinted, but let out a shout of alarm as the nature of his commander's predicament suddenly dawned on him.

I regained control of Orchus, but now the other soldiers had been alerted to our presence. "Come nearer and your commander is a dead man!" I shouted over the Andrian's shoulder. In fact, it was only a guess that Orchus was their leader. For the moment, though, the hoplites hesitated. But if even one came to the conclusion that our hostage was expendable, we were dead men. "Move!" I growled at Orchus. We were still thirty or forty paces from the main gate. Too far, I thought to myself. The hoplites began to converge on us.

The baiting from Orchus continued. "You're too late to help your *brothers*, boy. They hardly even put up a fight. Set their own compound on fire, by Zeus!"

"Shut up!" Twenty paces.

Orchus was undeterred. "Your sister was better, boy. Almost cut young Menekrates' throat with that pig-sticker of hers! Not much match against a veteran's spear though. Now she's naught but cinders and ashes, I reckon."

Meli. I blinked back the tears welling in my eyes. Lykos' grip on my shoulder tightened, his fingers digging into my flesh. My mind was screaming for revenge, but I could not kill Orchus yet. Ten paces. I twisted the sword viciously.

Orchus gasped from the pain but did not relent. "The young lord searched everywhere for you, boy. Said he wanted you to die slowly. Like a slave, he said."

The mercenary resisted as we drew closer to the door, the taunting continuing unabated "Couldn't find you, though. Had to be satisfied with the lives of your wife and boy."

"What did you say" I began to crush the scarred bastard's throat in the crook of my arm.

"Not right for a lady of her stature to marry a half-breed like you, he said. Broke the law, she did. She had to be punished, he said," Orchus managed to rasp. "Gods! I thought your boy would never stop his howling."

A slap on my back. "Daimon! We're at the entrance!" It was Lykos. "Kill him and go!"

Orchus heaved. I thought he was gasping for air, but it was laughter. "You'd better do it, boy! A corpse don't bite, eh?" His body convulsed with laughter. My muscles tensed to drive the sword home.

But I never had a chance. A roar like a bull hit me like a punch. A giant strode through the crowd of hoplites, shoving them aside as though they were children. His shield was half as large again as that of a normal man's. In his right hand he wielded not a spear but an enormous Spartan-style *kopis* sword. Bare-headed, the beast bellowed again, his hate-filled eyes fixed upon us.

Akras. The colossus of Syracuse had arrived.

The distraction gave Orchus his opportunity. He threw his head back, stunning me. He twisted violently out of my grasp, stumbling towards Akras and his men. "Kill him!" he shouted as he scrambled away.

A javelin skimmed over my shoulder as I sprinted after Lykos through the smoking gate. The heat struck me like a hammer blow. The better part of the courtyard's perimeter was either aflame or smouldering, burning wood cracking as though it were being hewn with axes. Embers swirled about like snowflakes, pricking exposed skin like tiny daggers.

Lykos had pulled up, a frozen form amidst the heat. His sword arm hung limply at his side. He was staring at the conflagration that was devouring the eastern portion of the compound. The room that

Lykos and Meli used as their quarters was there. "She is dead," he said, still not moving.

I choked back my own sorrow. There was nothing to be done but look for survivors in the eastern half of the compound before it too was consumed. I had to find Phaia. "We must go," I said through my tears. Lykos turned his head and looked at me blankly. "Brother," I said. "We must go." The words reached him, and he nodded. We turned away from the funeral pyre to the west.

Only now did we take in the full extent of the carnage of the *peripoli*'s last stand. The very ground was scorched and patches of flame still flickered, though there was no fuel visible. More horrific were the smoking corpses that lay strewn about, filling the air with the sickening odor of burning flesh. Half-seared faces peered from blackened helmets, their faces locked in a voiceless scream. I did not recognize them, and I understood that these were the corpses of the enemy, abandoned by their comrades who had fled the inferno.

"Over there," Lykos coughed, pointing to the far side of the courtyard.

The *peripoli* had set up a defensive barricade of benches, tables and anything else on hand. Ahead of me, Lykos disappeared through a gap in the makeshift wall and I ran after him, picking my way through the dead. The breach in the wall was glutted with both *peripoli* and enemy dead. I stepped through the gap.

I wish I had not. At least thirty slain *peripoli* were there, mixed among the enemy that they had managed to take with them. I scanned the scene desperately but did not see Meges or Phaia among them. But the others I recognized all too well.

The arms-master Heirax was there, leaning against the wall as though taking a rest. The Skythian was impaled by two spears, both snapped off where they had entered below his breast. The good-humored Kirphis had been gutted and lay on his side, his entrails spilling out onto the dirt. Lykos was kneeling by one of the bodies.

Hermon lay on his back, his eyes staring up into the glowing sky. A jagged gash ran deep into the left side of the *peripoli* commander's neck, the blood turned black from the heat. His breastplate bore the ragged holes of a dozen spear-thrusts.

"They used lamp-oil," Lykos said hollowly. He waved weakly at a number of sealed pots piled beside the altar. "Hermon set the bastards on fire rather than surrender." He looked up at me, and I could see where his tears had left tracks through the soot on his face.

An enormous crack made us both turn simultaneously. The lintel beam above the flaming western gate of the training yard had partially collapsed. It was the only remaining access to the yet unburnt parts of the compound. To where I had left Phaia and my son. We could not linger. "We must go," I implored.

Lykos slowly rose to his feet. A battle for emotions played across his face, but the soldier in him won out. "For Phaia," he said hoarsely.

As we emerged from behind the barricade, Lykos suddenly shouted a warning. I threw back just in time to avoid being skewered with a javelin.

Scrambling to my feet, I saw that five hoplites had overcome their reluctance to reenter the inferno of the compound, prodded on by something even more fearsome than the flames: Akras. Levelling his *kopis* sword at us, the giant roared, commanding the men to attack. Even so, the men were wary, the smoking corpses of their comrades a deterrent against rash charges.

"The oil!" Lykos shouted.

A flurry of oil-pots flew over the makeshift wall as we hurled them towards the approaching hoplites. The clay vessels shattered on impact, splattering the nearest two soldiers with slick oil. One of them screamed as the oil on his legs ignited.

"Through the west gate," Lykos yelled. "We can hold them off there. Now go!"

We dashed through the burning gate and into the eastern part of the compound. I spun to face whoever pursued us, my sword ready. Beside me stood Lykos, clutching one more pot of oil in his free hand. We were both breathing hard, glistening with sweat and dirty with black soot.

The looming figure of Akras appeared in the doorway.

"Daimon! Back!" Lykos screamed. Before Akras could bear down on us, Lykos swung the pot in an overhand arc. The incendiary missile sailed directly at its target. Akras jerked his shield around, its edge catching the pot and shattering it in a shower of fluid that coated the titan's right side with the volatile oil.

For a heartbeat nothing happened, but then almost magically, the oil ignited. Like a tormented beast, Akras roared as blue-green flame rippled wherever the oil had coated him. In an instant, his shield was completely engulfed. Still bellowing in pain, the Syracusan desperately worked to shake his shield free and at last it flew from his grasp.

Akras stood completely exposed, spots on his breastplate and face still smoking. With a scream of vengeance, Lykos lunged forward to finish off the foe who had slain so many Athenians. There was no grace in it. The *peripoli* captain leapt recklessly, his sword flashing downwards towards the giant's neck.

And the blade froze midway through its deadly arc.

In horror, I watched Akras move faster than should have been possible for a man of his size, catching Lykos' forearm in his enormous hand. He lifted Lykos skyward as though he were a child.

Akras' *kopis* drove upwards, plunging through Lykos' sternum with such savagery that it burst out of my friend's back. Impaled, Lykos convulsed weakly on the blade and then was still.

"No!" I screamed.

With brutal disdain, the Syracusan ripped the sword free and dropped Lykos' body aside as though he were no more than a sack of grain.

The giant's eyes fell upon me. Seared flesh smoked where his hair had caught fire, but he seemed oblivious to the pain. Roaring a challenge, he pummeled his chest with his free hand, daring me to meet him.

Rage surged within me. My war-cry rising in my chest, I prepared to throw myself at the monster that had just slain my friend. My brother.

A crack like a thunderbolt shattered the air, as though Zeus himself had interceded in the battle. The beam supporting the doorway groaned in one final protest and then surrendered to the inevitable. Still standing astride the body of Lykos, Akras threw himself back just as the entire wall collapsed in an explosion of flame and glowing cinders.

A fiery wall of rubble now separated me from the cemetery of *peripoli* that lay beyond. I do not know how long I stood there before the flame. I could not find the will to look away. Finally, though, a name stronger than my grief pushed its way to the surface of my mind: Phaia.

Abandoning Lykos in his pyre, I turned and ran.

THOUGH FLAMES HAD SO FAR SPARED the western half of the compound, the same could not be said for death and slaughter. When I burst into the kitchen, the tenuous hope I had been clinging to was shattered in an instant. I almost tripped over the body of Lampita lying on her side in a congealing red pool. Her eyes were wide and fierce, as they always were in life. By her hand was a long butcher's blade stained with gore. Lampita had not sold her life cheaply.

Lampita was not the only victim of the attackers' massacre. On one corner of the kitchen was a mass of bloody bodies, some draped over others. At first I thought they were all women, but behind them were children, young and old and babes in their first year, slain like their mothers. Fear ate at my guts as my eyes flicked from one corpse to another, but with guilty relief I saw neither Phaia nor Niko among them. I abandoned the dead and plunged deeper into the land of the dead.

I hurtled towards the storeroom that was my family's home. Around the last corner and I was there. I opened my mouth to call out to Phaia, but her name died on my lips.

Amid the bodies, my eyes fell upon Meges first. He sat slumped by the doorway, his head leaning forward so that his black oily hair obscured his face. His legs were splayed out and his arms hanging loosely by his sides, making him look like a drunk sleeping off a night's revelry. He would have toppled forward but for the broken spear pinning him to the wall. Foolishly I cried his name, but he did not move.

Before him lay three men, their limbs bent and necks turned in the unnatural angles that only the dead could assume. They were not *peripoli*. Meges had died protecting Phaia and my son.

I looked at the door to the storeroom. The canvas in the door hung limply, suspended from one corner of the door. Within there was only darkness and silence. I picked my way over the corpses and entered.

Phaia was the only one in the room. My wife lay on her back, her arms straight and slightly away from her sides with her palms turned upwards. Mercifully her eyes were closed. Of Niko I saw nothing, only his overturned cradle splashed with blood, and I knew he had been slain. Dropping my sword, I fell to my knees, moaning.

The tang of her blood filled the small space of the storeroom. My hand drifted to her stomach. My fingers paused at each of the tacky clumps where a blade had pierced her front. Gingerly I touched her cheek, my fingertips leaving crimson streaks on her face. I pulled her up to me and for some moments I held her to my chest as sobs wracked my body. I was alone.

I could not leave her there to be consumed by fire or to have her body thrown outside the walls like a traitor or criminal, rotting in the sun and consumed as carrion. I needed to bury her so that her shade would not wander the earth. Like my father. My mother. Neleus. Lykos. Meli. My son who had not even reached his first year. So many had died.

I rose, cradling Phaia in my arms. I have seen men wandering the battlefield after a battle, their eyes glazed and blind to the world around them. So must I have been at that moment.

I left Meges where he had fallen. It shames me to think of it even now, but Meges would have mocked me for my guilty conscience. The gods care not for the living or dead he had told me whenever the opportunity had arisen, and I encountered neither as I made my way through the compound.

The door through which Lykos and I had accompanied Thrasybulus and his family only a day earlier was still barred. Methodically, I lay Phaia on the ground, lifted the heavy beam, opened the door, and took Phaia in my arms once again. I stepped out into the streets of Piraeus and abandoned the dead to their fiery tomb.

AMID THE CHAOTIC STREETS I was but one more shadow. A few people pointed and fell back in fear as I carried Phaia, but I paid them no mind. The *peripoli* compound was only a short distance from the western edge of the port where I was heading.

The rubble of the old wall lay heaped where it had been cast down months before. No one had dared move the rocks and boulders. Any enemy could come into the city as they pleased. Or leave. Behind me the fire still filled the night with its glow, the heat of it still whispering at the back of my neck. But before me was the night, black as pitch, waiting. Only a heap of stones blocked my way.

"Halt!"

I stumbled to a stop and waited, swaying from grief and exhaustion like a drunkard.

"Turn around and face me!" the voice demanded. "Turn, or you will feel my spear in your back!"

I craved death. I wished to die there with Phaia in my arms, to embrace the nothingness of the shadow-world. No longer would I endure the torments of the gods.

I waited for the footsteps and the merciful snap of the spear-thrust that would end my existence. Yet only the hoarse rhythm of my own breathing filled my ears. I turned to face my executioner.

The soldier was my age, perhaps a few years older. He stood five paces away from me, his spear held level and pointed at my chest. He wore a scaled corselet and helmet polished to a high sheen, open-faced in the new style. The gear of a wealthy man.

The weight of Phaia's corpse in my arms pressed down. She seemed much heavier in death than in life. I looked away from the young spearman, looking down at my wife's face. Her skin was pale, like a statue. Tears sprung anew, dripping onto Phaia's spattered tunic.

I looked up at the young man. He had not moved. His spear-point quivered. Anger began to swell in me. "What are you waiting for?" I rasped through tears and mucus. "Do it! I am *peripoli*! I am an enemy!"

But still the guard hesitated. His eyes were open wide. The spear trembled.

"Do it!" I pleaded.

The man's face filled with shame. He straightened, raising his spear. For a moment, neither of us moved. He glanced at Phaia and back up to me, with sorrow in his eyes. "Go and bury your dead," he said. Then, he turned away from me.

I stared at the man's back, not understanding.

"Please," I whispered. But the man walked away.

Like the tiny spark in the kindling that glows and fades, the will to live fought and struggled to ignite. The flame took. The hoplite's mercy was the fuel, a mercy that the gods had denied me.

I turned again towards the remains of the wall. I hefted Phaia onto my shoulder and stepped through the gap and was swallowed by the night.

IT WAS MORNING WHEN I ARRIVED at the hunting lodge, exhausted and weaponless. Tibetos was waiting with a mule and supplies procured from a hamlet in the wide, flat river plain.

In clipped, flat words, I told him of the slaughter of the *peripoli* by Menekrates and the soldiers of the Tyrants. Tibetos wept unashamedly for them all while I knelt on the ground, stone-faced.

In a grove near the lodge we buried Phaia. I cleaned her face and wounds, arranging her hair and garments as best I could. She looked at peace. We go to the underworld in the form we hold at our deaths, and I would not send her there bloodied and dishevelled.

The earth was soft, but even so my fingernails were ragged and bloody by the time I performed the rites. While we toiled, the sky became overcast, the clouds darkening and the wind picking up. Isolated raindrops fell, causing tiny craters in the dust, each one sounding like someone tapping on a tabletop with his finger. Suddenly there was a whirlwind about us and the torrent that had been held back was unleashed. A late summer storm, a harbinger of the winter rains to come.

Piling stones upon Phaia's grave, I ignored the wind and rain and thunderclaps that grew ever louder. I told Tibetos to go back to the lodge to wait out the storm, but he would not abandon me. So we sat by the cairn in the raging darkness, illuminated by the lightning flashes in the sky.

With each jagged bolt I cursed Zeus. The Saviour. All my life I had offered prayers and sacrifices to the gods, as my father had done. But my piety had been incinerated in fire and death. I hurled insults at the sky, daring Zeus to strike me down. The cold lancets of rain drove into me. But I felt nothing but hatred and a thirst for vengeance.

There was only one path to retribution.

I was going to Thebes.

## CHAPTER 32

The raiders fled down the slope with stones and jeers pelting their backs in equal measure. A jubilant cry rose from the defenders on the ridge and even I allowed myself the grim hint of a smile. This initial skirmish had ended as an ignominious defeat for the forces of the Thirty Tyrants.

"Look at them run, Dammo!" Tibetos grinned at me, still twirling a stone in his sling. "All the way back to Athens. Turd-eaters!" he shouted at the attackers' backs. "All the way back to Athens!"

I grunted in agreement. Our fort was on a ridge called Phyle. Thrasybulus had chosen the location well. The crag holds a commanding view of the valley below, and no large force can approach undetected. If the heights are secured, a small group of well-armed men can easily hold off many times their number, as we had just proven.

Thrasybulus had been good to his word, naming me a *lochagos*, a captain. But there were few men for me to command. Of the hundred or so men who occupied the ridge, only half were warriors in their prime, among them a number of fugitive *peripoli* including Telekles and Sabas, the Cretan. The remainder were good for nothing except eating our food and griping. Some were metic merchants, their wealth confiscated by the Thirty. Others were former leaders of the democratic faction in Athens who were very fond of hearing their own voices. If words were spears, we could have brought Kritias and Lysander to their knees in a matter of days. I watched as Tibetos and the others hastened to strip the enemy corpses of their valuable armour and weapons. And I worried.

We had defeated a few hundred attackers. These had been the hotheads, eager for the glory, and they had paid the price for their rashness. Next time they would not be so foolish. Tomorrow they would send the full force of a thousand men camped in the valley below.

While I stood contemplating the discouraging prospect of fending off a thousand enemy fighters, Thrasybulus moved about congratulating the men. He saw me and strode over. "It was well done!" he boomed.

But I was in little mood for his optimism. "And what will we do when they send a thousand men tomorrow?" I challenged him, my voice loud enough to draw the looks of those nearby.

Thrasybulus smiled, but his eyes were iron. He put his arm around my shoulder. "Come with me, Daimon."

Below us, men scoured the slopes for items discarded during the enemy retreat. Everything was of value. Thrasybulus pointed at them. "Look at them, Daimon," he said. "Why do they fight?" I did not answer. "They fight because they have nothing. They have lost everything. Wealth, property, family. In exile, they would live little better than slaves. They are desperate." He turned to look at me directly. "Do not underestimate desperate men, Daimon."

"Yes, *strategos*," I said sullenly. I could not bring myself to share his optimism.

Thrasybulus sighed at my intransigence. "I need you, Daimon, to win battles like we did today. Men will hear of our success and join our cause."

"If they don't come soon, there will be nothing left to fight for," I said and pointed down to the valley. "We cannot stand against that many soldiers."

"If they move against us we will retreat into the mountains."

"If we retreat, they will have won all the same. The men will scatter and we will not have another chance!" I was frustrated and impatient, for I saw my only chance for vengeance slipping from my grasp, however tenuous it might have been.

"Who knows what opportunity the gods might provide us?" Thrasybulus said. "Nothing is certain, Daimon."

I snorted. "The gods? I would rather count on my own spear!"

"Then I will accept that as your word. But I need you to fight when others waver." He held out his hand.

Men were staring at us now. I could not dishonour Thrasybulus in front of them. I nodded, and we clasped hands. "I will fight for you, *strategos*. To the end." I meant it.

Thrasybulus hesitated. "I have received other news," he said.

"Good or bad?"

"I would say they are ill-tidings, but you might disagree. Alkibiades is dead," he said, waiting for my reaction.

In truth, I could not summon the joy I should have felt at the death of the man I had scorned for so long. "How?" I asked.

"Lysander's assassins caught up with him in Asia. Lysander saw him as a potential threat and had him killed," Thrasybulus said. I learned later that the Spartans had trapped the god-man in a house in Phrygia with his mistress and set fire to it. Alkibiades ran out with his sword and died under a hail of arrows. As I have said, I never questioned Alkibiades' courage. But I have never forgiven him for the death of my brother Heliodoros.

"He wanted you to like him," Thrasybulus added. "It vexed him that you were immune to his charms."

I scoffed at this. "And did you come under his spell, *strategos*?"

He thought about it for a moment. "I was jealous of his gifts. It bothered me that he squandered his talents on his own personal gain rather than for the benefit of Athens. But I confess that I liked him." He looked out at his men on the slopes below. "And now Lysander and his dogs in Athens are coming for us. But we will show him what those with right on their side can do, no?" He winked at me.

I watched thoughtfully as Thrasybulus went to encourage another group of men nearby. Thrasybulus fought for the democracy that was precious to him. But it was not my cause. I wished only for vengeance. But as I looked down towards the valley, that hope for revenge faltered. The soldier in me knew what was going to happen.

Tomorrow, or the next day, a hundred men would face one thousand. We would be crushed and the insignificant rebellion of Thrasybulus would be throttled in its infancy.

Something brushed my cheek. I wiped it away, annoyed. My finger was cold and wet. I lifted my head and peered at the sky. All about me, others did the same. Soft, white flakes swirled from the heavens.

It seemed as though the gods were listening to Thrasybulus after all.

It was spring. But it had begun to snow.


WHAT A GIFT THE GODS had sent! The first green shoots of spring growth were buried under a white blanket that often reached the middle of a man's thigh. No attack on our fort was possible now. But we could fall upon our enemies.

Our men were few in number and poorly-armed, but we were equipped to live off the land. The army of the Thirty was not. Their expedition had set out from Athens expecting a quick rout of the rebels, leaving them ill-prepared to keep men fed and warm in these conditions. Defeated by the weather, the enemy force began its retreat to Athens.

They were sheep to our wolves. Weighed down by their supplies, they moved slowly, even abandoning fully-laden carts. We carried only our weapons, and we moved swiftly over the paths the retreating soldiers had left for us. The snow muffled our approach, and we fell upon bands of stragglers before they even realized we were near. We slaughtered any that we came upon and left their naked corpses for the ravens.

It took several days to gather all the spoils. In one fell swoop, we had doubled our stocks of food. Atop Phyle, a great fire burned, and the smell of sizzling horse flesh filled the air. Men admired the pile of weapons and armour that had been harvested from the enemy.

But more than gaining plunder we had inspired hope.

Word of the victory spread. What had heretofore been a trickle of exiles turned into a steady stream. Mercenaries, attracted to conflict like flies to dung, found us too. They were hardened veterans from all over Greece for whom the thirty-year war had never ended, thieves, pillagers, and killers to a man. I was glad to have them. In a month our numbers swelled to more than seven hundred men.

The exiles brought with them word of the atrocities of Kritias and the Thirty. Thousands had been arrested and executed. Many more had fled and abandoned their property to the greedy Tyrants. The new corrupt regime was consolidating its power, eliminating its enemies and enriching itself.

My comrade Mnasyllus found his way to our camp. He had been on his family's farmstead when the *peripoli* compound burned. But his family had not escaped the purges of the Thirty. "My father was murdered like a dog," the big man told me, and we wept for our losses and swore vengeance. But I was happy to have him by my side once again.

Another addition surprised me. "Daimon!" I turned to see my former tutor Iasos. He must have been approaching sixty years, but he thrummed with good health. "A student of mine warned me that my name was on the list of proscribed citizens. It was time to leave. Let us make your father proud, *pai!*" he said. His weapons were well-used and well-maintained. I felt ashamed of how I had treated him when I was younger, for he had proven to be as loyal and good a man as I have ever known. I told him so.

"All youths are foolish and judge others too simply, but only a true fool never learns to admit his mistakes," Iasos said generously.

But our growing numbers bred other problems, for it is no small matter to feed and arm seven hundred men. Nor had the Tyrants forgotten us. Another army had come and camped in the valley. No snow would save us this time. Thrasybulus called a meeting to decide what should be done.

The former *strategos'* voice quelled the bickering in the tent. "The *lochagos* will report on what the *peripoli* have seen of the enemy camp," Thrasybulus said, giving me my cue to speak.

There was a derisive sniff. I glared at the source, Archinus, a wealthy democrat in exile. He was a supercilious coward with an oily tongue, just the type of man who thrived in the assembly. But he was not a warrior, a point I took great pleasure in rubbing his face in at every opportunity.

Archinus envied the authority that Thrasybulus had granted me, for he thought it should be his own, and he spread his poison against me. Once he had been careless enough to call me a Thracian barbarian, and I had seized him and threatened to cut his flapping tongue and nail it to his balding head. He had been justly wary of me since. Yet he had his supporters and had regained some of his courage now that he felt safe among them in the tent. Hostile faces stared back at me, formerly rich men forced to listen to the son of a slave. I smiled sardonically at them as I rose to speak.

"As you know, we have been patrolling the foothills and plains to the south on a daily basis. We have also made larger raids on farms to secure provisions. Until now, there has been little resistance from the Thirty, only the occasional patrol, but these were easily avoided or dealt with." We had brought back enough weapons and armour from the dead for everyone to understand what I meant by that statement.

"However, in the last few days, the Thirty have set up a large camp at the end of the valley. The camp is occupied by more than one thousand men, the Spartan garrison from Athens from the look of it, and two or three divisions of cavalry.

"They are building barriers across the valley. If they succeed, it will severely hamper our ability to enter the plains and raid the estates there. They have learned the folly of trying to attack our position, so it seems that the Thirty are going to cut our main supply lines."

I paused, glancing at Thrasybulus, who nodded almost imperceptibly. "If they are allowed to do this, they will then attempt to cut our remaining supply route from Thebes. If they succeed, we will starve before we ever have a chance to fight." The braying of Archinus and his clique erupted before I had even taken my seat.

The cowards called for every kind of caution under the sun. We should wait for more soldiers. We should hold our position. We should move our camp to another location. We should appeal to the Thebans for aid. I let my mind wander while the fools prattled on as though they were holding a debate in the assembly.

One bag of wind, Cephisophon, made the particularly inane suggestion of sending an embassy to the Thirty to see if terms could be negotiated. I laughed out loud at this, drawing irate stares from those in Archinus' faction.

"Why do you laugh, *pai?*" Archinus said, stressing the last word.

*Pai* can mean either child or slave, and it was clear what Archinus was insinuating. My bile rose but I did not take the bait. "The Thirty," I said through gritted teeth, "will not negotiate. And the other suggestions," I said with a dismissive wave, "will leave us without food or money within a month's time."

"And you have a better suggestion, do you, *pai?*" Archinus jabbed a finger at me. I wanted to tear it off and feed it to him. "Let us hear it then! It is sure to be wise and insightful. We are all ears!" he said in a tone dripping in condescension.

Thrasybulus arched an eyebrow but said nothing. He already knew what I was about to say, and now I did so with his tacit approval.

"We attack them," I said simply.

Archinus and his faction blustered in a predictable manner, throwing their arms in the air and rolling their eyes. For once, I sat calmly, letting their taunts and proclamations wash over me. It was a tactic I had seen my father use so many times before in the assembly. "The hot air blowing from the mouths of fools soon exhausts itself, like a summer storm," he often told me.

So now I let the wind spew from the fool's mouth. "And," Archinus said in his best rhetorician voice, "How do you propose we defeat them, *pai*? That is no ordinary army encamped in the valley, as you have said. It is a Spartan garrison, fully equipped and trained. Hardly half our number has full hoplite gear. And even if, with the help of the gods, we were able to match them, there are two entire divisions of cavalry. Our flanks would be cut to pieces!

"The young!" Archinus turned to appeal to his audience. "They are brave, yes! But sometimes to the point of foolhardiness!" A few laughed at the feeble attempt to undermine me. Archinus looked at me smugly.

I rose from my seat. "We need neither gods nor hoplites to defeat them," I said, raising my voice. "Not if we fight as the *peripoli* do. We hit them in their camp at dawn while they're still scratching their balls. We will cut through their camp like a scythe through ripe grain. But we must strike soon, before they build their defenses. But it is not for *cowards*," I added with a sneer towards Archinus.

I sat back down. The tent exploded into squawking debate once again. Archinus glared at me with undisguised loathing.

The mighty voice of Thrasybulus boomed. "Enough!" A reluctant silence filled the tent. "This plan has merit. If the omens are favourable, we attack at dawn." Does anyone challenge this?" Thrasybulus tone discouraged any such challenge. Archinus had lost the debate. "Then this meeting is dismissed."

The general and his supporters exited the tent first, leaving Archinus and his faction to mull over their defeat. I stayed on my stool, watching them as a hawk watches mice. Feeling my eyes on them, they mumbled feeble protests and pushed through the tent flaps one by one.

"Archinus!" I called. "Let us speak for a moment. I would not have us part company this way." Archinus hesitated at the exit, unsure of my motives. I smiled warmly. "Please," I said, my voice conciliatory. "We are allies in this after all, and I value your experience." I indicated the stool next to me.

Archinus regarded me suspiciously, but the man never could resist the opportunity to hear his own voice. He sniffed, raised his chin, and came to take his place.

He yelped in pain as I seized him by the ear and gave a vicious twist. He buckled and writhed, but I tightened my grip and jerked his head down so that he was bent over like some old man's bumboy. I leaned close to his other ear and spoke in a flat whisper. "If you call me '*pai*' again, I will gut you, ally or no. Do you understand, *old man*?" I twisted even more with the last words.

Archinus grunted, though whether it was in assent or just pain, I am not absolutely certain. I shoved him away. He clutched his injured ear, his eyes lit with pure hatred. I turned my back on him, an unwise decision in most cases, but I knew him for a coward.

Sure enough, no retaliation came. I pushed the tent flap aside and went out into the cool air of spring. It smelled of new life. It smelled of hope.

# CHAPTER 33

We flowed through the trees like ghosts in the half-light of dawn.

A lonely guard near the edge of the camp died without a sound. My sword hacked through the back of his neck as he tended a low fire. He toppled into the flickering coals with a soft crunch, sending an upward cascade of tiny, glowing cinders into the air. I glanced over at Mnasyllus beside me, who carried a smith's cudgel in one hand and a spear in the other. He nodded but did not stop.

To either side of me, the freedom fighters of Thrasybulus, spread out in a loose mass a hundred men wide, advanced on the enemy camp. I was in the fore with Mnasyllus, Telekles, and Tibetos, my two swords held low as I advanced in a loping crouch. We moved quickly, making no sound, slaying any we encountered. To my left was the first scream. The alarm was raised.

There was no more need for silence. Up and down our line, men howled their war-cries. Like a wolf-pack, we swept through the panicked camp, baying for the blood of our oppressors.

It was a slaughter. Many died in their tents, still groggy from their night's sleep. Some had been preparing their breakfasts or tending to their horses. Those who were armed scarcely had time to draw their weapons. A testament to their discipline, some of the Spartan-trained garrison had suppressed their panic and put up some resistance. But there were too many attackers and they were surrounded and stabbed and speared to death by our shadow army. Great numbers simply fled from the massacre, leaving their comrades to fall beneath our motley collection of axes, swords, and spears that were older than the men who wielded them. It made no difference in the end.

Riderless horses galloped wildly through the camp, their eyes rolling in terror. A few cavalrymen had actually managed to mount their beasts but to little effect. A spear-throw away from me, one rider was hauled from his horse by a fury of clawing, vengeful hands.

The thunderous voice of Thrasybulus reverberated above the chaos. "Hold the camp! Hold the camp! Do not pursue!"

It was a sage command, for scattered pursuers are vulnerable to organized counter-attacks, especially by men on horse. Like me, our men wore light armour, if they wore any protection at all. We had routed the enemy, but a careless pursuit could have easily turned the tide.

The cacophony of battle had subsided, replaced by the moans and cries of the mauled and dying. The shrieking of a wounded horse echoed through the camp at regular intervals. The coppery tang of blood lingered underneath the odors of smoke, leather, and horse dung permeating the air.

Men were already stripping the dead of armour, weapons, or anything else that had even a hint of value. Madness overcame many of our men as they ran to plunder the tents and wagons in a frenzied race to secure the best booty for themselves. Men who had been allies in the battle a few moments earlier now argued over looted goods. A mercenary casually speared a groaning hoplite where he lay on the ground. Throwing his own battered conical helmet away, he removed the high-quality one from the dead man's head and held it before his face, admiring the polished bronze. Seeing me, he bared his teeth in a growl, warning me to find another body to strip. I shrugged and let him have his prize.

Wandering through the camp, I nearly collided with Barates, the oft-wrong seer. The soothsayer's eyes widened at the sight of me. The obsequious *mantis* had shown up a month earlier, quickly attaching himself to Archinus. The seer had sacrificed a sheep the previous night and declared the omens to be poor, no doubt at the request of Archinus. Afterwards I had privately suggested that he make another sacrifice, and should the signs be inauspicious once again, I predicted he would end up with a second mouth across his throat. The portents of the second sacrifice were unambiguously positive in favour of an attack. Now amidst the carnage of our victory, I leered wickedly at the seer, and he scuttled away without a word.

I found Thrasybulus surveying the scene in the main clearing at the centre of the camp. His face and chest were splattered with blood. Beside him, conspicuously unsullied by the gore of battle, was that piece of weasel dung, Archinus. Seeing me approach, Thrasybulus threw open his arms and strode over to embrace me firmly. Archinus glowered.

Thrasybulus released me and stepped back, regarding the dark patches that likewise stained my front. "You have also done battle this day, I see."

"Those in the front ranks always do the heaviest lifting. I fear there was nothing left for those who arrived last," I tried to provoke Archinus, who wisely held his tongue.

Thrasybulus was uncharacteristically euphoric. It was only then that I understood that his outward display of confidence had masked his own corrupting doubts.

As he enthused over the victory, my attention wandered. At the edge of the clearing, a row of prisoners knelt in the dirt under guard. With bowed heads, the captives endured the curses and abuse of their captors. The guards spat on them and pricked them with their weapons. There would be no hostages this day. Once they had been interrogated, the prisoners were dead men. I felt no sympathy for them. The best they could hope for was a quick cut across the throat, though many of them would no doubt suffer worse fates. A desire for vengeance makes men cruel.

I was about to turn back to say something to Thrasybulus, but I halted abruptly. One prisoner had caught my eye. It was only because of the brightening morning light that I saw it.

A scarlet Spartan cloak, torn and dusty from the battle, hung limply over the kneeling man's shoulder and back. But there were many such cloaks about the camp, and it was nothing to set the man apart. It was his breastplate that held my gaze.

A familiar pattern of incised whorls traced their intricate path about the breast and abdomen of the armour. Below the left breast was an ancient rent in the metal, expertly mended but still plainly visible, damage caused by the spear-thrust of a Phocian hoplite.

My heart lurched. As a child I had gazed upon that cuirass in wonder and had endured countless blisters polishing its surface with sand and grit. I knew its lines and imperfections as well as anything in this world.

As if in a trance, I strode towards the kneeling prisoner. I came to a halt before him, but he did not look up. Grabbing the man's black hair, I yanked it hard so that I could see his face.

His dull eyes widened in astonished recognition.

It was my brother, Adrastos.

ADRASTOS LET OUT A WEAK LAUGH. "The gods have shit on me today."

My sword hissed as it slid from its tattered leather scabbard. I pressed the edge of the blade lightly against his throat.

My brother curled his lip. "This is the only way a barbarian like you could defeat me. Take my life then, coward."

I should have opened his throat. Yet still I hesitated.

"Coward!" he hissed.

"*Lochagos*," said Thrasybulus behind me. The usual resonating timbre of his voice had softened. The iron at my brother's gullet trembled, one stroke away from ending his life. "Daimon," Thrasybulus said, and I felt the weight of his hand on my shoulder.

I released Adrastos from my grasp and spun to face Thrasybulus. Sadness tinged his sombre expression. He knew my story well enough and would have guessed who it was that knelt before me.

"*Strategos*," I said. Tears threatened to flow down my face. "I have served you faithfully and well. You have rewarded me with respect and opportunity that few others have deigned to grant me. But now there is something I ask of you."

"If it is in my power, it shall be so."

"I demand justice."

"You shall have it."

I took a breath. "In the Thracian manner."

Thrasybulus pursed his lips slightly but nodded his assent. A small crowd had gathered, drawn to the drama by some silent call.

Adrastos snorted in contempt. "Thracian justice? Do they even know the word?"

My anger flooded back at the sound of his voice, but I suppressed the rage, letting it smoulder deep inside me. "You will be able to fight for your worthless life, brother."

"Only to be executed when I kill you?" he sneered.

"If I am defeated, you will be free to leave. I swear it."

My brother raised his voice so that the crowd could hear his words. "And I am to believe you? Why should I take the word of a barbarian slave?"

"You have my oath that you will be unharmed should you prevail," Thrasybulus replied, his words audible to all. There was a grumble of dissent from those gathered around us, for many had suffered greatly under the rule of the Thirty.

"I accept *your* oath," my brother responded to Thrasybulus, bowing his head mockingly.

"Do not test my patience." A rare edge of true anger crept into Thrasybulus' voice.

My brother merely laughed. "Keep your word then, O *strategos*. Unbind me, and let it be done. I can still be back in Athens before dinner."

FROM THE OTHER SIDE OF THE SMALL CLEARING, my father's shade watched me warily over the edge of his shield, his spear levelled at my chest.

Or so it seemed to me, for my brother bore more than a passing resemblance to our father, especially when clad in his armour. The Pegasus emblazoned on my father's *aspis* shield still soared proudly, as though untainted by the polluted soul of the man crouching behind it.

In contrast to my brother, I was helmetless and wore only my black horse-hoof corselet for protection. My *rhomphaia* had been lost in the conflagration of the *peripoli* compound, so I would fight with two swords in the Thracian manner, a *xiphos* in my left hand and a curved *maichera* in my right. I spun the weapons restlessly.

Spectators ringed the clearing. Word had spread, and there was not a man present who was not aware of my brother's crimes. There were some shouts of support, but most stood in grim silence, waiting to see justice done.

I offered prayers to no gods. Thrasybulus came forward. The murmur of the crowd died down to nothing. "Begin!" came the command from Thrasybulus.

Adrastos dropped into a defensive crouch. The tip of his spear tracked me as I paced back and forth, drawing closer to him with each turn.

"You are a coward!" Adrastos barked from behind his shield. "You have never beaten me, *Brother*. I will shame you in front of your bandit horde before you die." I did not respond. "Are you not eager to join your whore wife in Hades? Menekrates told me how he killed her. I will be merciful and make your death quick, unlike hers!"

It had ever been his trick, his power over me, to hound and prod me with insults, to goad me into a careless attack and use my own rage against me. The words bit, but I was a boy no longer. I was hunting him and he knew it.

We circled each other warily, the distance between us diminishing until I was so close I could have reached out and tapped his shield with my sword.

Adrastos continued his baiting. "Or perhaps I should sell you into slavery, like your half-breed son and little bitch sister? How long would you last in the mines, barbarian? Or as a slave rower on a grain ship?"

His words stunned me. Adrastos' spear snapped towards my chest as fast as a viper. Only a desperate pivot saved me before I stumbled out of range. As I recovered my balance, I glimpsed Archinus in the crowd. His eyes were hungry for my death.

I was shaken. I had thought my sister and my son dead. Had the mercenary Orchus not said so? Yet Adrastos had said they had been enslaved. "Where is Melitta?" I yelled. "Where is my son?"

Adrastos had found the chink in my armour and sought to exploit it. "Sold, like animals!" He lunged, and the spear tip tore off a black plate of my armour, leaving it hanging, and he danced out of range and continued to taunt me.

"Gone on a slave ship! To be with the helots in Sparta?" His spear flicked out and I leapt back. He laughed. "Or with the Persians? When your boy is old enough, they'll geld him like a yearling!"

My heart sank. If Meli and Niko lived, they could be anywhere. They had only been condemned to a slower death, and I felt hope slip from my grasp once more. But Adrastos had revealed too much, for I knew he was of no use to me. His life was forfeit, and ice filled my soul. But I would not let Adrastos see that. Not yet.

Feigning a broken spirit, I raised my twin blades half-heartedly and took a clumsy step towards my brother, leaving an opening.

The temptation was too great for Adrastos. His spear whipped out like a snake striking, aiming for my groin. It was a fine attack and would have skewered most men.

But I was faster.

I stepped towards him, letting my *xiphos* guide my brother's spear harmlessly past me, and I brought my foot up, planting a kick in the middle of his shield with all my strength. Even with the weight of his extra armour, my brother staggered back from the force of the blow, and once again I was out of the range of his spear.

"I gave you your chance, Brother," I called to him. For the first time, uncertainty flickered in the eyes that peered at me from behind the protection of my father's helmet.

Then I came at him. It was not how an Athenian or Spartan moved, but like a Thracian, all constant motion, unpredictable and flowing. With a zig-zagging lope, I bounded forwards, rapidly cutting the distance between us. With a shout, I made an arcing leap, focusing all of the power and momentum into a downward blow of my *maichera*.

Desperately, Adrastos heaved his shield upwards. The crack of the impact rang like a clap of thunder through the clearing and splinters of wood flew into the air as he reeled away from me.

He lashed out in a counter-attack, but the spear-thrust was wild and I turned to let it go past me. Like an enormous pair of shears, my swords chopped in opposite directions on the ash shaft of the spear before my brother could draw it back, shattering it like a piece of kindling. The amputated spear was still levelled at me impotently. Adrastos' attention flicked back to me, his fear apparent now.

He threw the useless weapon at me and I batted it away. He drew his sword. It did not matter to me. Let him cower behind his shield. It would not save him. I played with him, feinting and slashing from all directions. The heavy shield and armour drained his stamina and soon his mouth hung open as he gasped for breath, his blocks and parries becoming increasingly wild as he fended off each successive attack.

I had had enough.

I charged. He braced himself against his shield, but the impact never came. Dropping low, I rolled under his guard and I was suddenly behind him. I slashed at the back of his exposed knee and I felt the blade grate against the bones in his leg. With a scream, Adrastos dropped his sword and collapsed on his other knee, hamstrung. The encircling crowd of hardened soldiers gasped.

My brother struggled to rise, propping himself on his shield, but his ruined leg would not let him stand. I kicked him contemptuously in the centre of his back and he sprawled face forward into the packed dirt. He scrambled to free himself from the awkward shield and tried to crawl away from me, dragging his bloody leg behind him and moaning with each jerk of his body.

Tossing my swords aside, I went to him. I bent over and ripped the helmet savagely from his head and it struck the dusty earth with a muffled clang. Adrastos whimpered as I seized his breastplate and flipped him roughly onto his back, sitting down astride his stomach. I struck him hard in the face three times. He looked up at me dazed.

I leaned in close. "I will deny you an honourable death. I will leave your body unburied, like you did for Father. Your shade will never find peace." I whispered hoarsely.

A look of terror overcame him as he realized my intention. "No," he protested weakly, but my hands were already wrapping around his neck.

My brother's windpipe collapsed under my grasp. He punched me in the chest. He pulled and scratched at my arms. His bloodshot eyes bulged as my grip tightened, and his skin darkened into a terrible purple.

Then his body shook with outrage and with a final twitch he gave up his black soul.

His empty eyes stared at the sky. His tongue lolled grotesquely from his mouth. His last breath rasped from his body as I loosened my hold. I looked to the sky and howled, a sound that was more animal than man.

Madness overcame me. I lurched to my feet. Retrieving one of my swords, I returned to the corpse of my brother, taking it by the foot and dragging his flaccid deadness around the clearing. I roared in the grim faces that judged me. Some nodded approvingly, others gaped in wonder. I paused before Archinus, looming over him. His face was pale. I grimaced and he shrank before me, and those nearby laughed at his cowardice.

I bellowed a challenge. If anyone wished to claim my father's fine armour, they could fight me for it. But there was only silence. I grunted and began to strip the breastplate from Adrastos' limp body.

There were hushed voices, and the men began to disperse, off to collect their own spoils and the other supplies from the camp. A hand on my shoulder made me look up from my task impatiently. It was Thrasybulus.

For once, he was at a loss for words. Finally, he spoke. "It was a terrible thing to behold, Daimon," he said, and I felt resentment rising in my throat, for I heard disapproval in his voice. "But justly done, I think," he added, leaving me with my brother's corpse.

Turning back to my task, I was interrupted again by a cough. It was Tibetos. He squatted beside me and began to help.

"Thank you, Tibo," I said. My voice was hoarse.

"I hated the bastard too," he said quietly. In his voice, I heard the lifetime of abuse he had endured at my brother's hands. He spat fiercely in Adrastos' lifeless face and went back to untying a greave from my half-brother's calf. We worked in silence, each lost in his own thoughts.

We left Adrastos' dismembered corpse for the crows and foxes and other creatures that roam the night. May his shade forever roam those lands, lonely and unremembered.

My father's armour was heavy on our backs as we marched back to the camp at Phyle. Tibetos was the first to bring up the thought that weighed heavy on our hearts. "Do you think Adrastos was telling the truth about Meli? And Niko?"

If Adrastos had told the truth, then they had been put on a ship and condemned to a life of slavery, gone forever. I avoided the question, for I dared not hope that I could find them. "Orchus told me they were dead," was all I said.

My vengeance had not brought the release I sought, only more sorrow. Even in death Adrastos had cheated me one last time.

# CHAPTER 34

Tears streamed down the face of the herald from Eleusis. "They have executed every youth and man in the city, O Thrasybulus! My family! My kinsmen!"

Thrasybulus' face was grim. The Thirty had not waited long to avenge their defeat. But they had not attacked us. Instead the Tyrants had taken out their rage on the citizens of the holy sanctuary of Eleusis.

Cries of shock and outrage filled the tent. "Why would they attack Eleusis?" one gruff veteran demanded.

"They knew that many there were sympathetic to our cause and feared they would give us shelter," Thrasybulus responded. This was true, for many of the men who fought with us hailed from Eleusis.

"But to execute every man in the city!" The disbelief in the soldier's voice echoed the mood in the tent.

"That is the nature of the enemy we face," Thrasybulus said.

"We cannot let them go unpunished for this!" the tearful messenger implored Thrasybulus.

All eyes turned towards Thrasybulus. For a moment, he said nothing. But I saw his resolve harden, for I had seen it many times before. His decision had been made.

The leader of the rebellion stood up. The anger in his voice burned like hot iron. "Prepare the men. We march to Piraeus tonight!"


THE SOLDIERS IN PIRAEUS WOKE UP besieged by an enemy army. We had marched all night, appearing like ghosts outside the broken walls of the port at dawn. The inhabitants of Piraeus had hailed us as liberators and joined us in chasing the startled garrison away. A few skirmishes aside, it had been a bloodless victory. We jeered at the soldiers fleeing up the road back to Athens.

"They're running away like Phrygian chickens!" Mnasyllus laughed.

"Even Phrygian chickens couldn't run so fast," Tibetos chipped in.

The grateful men of Piraeus swelled our ranks. A few were wealthy enough to own their own armour, but most came from the poorer classes of merchants and tradesmen. Weapons that had remained hidden from the spies and informers of the Thirty were now proudly on display, as was the frantic joy of the liberated populace as they milled about in the streets.

I could not share in their celebration. For me, Piraeus was haunted by the angry dead. Their whispered laments drew me inexorably to the collapsed gate of the *peripoli* compound. Charred timbers protruded from the structure like great blackened ribs. A sooty odor lingered about its ruins, even nearly a year after its fiery destruction. The dead bade me enter, but my own sorrow and fear kept me frozen on the threshold.

A shout freed me from my state of paralysis. "Daimon! Daimon of the *peripoli*!" I turned to see a familiar figure trotting towards me. Timonax, the avuncular blacksmith, had made many weapons and tools for the *peripoli*, and I had spent many a happy hour assisting him at his forge. The grizzled craftsman pulled up in front of me, mouth agape. He looked as though I had returned from the Underworld. "It is you, lad!" he declared finally. His iron arms squeezed the air from my lungs as he embraced me. "Come with me, lad!" he said, and without explanation he hurried away from me.

I hastened after him, all the way to his smithy. Timonax spun suddenly and held up a finger. "Wait here!" He scurried off. When he returned, my chest tightened. My beautiful, deadly Whisper lay across his outstretched hands.

The Thracian *rhomphaia* flashed darkly as Timonax placed the sword gingerly in my palms. He had kept the blade oiled, and it glistened with its characteristic blue tinge. I gripped the hilt with two hands and felt the familiar heft of the weapon, so well-balanced despite its length. In my tremoring hands, she quivered as though alive. I looked at Timonax in awe.

"I dug up the weapons cache in the compound, after..." He did not finish the sentence. "I have safeguarded it for you, *pai*." The smith's eyes were filled with sadness. "I found this, too," Timonax said softly. He reached around his back to pull out something that had been concealed there.

I gasped, nearly dropping Whisper. Laid out on the wide, calloused palm of Timonax was the knife that I had given Meli so many years before.

Dropping to my knees before Timonax, I wept unashamedly for the dead and the lost. The blacksmith placed a burly hand on my shoulder with surprising gentleness and let me weep.

OUR COMMAND POST WAS A TAVERN beside the amphitheatre that lay at the base of the hill called Munychia that rose beside the harbour of the same name. Messengers came and went, reporting on the state of the defenses around the city, which was generally poor, as well as the supplies and men that we had managed to procure, which was more positive.

"How many men do we have?" Thrasybulus asked me.

"One thousand seven hundred. Perhaps another one hundred. It has been difficult to get exact numbers."

"And how many hoplites?"

"A thousand at most."

Thrasybulus creased his brow in thought. "It is still not enough to hold the walls if we are attacked. We would be too thinly stretched. We must begin to shore up the damaged sections of walls immediately."

"It will take time," I said doubtfully.

"Let us pray to the gods for time, then," Thrasybulus said.

"I'd rather have a thousand more men," I said, not sharing my general's faith in divine intervention.

My lack of faith was instantly justified. A soldier burst through the tavern door, his face flushed. Catching his breath, he made his report. "*Strategos!* An army has set out from Athens towards Piraeus!"

Looks of uncertainty flashed around the room, but Thrasybulus merely frowned. "How many?"

"Four or five thousand!" the soldier responded. "Including cavalry and the Spartan garrison!"

Everyone looked to Thrasybulus for his reaction. He narrowed his eyes as he weighed his options.

"Perhaps we can block their advance on the road?" someone piped up. It was that ass, Archinus.

"A thousand hoplites against five thousand on even ground?" I said dismissively. "They would crush us without breaking a sweat."

"The odds were almost the same at Marathon!" Archinus bleated, raising his hand in a dramatic fashion. There was a collective rolling of eyes among the veterans in the room, and Archinus could sense the lack of support for his plan. "We could —
"

Thrasybulus cut him off with a wave. "No, the road is lost."

"We could block off some streets. That would help offset their advantage in numbers," another captain suggested. This was a much more sensible plan, I thought, but still flawed. If Kritias and his forces pressed, they would still win, but they would take heavy losses in the street-to-street fighting. The prospect of so many casualties might discourage them from engaging us.

But Thrasybulus dismissed this strategy as well. "We could still only hold a small part of the city. We would be surrounded, and then Kritias might decide to simply starve us out. He would not even need to fight."

"Then we must retreat to Phyle!" Archinus proclaimed. "Fight from a position of strength."

"No." The word fell from Thrasybulus' mouth like a drumbeat, simple and final. "We will make our stand today."

"But how?" Archinus asked, openly incredulous now. "Our hoplites are outnumbered five to one!"

Thrasybulus faced him down. "Kritias is impatient. We are a challenge to his power. Every day we occupy Piraeus will undermine his authority. That is why he hastens to bring us to battle." He looked at each man as he spoke. "So we will give him the target he seeks, something too tempting to resist. But we will not fight from even ground. We will mass our entire force on the hill," he said pointing to the slopes of Munychia behind us.

I suspect that he had planned for this all along. That was how Thrasybulus always won battles, by taking away the advantages of a stronger enemy and fighting the battle he wanted to fight. Now, Munychia was his arena. The odds were still not good, but there was a glimmer of hope.

I had my own reasons to wish to bring the Tyrants to battle. As leader of the Thirty, Kritias himself would be obliged to fight. Menekrates would most likely be there, too.

And I would be waiting.

Men stood by, unsure of what to do next. A *strategos* devises plans, while a *lochagos* makes it happen. Rising to my feet, I did my duty as Thrasybulus' leading captain. "You heard the *strategos*!" I shouted at the assembled men. "Gather your gear and get on the hill. We have some tyrants to kill!"

FROM THE SLOPES OF MUNYCHIA, we could see the Tyrants' army approaching the base of the hill where we would make our stand. The gathering phalanx below was a forest of iron points rising from a field of bronze. Five thousand hoplites.

"Is that all?" I yelled so that all the men could hear. I strode out before them. I was clad in my father's fine armour for the clash to come. The bronze helm and breastplate were burnished to a high sheen and gleamed in the early afternoon sun. Underneath I was already drenched in sweat. "Ten drachmas to any man who kills more of them than me!" I shouted.

My bravado provoked an enthusiastic roar from our men. A captain can show no fear, for men can smell fear the way a dog can smell a bitch in heat. It infects them and drives them mad. So I spat and cursed and marched up and down our lines, slowly fanning the flames of anger in their hearts to the incandescent rage they would need in the battle ahead.

Thrasybulus had a thousand hoplites at most, most bearing ill-fitting or mismatched armour. More often one could see men with wicker *gephalos* shields and conical *pilos* hats, which offered some protection, but not against a fully-armoured opponent. Our remaining number consisted of lightly-armed slingers, javelin-men and bowmen, and many others with nothing more than sacks of rocks and ballast stones with which to pelt the enemy. It was not an army to inspire terror.

So I let our men see the confidence of the Demon of Thrace, as many had begun to call me. I played the part of the barbarian. I strutted and howled. Let them see my thirst for blood and wonder at it, if only to make them forget their own fear.

Finally I came to Thrasybulus, who hefted his own spear and led the cheer as I passed by. Barates the soothsayer stood at his side. I grinned wolfishly at the seer, and he dropped his eyes rather than meet my accusing stare.

Before we ascended the slopes of Munychia, Thrasybulus had called on Barates to make a sacrifice and read what omens the gods had sent us. Many of those present laughed aloud, for Barates' skills as a *mantis* did not enjoy great prestige, due in large part to my own ill words against him. His face reddened in shame at the laughter, but he carried out the sacrifice and read the sheep's entrails. He declared the signs propitious and that we would triumph that day. But, the seer added that one of our men would have to attack and be killed before the gods granted us victory. He stared at me as he said this, no doubt put up to it by Archinus, for I had seen the two in quiet conversation before Barates opened the sheep's throat.

"Your men are as eager as you, *lochagos*?" Thrasybulus asked, saving Barates from further intimidation.

"They are ready, *strategos*," I said with more confidence than I felt.

"Then take your position. I would have words with the men."

"Yes *strategos!*" I pivoted and strutted back to my position on the right flank, but not before stopping midway to shout curses at the army that had come to crush us. Behind me, the army roared its approval.

I took my place in the front rank. On my left was Telekles and on my right Mnasyllus. Tibetos and Sabas the Cretan had taken positions in the mass of slingers and archers behind the hoplites. We looked down the slope, ready to die for each other, united against the enemy.

The shrill drone of distant flutes drifted upwards as the Spartan garrison launched into their paean. All eyes were drawn to the base of the hill. A ripple passed through the great mass of hoplites assembled at the base of the hill as the phalanx shuffled into movement. Within moments, their pace had increased to a fast trudge, the soldiers leaning forward as they climbed the progressively steeper incline.

There is a moment before every battle when men's courage is stretched to the breaking point. Your bowels turn to liquid while your throat becomes as parched as a summer road. Phobos floats through the ranks unseen, stopping to whisper in your ears about the spear waiting to spill your guts, and about the loved ones that you will never see again. Your pounding heart echoes in your helmet and your breath rushes in and out like a bellows.

It was at that moment that Thrasybulus stepped forward out of the ranks. He strode out in front of our ragged lines, contemptuously turning his back to the five thousand men climbing the hill to kill us. Never had his thunderous voice found a better occasion. It was at that moment that I knew why men loved him, and why we would follow him into Underworld if he asked us.

The speeches of generals recorded in the histories are nothing like what is really said. Before a battle, men must be roused to anger, to hate, to a state of bloodlust greater than their fear.

Thrasybulus pointed his spear at the five thousand troops, and his booming voice drowned out the Spartan pipes, lifting away their power over us. "Do not fear the enemy's numbers, for we do not face hoplites today, but cowards! The men on their right wing fled your spears only four days ago, and they will flee once more today. Their left wing, their best men, only dared arrest us when we were unarmed in the agora! They murdered our families in our homes! But today we will punish them with sword and spear, and their blood will stain this hill like spilled wine.

"Do the gods not favor our cause? Did they not send the snows to protect us from our enemies? We have set up trophy after trophy, and the gods will grant us victory again today! Look at them!" Thrasybulus waved at the army climbing the hill. "Throw your javelins and stones and bullets. Do not fear a poor shot, for the shameful enemy is so tightly packed that you cannot fail to miss. Already they skulk behind their shields in fear, but more in shame, for they know the evil of their cause. Look at them struggle! They will be exhausted when they reach us, while we will be fresh and ready for slaughter! And should you fall today, be you poor or rich, your very name will be honoured like those who fought at Marathon for our freedom against others who would have made us slaves!"

His voice reached a crescendo. "Today, we retake what is ours! We take back our wives and children! We take back our honour!" Everyone roared in response. "Today, we will have justice!" Another louder roar. "Today the Tyrants will taste death!"

The hill erupted into a chant of death. I yelled as loud as anyone! I thought of my parents. I thought of Meli. Lykos. Phaia. As I screamed, hatred flooded into my heart.

"Charge when I start the paean!" Thrasybulus shouted. He strode back to his place on the left rank, oblivious of the army advancing behind him.

Kneeling with our shields grounded, we let the enemy come to us. Their line was ragged, broken up by the uneven ground.

Then something astounding happened. A lone soldier broke from our ranks and sprinted down the slope. Everyone rose to their feet to behold the spectacle. I snorted in astonishment as I realized the suicidal madman's identity. "Barates!" I exclaimed.

The seer was screaming incoherently. He ploughed into the front rank of the enemy. A flurry of spear-thrusts felled him and he vanished under trampling feet. The seer was a fraud and a fool, but he had wanted to die having made at least one accurate prediction. A brave fool in the end. I honoured the turd-sniffing charlatan as best I could. "Avenge Barates!" I shouted, eliciting a chorus of "Barates! Barates!" from our ranks.

The army of the Tyrants was only thirty paces away. The ground shook with their relentless footsteps. Our line drew tighter to form a wall of wood and bronze. Our javelineers and slingers hurled their missiles with abandon. The front ranks of the enemy raised their shields, advancing blind rather than face the barrage, but many still screamed as javelins, arrows, and bullets found gaps.

And then I saw Akras.

There was no mistaking the colossus, even among five thousand men. The enormous Syracusan was to my left, near the centre of the Tyrants' phalanx. Kritias would be with his bodyguard. And his vile son, Menekrates, most likely. My rage surged anew.

Only fifteen paces separated the lines now. My mouth was dry and my breakfast heaved in my guts. My sweating hand tightened and loosened on my shield's leather hand-grip. And I heard it. Above the shouts of the enemy, the tramping of feet, the clattering of metal and wood and the trilling of pipes it came. The voice of Thrasybulus sang the paean and then we were all screaming the war-cry.

And like water suddenly pouring out of an overturned vessel, we charged.

Metallic thunder surrounded me. I barreled down the hill at the enemy, my spear held above my shoulder. The enemy halted, burying themselves completely in the hollow of their shields, bracing for the impact to come. With my last step I hurled myself forward.

Up and down the line, the air reverberated with the crash of the two phalanxes. My fear was vaporized by the rush of battle. The *aristeia* seized me.

I thrust the spear down, my momentum driving the tip into the face of a hoplite in the second rank. The shield of the man behind me pressed into my back, along with the weight of ten more ranks of men, squeezing the breath from me. The pressure eased slightly with the recoil from the initial impact. I stabbed over the edge of my shield and felt the point deflect off of something metal.

Around me, the maelstrom of battle lashed at my senses, the shouts and screams and curses of men stabbing and hacking at each other, the clangs and cracks of iron beating down on wood as hoplites from both sides tried to open gaps in the enemy lines. The stink of hot dust and sweat and piss and blood flooded my nostrils with each breath.

And the spears came. A spear tip found a hole and punched my breastplate like a hammer, but my father's plate held. Another spear glanced off the left side of my head, and I heard the shaft scraping along my helmet. The jabbing spears of our own second and third ranks passed over each of my shoulders. Another enemy spear passed between my legs, narrowly missing my ankle, and I roared and stamped down on it with my front foot, snapping the shaft into splinters. I bashed my shield again into the red-crested man in front of me and thrust my spear once more over the top. This time the blow landed, catching the finely-armoured hoplite on the side of his neck, a jet of blood erupting as I quickly twisted out my spear and withdrew behind my shield. The man toppled sideways into a hoplite with a black-crested helmet who was stabbing at Telekles over his shield, knocking him off balance, and it gave Telekles the opening for a counterthrust that drove into the man's face. Another hoplite stepped into the gap left by his fallen comrades, but he lost his footing and tumbled in front of me, and I chopped the bronze rim of my shield down on the back of his neck, but another screaming soldier struggled forward to take his place.

The fifty ranks of the Tyrants' phalanx was like an immovable boulder. Shield battered shield, spears jabbed and probed trying to find targets, and swords hacked and stabbed, but the sheer mass of the men held us up. They would wear us down with numbers. I could sense our line wavering.

My spear lodged in a shield and I let go of it. I drew my *xiphos* sword and stabbed at the face of the enemy. My left arm was numb from taking shattering blow after shattering blow on the heavy shield.

A weaponless soldier suddenly leapt forward and grasped the top of my shield. Grimacing he pulled my shield down with all his weight, exposing me to the killing iron of his comrades. He howled in victory but his bare-toothed visage suddenly vanished as a huge stone came hurling from the sky and crushed his face to a pulp, and he toppled backwards and disappeared.

Pieces of rubble and ballast stones were like a rain of boulders on the enemy, and no matter where they fell, they did damage, staving in helmets, breaking shoulders or crushing feet. If someone raised his shield to ward off a missile, the entire line weakened. The defense of the enemy was breaking, and gaps were opening along the entire battle line.

As javelins and stones sailed overhead, I stepped into the gap that had just appeared before me, tearing into the unprotected flanks of the hoplites to my sides. In my state of battle-madness, the enemy seemed to move as if submerged in water. To my left, I chopped into an unprotected thigh, and as my first victim fell screaming, I wheeled to the right and sheared clean through the muscle and bone of a man's shield-arm. In the chaos around me, I did not know what was happening five paces to either side of me, but I did not care. My only thought was to kill as many of the bastards as I could.

But then I sensed it.

There is a feeling in a battle, when the *trope*, the rout, begins. The pressure opposing your advance loses a fraction of its vigour, like rain letting up slightly after the heaviest part of a downpour. The enemy phalanx begins to loosen, a hitherto impenetrable wall becomes porous.

And so we, too, started pushing deeper and deeper. There was more room to swing a shield and weapon. We plunged ever forward, slashing and stabbing and bashing any target that presented itself.

Among our foes, soldiers with more experience or presence of mind locked their shields into tight knots and edged back away from the melee, while those unfortunate to be caught alone were set upon by the frenzied spears and swords of men fuelled by a lust for vengeance against their oppressors.

A space opened before me and I darted through. I was suddenly alone without my comrades. But I did not care, for not five paces in front of me was the man I had been seeking, the only hoplite instantly recognizable amidst the carnage on the slopes of Munychia.

Akras.

WHILE THOSE FURTHER DOWN THE HILL were fleeing the relentless rain of missiles, Lykos' killer stood like a breakwater as waves of soldiers crashed and shattered against him.

The Tyrant Kritias sheltered behind the giant Syracusan. His white-bearded face easily was framed by a glorious helmet crowned with a striped black and white crest. He scanned to and fro, searching for an escape from his besieged position and shouting at those around him to fight to the death. I threw my *xiphos* sword aside and freed Whisper from her scabbard.

Akras was helmetless. The burnt left side of his face twisted grotesquely as he roared at the enemy that beset him on all sides. His scything *kopis* cut down any that ventured near and in his left hand he wielded a spear with equal savagery. A few patches of shining bronze peeked through a breastplate that glistened with gore. Some of the blood must have been his own, for his arms and legs bore numerous wounds, but these had not the least effect on him.

Two hoplites ahead of me made their attempt on the giant. Akras skewered the first of them clean through the belly with the spear, two feet of the weapon protruding from the brave man's back. Akras, still clutching the spear, lifted the flailing man off his feet and heaved him into his comrade, who stumbled from the impact. Before the second man could recover, the Syracusan's *kopis* clove him shoulder to breastbone.

What the man could not accomplish in life he achieved in death. His corpse clung stubbornly to Akras' blade as the mercenary attempted to wrench the weapon free, but to the monster's frustration, the *kopis* stayed firmly embedded in the man's chest. I sprang forward.

Akras saw me coming. With a violent twist of his torso, he pivoted away from me as Whisper bit deeply into his exposed shoulder and he roared in pain. But it was not a crippling blow, for no sooner had I struck him than he finally ripped his sword free, whipping it towards my neck. I dropped low and the blade sliced the air above my head. Gods, for a large man he moved fast.

Clenching his teeth, Akras raised the *kopis* high and chopped down. The body under his foot shifted, throwing him off balance and saving my life, for the stroke struck my upraised shield with less force than it would have. Even so, the numbing blow left my *aspis* shattered, leaving splintered fragments of wood dangling uselessly from the shield's leather covering. Instinctively, I ducked under another swing meant to decapitate me and let the giant's momentum expose his own flank. With both hands now free, I whipped Whisper's hooked tip across the monster's waist.

It was a perfect attack. Whisper's point slashed across his side under his breastplate. The *rhomphaia* tore deep through his vitals and blood spouted from the fatal opening.

But Akras was not dead yet. Too late, I saw his backhanded recovery coming. Everything went white as his sword-wielding right fist clubbed me in the side of the head. Whisper sailed from my grasp, and I fell to my hands and knees, stunned, and my helmet tumbled to the ground. My ears still ringing, I struggled to my knees.

Even as his lifeblood left him, Akras raised his *kopis* in a two-handed grip above his head. And he paused. A wicked grin of recognition spread across his face. He drew a deep breath and flexed again, getting ready to savour my death. I raised my arm in a vain gesture to ward off the killing blow.

The blow never fell. A black circle the size of a walnut suddenly materialized in the giant's forehead, like a cyclopean eye. Akras became rigid, his teeth bared in a silent roar. In his hands, the *kopis* began to quiver as his eyes rolled upwards, trying in vain to see the object that had embedded itself in his skull. Then, like a tree that has received the last, critical blow of the woodsman's axe, he tottered for a moment, as though unsure in which direction he should fall.

After what seemed to be an eternity, he finally plummeted earthwards where I knelt in front of him.

I heaved myself to one side, barely avoiding being crushed by Akras' hulking corpse as he crashed face-first into the ground beside me. Looking up, I found my focus once again as my eyes fell on Kritias.

His champion slain, Kritias was unprotected. The Tyrant of Athens shouted orders and gestured wildly with his sword in an attempt to form his broken ranks into some kind of coherent line.

The oversized *kopis* of Akras lay before me. Seizing it, I rose from the ground and bounded towards Kritias in three great strides, a howl rising in my throat. The Tyrant jerked his head towards the unearthly wail and found a red-haired barbarian bearing down on him. His jaw dropped in fear as he saw my face. He knew me. I raised the huge sword two-handed, such was its weight.

Kritias tried to say something. Whether it was to warn his men, to beg for his life, to curse me, I will never know, for the words never left his lips. Like a woodman's axe, the *kopis* hurtled downward, driven by its weight and my fury. The blow caught Kritias on the shoulder at the nape of his neck, and it hewed through his aristocrat's torso and ribs and beautiful armour in a spray of blood, right down to his black heart.

Many on the hill had seen Kritias and Akras slain, and like a ripple from a stone dropped in water a wave of defeat passed through the Tyrants' army. Then, their will to fight broken, thousands of men turned and fled down the slope of Munychia back to the streets of Piraeus.

I did not pursue. The bloodlust had left my body as suddenly as it had possessed me and was replaced by a wave of pain and exhaustion. I swayed unsteadily on my feet and noticed with some surprise that a few shattered remnants of my shield, my father's shield, still hung from the strap on my arm. I shook them off, and they fell to the earth with a clatter.

My fellow soldiers sprinted past me down the hill, turning their merciless spears and swords on the backs of their former oppressors. Those attempting to surrender were given no quarter, and many fell to angry iron with their hands raised meekly in supplication. Far down the hill, the hoplites who had been fortunate enough to be in the rear ranks were streaming back to the streets of Piraeus, eager to escape the bloodbath on the hill above them.

"Hold! Hold! Do not pursue!" The mighty voice of Thrasybulus echoed over the battlefield as though Zeus himself commanded it. "Hold! Hold!" It was a prudent order. We were still greatly outnumbered, even by the survivors, and a reckless pursuit could easily turn into a rout of our own men if the soldiers of the Thirty managed to rally a defense.

Somehow the words penetrated the rage and lust for revenge that drove the men. At the base of the hill, men ceased their pursuit, allowing the last stragglers to dash ignominiously for the safety of the streets.

A roar of victory rang out on the slopes of Munychia.

As I bent over to retrieve Whisper from where she had fallen, a familiar voice called out behind me. "Dammo!" I turned to see Tibetos coming towards me, picking his way through fallen bodies. His olive face was split by a wide grin. In his right hand, his sling twirled idly. "It was a lucky shot," he said, dipping his head towards the body of Akras.

I let out a breathless laugh and stepped towards Tibetos. I embraced him with tears in my eyes. A moment of sunlight, but my mood darkened once again.

I pointed to the corpse at my feet. "Kritias." The Tyrant lay on his side, his face frozen in astonishment. I grasped the hilt of the *kopis* embedded in his chest. I wrenched it free and a gush of dark blood welled out from the slain tyrant's corpse. I wondered about what Kritias had said about the gods, whether they existed or not. I had sent him to find out. But as much as I hated the Kritias, there was another whose death I sought.

"Where is Menekrates?" I asked, as much to myself as to Tibetos. We examined the dead lying nearby, turning over bodies and removing helmets, but Kritias' son was not among them.

The thought that Menekrates might have escaped my vengeance corroded my soul, even as men came over to inspect the bodies of Akras and Kritias. They marvelled at the giant of Syracuse. They prodded at the fatal lead bullet lodged in the giant's forehead, a bullet launched by Tibetos, a former slave who had slain the most fearsome warrior in Greece.

A rough hand on the back of my neck pulled me away from my thoughts. "A great victory, Daimon," Thrasybulus said. "A great victory." There was a weariness in his voice, as though he had finally exhausted the well of energy that had driven him for so long. His splattered breastplate bore three great dents where the armour had turned away spear-thrusts

"A great victory, *strategos*," I agreed, pointing at the body of Kritias.

Thrasybulus nodded his head. He pursed his lips in thought as he gazed at the man who had been his enemy until only a few moments earlier. "He was a brilliant man, you know," he said at last.

"In my experience, they are the worst kind, *strategos*," I said.

Thrasybulus left the comment unanswered. "Let us set up a trophy," he said.

"Use the armour of Akras," I said pointing to where Tibetos stood next to the fallen giant. Telekles, Mnasyllus and the Cretan bowman Sabas had found us. Tibetos was retelling his tale to them and a growing cluster of gawking men. I handed Akras' *kopis* to an awed Mnasyllus, for he was the only man I knew mighty enough to wield it.

Soon, the empty shell of Akras' armour was overlooking the streets of Piraeus below. The defeated army would send a herald to ask for a truce to claim their dead from the field.

I sat down beside the earthly remains of Kritias. Someone would come to claim the Tyrant's body. And I would be waiting.

A TRUCE GRANTED, SOLDIERS OF THE THIRTY trickled out from the streets of Piraeus, their heads hung in shame. They listlessly scaled the rise of the hill they had climbed earlier that day, this time seeking their dead instead of victory.

My pulse echoed in my ears as I strained to identify Menekrates among those coming up the hill. For when he came to claim his father's body, I would kill him, truce or no.

Some of the defeated came to where I waited, but I warned them off with a growl, telling them to spread the word that I would only release the body of Kritias to Menekrates.

At last, a familiar face appeared. I rose to my feet, my fingers playing on Whisper's hilt in restless anticipation. I scowled with hatred as the figure approached me.

"My brothers and I have come to claim the body of my uncle." It was Aristokles, the nephew of Kritias. Plato, they called him.

"Then you will die trying," I said coldly. "Send Menekrates."

Plato blinked in surprise at my blunt refusal. "But there is a truce, witnessed by gods and men!" he protested. He swallowed hard before drawing himself up. He attempted to infuse his voice with aristocratic authority. "You are obliged to release the body to me!"

In response, Whisper hissed from her scabbard. Plato leapt back in fear, his hands raised before him. But I did not strike him down. Instead, I plunged the sword into the chest of the dead Kritias.

Plato recoiled in shock. "What are you doing?"

I withdrew the blade and drove it into the dead Tyrant's neck, keeping my eyes locked on Plato. "Where is Menekrates?" I demanded coldly.

He ignored my question, stepping forward towards me. "You dare defile a corpse? You pollute yourself by your actions! You show contempt for the laws of gods and men, *kakos daimon*! You have no honour —"

With a roar I seized Plato by his tunic and in one motion slammed him to the ground. He hit the earth like a sack of grain, the air rushing from him in a whoosh. In an instant I was upon him. My fist rose and fell three times in quick succession. I heaved him up so that his dazed, bloodied face was only inches from mine.

"You dare speak of honour?" I shouted, my spittle flecking his face. Plato was shaking in terror. "You told Menekrates you saw me on the Long Walls!"

"I did not!" he stammered, denying the charge.

I ignored the lie. "Now you come to claim the body of a monster, and you lecture me on honour? You defend Menekrates, who murdered my mother on the altar where she had begged for mercy? You ally yourself with the man who murdered my wife? Who sold my sister and son into slavery?" My voice kept rising as madness took hold of me.

"I do not know where Menekrates is!" Plato pleaded desperately. He looked to his brothers, but Tibetos had drawn his sword as a warning not to interfere. Plato's eyes darted manically as he kept looking from one of my eyes to the other. "He fled after the battle!"

Meli's knife flew from its sheath at my waist. I pressed its edge into Plato's throat. I leaned in closer so that our faces were almost touching. "Then you will die in his place this day!" I whispered hoarsely.

"I know where your son is!" Plato shrieked.

I froze. My grip tightened on the knife handle.

"I know where your son is," he repeated frantically, realizing that his life was balanced precariously on the truth of this claim. Seeing that his words had just prolonged his existence, Plato offered more details. "Menekrates sold him as a slave, but he is still in the city. I can protect him." The words spilled out in a torrent.

"And what of my sister?"

Plato hesitated. I applied more pressure to the blade. "I do not know her whereabouts. She was sold to a slave trader who left the city soon after..." His words trailed off. "But let me leave with the body of my uncle, and I will make sure that your son is safe." His lips were trembling.

I had no choice. I removed the blade from his throat and rose unsteadily to my feet. Exhaustion and hopelessness extinguished the fire in my belly. Meli was gone. Menekrates had fled beyond my reach. But I could still rescue my son. For Phaia.

I waved at the naked corpse of Kritias. "Take him," I said flatly. Plato scrambled to his feet, his expression wary. "Take him and be gone."

Plato hurriedly motioned for his two brothers to help him retrieve Kritias before I changed my mind. As the three men hauled the limp body of the former tyrant down the hill, I called out. "Aristokles!" He turned, a fearful expression on his face. "I will know my son when I see him, so do not attempt to play me false. If any harm comes to him, the price will be paid with your blood. This I swear." He nodded weakly before turning and rushing to catch up with his brothers, who were already at the bottom of the hill.

I plopped heavily on the ground, watching him go. "Did I do the right thing, Tibo?"

"It was what Phaia would have wanted. And I will help you keep your oath, if it comes to it."

I rubbed my face, suddenly feeling much older than my twenty-four years. Exhaling slowly, I gazed at the scene about me.

Many more men combed the hillside, retrieving their dead. There were some heckles and taunts to be heard, but this was the exception. In many more cases, men wept, embracing their former enemies like long-lost brothers, for many had fought for the Tyrants unwillingly, and now their shame had become manifest. I sat alone with Tibetos, watching friends and kin reunite. No one approached us, a slave and the son of a slave, for we had ever been excluded from their world.

The soldiers of the Thirty began to disperse, carrying their dead back to the carts on the Bendis Road at the base of the hill. Yet many remained, their hearts changed by deeper loyalties than politics and faction.

Some twenty paces from me, one such man stood watching his comrades depart. There was anguish in his features as he struggled with the decision of whether to stay or leave. He shifted slightly, and I had a clearer view of his face. I inhaled sharply. I recognized him.

I shuffled to my feet, a sudden urgency seizing me. "You there!" I shouted, striding towards him.

He turned his gaze towards me. His eyes grew round in fearful recognition as he saw my wild-haired, bloodstained figure striding purposefully in his direction. He looked to be about to bolt, but I called again.

"Do not run! I would have words with you."

I came to a stop before him. He opened his mouth to speak, but no words came, for shame had seized hold of his tongue.

"It is you," I said, and he nodded. Sadness welled up inside me and tears blurred my vision. For I was remembering the night when I carried my Phaia's bloodied and defiled body on the streets of Piraeus. And I remembered the man who had let me go, the soldier who had chosen mercy over duty. He stood before me now.

The man found his voice at last. "I have thought about you many times since that night, and what might have become of you. Whatever else has happened, I am happy to see that you live."

I regained control of my emotions, forcing down the lump in my throat. "What is your name, brother?" I asked hoarsely.

"Stachys of the deme Themakos," he said

"Daimon, son of Nikodromos," I said, my voice stronger. I held out my hand. "Will you not join us, Stachys? I will speak for you, if you so wish."

"I wish it to be so," and he clasped my hand.

On the hill of Munychia, I took my former enemy and newest comrade and introduced him to Tibetos, my oldest friend.

CHAPTER 35

Time was on our side.

Thrasybulus controlled the port, and with no food reaching Athens, the city would slowly starve. Eventually, the remaining Tyrants would have no choice but to sue for peace. So for the next month we waited.

The respite did not mean we remained idle. Men were put to work repairing the gaps in the walls around the port. More exiles, hearing of the victory on Munychia, returned to join the cause of Thrasybulus.

And word of his promise spread. Freed slaves and metics who fought with us would be rewarded with full Athenian citizenship when the democracy was restored. It was a great incentive, a prize worth more than gold for many.

Citizenship. The chance to stand as an equal in my city. My lifelong goal was tantalizingly within reach. I would bestow the gift of citizenship upon my son so that he could stand proudly not as the son of a slave but the son of two citizens. But first Athens had to surrender to Thrasybulus.

A lack of arms was still a problem. Despite the weapons and armour gained at Munychia, we were still short. With those who had defected from the Thirty, our forces now numbered some three thousand. But only half of them could be equipped as hoplites. The sounds of industry rang out around the street as craftsmen hurried to meet the demand for shields, spears, and swords.

Plato sent no word of my son. Madness would have consumed me had I not found refuge in work. My days were spent in the smithy of Timonax, hammering out the dents in breast-plates and helmets, sharpening old blades and crafting new spear-points.

I quickly fell into the old rhythm I had known with Neleus. I woke up early, even before the slaves, to stoke the fire and build up the heat. From dawn to dusk I hammered and pounded, hardly taking a break for water or food. As the sky darkened, I would tumble exhausted onto the straw-stuffed sack Timonax and his wife had provided for me. "You will wear yourself out, lad!" Timonax admonished me repeatedly. I would just grunt and smile at him through the sweaty soot on my face before returning to work.

Until one day a messenger came. It was not from Plato, but Thrasybulus, an urgent summons from the *strategos*. The craven leaders in Athens had not been idle either. The cowards dared not face us in open battle, so they had called on their strongest allies.

The Spartans were coming.

THE SPARTANS BESIEGED US BY LAND and sea. Lysander blockaded the harbour while the Spartan king Pausanias encamped his army a short distance from the growing walls of Piraeus.

In a pitched battle, we could not hope to match the Spartans, for we had neither the numbers nor the arms nor the experience to match them in the field.

Yet neither Pausanias nor Lysander was foolish enough to assault our stronghold. Outnumbered though we may have been, they would have suffered heavy losses in street fighting, where numbers counted for little. But stone walls could not fill our bellies. Now it was the Spartans who were content to starve us into submission.

The walls around Piraeus grew ever higher with each passing day. Every able man put in his daily quota of hours sweating and hauling rocks to shore up the defenses. Thrasybulus joined us there, stripped to the waist and bellowing work songs, his voice surely carrying to the Spartan camp half a mile away.

When the morning sun became oppressive, we rested in the shade, swigging from jugs that contained wine so cut by water that hardly any wine remained. But we were as hungry as the increasingly vicious feral dogs that fought each other over even the tiniest morsel of food.

The curs were an entertainment to us, for all the contestants of cock-fights had found their way into cooking pots long ago. The mongrels were given names and bored men put wagers on the outcomes of their encounters.

There was one beast that no one bet against, a great hound dubbed Akras, for it dwarfed the other strays just as Akras the Syracusan had towered over men. The monster had taken to hunting the other dogs.

One morning Akras had killed an old bitch we called Agapia, though I cannot recall how she came by the name. The hound dragged its victim to the shade of a nearby wall and began to feed.

Drawn by the scent of blood, other strays gathered. Tremoring with hunger, the starving creatures were fixed on Akras but kept a wary distance from him. "Look at the others," Telekles said, pointing. "They dare not approach, even to steal a scrap!"

The smaller dogs had tightened their circle. Akras raised his head and let out a rumbling growl. A mangy tan dog darted forward, attempting to snatch a shred of flesh. Akras snapped his jaws, barely missing the tan's neck at it turned and fled.

You could see their desperation, their fear. But I saw something else. "A drachma that Akras will fall," I said suddenly. A flurry of wagers were taken against me. All eyes turned to the dogs.

"Can you cover your losses, Tyrant-Slayer?" Telekles joked, using my most recently-acquired nickname. "Akras is immovable. The wall is behind him. He just needs to sit there." I waved him off. I could see what Telekles could not. The pack had a plan.

The other dogs continued to pester the enormous hound, who was increasingly put out. Then the first success came. As Akras bit at one dog, another darted in and nipped at the enormous hound's haunch.

The black beast leapt to its feet and lunged after the dog that had the temerity to attack him. It was a mistake. In his anger, the hound stepped away from the wall. The frenzied pack immediately surrounded him on all sides, harrying him relentlessly with nips and bites.

The tan was not fast enough. Akras clamped his jaws on its throat and shook it violently, but this only drove the other dogs to new heights of aggression and they fell upon their oppressor from all sides, gnashing at the black beast's flank and legs.

With a yelp, Akras dropped the tan's limp corpse. Mauled and torn, the whimpering hound bolted and disappeared into an alley. The remaining dogs did not pursue, instead falling ravenously upon the abandoned carcasses.

Around me, the others shook their heads in wonder. I was smiling, and Telekles and those who had bet against me thought it was because I had won the wager.

But I was thinking about something else. I knew how we could defeat the Spartan army that besieged us. Without a word, I left my comrades still debating. I had to see Thrasybulus. I had a proposal for him.

THRASYBULUS HAD ACCEPTED my plan. Now, for the fifth morning in a row, dawn in the Spartan camp was greeted by howls of despair. Hidden in a grassy depression less than a bowshot away, Sabas and I listened to their anguished cries.

"They found them," I whispered. Sabas bobbed his head once in silent agreement.

The Spartans had discovered the corpses Sabas and I had left them. One a perimeter guard with an arrow through his neck and the other a Spartan whose throat I had slashed while he slept by a fire near the edge of camp. The clamour of the enemy reached our ears where we hid as they searched for the killers who had so recently been in their midst.

For the past five nights, we had struck, claiming our victims under the darkness of a moonless sky. The first night had been the easiest. We had simply walked into their camp. There were a few hundred elite Spartan warriors, but the bulk of the army was made up of soldiers conscripted from the various cities under the Spartan hegemony. No one had challenged us. Sabas and I had just been two more soldiers. We left five men dead in their tents and then disappeared into the night.

On the second night, we killed three more. From then on, the men of the Spartan army had been more wary, posting guards and tightening the perimeter of their camp. But Meges had taught me well and the Cretan Sabas and his hound Argos moved as silently as wolves. Men get careless. They get tired. They go to relieve themselves away from camp. And they die. Every morning the Spartans and their allies had found the bodies, and every morning their rage grew.

Like small dogs, we nipped and bit and harassed the great beast that was the Spartan army.

I peeked over the edge of the hollow towards the enemy camp. Some men scurried about in vain, while others stood gazing back in our direction towards the walls of Piraeus, the source of the bane that haunted their camp each night. The ruddy dawn sky brightened with every heart-beat. The longer Sabas and I tarried, the greater the danger that we would be spotted.

That was exactly what I wanted.

"Let's go," I whispered, and Sabas and I crept from our hole.

We crouched low as we moved, but we were deliberately careless, moving too quickly and letting our heads bob too much. Just conspicuous enough to be spotted by a sharp-eyed observer in the Spartan camp.

Behind us, there was a shout and a great cry went up as every man in the camp turned their eyes towards Sabas and me, the authors of their recent misery and frustration.

Loosing one more provocative arrow, Sabas turned to me. "The fish are biting!" A group of twenty or so men was already bearing down on us in a dead sprint, screaming for our blood. The Cretan archer was grinning maniacally, delighted at the novelty of the pursuit. He was truly mad.

We bolted towards Piraeus. I forced a stumble, falling on my face. Sabas, laughing but acting the part of a loyal comrade, did not abandon me but turned to help me to my feet. Our pursuers closed the gap on us with alarming speed and we were still far from the walls of Piraeus. The pounding of footsteps behind us grew louder.

And then the missiles flew.

Our own men sprung their ambush. Javelins, arrows, and slung bullets rained down on our pursuers without mercy and they died screaming. The hail of wood and stone and metal ceased, and ruthlessly we fell upon the few survivors with spear and sword. Whisper flew in my hand, cutting through air and flesh with cold efficiency.

Only a few hundred paces away, stunned grief spread among the enemy as they witnessed the slaughter of their fellows. A howl rose in the Spartan camp, building into a roar like the sound of an ocean gale. Around me, men unconsciously stepped backwards, wishing to be back behind the protective walls of Piraeus. The sleeping beast had awoken and only needed to be prodded. I would give them all the prodding they needed.

"Hold your ground!" I shouted. "We need to provoke them! Do it!"

Our men heard my call. Screaming curses, our hundred fighters raised their swords and spears, shaking them defiantly at the army that faced them across the plain. It was like pissing into a waterfall, but the men played their parts, leaping and parading and baring their arses with abandon. But the Spartans were too disciplined. They would not come.

Fortune smiled upon me, for among the dead I found what I needed to stoke the fire of their rage. The long, carefully plaited braids marked the dead man as a Spartiate, one of the elite warriors of Sparta's society. In three quick blows, Whisper severed the brute's head from his body.

Holding the head aloft by its black braids, I strode out twenty paces in front of the others. I halted, standing with my *rhomphaia* in one hand and the gruesome trophy in the other. Time stretched as I let every man in the Spartan army behold me and I felt their hatred upon me. Then with a heave and a scream, I spun and hurled the head back towards them. It was like throwing a stone at a hive of angry bees. I turned my back to them and strode contemptuously back to my men.

A great wail came from the Spartans and their allies. I could almost feel the impact of their fury as it washed over us. By now, some of the Spartan cavalry had mounted their beasts.

"Time to leave," I shouted. The men needed little encouragement, fleeing apace towards the shelter of Piraeus. Sabas and I glanced at each other before turning tail and making our own mad dash back to the walls.

The pounding of hooves grew louder as the Spartan riders bore down on us. An errant javelin sailed wide to stick firm into the earth on my right side. The next one would surely find its mark. My heart thudded in my chest.

The lithe, light-footed Sabas had pulled ahead of me. With a sudden spurt, he made it through the gate where a throng of shouting men waved him in. They screamed encouragement at me, and just when I thought my lungs must explode, I was in.

"Close the gates! Close the gates!" someone yelled. With a reluctant groan, the massive wooden doors came together. A team of men hefted the huge crossbeam into place. I was doubled over with dry heaves, but despite their best efforts, my guts remained stubbornly inside me.

Sabas, panting but grinning, helped me stand upright. "Do you think it worked?" he asked.

Mnasyllus had climbed up some rubble and was perched so that he was peering over the wall. I called up to him between gasps. "What are the Spartans doing now?" I waited in uncertain anticipation, for the success of the ruse depended on his response.

Always deliberate in his actions and words, Mnasyllus ignored my urgent query. Instead, he leaned forward a few inches, as though that would help him better discern the activity across the plain.

"Come on, man! What is happening?" My frustration was mounting.

After what seemed to be an age, Mnasyllus turned and looked down at me. A wide smile split his face. "They are starting to form ranks!" he said. "They're attacking!"

Sabas slapped my back. "You're a good fisherman, Dammo!"

As honour demanded, an army of thousands of enraged Spartans and their allies was marching on the walls of Piraeus, seeking revenge for their slain comrades.

"Where are my helmet and shield?" I yelled to no one in particular. I had Spartans to kill.

The vaunted discipline of the Spartans was hardly in evidence. Gripped by the desire to revenge themselves upon their impudent tormenters, the mob that threw itself at the unfinished walls only had the barest semblance of a phalanx. Our harried defenders retreated from the ramparts under a barrage of missiles. The first of the enemy scrambled over the walls, opening the gate for their fellows outside.

"Fall back!" Thrasybulus boomed. Unlike my black cuirass, his armour gleamed in glorious resplendence. He was a *strategos* of the best sort, in the thick of battle with those he led. Our eyes met and that wordless understanding of comrades in battle passed between us. The dice had been thrown, and the prize awaited those bold enough to take it.

"Fall back!" I echoed, and others took up the call. Attackers were already scrabbling to the top of the walls, baying for our blood, only to see our backs as we fled.

To an outsider, it would seem that we were beaten. But our retreat before the battle had even been joined was not a failure.

It was a trap.

Neleus had told me time and time again. The Spartans won battles because they chose the time and location that was to their advantage. But not today. Today the battlefield was of my choosing.

In the plains, we could not win. But in the streets of Piraeus, the Spartans' numbers counted for nothing. Pursuing us up the main street, they would not see that the side streets had become dead ends, sealed off by barricades of rubble. It was the same stone from walls that the people of Athens had pulled down under the gloating gazes of their conquerors while flutes trilled. Now that same stone would form the walls of the conquerors' tombs.

The main street had become a channel. Like a sluice, the road would guide the flood of invaders towards the theatre, where a slaughterhouse awaited them.

Our retreating band of hoplites came around the last turn in the road. A wall of bronze twenty men wide and twenty men deep sealed the road, their shields locked as tightly as the best Spartan formation. Our appearance told them that the enemy was not far behind.

We late arrivals took our places in the front rank, Thrasybulus on my left, Mnasyllus on my right. My spear rested on my shoulder, as did the shafts of the spears of the two hoplites behind me. Whisper hung under my arm. I closed my eyes and took a deep breath, the odor of dust, heat, metal and sweat-soaked cotton and leather filling my nostrils. My heart pounded. I was alive. My eyes flicked open.

And the enemy were there.

It was more a horde than a phalanx. There were men of Sparta mixed among them, the distinct lambda sigils emblazoned on their shields.

Seeing our phalanx blocking the road, the hoplites began to fall into ranks. A Spartan commander, his helmet distinguished by an enormous horizontal crest of alternating red and white bands, strode before them, barking orders and radiating authority. His crimson cloak billowed behind him. He was magnificent and fearless.

The Spartans filled the front rows of their formation with their allies filling the rear. A uniform line of lambda shields faced us, and fear tickled the back of my neck, for no man can see such a thing and not tremble. The enemy numbers swelled as more and more of their comrades reached the scene of the standoff, pushing those already present towards us.

The commander, in the centre of the line, let out his people's ancient war-cry, and in an instant, the rest of the Spartans took up the paean. Like great armoured crabs, they came at us with their distinct side-to-side marching style. The discipline of it was mesmerizing.

Our own lines stood fast.

"Now! Now!" bellowed Thrasybulus.

Hundreds of figures, men and women, revealed themselves of the rooftops and began to hurl death down on the massed enemy troops. Stones, javelins and even roof-tiles plunged down into the helpless Spartan formation. Somewhere Sabas was piercing any exposed flesh with his deadly shafts, while Tibetos and his fellow slingers brutalized the trapped men with lead and stone. The hapless Spartans raised their shields above their heads to ward off the rain of missiles. The pressure of soldiers still arriving from the back prevented their suffering comrades at the front from retreating.

"*Alalalala!*" Thrasybulus began our own paean and our phalanx ground into motion. It was not as beautiful as the Spartans' choreographed charge, but it was relentless and focused, like a mallet driving onto a wooden peg.

Howling our war-cry, we drove into the stalled Spartan advance. My spear blows struck mercilessly. I drew back my arm again and again, but it was a mindless blur and I cannot recall how many times the point landed true, except for the last when the spear-tip became lodged in the bone and bronze of a Spartan's chest. I released my grip and the dead man toppled backwards. Weaponless, I buried my shoulder in the curve of my shield and ground forward with all my strength.

All around me, the Spartans could not check our momentum. Too many were defending themselves from the missiles above instead of bracing the front lines of their formation, and every shove and bash of our shields drove the enemy back. Soon we were trampling their dead and wounded, stamping skulls and snapping limbs, crushing them under our inexorable push. The narrow confines of the street only amplified the cries of the wounded and the dying. The Spartan phalanx was shattered.

Now the enemy struggled to escape the slaughter, fighting to put space between themselves and our blades. As his men shoved past him, the Spartan leader roared out in frustration. "By the twin gods, are there no men among you? Do you all fight from afar like barbarians?"

My hand found the extended handle of my *rhomphaia*. My palm wrapped about Whisper's corded hilt and the blade slid smoothly from the scabbard like a great serpent's fang. I stepped forward over a writhing body, screaming my challenge. The Spartan's eyes locked on me and he crouched low, bracing his shoulder inside the concave lambda shield.

From behind the great plumed helmet, his eyes shot fire at me. "Come!" he roared.

There was no need to accept the challenge, for the Spartans were suffering a defeat. But the battle madness was upon me. The *aristeia*.

My shield was hindering me and I cast it off. I raised the huge arcing blade of the *rhomphaia* above me in a two-handed grip. It was madness, but only the mad can win their reputations. At that moment, I was my truest self. I was Greek. I was Thracian. I was a warrior. I was death.

In three loping steps, I was upon him. His spear snaked out in a flash, but I was gone, rolling down the shaft and letting my momentum take me to him. I crashed my shoulder into the lambda, driving the Spartan back. Before he could recover his balance, I spun again, the rotation of my body whipping the trailing *rhomphaia* blade into an unstoppable, accelerating arc.

Whisper's tip took the Spartan cleanly in the neck in the small space between his helmet and his breastplate. The *rhomphaia* bit deep, almost severing his head in a spray of crimson and his head flapped back. The commander collapsed in a heap at my feet.

My enemy vanquished, I howled in Thracian, challenging anyone to face me. I was outside myself.

But no one stepped forward. Only fearful stares met my gaze. The enemy pushed and shoved, not towards me but away. And I saw something rarely seen before or since that time.

The prediction that my friend and mentor Neleus had made long ago was coming to pass.

The Spartans were fleeing for their lives.

STARING IN STUNNED WONDER, I watched as our own soldiers streamed past me in pursuit of the routed enemy. Exhaustion seized me. I tipped back my helmet and sucked in deep, replenishing breaths.

"You have given us victory, Daimon. You are truly the son of a *strategos*." It was Thrasybulus, his helmet also tilted back. He looked at me appraisingly. "And something more, I think."

I was strangely embarrassed by his praise. "You have led us to this point, *strategos*. This day would not have been possible without you."

He gave a shake of his head but did not contradict me. He glanced down at the corpse of the Spartan commander. "I saw you strike him down. It was a fearsome blow," he said.

"Some kind of captain, I think." It already seemed to have happened an age ago.

Thrasybulus laughed. "A captain? Look at the helmet, lad," he said pointing his spear towards the red and white plume. "That is a *polemarch* lying at your feet!"

I blinked in stunned silence. A *polemarch* was the equivalent of an Athenian *strategos*, a general. The man I had cut down was one of the highest-ranking men in the rigid Spartan hierarchy. A small crowd had gathered around us to look at the dead Spartan leader.

"Your plan worked, Daimon," Thrasybulus said.

"It depends on Pausanias," I said. I tried to sound confident, but in truth I was uncertain. What would the Spartan king do? The defeat would weaken his position, or so we hoped. His Peloponnesian allies would not want to besiege Piraeus indefinitely, for the harvest was soon approaching and they would be eager to return to their homes. The king would be forced to negotiate. This was our aim.

I looked about at the devastation we had wrought. The street was cluttered with the fallen and their scattered weapons. The chaotic din of battle was gone, replaced by moans of the wounded and hushed conversations among the few soldiers who had not taken off in pursuit of the routed foe. As if from nowhere, women and children who had remained hidden were suddenly present, picking their way among the bodies, looking for items to plunder. A haggard-looking woman knelt close to a groaning Spartan. Her face was emotionless as she dispatched the scarlet-cloaked warrior with a quick dagger-cut across the throat. I shivered at her cold efficiency.

From the direction of the city gate came the peals of a distant trumpet. My attention snapped away from the predations of the old woman. Every man stood frozen, all ears turned towards the distant wailing as the trumpeter sounded his horn again and again.

Thrasybulus frowned. "It is outside the city."

The hair on my neck stood on end, for in my heart I knew something was wrong. It was the Spartan call to battle.

The look of surprise on the face of Thrasybulus was quickly replaced by one of grim determination. "To me! To me!" His voice rang through the street. "To the gate!" He slammed down his helmet and began running, a gaggle of hoplites and lightly-armed troops trailing behind him. I hastily lowered my own helmet and grabbed the fallen Spartan general's lambda-emblazoned shield and spear from the ground.

When I caught up to the *strategos* at the gate, he was getting a frantic report from a hoplite. I looked about in shock, for there was barely a man in sight.

"It was Archinus, *strategos!*" the man said hurriedly. "He ordered the men to continue the pursuit outside the city and press our advantage!"

I had never seen Thrasybulus so angry in all the time I had known him. His face was red with fury. "Hades take the fool!" he shouted, taking out his rage on the terrified young hoplite. "Damn the fool to Hades!"

Thrasybulus was right to be furious, for he had expressly ordered that the hoplites not pursue the enemy beyond the safety of the walls. The idiotic zeal of that windbag Archinus exposed our forces to a Spartan counterattack. In the plain beyond the walls the Spartan trumpet continued its plaintive cry. And then a new sound. The chant of the Spartan paean.

CHAPTER 36

Only the inspired generalship of Thrasybulus prevented the total destruction of our forces. But as it was, we still suffered heavy losses.

More than one hundred of our soldiers were isolated and driven like sheep into the marshes north of Piraeus, where they were butchered to a man. The Spartan cavalry ran amok, riding down any man who had been foolish enough to become separated from the main body.

The thunderous voice of Thrasybulus echoed over the battlefield. "Form ranks! Form ranks!" Men desperate for salvation rallied to the *strategos*. By some miracle, we were able to match the Spartan line, though their phalanx was more than twice as deep as our own. But we did not press forward, for to do so would have meant certain defeat. Instead, the *strategos* began the most difficult of manoeuvres: the ordered retreat of a phalanx.

It is no easy thing for a phalanx to retreat. To step backwards in full armour while maintaining your lines is a challenge in any circumstances. Doing it while facing a phalanx of thousands of screaming Peloponnesians is nearly impossible.

It was a manoeuvre that the Spartans practiced, but we lacked their polished discipline. Yet certain death awaited those who strayed from our ranks. Fear and the will of Thrasybulus held the ragged body of soldiers together as we retreated with painful slowness.

"Back-step!" The phalanx lurched back one more shuffling stride towards Piraeus.

The Spartan cavalry harried the vulnerable edges of our lines but were driven back by slingers and javelin-men.

Our line of twenty men stretched across the city gate, sealing it off. The shield of the man behind me pressed into my back, and so it went twenty or thirty men deep.

"Front rank! Kneel!" Thrasybulus bellowed.

With the others in the front row, I dropped to one knee. My recently acquired lambda shield anchored itself firmly on the ground, buttressed solidly by the weight of my armoured body.

"Second rank! Forward!"

The men behind us filled the gaps between the kneeling first rank, a clacking thump filling the air as they locked their shields in a row above ours. Through a small gap I spied the massed Spartan lines that faced us, just out of range of our slingers and javelineers atop the wall. We were vastly outnumbered. The enemy could simply overwhelm us and the rebellion of Thrasybulus would be no more.

But it would cost them many dead and wounded to do so. A seamless wall of shields bristling with spear-points filled the wide gate. Our men on the walls could be swept away with some effort, but the Spartans and their allies had already had a taste of the battering that would fall on them, and the memory of it must have given them pause.

An eerie quiet had descended. Each side stared at the other, unmoving. Then a trumpet rang from somewhere behind the Spartan ranks. It sounded five times. The great body of men began to draw back towards their camp.

The Spartans had their fill of bloodshed for one day.


"YOU SHIT-EATING IDIOT!" I pinned Archinus against a wall with my forearm across his throat. He gasped pitifully as he tried to suck in some air. "How many men died today because of your stupidity, old man? Yet you still live, protected by the shields of your betters!" I increased the pressure and his face went from red to purple. I did not care if the arrogant fool died right there.

We were ringed by a crowd of onlookers. No one lifted a finger to stop me from squeezing the life out of Archinus.

"Move! Move!" a familiar voice boomed from the back of the crowd. I pressed harder. The firm hand of Thrasybulus seized me by the shoulder and jerked me away from Archinus. I spun to face him. "Daimon! What are you doing?" he demanded.

"Giving this fool the justice he deserves!" I growled, pointing an accusing finger at Archinus. He was on his knees, rubbing his throat and taking great gulps of air.

"It is not the time or place!" Thrasybulus shouted in exasperation. "We cannot fight amongst each other while victory is within our grasp."

I stared at him as though he were mad. "What victory?" I exclaimed. "This worthless dung-heap has brought us defeat!" Archinus had staggered to his feet and still looked at me fearfully.

"Come and see for yourself, if you wish."

We stared hard at each other while those around us watched the standoff. My rage at Archinus began to subside. "You speak the truth?" I ventured sceptically.

"Come and see," Thrasybulus repeated, extending an arm away from where I stood.

I shot a look at Archinus. His sudden reprieve had put some defiance back in his eyes. I stepped towards him with a growl and his courage left him as he scurried away.

"The Spartan herald is waiting," Thrasybulus said. His words had the desired effect. The tired *strategos* smiled wanly at my surprised expression. "More interesting than killing Archinus, yes?"

Intrigued, I followed Thrasybulus. From the soldiers around us, murmurs regarding the arrival of the herald filled the air.

The herald himself was a paragon of Spartan virtue. He was immaculate in his posture and dress, his scarlet cloak accentuating his imposing figure rather than hiding it. Only a Spartan could stand with such cool disdain amidst the stares that were an odd mix of hostility, curiosity, and awe. His dark eyes locked on Thrasybulus like a hawk focusing on its prey. Thrasybulus stopped in front of the herald. He said nothing, waiting for the Spartan to address him first.

After a considerable pause, the Spartan deigned to speak, though he gave no impression of having conceded anything in this first battle of diplomacy. "You are Thrasybulus," he stated. The words rolled out in a thick Doric accent

"I am," Thrasybulus replied,

"You shall come with me," the Spartan ordered.

"Do you come from Lysander?" Thrasybulus inquired of the man.

The Spartan's eyebrow rose ever so slightly, and he answered in the curt manner so typical of his tribe. "King Pausanias."

Thrasybulus pursed his lips in thought. "Then I will accompany you, Spartan."

The Spartan glanced over at me. His heretofore expressionless eyes narrowed a fraction as they fell on the *rhomphaia* slung over my back. "Him, too." I frowned.

"Done," Thrasybulus responded without hesitation.

We went to fetch horses. Once out of sight of the herald, I asked Thrasybulus, "What interest do the Spartans have in me?"

"I don't know, but I suspect that it is related to the dead *polemarch* you left lying on the street," Thrasybulus said.

Another thought pestered me. "And why does it matter that the herald is from Pausanias and not from Lysander?"

"Politics, lad. Always politics," Thrasybulus said. I pressed him to elaborate. "Lysander's power has grown to rival that of the King Pausanias, but he is not yet strong enough to seize power for himself. Right now, Lysander is the hegemon of Athens, but if Pausanias negotiates a truce with us…" He let the sentence hang.

"He will undermine Lysander!" I exclaimed.

"Victory is never achieved on the battlefield alone," Thrasybulus said sagely. "Though a sharp spear never hurts in making negotiations proceed more smoothly," he added.

The Spartan led us back to his camp. From the back of my horse, I could feel the resentful stares that followed our silent procession, but the presence of the herald protected us until we reached the king's tent.

Two Spartan guards stepped aside to let us pass. The herald led Thrasybulus inside, and I took up the rear. I had no idea what to expect.

All eyes turned on us as we entered. The scrutiny of the powerful men assembled in the tent was oppressive. I scowled at them, putting on airs of simmering bravado, if only to hide how far out of my depth I felt.

In the centre sat Pausanias, the Spartan king. He was not ostentatious in the manner of Persian kings and satraps. It was only his bearing and finely made bracers that set him apart from the others. His physique was still imposing, despite being more than a decade older than Thrasybulus, and his hair and beard were shot through with grey. He rose when Thrasybulus entered, others in the tent following his lead.

"I welcome you, O Thrasybulus, son of Lykos," he intoned richly, the normally plodding Doric words coming out lightly from his lips. "Please sit and enjoy our hospitality." The king indicated the simple leather stool that sat empty at his side. If there was an insult here, it was not apparent, for even the king's seat was of the same spare functionality.

Thrasybulus played his role. "I am grateful for your hospitality, O King," he replied. Pausanias extended his right arm, and the two men clasped hands. No stool was offered to me.

Besides two more guards who had obviously been chosen for their enormous size, there were six more men in the tent. Two men I guessed to be *polemarchs*, for they were older and dressed very much like the man I had killed in Piraeus. On the King's left side stood three robed men who were obviously not Spartans. Their faces were tired, their shoulders sagged, and the odour of defeat hung about them.

One Spartan, however, I knew, and unlike the others, he stared at me rather than Thrasybulus and King Pausanias. His eyes blazed with black fire within a face that could have been cut from stone.

Lysander.

His white cloak was dull in the confines of the tent, but his armour shone with status and wealth. Any outsider would have thought him the King rather than the modestly-attired Pausanias. He regarded me with pure malice.

Finally Lysander could restrain himself no longer. "Is this the man who killed Chairon?" he demanded, pointing at me.

Pausanias looked irritated. He spoke to Thrasybulus, ignoring Lysander. "Chairon was a *polemarch* slain in Piraeus. His is a great loss." The King's tone suggested that he felt otherwise.

"Daimon, son of Nikodromos, slew such a man," Thrasybulus confirmed.

Lysander took a half-step towards me, his hand already reaching for the sword at his side. Pausanias moved smoothly between me and Lysander. "Then it was well done!" The king looked at me appraisingly, as if looking for something. With effort, I held his stare as he addressed Thrasybulus again. "As well done as your plan to lure my army into Piraeus, *strategos*. It was worthy of a Spartan!"

"Alas, O Pausanias, it was not my idea, though I supported its execution."

Pausanias took his meaning and gazed at me more penetratingly than before. His eyelid twitched. As I saw the cold calculations going through his mind, I was aware that the shears of the Moirai were hovering over my thread, ready to sever it. But Pausanias smiled and turned his hands upwards as though to concede the point. "Then it was well done, Daimon, son of Nikodromos," he repeated. Lysander glared at me.

The King turned away to address Thrasybulus once again. Released from the king's attention, I let myself swallow hard.

"But let us look to the future, *strategos*, a future in which Sparta and Athens are allies, as in the old times. The Persians grow bold once again, and it only aids them if we Hellenes continue to bicker amongst ourselves." The wily king did not mention that Sparta had been gladly taking Persian gold for years. "Thus," Pausanias continued, "I have invited representatives from your city so that peace may be restored to the city of Athens." The three depressed-looking men from the city shrank even more.

To call what followed negotiations would be absurd, for Pausanias dictated what would be. The citizens of Athens and Piraeus would cease hostilities immediately. Democracy would be restored, the King declared, and Sparta and Athens would be allies. At each pronouncement, Thrasybulus too bowed his head in acknowledgement. Yet it was not in defeat but in triumph. Pausanias was giving him everything he had fought for. The ambassadors from Athens hung their heads in silent defeat, for the return of democracy meant the end of their own rule. In only a few moments, the King had changed the fate of all those present. My own heart surged with fearful hope that I would soon be reunited with my son. But had Plato kept his word?

Lysander was on the verge of exploding. He had been shut out by the manoeuvres of Pausanias and the tacit agreement of his new ally Thrasybulus. The power and wealth of Athens had been his through the tyranny of Kritias and the Thirty, but like a man who grasps a handful of sand, he could only watch helplessly as it slipped away through his fingers.

He caught me watching him. His hard, black eyes bored into me, but he could do nothing. I raised my chin defiantly and turned my attention back to Pausanias.

For there was something else I craved. Menekrates. The son of Kritias still lived, taking refuge in Eleusis with the remnants of the Thirty and their followers. I hungered for justice. Yet the king had not mentioned what would become of them.

When Pausanias seemed to be concluding the terms of the amnesty, I could restrain myself no longer. "What of those who fled to Eleusis? What justice will they face for their crimes?" I blurted.

Pausanias frowned at the interruption. Thrasybulus' expression warned me that I had overstepped. I did not care. But my impatience was my downfall.

Lysander's humourless eyes brightened with understanding of what it was I desired most. The corners of his mouth curled upwards, and my hackles rose from the chill it sent over me. I knew I had erred in some way.

Lysander rose to his feet. "It seems to me that the King's amnesty extends to all Athenians."

Pausanias nodded. "It is so," he said magnanimously.

"Yet the leaders of the previous government of Athens would live under the constant threat of violence from undesirable elements who may not respect the authority of the King." Lysander's gaze rested firmly on me as he spoke.

"It would be so," Pausanias conceded.

Lysander revealed his masterstroke. "Therefore, it is my proposal that the remaining Thirty and their followers should find refuge in the city of Eleusis. I, Lysander, personally give my pledge to guarantee their safety and autonomy." This was the small victory Lysander had been seeking. He had lost Athens, yet he would maintain a base of power in Attica. And at the same time he could hurt me by stealing away my chance at vengeance.

Pausanias knew he had been outmanoeuvred, but it seemed a small concession. "That is most reasonable. Peace must be preserved, do you not agree, O Thrasybulus?"

"I do, O King," Thrasybulus said, his eyes on me. A sense of betrayal flooded over me, and I glared at my *strategos*. Lysander smiled icily, basking in the discord he had sown.

"Then return to your cities," Pausanias commanded, "and deliver my message." The negotiations were at an end.

I was livid. Thrasybulus was giving his leave to Pausanias, but he glanced over at me with concern. Perhaps he was worried that I would erupt into violence there and then. It was a possibility. But I was also angry at myself, for I had underestimated Lysander, and he had made me pay the price.

I made to leave the tent, but a hand on my shoulder stopped me. It was Lysander. The most powerful man in Greece leaned in close. "You have made an enemy today, *pai*," he said in a voice so low that only I could hear it.

But I did not fear him. In a voice even lower than that of Lysander, barely a growl at the back of my throat, I spoke. "I have slain tyrants and *polemarchs*. I will cut you down here and now, truce or no truce."

Lysander knew that I was not bluffing. Removing his hand, he laughed softly. "You should have been born a Spartan, Daimon, son of Nikodromos," he said, and he was gone. Not for the last time, I had underestimated the Spartan Hegemon.

I did not look back, nor did I wait for Thrasybulus. I strode through the Spartan camp scowling, oblivious of the hostile stares that followed me. To the crows with them. To Hades with Thrasybulus and Lysander and Pausanias. I was master of my own destiny.

Our mounts were where we had tethered them. No one impeded me as I untied my horse and leapt on its back. As I steered my horse around, a familiar shout made me pull up on the reins.

"Daimon! Wait!" Thrasybulus had rushed after me. As he drew near, he must have seen the murder in my eyes, for he raised his palms in supplication. "Patience! All will come!"

"You have betrayed me!" I pointed an accusing finger at him. "You have bartered away my vengeance! You have let the killers of my family survive! The same men who murdered Lykos! Do you not even care about avenging your own brother?" I asked viciously.

The stern demeanor of Thrasybulus cracked. I saw the pain on his face. "You must be patient, Daimon!" he repeated imploringly.

But I was lost to him. The saviour of Athens could only watch helplessly as I rode away, not towards Piraeus but to Athens.

There was something I needed to do.

I was going to find Plato.

And my son.

# Part Four

# Blade

CHAPTER 37

The messenger had summoned me to the home of Thrasybulus. The young man had been insistent. Reluctantly, I had relented, and now I stood in the courtyard of the leading citizen in Athens. "How is your son?" Thrasybulus asked me. It was the first time we had spoken in almost a year. Before I could respond, Thrasybulus' young son came screeching through the courtyard, pursued by his giggling older sister, Thaïs. The boy pulled up short and seeing my stern visage staring down at him burst into tears. His sister stopped too, regarding me with wide-eyed surprise in the manner of children. "Thaïs," Thrasybulus told his daughter, "take your brother upstairs to your mother. Your uncle and I are discussing important matters."

The wide-eyed girl said nothing, but took the hand of her snuffling brother and led him away, taking one last glance over her shoulder before they both disappeared. Smiling with a father's pride, Thrasybulus turned back to me and repeated his question. "And your son?"

My son was nearing three years old, healthy and full of rambunctious energy. But I was not going to give Thrasybulus the satisfaction of courtesy. I swatted away his olive branch with disdain. "Did you summon me here to prattle on about family?" I said truculently.

A pained expression passed across the face of my former *strategos*. "I am truly sorry, Daimon. I did everything in my power to help you."

I scoffed. "You speak of the promise you failed to honour? Full citizenship for those who fought against the tyrants, be he slave or foreigner? You used us for your own ends and then abandoned us!"

"You did not make it easy, Daimon!" Thrasybulus shot back angrily. He had aged much in the last year, his once dark hair now mostly gray. He waved a hand at me. "You have made an enemy of every influential man in Athens, Archinus above all. Archinus is a fool, but he commands great respect in the assembly. I was only one voice against many."

My pride and bitterness blinded me to the truth of his words. Thrasybulus had indeed put forward a motion in the assembly to grant citizenship to all those who had fought to topple the Tyrants. And the coward Archinus saw the chance for revenge, for he hated me. The lying snake knew the pettiness of the mob of the assembly. The *demos* – the People – were ever jealous of their status as citizens and were loath to share that privilege with outsiders, even those who had saved them from tyranny. Under the direction of Archinus, prominent citizens had lined up to speak in opposition to Thrasybulus' proposal. In all the speeches, my name was never mentioned, but everyone knew it was I they spoke of, for Archinus had spread his poison against me. And the people listened. Thrasybulus' motion was defeated. And I was still an outsider.

Thrasybulus leaned heavily on the courtyard altar. His eyes were closed as he calmed himself after his uncharacteristic outburst. "I helped you as much as I could."

It was true. Thrasybulus could not change the vote of the assembly, but he had used his influence to obtain an *enktesis* for me, a rare grant that allowed a non-citizen to own property. My father's house was now mine, though I had shown little gratitude.

He opened his eyes and looked at me solemnly. "They say you destroyed the altar in your home."

My silence confirmed the truth of this. With a quarryman's hammer and chisel and cold anger, I had reduced the ancient altar to a pile of rubble. Never again would the gods taste my sacrifice, nor would I beg their intervention. Rumours of my blasphemy against the gods spread. When I walked through the agora, I was followed by whispers of '*kakos daimon.*'

Thrasybulus sighed at my intransigence, suddenly reminding me of my father. "You are correct in saying that I have not called you here to speak of family. I have received news," he said, "of Eleusis."

My throat tightened. Eleusis. The last refuge of Menekrates and the remnants of the Thirty, hidden behind the stout walls of that sacred city.

Thrasybulus continued. "They have been hiring mercenaries in great numbers. They are planning an attack."

Athens was not the power she once was. Sparta did not interfere in affairs of the polis, but neither did it allow Athens to rebuild her walls or her navy. The city was weak and vulnerable, always under the Spartan thumb.

"Lysander?" I asked. Lysander still worked secretly to undermine the agreement between King Pausanias and Thrasybulus that kept Athens free.

Thrasybulus shrugged. "His hand is in it, but he is too cautious by far to reveal his involvement."

"How many men do they have?" I asked.

"Not enough," he said. "Yet."

"Will Athens attack?"

"Lysander thinks that we are still divided, but he is wrong. We can still muster a large force. We will besiege them, and they will see that they cannot defeat us. When they come to this realization, they will sue for negotiations."

His last words hung in the air, but their true meaning he left unsaid. But I heard him nevertheless.

"Will Menekrates be there?" I asked softly.

"He is one of the leaders, I am led to understand." He paused, considering his next words. "I cannot replace what you have lost, but I can give this to you, Daimon," he said, leaving much unspoken.

Thrasybulus was offering me an opportunity.

I took it.


THE SIEGE WAS A SUCCESS. When no force came from Sparta to drive our force of five thousand men away, the mercenary army of the surviving Tyrants knew their cause was hopeless. And as Thrasybulus had predicted, the leaders offered to negotiate a truce. The snakes were coaxed from their holes for a parley to be held on neutral ground at a crumbling temple outside of the sacred city.

The temple had been razed by the Persian army of Xerxes generations earlier. Much of the stone had vanished, most likely scavenged by local farmers to mark their field boundaries or to repair their buildings after years of neglect. Now little more than an ancient weathered altar remained.

The delegation of the remaining Tyrants awaited us. A few hundred hoplites stood in formation behind them. Our own delegation only had thirty men. As we drew closer, I could make out their individual faces.

Menekrates was there, with the scar-faced Andrian Orchus a pace behind him. The son of Kritias smirked smugly at our small force, but behind his twisted nose, his black eyes watched warily as we approached.

We stopped twenty paces away. I stepped forward and removed my helmet. Menekrates froze. His face slackened and he stared in disbelief. He began to squirm under my stone-faced gaze. Orchus' eyes narrowed slightly. There was a ripple of voices among the delegation of the Thirty, for I was not what they had expected.

One of the remaining Thirty stepped forward. "Where is Thrasybulus?" he demanded. His name was Melobius. Or Pheido. I forget. The frightened old men all looked the same to me.

"I am Daimon, son of Nikodromos. I have been given authority to negotiate on behalf of Athens," I proclaimed. The former Tyrants looked at me uneasily. If they had not recognized my face, they knew my name and reputation. Yet I made no aggressive moves. I spread my empty hands in a gesture of conciliation. "Let us make the truce and be done with it!"

Menekrates' eyes darted about nervously, looking for the hidden danger. My men stood at ease, though we were greatly outnumbered. Seeing no threat, Menekrates seemed to regain some courage, enough to curl his lip at me.

"What are your terms then?" the old man asked. There was a trace of hope in his voice.

"These are my terms," I responded. I moved aside to reveal the shrunken form hidden in my shadow. The blood drained from Menekrates' face.

Meli stepped forward.

It had taken a year. A year of searching and questioning, bribes, and intimidation. But I had found her. She had not been far from the city. Menekrates had condemned her to a slow death in the silver mines of Laurion. Mine operators preferred children and girls whose thin bodies could squeeze into the myriad tunnels that penetrated deep into the earth. Most were lucky to survive three months before the passages became their tombs. Meli had survived for more than a year.

The withered form that had emerged into the light made me cry. Meli's flesh barely masked her bones, the fiery red of her hair smothered by the choking black dust of the tunnels. Yet her eyes had still burned with hate. And madness.

Now, almost a year later, she stood before me in a simple tunic, her thick hair unbound and radiating like waves of flame. Her limbs, never recovering their lithe grace, had transformed into cords of sinew as tough as rope. She was an *empousa*, a creature of Hades that fed on the blood of the living. As she had promised Menekrates in the courtyard of Kritias many years earlier, she had come from the Underworld to claim him.

Meli drew something from behind her back. Menekrates' eyes widened in fear as he saw the small, curved blade in my sister's delicate hand. He knew the knife. It had bitten him twice before.

"My terms are these," I repeated more loudly. "I speak to the soldiers present. Athens has no quarrel with you. If you return to Eleusis now, no harm will come to you. If you choose to fight, a squadron of cavalry only awaits my signal to come and cut you down to the last man." A trumpet sounded in the north. The heads of the soldiers and their masters swivelled towards the signal to see five hundred horses appear over a rise in the distance. "The tyrants you serve will have their justice today. What say you, soldiers?"

Menekrates and his companions shuffled about in confusion. "To arms!" Menekrates shouted, drawing his sword. The mercenaries did not move.

"Defend us!" a former tyrant cried, desperation creeping into his voice. The mercenaries exchanged looks with each other, and by tacit agreement, they turned almost simultaneously and began to flee back towards Eleusis. One of the tyrants attempted to join them, but an arrow from Sabas' enormous Phrygian bow took him between the shoulder blades before he had gone twenty paces.

Abandoned, the Tyrants looked for an escape, but my men had already spread out to surround them. A few of the former overlords of Athens drew their weapons, others began to plead for their lives. Their words fell on deaf ears.

Only too late did their panicked eyes fall on my grim, unmoving companions. Tibetos, Mnasyllus, Telekles and the other *peripoli* who had escaped the massacre of their brothers. Men of Eleusis who had seen their kinfolk slaughtered and enslaved at the order of the Tyrants. Stachys, Podaroes, and other Athenians who only wished to drown their shame in the blood of their former rulers. There was not a man present who would give mercy. I had made sure of it.

"Orchus! To me!" Menekrates yelled. But the wily veteran was nowhere to be seen. A wild look took hold of Menekrates when he realized his stalwart bodyguard had deserted him. I cursed inwardly, for I had not seen the Andrian mercenary slip away.

Thoughts of Orchus vanished as Menekrates suddenly scrambled atop of the ancient altar. "I am a supplicant! I claim the protection of the gods!" In a final bid for their lives, some of the other Tyrants followed the lead of Menekrates and clasped the altar, babbling incoherently about how the laws of the gods must be respected.

I laughed coldly. "I remember my mother invoked the same laws, and the gods failed her. Let us see if the gods hear your pleas and protect you from me this day!"

"I have money!" Menekrates screamed.

"Forward!" I yelled. I stood with my hand on Meli's shoulder as my companions fell upon the evil men who had once held power over them so cruelly.

The last of the tyrants fell screaming under the spears and swords of my men. The merciless arrows of Sabas brought down two men as they fled in vain. The killing was done swiftly. Except for one.

Tibetos, slave no more, held Menekrates down on the altar with the help of Telekles. Menekrates strained to free himself, but he was held fast.

Menekrates was a coward, and he begged for his life. "It was my father! He instructed me to do those things!" The lies spilled easily from his lips. "Don't kill me!"

I stared down at the man who had taken so much from me. "*I'm* not going to kill you," I said softly.

Menekrates stopped struggling and stared at me in disbelief. I moved to one side and Meli took my place beside the altar. Menekrates' eyes bulged in terror at the gaunt face of my sister, the *empousa*, the flaming-haired daughter of Hekate, risen from the underworld in search of blood. And she had come to claim her victim.

Under the blue skies of Eleusis, I gave the gods one last gift, though I had sworn never to offer them anything again. Menekrates' screams filled the plain. Meli's knife plunged downwards, and the ancient altar once again tasted a man's blood after an absence of countless years.

And the gods were silent.

*

THAT WAS NEARLY SIXTY YEARS AGO.

Now they are all gone. Meli. Tibetos. Zyraxes. Thrasybulus. They are nothing but shadows in the mind of an old man whose memory grows dimmer with each passing moon. I spend my days yelling at my insolent slaves. They steal from me without fear and hide when I call for them. They do not fear me, for they only see an aged man, not Daimon, the warrior who once defied the gods and made tyrants tremble.

I wonder about the gods. On some days I think that my longevity proves their powerlessness over me. The pious and superstitious have all had their light snuffed out by violence or sickness or time, but I offer neither sacrifice nor prayer, yet I have now passed more than eighty years, by my reckoning. But more often, I think that the gods have kept me alive as a punishment for turning my back on them so long ago. It is their revenge for my hubris and arrogance, to make me watch the passing of those I love, leaving me to wallow in loneliness and decrepitude.

For I long to talk with my comrades over wine and figs and bread, regaling each other with exaggerated tales of shattered spears and vanquished enemies. I want to enjoy the silent companionship of Tibetos, as I did so often, for there was nothing that needed to be said between us. I wish to laugh at the sharp-tongued jests of Podaroes, for it has been many years since I last smiled. I would give much to bask in the wise words of Lykos and Thrasybulus. I yearn to hear the lilt of my mother's Thracian voice. I miss them.

But I miss Phaia most of all.

Will she recognize me when I join her in the Underworld? I will go there bent and withered, my red hair long ago turned white, while her shade will still be as young and beautiful as the day she was taken from me. Will she still love the man I have become? Or perhaps she has gone to the place that was promised to her, and I will bear eternity alone. I do not know.

In my dreams, she comes to me, and I smile with joy, for she is as beautiful and kind and clever as she was in life. But when I awake with my face wet with tears, the vision evaporates like morning mist burning off in the heat of the rising sun, and no matter how hard I try, I cannot conjure her back. And the gods laugh at me.

Let them laugh. They too cannot escape the fates that the three Moirai weave for them. One day their bright threads will be cut like all the rest. In the end, we are all mortals.

And the gods cannot change the past, whatever their powers may be. I hold on to those memories and know that they are mine.

There was a day when Phaia and I climbed to the top of Munychia, long before its soil was soaked with the blood of Tyrants. From its peak we watched the setting sun.

I remember the weight of her head on my shoulder. "There is no war up here, Daimon," she said.

"There is always war," I said. I was right in this, for there has never been a time in my life when war did not stalk the world.

"No, at this moment. There is no war *here*. This moment will always exist, outside the gods." She often spoke this way of time and the cosmos, but I could only smile and hold her close to me, for I did not understand her at that time.

"What do you want to *be*, Daimon?" she asked.

I tensed in surprise. My father had posed the same question many years earlier. I had told him I wanted to be feared by my enemies, and he had laughed at my foolishness. But the gods heard my plea, and cruelly they granted my wish, for I am nothing if not feared.

But when Phaia asked, there was only one truth that I could speak. "I want to be with you," I told her. I think my father would have smiled.

The Fates and the gods would not grant me that. Only more sadness and endless war. But the Moirai gave me something else. They gave me immortality in my name and reputation.

I am Daimon, son of Nikodromos.

I am the Demon of Athens.

# AUTHOR'S NOTE

In the second century AD, Pausanias, perhaps the world's first travel writer, wrote this description of the tombs of famous Athenians that lined a road outside the city's walls: "And of all the graves, the first is that of Thrasybulus, son of Lycus, *in all respects the greatest of Athenians, whether they lived before him or after him.*" When one considers all the giants that ancient Athens produced – Solon, Themistocles, and Pericles, to name but a few – it is obvious that this is no small claim.

Yet one would be hard-pressed to find someone outside the field of classics who recognizes the name Thrasybulus. Many would know of the battle that occurred at Marathon or of the last stand of the Three Hundred Spartans at Thermopylae, but the name of the man who was held in greatest esteem by many ancient Greeks themselves, and later the Romans, would most likely draw blank stares.

When I first heard of the story of Thrasybulus and his improbable triumph over the Thirty Tyrants, I immediately wanted to share the amazing tale with anyone who expressed even the slightest interest in the ancient world. My excited descriptions, however, could not even come close to doing justice to the story of a tiny, rag-tag army huddling in the mountains and how this force managed to overcome the greatest power in the Greek world. Over time, my own narrative began to coalesce in my mind, the seeds of the story contained within these pages.

Getting the story from my imagination to the page was a long struggle. Not only did I face the obstacles of any first-time author, but I also came to realize the amount of research required to produce a historical novel. Perhaps the most useful book (and the most difficult to acquire) was *Thrasybulus and the Athenian Democracy: The Life of an Athenian Statesman* by Robert J. Buck. This thin volume collects all that is known about Thrasybulus, including his reputation for having the loudest voice in Athens. It also provides the most complete timeline for the movements of Thrasybulus and the major events that take place in Daimon's story. For triremes and naval warfare, I depended heavily on *The Athenian Trireme: The*

*History and Reconstruction of an Ancient Greek Warship* by J.S. Morrison *et al*, and *The Battle of Arginusae: Victory at Sea and its Tragic Aftermath in the Final Years of the Peloponnesian War* by Debra Hamel. These volumes provided invaluable information about the ships that were so essential to Athens' very survival. For hoplite warfare, I found the bulk of my information in *The Western Way of War: Infantry Battle in Classical Greece* by Victor Davis Hanson, and *Military Theory and Practice in the Age of Xenophon* (another extremely hard-to-find volume!) by J.K. Anderson. Surprisingly little is known about the details of daily life in ancient Greece, but *Daily Life of the Ancient Greeks* by Robert Garland gave me many snippets that found their way into the story. Of course, Thucydides and Xenophon were never far out of reach, and the *Landmark Thucydides* and the *Landmark Xenophon* are unmatched in their field, in my opinion.

Other gaps in my knowledge, however, required more 'creative embellishment'. Very little is known about the *peripoli*. Thucydides mentions that one of the *peripoli* was involved in the assassination of Phrynichus, and that the commander of the *peripoli* was named Hermon. They seemed to be some kind of border patrol and the famous general Demosthenes may have used them in ambush-style assaults that became more common as the Peloponnesian War progressed. Other than that, nothing else is known, and almost everything in this book is a product of my imagination.

In addition, little is known about ancient Thrace except the odd detail that Greek writers such as Xenophon mention in passing. However, *Thracian Peltasts and their Influence on Greek Warfare* by J.P.G. Best gave me enough to work with. Finally, the Eleusinian Mysteries that were so important to Phaia and many other Greeks and Romans certainly live up to their name! *The Road to Eleusis: Unveiling the Secret of the Mysteries* by R. Gordon Wasson was a very interesting read, especially regarding the possible pharmacological nature of the visions experienced by the pilgrims.

The overthrow of the Thirty Tyrants on the slopes of Munychia does not mark an end to the struggle for hegemony in Greece, but rather the beginning of a chaotic period in which old enemies and new allies vie for power and survival. It is a tale that needs to be told and in which Thrasybulus plays a prominent role. And so will

Daimon, the Demon of Athens, gods willing, for he still has a long road to travel.

# ABOUT THE AUTHOR

Martin Sulev graduated from the University of Toronto with a degree in Palaeontology but now wishes he had studied Classics. He has worked as a freelance writer in the ESL industry and has contributed translations of Chinese short stories to two anthologies published by Cornell University. Tyranny is his first novel. He currently lives in Toronto with his wife and son.

More information on upcoming Demon of Athens novels can be found at:

www.martinsulev.com

Follow on Twitter @MSulev

Facebook: @MartinSulevAuthor

Tyranny

**AVAILABLE NOW!**

# GOD OF SPARTA
## Demon of Athens Book 2

Sparta has imposed an uncomfortable peace over all of Greece and the once-mighty Athens is little more than a servant of its former enemy. Thrasybulus, the great general and leading politician in Athens, is working secretly to make his weakened city strong enough to throw off the Spartan yoke. But when an urgent plea for aid comes from the Oracle of Delphi, Thrasybulus sends Daimon, his most trusted agent, on a secret mission to the holy sanctuary, where the young warrior and his companions uncover a conspiracy that will destroy any hope for Athens should it succeed. Forced into a shadowy world of politics and violence, only Daimon can thwart the plot and save Athens, a city that hates and rejects him. But to do so, he must defeat a god, as well as the ghosts that haunt his soul...